WINTER FIRES

Cutter drew her close caressing her arm. Dav shoulder, keeping her e her window visible fror

"I can see my house that's my room. Can you see me all the time when I'm in there? Will Bennett be able to when he's playing up here?"

"He will if you don't keep your curtains closed," Cutter said dryly. "You should keep your blinds down anyway. Not all Peeping Toms are preadolescent, you know."

"Tell me you haven't looked a time or two." She dared him to tell her an untruth.

Cutter gave a guilty chuckle. She already knew the answer to that one. He *had* looked. And tonight she'd caught him at it.

Leaning her head back against the wall, Davalyn said softly, "Maybe . . . maybe I don't want to close my curtains. Maybe I *want* someone to look."

Cutter tensed. A tiny war was being waged in the very fiber of his flesh. Stay or go? Run or hold fast? He let the sweet smell of her hair wash over him. She smelled like summer. Like sweet honeysuckle on the vine. He let the sound of her breathing—a slow exhalation of warmth—draw him closer for comfort. It took a while for him to find his voice. And when he did, it sounded raspy to his own ears.

"Maybe more than look?" he suggested.

Countless heartbeats marked the time before she answered, "May

BOOK YOUR PLACE ON OUR WEBSITE AND MAKE THE ARABESQUE ROMANCE CONNECTION!

We've created a customized website just for our very special Arabesque readers, where you can get the inside scoop on everything that's going on with Arabesque romance novels.

When you come online, you'll have the exciting opportunity to:

- View covers of upcoming books

- Learn about our future publishing schedule (listed by publication month and author)

- Find out when your favorite authors will be visiting a city near you

- Search for and order backlist books

- Check out author bios and background information

- Send e-mail to your favorite authors

- Join us in weekly chats with authors, readers and other guests

- Get writing guidelines

- AND MUCH MORE!

Visit our website at
http://www.arabesquebooks.com

Winter FIRES

Geri Guillaume

ARABESQUE

BET BOOKS

BET Publications, LLC
http://www.bet.com
http://www.arabesquebooks.com

They say that everything is bigger in Texas. If that's true, then the people who helped me to fashion this book are not only the wind beneath my wings, but provided gale-force strength to help me finish. This book is dedicated to all of you. For Robert and Donna, my best friends and hardest critics. For Sara Camilli, my agent and velvet-whip cracker. For Bindu Adai, my expert on all things romantic. For Joanne Zwiers, for her almost scarily sympathetic sisterhood. For Heather Brixey, whose creative brainstorms inspired (and amused) us all. For Joe Sanchez, fighting fires in the field and on "The Network," and for Tammey Dunn and Stacy Joseph, the ladies of AKA. Thank you all.

One

Summer 1985

"Hey! Who turned off my jam?"

Donovan Bowers's voice was filled with obvious irritation, even though it was partially muffled, as he
eased his head from underneath the dented hood of his
1972 Impala. As Donovan straightened his lanky frame,
he was careful not to catch the back of his neck against
the hood, which was propped up with half of a wooden
broomstick handle. The original metal hood prop for the
'72 was serving a better purpose leaning against the
back end of his boom box.

Turning his head to the right, Donovan glanced over
at his next-door neighbor Cutter McCall, who was sys-
tematically matching the grease-covered orange spark
plug wires that he'd pulled out of the Impala with the
new gray replacement plug wires.

Cutter sat straddling an old metal-frame folding
chair. The blue vinyl covering was cracked with tufts of
white stuffing poking through where strips of gray duct
tape didn't quite cover. The bottom of the seat was
bowed and looked as if it could collapse under Cutter's
bulk. Only seventeen years old, Cutter already carried
the height and weight of a fully grown man. Strong

back, tight biceps, wide shoulders that looked as if they could withstand the weight of a three-quarter-ton truck.

"Hey, man. You turn off my music?" Donovan asked, throwing a grease-stained rug at Cutter's head to get his attention.

His friend's fascination with tinkering on cars was almost childlike. Cutter was a true gear head. Give him a shoe box, some roller skate wheels, and a rubber band and he could probably put together a ride that would rival any of NASCAR's best.

Cutter reached up, snatched the rag out of midair, and tucked it into the back pocket of his acid-washed, button-fly Levi's.

"Don't look at me," Cutter said, draping another plug wire match across the back of the chair. "I didn't touch your boom box."

It was Saturday morning and they'd been listening to Casey Kasem count down the weekly Top 40 songs since nine o'clock. The music was taking Donovan's mind off the oppressive Texas heat and the sweat that collected on his face and made his dark blue coveralls cling to his sticky, wet back. The fan blowing from the open garage door brought in the smell of the salty Galveston Bay, with none of its coolness.

After the commercial break, and almost two hours of waiting, listening to the music through the boom box's static bursts, Donovan was just about to find out who'd knocked Whitney Houston's "You Give Good Love" out of the number-three spot.

Donovan just *had* to know who had the nerve to step on his woman's right to be number one. That's right, his woman.

Ahhh, Whitney. If only she knew how many hours he'd spent staring at her eight-by-ten autographed glossy, watching and waiting for her videos, and dreaming of the moment when he would pull up to her mansion and announce himself as her main man.

But first things first. He wasn't going anywhere unless he could get the car running. To do that, he had to have the music going.

He rested grimy hands on the chassis, not minding the grease stains that he'd left behind. The stains blended in with the rust and the spots of primer paint. Stains didn't matter much to Donovan now. He was going to get his baby painted two-toned cherry red and antique white as soon as she was running. He didn't even mind the raw, scraped knuckles from trying to use an ill-fitting socket wrench to yank out burned-out spark plugs. But he did mind having his groove interrupted. He minded a lot.

"Come on, Cutter. Stop messin' around, man!" Donovan snapped. "Get the jams going again so we can get this baby cranked up."

"Van, how could I touch your box and I'm sittin' way over here?" Cutter patted the folding chair for emphasis.

Cutter knew better than to touch Donovan's radio while he was working. Donovan was sixteen, with a learner's permit burning up his back pocket. His old man had told him that if he could get the '72 running, he could drive it. Days, nights, and weekends—whenever and however Donovan could get spare time, he used it to work on the car. Anything that interfered with that goal was just asking for it.

And that's exactly what Van's pesky little sister is doing, Cutter thought, glaring from underneath his brows at a petite figure hunkering down behind the car. She was just asking for it.

She pressed one hand over her mouth and from the

other hand dangled the power cord from the boom box. She'd yanked out the cord just in time to hear Donovan singing loudly, vigorously, to the last song in the countdown. Even Cutter had to cringe. Donovan had more volume than talent.

Yep, she is definitely asking for it, Cutter thought as he formed his calloused hand into a mock pistol, index finger pointing at the ground, and drew Donovan's attention to a bright pink reflection against the Impala. He bent his thumb and made the soft sound of a gunshot. Davalyn responded by flashing him her own little finger.

"Van, your sister just shot the bird at me," Cutter tattled. "Man, I'm telling you, you'd better do something about that girl. She's gonna get hurt."

Donovan spun around. "Davalyn! You little snot!"

He picked up a burned-out spark plug and hurled it at his eight-year-old sister. The plug ricocheted off a weight bench and sailed past her. Just barely missing her head, the spark plug skidded along the concrete garage floor until it rested in the far corner of the garage, spinning like a pop bottle in a kissing game until it came to a halt under the last tier of a four-tier gray metal shelf holding an assortment of tools, half-empty paint cans, back issues of old magazines, and anything else that couldn't find a proper place in the Bower house.

"How many times do I have to tell you to stay out of my garage!" Donovan yelled at her.

"It's not your garage, spaz. I don't see your name on it." Davalyn stood up, placed one hand on the jutting hip of her lace-trimmed bumble-gum-colored pink biker shorts, and challenged him.

"You see this car? This is my car." Donovan slapped

his hand against the bumper, making the broom handle waver precariously.

"See these tools? These are my tools." He pulled out a socket wrench and a pair of pliers from the open pocket of his dark blue coveralls. "My radio. My garage. And I'm not telling you again to keep away from all of it, Dav. I mean it!"

"I mean it," Davalyn mimicked, screwing up her face and sticking out her tongue.

"You'd better get outta here, baby girl," Cutter warned. "Nobody's playin' with you now."

This time, Donovan picked up a twelve-inch crescent wrench and waved it back and forth like a club. "So help me, Dav, if you don't—"

"You'd better not. I'm gonna tell," Davalyn threatened, but she backed away toward the door connecting the house and the garage.

"Who're you gonna tell?" Donovan advanced on her. "The folks are gone. You're all alone. Nobody to help you out. You keep messin' with me and your butt's mine, you little snot."

"Jerk face!" she responded defiantly, but she glanced over at Cutter to see if there would be any support coming from that corner.

Cutter deliberately lowered his head, interested once again in making sure the old plug wires perfectly matched the originals. He hated it when he got almost down to the last set and found that he'd miscalculated and had to pull them all out again to start over.

Donovan raised the wrench again. Davalyn screeched and jerked on the garage door. Heavy steel combined with a doorknob coated with grime worked against her. It took Davalyn a couple of tugs before she was able to swing the door open and duck back inside.

"And stay out!" Donovan insisted. A can of WD-40 hurled at the door provided a suitable thump to keep her from sticking her head out again.

"Man! I can't stand her. She gets on my last nerve. Cutter, you're so lucky that you're an only child."

"Is that what you think?" Cutter looked up at his friend, his expression amused.

"That's what I know," Donovan said, utterly convinced. "You don't have anybody hangin' around you, gettin' on your nerves. Nobody to spy on you, snitch on you, get you into trouble. That girl's *always* tellin' on me."

"Maybe you oughta try stayin' your butt out of trouble," Cutter suggested.

"Oh, my God . . . like you're so totally, like . . . Mr. Perfect," Donovan mimicked Valley Girl speech, fluttering his eyelashes and flinging back imaginary long hair over his shoulder.

"Never said I was. But like *you* said, I don't have anybody to tell on me, either. Nobody to blame if somethin' goes wrong around the house. Think about that. If somethin' is screwed up around the house, it's either me or my old man who did it. And you know how he is. He would rather have a red-hot poker shoved through his tongue than admit that he's wrong. You're the lucky one, Van. Your folks are so cool. 'Specially your dad. The way he's always spendin' time with you. Sometimes I wish . . ." Cutter didn't finish the sentence. They both knew what he wished. It was evident in the way that Cutter spent more hours at Donovan's house than at his own.

Donovan's expression shifted, serious now. "You know what they say, don't you? That grass always looks greener over there. . . . It's not all that green around here now. The way my folks have been actin' lately. I don't know about them, Cutter."

"Your folks still thinkin' about splittin' up?" Cutter asked.

"More than thinkin' about it. They're always talkin' about it now. Fightin' about it so loud that last week one of the neighbors had to call the cops on them. It's all they ever do, Cutter." His voice broke as he turned back to the Impala. "I can't wait until I get this baby runnin' so I can get up outta here, Cutter, man."

"If your folks split, where's the little snot gonna go? Who gets her?"

"Why do you wanna know?" Donovan laughed at his friend.

"I just wanna know so whichever parent gets her, I'm somewhere a thousand miles away. A running head start. That's all I'm askin' for."

"Since you're so worried about the little snot, you can do me a favor. Why don't you take her off my hands? Let her go live with you and your dad. Then you can see what it's like having a baby sister like Dav all for your very own. Dav would go for that." He paused dramatically, a crooked grin brightening his expression. "I think she has a thing for you anyway."

"Thing? What kind of a thing?" Cutter asked suspiciously.

"You know what I'm talking about. A thing. A crush. A hard case of puppy love."

"What are you talking about? She's just a kid." Cutter quickly dismissed the idea.

"I'm serious." Donovan's voice dropped to a conspiratorial whisper. "The other day I heard her in her room playin' with her Barbie dolls. And guess what? You were supposed to be the Ken doll. And she was the Barbie.

And Barbie and Ken were cruisin' in that pink toy 'Vette."

"Come on, Van. You know that ain't even funny."

"But that ain't all," Donovan continued, laughing so hard that he could barely catch his breath. "Peep this. She had a whole bunch of other little dolls crammed in the back. Yeah, buddy, I think Dav has plans for you."

Cutter glared at Donovan. "I think you've been breathin' exhaust fumes from that '72 for too long. Lift that garage door a little higher. Turn that fan up a notch or two. Me and the little snot? Not in this lifetime."

Donovan ignored the glare and the scowl from Cutter and tunelessly started to whistle the Wedding March through his teeth. "Tum-tum-dah-dum . . . Tum-tum-dah-dum . . ."

"I said quit it. You play too much, Van. Me and the little snot? Come on, man. That grosses me out just thinking about it. Besides, I've got my own plans. And they definitely don't include your baby sister. If you would go on ahead and hook me up with Angela Bennett . . ." Cutter lifted his eyebrows meaningfully.

Donovan threw up his hands. "Man, you still stuck on that girl? That girl doesn't want you."

"That's because she don't know me. And she don't know me because you won't set us up. I thought I was your boy, Van. I thought you were going to talk to her for me."

"I told you I'm working on it," Donovan promised.

"Work? What work you gotta do? You see the girl every day. All you gotta do is set us up. I can take care of the rest myself."

"How am I going to get a word in for you while I'm working the grill and she's up front on the register? The assistant manager pitches a hissy fit every time I even think about leaving the grill. I gotta ask permission just to take a bathroom break."

"You gotta admit, Van, the girl is fine!" Cutter sighed. "I gotta have that girl. Those lips, those hips, the way she works it when she walks." Cutter held out his hands, indicating the curve of a young girl's body.

"Cutter, I'm your friend. And you know I've got your back, but I don't think you've got a chance with her. I heard from Carly in first period who said that Shantal told her during gym that Angela said when they were getting off the bus that she's not interested in you. You've got too many strikes against you."

"Strikes? What kind of strikes? Like what?" Cutter leaned his forearms against the back of the chair, his face intense.

"First of all, you're a gearhead. Everybody knows that Angela's got this thing against guys and grease. You wouldn't be able to get her within ten feet of this garage. She can't stand the smell of exhaust fumes. She would spaz out and die if she ever got a really good look at the grease under your fingernails."

Cutter examined his hands, pulled out a pocketknife, and began to work at the dark black half-moons. "I can fix that. But what else don't she like about me?"

"You don't talk good English," Donovan said bluntly. "Sometimes you sound ignorant, straight up out of the boonies. Angela doesn't hide the fact that she wants a brother with class. Hell, she wants a brother who showed up for class every once in a while."

"I got a C minus in Mr. Wharton's English class," Cutter objected.

"That's only because you rebuilt his transmission during auto shop. Saved him a trip to the used-car lot to replace that wreck he was driving. Otherwise you were headed straight for an F. And I don't mean finish line."

"I graduated, didn't I?" Cutter growled.

"Barely. Cutter, man." Donovan leaned back under the hood, as much to keep from looking at his friend's dejected expression as he wanted to fix his car. "Sometimes I don't get you. You're smart. Real smart. One of the sharpest bloods I know. You could ace a test without ever crackin' a book. If you wanted to, you coulda been valedictorian. But you hardly ever studied. Didn't turn in your assignments. Only half-assed paid attention in class. Pretty clear to me that you didn't care about school."

"I cared about Angela," Cutter said forcefully.

"If she wasn't there, I don't think you would have been, either. You cut class more times than I could count and when you did show up it was like you weren't really there. Yeah, you got your diploma, but did any of it stick? What kind of job you gonna get with half a head of knowledge?"

"I know everything I need to know. And I've got these." Cutter held up his two hands. "What my head don't know, my hands do."

"The girl likes money, Cutter. Boys like you and me aren't exactly rollin' in the lean green, if you know what I mean."

"Your pops said I could work with him at the garage as much as I wanted. Get as much overtime as I need. I can make the money, Van. Come on, man. Work with me, here."

"You sure you want me to hook the two of you up? I don't know, Cutter. You and Angela. I just can't see the two of you together." Donovan held out his hands, thumbs together, trying to frame Cutter's image. He tilted left, then right, and shook his head in denial.

"And I can't see you and Whitney Houston gettin' it on. But that's not stopping you from tryin', is it?"

"You got that right. You just wait till I get this baby on the road."

"You said that if I help you get this car working for you, you'd work on Angela for me. All we got left is to change out the plugs and wires, replace the air filter—"

"Change out the transmission fluid and filter, flush the radiator, Freon in the air conditioner," Donovan continued glumly. Seemed like he'd been working forever on the Impala and was nowhere near getting closer to tracking down Whitney.

Cutter stood up. The folding chair seemingly sighing with relief as it was released of his bulk. He clamped a large hand over Donovan's slender shoulder.

"We'll get it done," he promised. "You've got my word on that."

"And the first thing we're going to do after we get her running is to head east to find Whitney. Right?"

Cutter started to answer, but an eerie feeling came over him. He felt the hairs on the back of his neck rise as if being watched. He started to shrug it off, but then he caught a movement out of the corner of his eye. A flash of pink through a tiny crack in the door. Shoulder-length pigtails swinging with baubles and bows. A saucy tongue poking out. Van's sister, Davalyn, back again for more trouble.

"Right after we drop your baby sister off a cliff somewhere," Cutter suggested.

"You're on!" Donovan said enthusiastically.

Cutter saw Davalyn glare her meanest look at her brother, then slowly nod her head, her little mouth spreading in a wide smile. It creeped Cutter out, imagining that much evil in so small a package.

"Van," Cutter said slowly, tapping his friend on the shoulder.

"Huh?"

"I'm not sure . . . but I think your sister is planning something. She's gonna get you back for chasing her out of here," Cutter predicted.

"She's always planning something." Donovan dismissed the warning. "Come on. Let's get these plugs and wires back in and check that distributor cap one more time."

Cutter started to hand Donovan the wires, but he couldn't shake the feeling that maybe they shouldn't be here. Maybe he should go inside to check on her. "Van, you sure that you don't wanna go in? You should have seen the look she gave you."

"Man, I ain't studyin' on her." Donovan waved the thought aside and leaned over the hood of the engine, stretching the first set of wires from distributor cap to spark plug.

He managed to keep up his air of nonchalance for an impressive twenty seconds. Then, muttering a low curse, he followed after his sister. "If that girl gets me into trouble, I'm gonna kill her. Nobody will blame me, either. Justifiable homicide."

"More like temporary insanity," Cutter shot back. Grinning and shaking his head, he trailed a step or two behind Donovan. Same ol', same ol' routine. Davalyn would probably be inside doing something to set Van off and Van would have to go chasing after her.

To keep the two of them from tearing each other to pieces, he'd have to physically separate them. It wasn't as easy as it looked. Van was wiry, but he was a lot stronger than outward appearances. And Davalyn was short and wiggly. If Cutter wasn't careful, she'd squiggle right out of his grasp. It was as close to having a sibling knock-down-drag-out as he'd ever get. Maybe not the best way to spend a Saturday morning, but the alternative was hanging out at his own house—all alone. It wasn't something he enjoyed. Maybe that was one of the reasons he spent so much time at the Bowerses'.

Donovan opened the garage door leading to the kitchen and stopped so quickly that Cutter almost collided with him. He made a strange, strangled sound of despair—something between a gurgle and an enraged bellow.

"I'm gonna kill you, Davalyn! I swear I'm gonna wring your scrawny neck."

Davalyn froze with her hand poised in midair. Her expression was dazed, hypnotized by the lure of flames flickering on the stove's gas burners. But at Donovan's interruption, her expression changed from fascination to fear. She wasn't expecting Donovan to come back inside the house so soon. Her work of sibling sabotage was not done. She stood on a chair holding a pair of plastic salad tongs in her hand. Clamped between the melting tongs was a smoldering photograph of Donovan and Whitney Houston over the burner eye. Blue flame licked at the photograph, curling up the edge to black and gray ash. Donovan was frozen to the spot. He could only stare in disbelief.

That photo represented the best day of his life. He'd lucked out, beating out hundreds of others by constantly pressing the speed dial button on the telephone to be the seventh caller into the radio station. All he had to do was give the "phrase that pays" and sing the lyrics to the mystery song for the evening.

Limo ride, front-row seats, backstage passes for himself and three other of his closest friends. And Whitney herself had hugged and kissed him—braces fixing his buck teeth, jheri curl, acne, and all. If he'd died and gone to heaven that night, he would have wrestled Saint Peter himself to get him back to earth. That's when he'd forever dedicated his heart and soul to Whitney. And Davalyn had ruined it. His little snot of a sister had ruined it all!

Quicker than Cutter could stop him, Donovan crossed the linoleum floor and yanked Davalyn by the arm. For a moment, her feet dangled in midair.

"You are dead meat this time, you little snot!"

"Donovan! Let her go, man!" Cutter shouted. He didn't like the way Davalyn's elbow popped as Donovan jerked his sister around like one of her dolls. Donovan glared over his shoulder at Cutter. His expression was hard.

"Now!" Cutter snapped, sounding more like his father than he ever thought he could.

Donovan splayed his fingers open wide. "There? You happy?" he snarled.

Davalyn cried out as she tumbled to the floor, her left forearm grazing the stove as she tried to break her fall. But Donovan wasn't listening. Wasn't caring. He pried what was left of the photograph from her clenched finger and tried to salvage what he could. All that was left of Whitney's embrace was one hand peeking out from behind his waist. Who would believe him now? Without that photograph, who would ever believe that he'd once held Whitney Houston in his arms?

Sobbing and clutching her arm, Davalyn huddled on the floor. When Cutter knelt down beside her to examine her arm, she jerked away from him.

"Don't touch it! It hurts," she whined.

"Let me take a look at your arm, Dav," he insisted.

"No! It hurts. . . . It hurts too much!"

"I know it does," he soothed. "But you gotta let me see."

When she curled up, cradling her arm tightly, Cutter turned with exasperation to her brother. "Van, your sister's hurt and she won't let me take a look. Make her."

"I don't care!" Donovan said savagely. "I don't care if she's fried crispier than the Colonel's best."

"Come on, Van. You know you don't mean that. She might need a doctor."

"I said I don't care. Look what she did! You see what she did?" He shook the ruined photograph at Cutter and more ashes flaked away, drifting to the floor. That only made him madder. Now, not only was he going to be in trouble for letting Davalyn play around the stove as she was expressly forbidden to do, but he was going to have to mop up the charred, ashy mess that she'd made.

"I told you to leave my stuff alone, you little snot! I'm gonna teach you one way or another that I mean it."

"What are you going to do?" Davalyn's eyes grew large as Donovan peeled his coveralls from his shoulders, pushed them down past his waist, and unhooked his belt clasp to draw the wide leather out of the pants loops with a vicious yank.

"Hey . . . hey, wait a minute, Van. What do you think you're doing with that?" Cutter interjected. He shifted, positioning himself between Davalyn and her brother.

"She needs her tail whupped," Donovan insisted. "She's a total brat."

"Yeah, she's a brat," Cutter agreed quickly. "But that's not going to make it right, Van. Come on, now, put your clothes back on."

Cutter had enough unions with his own behind and his father's strap to know that it didn't fix anything. Anything he wanted to do, he did, even with the threat of a whipping hanging over his head. Knowing that he could be caught—and whipped—just made him that

more cunning, that more creative about breaking the
rules. And since he was probably going to be beat anyway, he always made damned sure that he enjoyed
whatever it was that was eventually going to see him
into trouble.

Now that he was six feet one and outweighed his father by at least twenty pounds, he hadn't seen that old
strap in quite a while. But that didn't stop his father
from threatening to drag it out every now and then. In
fact, the last time his father held the strap in front of him
as a threat *was* the last time. Calvin McCall, knowing
that Cutter probably wouldn't stand for a whipping, simply announced as he held the double-thick leather strap
in front of him, "See this, boy? Remember this? Gettin'
too big to lay this 'cross your backside. Though I ain't
sayin' that you don't need it every now and then. I can't
whip ya. And I sure as hell won't chase after you if you
take off runnin'. So next time you buck up against me,
boy, I'll just shoot you. Got my thirty-eight already
loaded."

In the state that Donovan was in, Cutter knew that
once he laid that strap across his sister, he wouldn't be
able to stop.

"Move out of the way, Cutter. I'm only going to beat
her to within an inch of her life," Donovan promised,
confirming Cutter's suspicion.

"No, you're not," Cutter said calmly, coolly. He felt
Davalyn clutch at his back. Her tiny hands grabbing
handfuls of his shirt. He tried not to grimace when he
heard her sniffle, then wipe her runny nose on the material.

"I can't believe you're takin' her side," Donovan complained.

"I'm *not* takin' her side. I'm just tryin' to keep your

folks from gettin' on your case. What do you think they're gonna say when they see how messed up her arm is? Huh? Take a minute to think about that. You'll be grounded until Whitney's old, married, with kids of her own. Is getting back at her worth that?"

That seemed to calm Donovan down. At the very least, give him reason enough to pause.

"Let me see your arm, snot," Donovan said tightly.

Davalyn hesitated until Cutter said, "Go on, baby girl. Let him take a look at it."

She held up her arm, showing a large half-moon-shaped burn. Light brown skin wrinkled to dark brown.

Donovan chewed his lip in indecision, hints of remorse. "Jeez, Cutter. That don't look too good."

"Nope," Cutter agreed. "Sure don't."

"You're a lot of help."

"So, I skipped the first-aid part in health class."

"We gotta do something."

Davalyn sat cross-legged between them, cradling her arm, hiccupping, sobbing, and threatening to get them both into a world of trouble.

"Okay . . . uh . . . let me think . . . oh! Yeah. When my pops burns himself, and he usually does when he tries to cook, he always puts butter on the spot." Cutter snapped his finger in remembrance.

"Butter?" Donovan asked doubtfully. "Your father drinks when he cooks. And cooks when he drinks. You sure he knows what he's doin'?"

Cutter shrugged. "You got me. But as soon as he smears butter on the spot, he stops his cussin'. It has to do something for him."

"I guess it's either that or try to call my folks to get her to the doctor. Look on the door on the fridge, Cutter. I think there's half a stick in there."

"You're not putting that on me!" Davalyn howled.

"Stop your whining," Donovan snapped, grabbing her wrist. Davalyn wrestled with her brother for possession of her arm. When he leaned over her, she kicked out, catching him in the stomach with the heel of her foot. Donovan doubled over.

"Fine, let your arm fall off, for all I care."

"Come on, Dav," Cutter coaxed. "This'll make it feel better," he promised. He dug his fingers into the chilled, congealed margarine. "I swear."

She hesitated a moment, then slowly held her arm out to him. Cutter took her hand in his, steadying her when she flinched at his first touch. "See if you can find a bandage or some gauze or something," he directed Donovan.

"You are so gonna get it, Donovan," Davalyn threatened. "When Mama finds out about this—"

"I'll tell her you were playin' on the stove and burned up my photo. If I get a whuppin', you know you will, too."

Davalyn paused, considering her options. She glanced up at Cutter for a suggestion on what to do now.

"Better listen to him, Dav."

By the time Donovan returned with a roll of gauze and masking tape, Cutter had smeared half a stick of margarine up and down her arm.

"I'll tell you what, you little snot, you keep your mouth shut and I will, too. What do you say? We got a deal?"

"How do I know you won't tell on me?"

"You're just gonna have to trust me."

"Yeah, like that's gonna happen," Cutter muttered under his breath. "There, all done," he announced, checking out his field dressing.

She flexed her arm. "Thanks," she said grudgingly.

"Don't mention it."

"Ever," Donovan said with feeling. He could only imagine the trouble they'd all be in if his folks ever got a good look at the scar. He would just have to become Davalyn's fashion consultant for the next few weeks, making sure that she wore long sleeves even though it was summertime. If his parents said anything about it, he'd just blame it on her being weird again.

"You keep that bandage on until I tell you that you can take it off. You got that, you little snot? Keep it on."

Even as he spoke, the adhesive on the bandage was already starting to peel away. The burn looked raw and inflamed.

"I don't like the look of that," Cutter muttered, examining her arm again. He shook his head, then nodded once, as if he'd come to an internal decision.

"Come on, snot," he said, scooping Davalyn up into his arms.

"Where are you going?" Donovan asked. Cutter had that look on his face. That look said that no matter what anyone said or did, he was going to do what he wanted to do. At six feet one, almost two hundred pounds, nobody was going to stop him, either.

"What we shoulda done in the first place, Van. This girl needs a doctor."

"If my folks find out I let Dav get hurt, I'm toast, Cutter. You know that." Donovan reached for his sister. "Put her down. Her arm is fine."

Cutter wrestled to keep hold of Davalyn. One arm held her protectively to his chest. He shoved Donovan back with his free hand. "Cut it out, Van. I'm taking her to a clinic I know. They don't ask a lot of questions. You know it's the right thing to do. They'll fix her up right. We'll take my old man's car."

"I thought he took the keys from you when he caught you drag-stripping up the 146, hell-bent for Seabrook."

"I got my own set of keys," Cutter confessed. "We'll be there and back before the old man sleeps off his drunk."

Donovan sighed through his nose, cursing his bad luck.

"All right, then. Fine. We'll go!" he relented, reaching for the keys to lock up the house. "But if I get busted because of this, Cutter . . . if my pops takes away this car and I don't get a chance to hook up with Whitney, it's you and me, in the backyard, bare fists, no holds barred, last man standing. You got that?"

Cutter pointed at Donovan, making it a date. Because there was no way on God's green earth that the Bowers parents wouldn't find out about this. Not with the "mouth of the South" waiting to snitch on them.

"You know you don't want to fight me, Van. The last time we did, you know I kicked your tail," Cutter reminded him.

"Man, that was when I was in the fourth grade after you took my lunch. I was weak from hunger. You know good and well that you couldn't beat me now."

"Try me," Cutter said, swaggering with confidence. "It'd be your own funeral. Say good-bye to your brother, Dav. 'Cause when we get back, I'm gonna have to put him six feet under."

"Bring it on!" Donovan challenged.

Two

"I'm taking this stupid thing off! I look dumb."

Bennett McCall was only eight years old, yet he had his own well-defined sense of fashion. He knew what worked for him and what didn't. He and his dad had had many a morning battle over just that very issue. Though Bennett thought his dad was cool in so many other ways, picking the right clothes for him just wasn't one of those ways.

The dark-blue-and-yellow-paisley clip-on tie that Cutter McCall had firmly affixed to Bennett's short-sleeved, button-down, heavily starched white shirt definitely was not working. Not for him. This was as bad as his Sunday-morning church clothes. He could have dealt with it if his dad hadn't made him put on that geeky-looking jacket as they headed out the door.

Bennett had tried to draw a virtual line in the sand— digging in his loafer-style heels, thrusting his fists deep into his khaki pants pockets, and threatening without words to make the rest of the day miserable for the both of them if he made him wear that dumb blue jacket. It wasn't Sunday morning. It was a Saturday. It should have been a day for his favorite outfit, a pair of wide-leg black jeans and his purple Dragon Ball Z T-shirt.

But his dad wasn't going for that. Not this time. No matter how much he huffed and dragged his feet, he was going to go out the door looking like a doofus and there was nothing that he could do about it.

"You don't look dumb. You look handsome." Cutter squatted down in front of his son. He adjusted Bennett's tie and collar. "My little man. I can't believe how fast you're growing. Didn't I just get these pants for you last week? And now look at you. Busting out of them already."

Bennett leaped on what he thought was the perfect opening for him to let his dad know just how much he didn't want to wear a miniature version of what his dad was wearing. "I do look dumb."

"Everybody will just think you're my Mini Me," Cutter teased.

"So why can't we go back home and change? It's right next door. I'll run real fast and—"

"No can do, little man. We're late enough as it is," Cutter said, glancing at his watch.

"A few minutes more won't hurt, then, will it?" Bennett pressed. A little too hard. He could see that he'd pushed too far in his dad's expression—the way his jaw got all tight and his voice dropped to a low, gravelly whisper. His father wasn't a yeller. When he got mad, he got quiet. Really quiet.

Bennett was convinced that was one of the reasons he was so surprised when his dad and mom sat him down to tell him that they were getting a divorce. He had no idea. Never saw it coming. Never *heard* it coming.

"We're not going back, Bennett," Cutter said, an air of finality in his voice that Bennett could not mistake.

"Yes, sir," Bennett mumbled his acquiescence. When his dad had picked him up at his mom's house, he'd already been late. That made his mom mad. Since she was living with her new husband, she didn't bother to hide the fact that she was mad. Just started yelling at him right in the doorway.

"You said you'd be here by one o'clock, Cutter. It's almost three."

"I know what time it is, Angela," Cutter retorted.

"You aren't the only one with things to do. You have absolutely no regard for anyone else, you selfish bas—"

"Bennett, go to your room and start getting dressed." Cutter had interrupted his mom, which made her even madder. He had to close the door to block out some of the things she'd called him.

When he finally came out, dressed in the outfit she'd laid out for him, he hadn't taken that moment to complain about the choices. Both of them looked as if they would not put up with any nonsense from him today.

His dad didn't seem to get into a better mood until he'd put several miles between them. Now that they were back home, Bennett had seized the opportunity to get into something more to his liking and was gently rebuffed.

Cutter rubbed his hand affectionately over his son's freshly cut hair. "I'll tell you what, Bennett, you wear the tie long enough to pay your respects to everybody. Say your hellos like a good boy and then I'll let you take it off. Half an hour at the most. Sound like a deal to you?"

"I guess so," Bennett said with a heavy sigh. "But I still don't see why I havta wear a stupid tie. I don't know anybody in there. They won't care if I'm wearing a tie or not."

"What do you mean you don't know anybody in there? You know Uncle Van."

Bennett's face broke into a wide, gap-toothed grin. Sure, he knew Uncle Van. His dad's best friend. More like a brother. If Uncle Van wasn't at their house, they were at his. Uncle Van was the one who once gave him five bucks when the tooth fairy somehow missed his house and forgot to pick up his tooth when he lost his first front tooth. Uncle Van brought him McDonald's Happy Meals on the days he forgot to take his lunch when his dad was on his shift at the fire station.

When he and his dad were both at the garage, working on cars, fixing up trucks, Uncle Van let him sit behind the wheel of some of the really cool cars and didn't yell at him when he blew the horn or changed the music on the radio stations. Long, tall, goofy Uncle Van. Yeah, he knew him. They were going to see him now.

But Uncle Van wouldn't be in a goofy mood today. And hadn't been since the beginning of the week. He hadn't been the same since Uncle Van's dad, Mr. Vincent, had passed out, collapsed on the floor of his office just a couple of days ago.

Uncle Van hadn't cracked a smile, told a joke since they all met up at the hospital to say their last good-byes to the man Bennett had come to think of as a third grandpa. Grandpa Vincent—as much a part of his family as anyone.

Bennett's mother, Angela, wouldn't let him go to the wake to pay his respects to Grandpa Vincent. In that fighting-but-not-really-fighting kinda way, Angela had told Cutter that it would probably traumatize him to see a dead body at such a young age. So, he didn't get a chance to pay his final respects like a big boy. And his dad had been in the middle of responding to a two-alarm fire when Uncle Van laid his father to rest at the cemetery. So, they visited the grave site on their own today, after everyone else had gone.

Now they were on their way to Uncle Van's house when all the other relatives would all come by to pay their final respects. He wanted his son to help honor the memory of Vincent Bowers—the man who'd opened his home to him, given him a job right out of high school, and in his last will and testament left him a way to support himself and his son. Cutter figured when he died, he would pass the shop on to Bennett.

Thanks to Mr. Bowers, he and Donovan were now co-owners of his custom detail shop. Cutter supposed that shop was a third home to him—where he'd spent many an hour and several customers had spent many a dollar to have their dream cars refurbished to near-mint condition and perfect running order. The shop was thriving, with folks coming as far as Houston to get the special treatment their coveted vehicles desired. Vincent Bowers was a fair man, a hard worker, and a good friend. Cutter already missed him.

"Who all's gonna be there?" Bennett asked.

"Who's gonna be there?" Cutter did his duty to correct his son's grammar.

"You mean you don't know?" Bennett sounded surprised.

"Of course I know." Cutter tried not laugh. "Uncle Van's gonna be there, and all Mr. Bowers's friends and folks from the garage."

"All them folks can't fit in their house, Dad."

"Those folks," Cutter said automatically. "I know. It's gonna be crowded in there. Mr. Bowers was a good man."

"You loved him," Bennett said insightfully.

When Cutter remained quiet, emotion choking him to silence, Bennett continued.

"It's all right, Dad. Mama says it's all right for grown folks to tell each other that they love each other."

"Is that a fact?" Cutter tried to shield the sarcasm in his voice. Angela Bennett-McCall said many things. Not all worth repeating, as Bennett was fond of doing. But Cutter had made a vow to himself. He wouldn't let his own relationship with his ex-wife, the mother of his son, affect Bennett's relationship with her. He would never speak negatively of her or cause Bennett to think so of her.

"Did you love Uncle Van's dad better than my grandpa?" Bennett wanted to know. "Did you love him better than you did Grandpa Calvin?"

"Why would you ask that, Bennett?" Cutter asked.

Bennett shrugged his thin shoulders. "I dunno. It's just that you didn't cry when Grandpa Calvin died. And you *did* when Mr. Bowers died. I saw you. Your eyes were all red and puffed up."

"How do you know I didn't cry when Grandpa died?" Cutter's mind flashed back to he, Bennett, Donovan, and Angela all standing at the grave site. He wondered how Bennett could have remembered that day. He was just a baby. Just four years old.

Maybe he'd been a little stoic. It was the only way he could have dealt with the loss. He and his dad were just starting to warm to each other—with Bennett being the reason. Maybe Bill Cosby's routine about "old folks tryin' to get into heaven" held more truth than humor. The birth of Bennett changed them all. Even Calvin McCall.

"I didn't see you cry, Dad. Not like I saw you cry

when Uncle Van told you about Mr. Bowers when we got to the hospital to see him. You don't have to be ashamed to tell me, Dad. Mama says it's all right for grown folks to cry."

Cutter considered his words carefully. Though he and his own father had never quite clicked, Calvin McCall had been the perfect grandfather to Bennett. The years had mellowed him. Somehow, during the passage of time, he'd learned to laugh instead of pass a lick, care instead of cuss. He never raised his voice to his grandson, let alone his hand. Cutter supposed that he'd taken more than enough licks from Calvin McCall to make sure that his own son was spared.

"Well, Bennett," Cutter said, carefully choosing his words, "sometimes people cry on the inside. It doesn't mean they don't feel the same way. They're just more private about it."

"Uncle Van wasn't private about it. Cried out loud like a big baby."

"Let him cry and don't you tease him about it, either, when you see him today," Cutter warned. He stood at the front gate of the chain-link fence, pausing a bit before heading up the walkway leading to the front door. He took a moment to straighten Bennett's tie. Then he held out his thumb—though not to give his son the thumbs-up sign.

Knowing the drill, Bennett leaned forward, stuck out his tongue, and moistened the ball of his father's thumb.

As Cutter smoothed over his son's thick, unruly eyebrows, he said solemnly, "Uncle Van was very close to his dad. His dad raised him when he and Mrs. Bowers separated. Mr. Bowers was pretty much all Uncle Van had since his mom took his sister when she left. Do you remember Uncle Van's sister, Davalyn?"

"Kinda. Sorta." Bennett shrugged, then admitted, "Not really. I mean, I know that Uncle Van has pictures of her around, but I don't remember anything about her."

"It's okay if you don't remember her, Bennett. She remembers you. And just so you'll know, she looks a lot like Uncle Van. You'll like her," Cutter assured him, rubbing his son on the head. He paused, giving Bennett an odd, reflective look. There was no small wonder why Bennett wouldn't remember Davalyn. He only remembered a handful of times when she'd come back to Kemah to visit. The last time was about six years ago. Bennett wouldn't remember her holding him, feeding him, and changing his diaper. He certainly wouldn't remember the look on her face when, as soon as she'd opened the diaper, he'd squirted her. But Cutter remembered. He remembered how hard he'd laughed and how she'd thrown the wet Pamper at him in retaliation. He also remembered how irritated Angela was. Said that Van's sister didn't know anything about taking care of babies and that she didn't want Davalyn anywhere around him—especially if she wasn't around to keep an eye on all of them.

He had more than enough memories of Davalyn Bowers for the both of them. When he and Donovan were in grade school, he had been there to console Donovan when his parents brought the squalling bundle of diapers-and-doo-doo home. In junior high, he'd helped Donovan to entertain the persistent toddler when his parents had to work. And in high school, he was the one coming up with the perfect plans to "ditch the snitch" when he and Donovan wanted to sneak off to race the stock cars they'd pieced together from junked cars.

"You know, in some ways, you kinda remind me of her," Cutter said as if the comparison just came to him.

"You trying to punk me, Dad? Trying to say that I act like a girl?" Bennett screwed up his face, narrowed his eyes in obvious displeasure at the comparison. He'd heard Uncle Van and his dad talking about how it used to be when they were all growing up. This Davalyn person didn't sound to him like anyone he wanted to be like. She sounded like a pest, very much like the girls in his class.

"No, Bennett." Cutter burst into laughter, drawing the attention of several somber mourners filing out the front door of the Bowers home. He quickly composed his face into the appropriately respectful expression the occasion called for.

"When Davalyn was your age, she was . . . Let me see. How should I say this? Little Miss Davalyn had her own mind and wasn't shy about giving you a piece of it. If she didn't like something, she was real quick about letting you know it."

"Oh. Okay." Bennett seemed satisfied with the answer. His dad had always encouraged him to speak his mind. He might not always get his way or what he wanted, but at least he was always heard.

"How come I don't remember her?"

"I told you. When Uncle Van and his sister were kids, their folks split up."

"Just like you and Mom," Bennett was quick to point out.

"Something like that," Cutter said, his voice cracking just a little with thinly disguised emotion. Though it had been four years, his divorce from Angela Bennett-McCall was still too new, too raw. Losing his father that year and the breakup of his marriage was hard on him.

He was still reeling from the emotional impact of it all. Even though his son, Bennett, seemed to be adjusting to the idea that two of the people he loved most in the world didn't love each other anymore, Cutter still had a hard time talking about it. He had a hard time accepting that something he'd poured so much love and effort into didn't work.

"Uncle Van's mother took Davalyn to live with her family in Maryland and Uncle Van stayed here to live with his dad."

"Just like you and me, huh, Dad?"

"Just like you and me, little man," Cutter echoed, his expression softening. "Come on. Let's go inside. Uncle Van's probably wondering where we are by now."

Cutter pulled on the handle of the screen door and stepped into the foyer. The first thing that hit him was how incredibly quiet the house was. Even though every room was thick with bodies, the house seemed eerily quiet. Folks talked in hushed tones as if the dead could still hear. There was music playing. A piano. Instrumentals of Mr. Bowers's favorite hymns. As he made his way through the entryway, he turned to the right toward the arched entry of the main sitting room.

Some folks he recognized, others he didn't. As he'd told Bennett, Vincent Bowers had been a well-liked, well-respected man. He expected that people would be coming in and out of the house for hours. He'd called Donovan to warn him that he'd be late.

"Don't worry about it, man. Folks are still coming by. The house is crammed with people."

"You doin' all right?" Cutter heard the strain in his friend's voice. He could empathize with him, knew what he was going through. Right now, he was imagining that all Van wanted to do was to go off somewhere, quiet and peaceful, and acknowledge his father's passing in his own way, without worrying what anybody else thought.

"I'm okay," Donovan said, his tone listless.

"You hang in there, Van. If you need a place to chill, you know where my key is. Let yourself in. I'm on my way."

Cutter and Bennett finally arrived, almost an hour and a half late. He would have been on time if he hadn't joined the crew that responded to a two-alarm fire at an apartment complex before heading out to pick up Bennett. He'd picked up the alarm on the two-way radio he always carried with him as a Kemah volunteer firefighter.

The apartment complex wasn't very large—eight buildings at the most, with only six currently being occupied. It was an old complex that was built before city ordinances required most of the basic fire containment measures. It had few working smoke detectors, no up-to-code fire walls, and limited access to hydrants for the Kemah Volunteer Fire Department to tap into.

By the time the pumper truck arrived, three of the buildings were fully engaged. Orange flames shot into the air; thick plumes of black smoke cut visibility down to a few feet. Coupled with high winds and low water pressure, it was all that Cutter and the rest of the KVFD could do to contain the blaze.

He'd showered and changed at the station as quickly as he could. But not quick enough. He missed the funeral service. Cutter told himself that he was doing his duty, that he had to be there with the KVFD. But inside, he knew that he wasn't ready to face the fact that Mr. Bowers was gone. His friend, his mentor, was now six feet under the ground.

"There's Uncle Van!" Bennett pointed excitedly across the room, breaking into Cutter's morbid thoughts.

Three

Cutter craned his neck, spotting his friend across the room talking to his mother. Dana Bowers and her daughter, Davalyn, had flown in from Maryland as soon as she'd heard that Mr. Bowers was in the hospital. But he'd passed so quickly after collapsing that there was no time for last words, no bedside good-byes. He was gone by the time they made it to the hospital.

All of their good-byes were spoken at the church during the final viewing and at the graveside interment. Mr. Bowers had never remarried, but Dana Bowers had. Cutter watched her, noting that she looked no less mournful than people who'd been his friends for years. He didn't think it was an act for appearance' sake. Her tears were genuine.

Though Dana Bowers had put on a few pounds since he'd remembered her last and was sporting a different color hair—brighter, sassier—Cutter recognized her immediately. There was no mistaking the distinctly long, oval face—almost a trademark of the Bowers family. Her large, dark eyes were red, swollen with tears of unrestrained sorrow. She was impeccably dressed in a Chanel suit, a strand of twelve-inch pearls with matching earrings. Her legs were crossed at her ankles, drawn to the left of the chair.

Dana Bowers looked up, catching his eye. She held her hands to him, one hand balled tight, crumpling a well-used piece of tissue. Cutter saw her lean forward to address Donovan.

Donovan looked over his shoulder, waved them over as Cutter approached. He held out to clasp Donovan's hand in a brotherly fashion.

"Sorry I'm late." He made his apologies as Donovan clasped him in a warm embrace.

"Don't worry about it, Cutter. Dad knows your thoughts were with him."

"I'm so sorry, Van. I sure am gonna miss that old man." Cutter shook his head.

"Clayton McCall," Dana Bowers called out to him. "Get yourself over here, boy."

Cutter forced himself not to frown at the use of his birth name. She was the only one who could call him Clayton and not get knocked flat on their butt for it. Nobody called him Clayton. Nobody. He couldn't remember when was the last time someone had. Wait . . . Yes, he could. One summer, Davalyn had come down to visit her dad. She must have been about thirteen years old then; wanting to sound grown-up, she called him "Clayton."

When he ignored her, teased her about her stork legs and braces, she and a group of her girlfriends took turns playing phone pranks, calling him, asking to speak to him, and giving Angela the impression that they were some of the hot-rod honeys who hung around the unofficial tracks, looking for fast action.

Mr. Bowers had only laughed when he'd complained to him. So, he'd called Van's mom to put a stop to it. She did, threatening to yank Davalyn back to Maryland so fast, it would jerk a knot in her.

Hearing her loving, scolding tone almost made him feel like old times, but then he was quickly reminded of the reason she was here. It was the look of sorrow on her face that did it. His mind raced to remember her married name. She wasn't a Bowers anymore and hadn't been for some time.

"Ms. Dana," he improvised, kneeling down before her and allowing her to enfold him in her ample arms. "My sympathies to you and your family. I'm sorry I missed the funeral."

"You're such a sweet boy," she murmured, patting his head. "Always were. You were one of the few of Donovan's friends that I could tolerate being around."

Donovan groaned at that, but couldn't deny it. When they were kids, if he'd asked for anyone to stay over more than a couple of hours, his mother usually made sure that the stay wasn't a pleasant one. But with Cutter, things were different.

"Are you doin' all right? Can I get you anything?" Cutter offered.

"No, I'm fine. Thank you for asking." She then leaned back in her chair, her hands clasped in front of her. "My goodness, Clayton. You have grown up to be a fine young man."

"Thank you, Ms. Dana."

She glanced at the miniature version of Cutter. "And this is your son?"

"Yes, ma'am. Bennett," he introduced, ushering his son forward.

"Clayton, if you didn't put your mark on that boy," she marveled. "He looks just like you. Like you just spat that boy out." She shook her head; from the faraway look in her eyes, Cutter got the impression that for a brief moment she'd taken herself back in time—to a time when he and Donovan were this young and wreaking havoc in her household.

They stood in front of her for a while, chatting about things Cutter would later forget. It was just busy talk, meant to take one's mind off why they were really there. Perhaps something of his distraction communicated itself to Dana Bowers.

She paused, tilting her head to regard him curiously.

"You and Angela aren't together anymore, are you?"

"No, ma'am," Cutter said, shifting uncomfortably. She should know that. It had been four years.

"My memory isn't what it should be," she said, though Cutter suspected that her mind was as sharp as ever.

"Davalyn's around here somewhere," Dana Bowers said, pointedly looking around. "Have you seen her yet?"

"No, ma'am. Not yet. In fact, not in a good long while."

"About six years," she supplied.

Davalyn hadn't been able to make it down for his wedding. And he was on vacation with Angela and Bennett when Donovan asked if he had wanted to drive out to Maryland to attend her high school graduation ceremony. Wanted to go—yes. Able to go, definitely not. In fact, Angela had even given him attitude just for hesitating in responding to Donovan. It made her mad to think he'd go rushing off to celebrate some other woman's achievements, even if that other woman was just Davalyn. Little Davalyn Bowers. As much a sister to him as Donovan was his brother.

"Come on," Donovan had almost pleaded. "You only get one big high school graduation in your life."

Cutter could only shake his head. "Sorry, Van, but

Angela has been planning this vacation for months. I can't go. I'll get Dav a present and you can tell her how much I wanted to be there."

To which Donovan promptly responded with the sound of a whip crack, "You're whipped, man. Go on. Admit it. And have been since high school."

"Say what you want to," Cutter had replied. Years of friendship restrained him from cracking Donovan's skull for that slur. "But you know Angela and me have been goin' through some things. This may be the last chance I get to get our marriage back on track."

Cutter spent the next two years working on that track. Even though Davalyn attended the University of Texas in Austin—just a few hours' drive from Kemah—he wasn't able to make that graduation, either. A stint in the hospital when Angela miscarried for the third time made sure that Cutter stayed diligently, faithfully, by her side.

More opportunities than he cared to admit passed by to see Davalyn again. He'd been at Van's house a couple of times when she called her brother and they'd chatted. A few postcards, an exchange of e-mails, passing on pictures of noted occasions in each other's lives—so they hadn't completely lost touch. But there was nothing like seeing someone in the flesh to stir up old memories.

"You're not the only one who's all grown-up, Clayton McCall."

A voice—low-pitched, cultivated but clear—cut through the hushed tones of conversation and caressed his left ear, even as he felt a small, well-manicured hand tap, then squeeze his right shoulder.

Cutter half turned. His freshly shaved cheek grazed silky dark hair that was lightly scented with some sort of floral shampoo. Honeysuckle. He could not mistake *that* scent. The fence that separated their two houses was choked with the fragrant vine in the summertime. He and Donovan had spent countless hours every summer trying to keep the vine from overtaking the rest of the Bowers yard.

He swallowed hard, trying to clear the mouth that had suddenly gone dry as Davalyn Bowers stepped from behind him. She crossed her arms at her waist and lifted a finely arched eyebrow at him. She wasn't smiling as she made a show of glancing at her watch and tapping on the crystal as if to emphasize the lateness of the hour.

Memory played tricks on his mind. For a moment, he didn't see Davalyn as she was now—a slender five-foot-seven frame dressed in a black tailored jacket and skirt that showed off to her advantage long, lean legs toned by hours of diligent workouts.

He didn't see polish and sophistication. Instead, he saw braids, bows, and Barbie dolls. When she spoke, he hadn't heard the soft drawl, a mixture of Texas twang and Southern gentility, but childhood jump rope chants and the taunts of sibling rivalry. For a moment, he was seventeen again, back in the Bowerses' garage working on that '72 Impala.

Then Davalyn surprised. She flung her arms open wide and launched herself into Cutter's arms. Wrapping her arms around his neck, she lifted up on tiptoes and pressed her lips to his cheek in an unrestrained display of affection. In an automatic response, Cutter hugged her back, his chin resting on the top of her head. Closing his eyes, he squeezed her tight in an unspoken apology.

"It's so good to see you again, Cutter," Davalyn murmured against his chest. "It's been such a long time."

"Way too long," Cutter agreed, and squeezed tighter when he felt the long, lean lines of her body mold into his. In a flash, Cutter's mind ended its brief trip back down memory lane and brought him screeching back to the present with acute awareness. He wasn't seventeen. He was thirty-six, seeing and hearing Davalyn for who and what she was. And what his body was telling him was that little Davalyn Bowers was now every inch a fully grown woman—and all that implied.

Whoa! Down, boy.

Cutter's mind quickly reined in his body's unexpected response to Davalyn—a response that was moving with determination from friendly, brotherly affection to unexpected arousal. Too long indeed. It had been a long time since he held a woman against him quite like this.

Raw wounds of a bitter divorce had played havoc with emotions, leaving him wary of opening himself up again to these kinds of feelings. He'd been on several dates, setups from well-meaning friends, casual get-togethers, even a few on-line dating services. But he'd always been careful to keep his heart out of it, even when a cool head didn't always prevail.

His attitude toward the fairer sex would probably hurt him in the end. He'd have to carry the badge of being a player for a little while longer, yet he was a big boy. He knew the difference between sex with a woman for the sake of companionship and a woman who aroused his senses. He'd been on the lookout for a woman who, without obviously trying, could make him forget himself. Four years of an emotional dry spell. He'd finally hit on one that just might make it past his emotional armor and it had to be Davalyn Bowers—a woman as near to being a sister as any woman could claim to be.

Damn it. Sometimes life just wasn't fair. First he'd lost a man who was like a father to him and now *this!*

Cutter placed his hands gingerly at Davalyn's waist and pulled her away from him, saying, "I'm just sorry that we had to meet up under these circumstances, Dav."

Her soft smile was mournful. But even through the sadness, he was stunned by the incredible beauty of that smile. It was a little shy, even hesitant; at the same time, it was tinged with a pure sensuality that made him want to put a little more distance between them. If she had any inclination of what he'd been thinking, feeling, she didn't show it.

"I guess what they say is true. Families only get together for weddings and funerals."

"You didn't make it to my wedding," he reminded her.

She lowered her eyes so that he couldn't see her expression. "I know, Cutter."

Cutter placed his index finger under her chin, lifting it to meet his gaze. "That's all right, baby girl," he said, falling into the easy old familiarity with her. "I forgive you for not making it."

Davalyn's smile broadened. She raised a little on tiptoe and whispered in his ear, "And I forgive you for getting married without me."

Four

I wish I had my camera with me to capture the expression on your face, Davalyn thought as Cutter held her out at arm's length. His expression was classic—a mixture of pleasurable recognition, mild embarrassment, and not a small amount of surprise.

Donovan eased beside Cutter, placed his hand under his chin, and lifted. "Drop something, Cutter? Like your jaw?"

Davalyn shot her brother an affectionately annoyed look. "Okay, Van. You only get to say that one more time before I button your lips together. All right?"

Since she'd come back, he'd been telling that same joke to anyone who'd listen. Yes, she'd changed. She didn't know why everyone was so surprised. What were they expecting to find? Their baby girl? Many years had passed since she'd moved away. Almost twenty. And the last time she and Cutter had seen each other in person had been about six years ago, when she'd come down to spend Thanksgiving with Van and her father. But people change. *She'd* changed. That shouldn't have come as such a big surprise to him.

If nothing else, he must have seen some of the pictures that she'd sent to Donovan and him over the years that marked how much she'd changed. She'd even sporadically gotten a few pictures from Cutter himself—pictures of Donovan and him at the grand opening of the third body shop, or hanging out during a few of their joint vacations, and pictures of himself, all decked out in full firefighter's gear, when he became a Kemah volunteer firefighter.

When he'd finally broken down and bought a personal computer, he'd sent her a few electronic photos of his wedding and early pictures of his son, Bennett.

As she stood there, scrutinizing him, the more she realized that those photographs didn't quite tell the whole picture. She didn't remember him being so . . . so . . . so . . . well, damned memorable, either. Flat photos couldn't really do justice to Cutter McCall in the flesh. As she held on to him, she could feel the hard, sinewy strength of his arms through his suit jacket.

He'd lost a few pounds since she'd received the last photo taken about five years ago, too. She saw that in the lean, chiseled line of his jaw. Cutter had always been a big boy. She remembered him literally dwarfing her when she was a kid. Sometimes his size worked to her advantage. None of the bullies at her school dared mess with her after they saw him and Donovan walking her to school. And Davalyn always made sure at the start of each new school year that along with new clothes, backpacks, and lunch boxes she had a pair of dedicated bodyguards to accompany her.

Other times, his size was a liability for her. She'd lost count of how many times he literally had her in tears—not with rage but with laughter as he or Donovan pinned her down and tickled her until she was gasping for mercy. Or, when they really didn't want to be saddled with a tagalong, their speed and quick thinking often left her standing, stomping her foot, and threatening to tell their parents that they'd left her alone.

Let's see him try to duck me now, Davalyn thought with satisfaction. She was a little older now. A little taller and a whole lot smarter. She wouldn't fall for those "I think your Barbie doll is calling you" or "Daddy has some candy for you" tricks again. No siree. She'd learned a few things since she'd been away.

Cutter held her at arm's length, a sheepish smile touching his lips.

Davalyn was content to stand there—enjoying this connection with her past that she could never quite make herself give up. She didn't know how long she stood there until Deacon Hargrove cleared his throat. Maybe it was a little longer than a moment that they stood there. Time was definitely playing tricks on her mind. Passing years had compressed to mere minutes while memories raced through her mind.

"What did you do to your hair?" Cutter asked, involuntarily reaching for one tendril curled loosely around her ear.

"Do you like it?" She spun around, giving him the full effect of the ebony natural curls and styling-mousse-sculpted spikes.

"I don't know." His tone was dubious. "I think that might take some getting used to."

"The way you're acting, maybe it would help if I stuck a big pink bow up on top?" she suggested.

Cutter chuckled. "It kinda reminds me of that haircut that Halle Berry wore in that movie with John Travolta. What was the name of that movie? Something about a big fish." He snapped his fingers, trying to bring the movie to mind.

"Hey, didn't Halle go topless in that movie?" Donovan recalled.

"Donovan," Dana said severely. Her tone clearly indicated how inappropriate she thought the comment was.

"Sorry," Donovan muttered, clearing his throat.

"Thank you for the floral arrangement, Cutter," Davalyn said, smoothly changing the subject. "It was a lovely gesture."

"Seems small. Mr. Bowers did so much for me and my family."

"Speaking of family," Davalyn said warmly. She looked past Cutter and into a pair of curious brown eyes staring up at her. Leaning forward with her hands on her knees, she continued. "Oh, tell me this isn't Bennett." She glanced up at Cutter. "He's grown so tall! The last picture you sent me, he was what . . . three or four years old?"

Cutter shrugged apologetically. "Three, I think."

"You think?" Davalyn teased him. "Don't you know? You're a grown-up man with responsibilities. You're supposed to stay on top of important stuff like that, Cutter."

"I never was good about that kinda stuff. Cards and letters and remembering important dates like birthdays or anniversaries."

Probably another reason why his ex-wife had been so frustrated with him. She had an anniversary date for everything. Their first date and kiss. Their first dance. Their first argument. Bennett's first steps and the first day of school. Cutter had always been there and enjoyed the moment, but couldn't always put a time and date to when they occurred.

He placed his hand on his son's shoulder, guiding him

off the seat and toward Davalyn. "Say hello to Ms. Davalyn, Bennett."

Bennett edged forward slowly, his hands thrust deep into his pockets. "Hello," he mumbled.

"It's a pleasure to see you again, Bennett." Davalyn held out her hand to him. "You probably don't remember me. The last time we met, you were sitting on my lap. Your dad was trying to make you eat some nasty old vegetables. But I saved you and we wound up having chocolate chip cookies and marshmallows for dinner."

Bennett paused, considering whether to take it, until he felt a light, encouraging squeeze on his shoulder. When he held out his hand reluctantly to her, Davalyn took it and shook it gently.

"Nice to meet you, ma'am," he responded.

"And so polite," Davalyn remarked. She turned to Cutter, her dark eyes sparkling with mischief. "He obviously didn't get that from *your* side of the family."

Cutter gave a soft snort of derision.

"Clayton and Bennett have just arrived," Dana Bowers informed her daughter. "If you're taking a break from the piano, Davalyn, why don't you show them to the kitchen for something to eat? There's enough food there to feed an army. I'm telling everybody to take some home with them when they leave."

"That was you on the piano?" Cutter asked, sounding impressed. "When did you learn to play the piano, Dav?"

"I can see I'm going to have to get you all caught up. Bring you up to speed on the last few years of my life, *Clayton.*"

Five

Davalyn lifted an index finger, then crooked it, motioning for Cutter and Bennett to follow her. Cutter tried not to notice the distinctive sway of her bottom as she weaved her way through the room. Kinda hard not to, though. No lie. Davalyn had a nice, narrow waistline, flaring out to a set of well-shaped hips. The girl's gifts were natural. He'd stake his *almost* undeserved reputation as a player on that one. He didn't mean any disrespect to her or her deceased father. But he was who he was—and he couldn't deny his eyes. He followed behind her, concentrating on keeping his eyes trained between her shoulder blades.

The Bowers home wasn't that large. The kitchen wasn't far from the formal living room, where most of the mourners congregated. Still, it took several minutes to weave their way through. Well-meaning mourners continuously stopped Davalyn to express their sentiments.

"So sorry for your loss."

"Mr. Bowers was a good man."

"He surely will be missed."

"I guess that makes Donovan the man of the house now."

By the time they'd reached the kitchen, Cutter could

see the relief on Davalyn's face. The kitchen was practically empty, since those who'd arrived early had already eaten their fill.

"I think if I hear one more time how Donovan's now the man of the house, I'm going to scream my head off," Davalyn stated, giving fair warning.

"Don't mind them, Dav. You know folks mean well."

"I know. I know. I don't mean to sound ungrateful for their well-wishes, it's just that . . ." She shrugged her shoulder, trying to shake off her irritation. "I don't know. I can't explain it."

"I know how you feel," he went on. "When my old man passed, everybody kept telling me to be strong. To rejoice. That he's in a better place." Cutter made a soft sound of derision. "I knew better than that. Couldn't stand to hear all of that crap. That mean old sumbitch ain't doing nuthin' but fryin' where he lies."

"Cutter!" Davalyn clamped her hand over her mouth. She looked over at Bennett and tried to compose her expression. "That's not funny. You shouldn't talk about your father that way. Bennett, why don't you go over to the table and pick out what you want to eat?" she suggested. "I'll help you serve up a plate after I've had a word or two with your dad."

Cutter grinned at her. "Taking me to the woodshed, Dav?"

"Somebody should. Why do you want to talk that way about your father in front of him?"

"Old Calvin always said to tell the truth and shame the devil. The point is, folks came to see him in death who never gave him the time of day in life. When they crowded around after the funeral, it was like buzzards hovering over a kill. They all seemed so phony somehow. Those people didn't have any idea what kind of man he was. Nobody really knew him."

"You did."

"Which gives me the right to say whatever I want about him. I'm qualified to tell the truth. Those other folks weren't. I know it's not like that with your father, Dav. Mr. Bowers really was a good man. But you don't need anybody to tell you that. They're just here for the food and to gossip about how he divided up what he had."

"I think Mama's disappointed that there wasn't more to go around," Davalyn confessed. "Dad didn't have much. You and Van got the shop. Van and I got the house. Mama got whatever he had left in his savings. And that wasn't much. Most of that will go to taxes anyway."

"All of his wealth was in his relationships," Cutter said gently. "He had a lot of true friends."

"Friends rich and funds poor. It won't take Mama long to take care of the rest of his estate business. And then she'll be going back."

"What about you?"

She stared oddly at him. "I'm going back with her. But only long enough to ship the rest of my things back here."

"Here? You're coming here? I thought you were taking that offer in Austin. The last time I talked to you, you were so excited about it. An investigator for the state fire marshal's office."

"No," she said slowly, folding her arm across her chest. "I'm taking a job here, covering the Kemah, Clear Lake, Seabrook, and Galveston area."

"Oh . . . well, congratulations. You sure landed a sweet deal," he remarked. "How lucky is that?"

"Luck? Luck!" She stabbed his chest with her index finger. "Luck had nothing to do with it, buddy boy. Hard work and sacrifice. Jeez, Cutter. Didn't you read any of the letters that I sent you? What do you think I've been doing the last few years since I got my degree? Sitting on my thumbs? I've been taking every course I can get my hands on to become a certified fire investigator—hazardous-materials control, emergency response, gas-and-electric-appliance fires, fire causation. If it burns, blows up, or reacts, I'm gonna find it. My résumé looks damned good and that's what got me the job. Not luck." She stopped, realizing that she'd gotten flustered. Davalyn figured that she wasn't really lashing out at Cutter, she was reacting to the loss of her father.

Cutter mentally crossed his fingers against the tiny stretch of the truth. "Of course I've read all your letters, Dav. You sent one about six months ago, right?"

Bennett heard their raised voices and thought they might be fighting. It surprised him, seeing his dad argue with a woman who wasn't his mom. He drifted over to them.

"Try three weeks ago, Dad," Bennett offered. "A pink envelope, Ms. Davalyn, with a rose on the corner?"

"That's right, Bennett," Davalyn said, shooting Cutter an amused look.

Pleased with the success of his memory, Bennett went on excitedly. "I think it's the one sitting on the desk with all those letters Dad said that he was going to throw away."

Cutter made a face like a man cut to the quick. "Junk mail, Dav. Not your letter."

"Don'tcha just love kids? So brutally honest," Davalyn said, smiling. "I e-mailed you and Van. I was on my way back here, back home, even before . . . That is . . . if Dad hadn't . . . Well, let's just say that he moved up my timetable sooner than I expected." Her voice suddenly broke as she choked on unshed tears.

Davalyn made herself suddenly busy, rummaging on the table set up to hold the covered dishes brought by the mourners, gathering paper plates and plastic ware for Cutter and Bennett. She wiped her hand across her eyes, muttering, "I know there are some napkins around here somewhere. Look at all of this food. Who's gonna clean up all of this?"

"Don't worry about it, Dav," Cutter said gently, taking the utensils out of her hands.

Davalyn stepped back, folded her arms, and leaned back against the kitchen counter. Staring at a point somewhere near the pointed toe of her sling-back black pumps, she shook her head.

"Sorry, Cutter. Guess I'm not taking this very well. You'd think that after all the years I'd been away that I could get used to the thought that he's gone. He's really gone."

"Not as long as we remember him," Cutter said fiercely.

Davalyn's smile was reluctant. "That sounds like the right thing to say at a time like this. And maybe, in a while, when it doesn't hurt so much to think about his passing, I'll believe it. But here, today . . . just let me wallow in my total denial. Okay?"

"A little wallowing is good for the soul," Cutter agreed. "We've all done it, Dav. So don't feel like you've got a lock on pain. If you need to talk to someone, I'm here." He placed a hand lightly on her shoulder.

She covered his hand with her own and squeezed gently. Cutter lifted his hand and, with the back of it, brushed away the remnants of a tear against her cheek. When she looked up at him, for one wild, insanely impossible moment, Cutter thought that maybe he should kiss her. It surprised him how much he wanted to. When he stepped a little closer, and she didn't back away, Cutter sensed that maybe she wanted him to kiss her, too. Something in those big dark eyes, glistening with tears, glowing with gratitude.

As quickly as it took the tear to dry, the mood, the moment, and the opportunity disappeared. The tugs on his attention came from multiple angles.

"Da-*aaahhhd,*" Bennett complained from the serving table, pointing to the food.

At the same time, in his jacket pocket, his cell phone buzzed against his chest. Cutter knew that it wasn't the station calling for him. He'd already arranged for someone to take his shift. He reached into his jacket pocket, checking the caller ID before answering.

Bennett came up from behind him, tugged on his father's jacket with one hand, and clutched at his rumbling stomach with the other. "Dad, can you fix me a plate now?"

"Yeah, sure. Sorry, son. In a minute."

Cutter indicated that he needed to take the call by stepping aside and lowering his voice before answering. "Yeah. Hey, uh . . . What's up?"

A brief pause, then Cutter looked briefly over his shoulder at Davalyn. She raised her eyebrow in question but said nothing. He wasn't offering any explanations, so she let it go. Still, it didn't escape her notice that Cutter was carefully avoiding mentioning the name of the person he was talking to. Instinct told her that it wasn't business on the other end of that line.

"Come on, Bennett," Davalyn offered.

She picked up a plate and placed a thick wedge of the four-layer double-chocolate cake with sweet cream-cheese icing, then handed Bennett a fork.

Cutter opened his mouth to protest, but Davalyn gave him another look, raising that active eyebrow again. "You were going to say something?"

He shook his head, then said into the phone, "Can I call you back later? Okay. Me too. Bye."

When he returned to Bennett and Davalyn, his tone was overly enthusiastic. "That's a big slice a cake you got there, young man. Tooth fairy's gonna have a field day with you."

"If she gives you any problems, Bennett, you tell her to come see me," Davalyn said.

Cutter didn't argue. It was important to him for Bennett to like Davalyn. Now that she was back, he imagined that the three of them—Donovan, Davalyn, and he himself—would fall back into their old trio. The more comfortable Bennett was around her, the better. A stable female presence in his life certainly couldn't hurt.

After the judge had granted him custody of Bennett, though Angela had fought long and hard to keep him, she'd shown a surprising lack of interest in their son. Four years since the ink had dried on the page and he was still reminding her what time she was supposed to pick him up. If he was a little late picking Bennett up, she gave him grief about it.

"There you go, Bennett," Davalyn said, setting the plate into his outstretched hands. "Think you can handle a slice like that?"

"Yes, ma'am. No problemo!" Bennett showed honest enthusiasm.

"You'll spoil his appetite, Dav," Cutter warned her.

"If making him wear that tie didn't spoil his appetite, nothing will," she quipped.

Cutter found himself at a loss for words. His sense of the moment was all skewed. He had been looking forward to seeing Davalyn again. After all, she was Donovan's sister—as good as family. But with each passing moment, something in the back of his mind was telling him that verbally sparring with Davalyn, as they'd done when they were kids, would not be the same. The dynamics between them had somehow changed. He didn't think he could easily get the upper hand like he could when they were kids. Not having the last word was going to take some getting used to.

When they were kids and she got tired of arguing with him, her response to him was limited to two weapons in her arsenal. Either she'd run and tell her parents or she'd make a face at him. Stick out her tongue. With either, he'd always felt as if he were the victor.

Now, as she stood at the kitchen table, using her tongue to unceremoniously dab at the dribbles of incidental frosting on her fingers, Cutter found that her arsenal of weapons was infinitely more sophisticated. Eminently more effective.

"Careful, Bennett. Don't spill anything on that suit. You're gonna have to wear it to church tomorrow."

Davalyn gave a short burst of laughter, then covered her mouth with her hand.

"What's so funny?" Cutter asked. He was stung. He might not be the perfect role model for his son, but he was trying to do right by him. Spiritual guidance was top on the list, even if fashion guidance wasn't.

"Nothing." She waved her hand, pressing her lips together to stifle another outburst.

"No, really. I want to know," Cutter insisted.

Davalyn sighed, considering whether or not to go on. "I was just remembering that time you and Van didn't change after church and went straight to the garage to work on that raggedy old Impala."

"You're gonna have to narrow that one down, Dav. That only happened . . . let me see . . . almost every Sunday for about a year," Cutter retorted.

"Come on, Cutter. Stay with me here. Think about it. You and Van, Sunday best, neckties—"

Cutter groaned loudly. "Oh man! Why'd you have to bring that up, Dav? I'd almost forgotten about that." It wasn't exactly one of their shining moments in their auto-repair-and-restoration history. It was a tale second only to the time the police raided their favorite dragstrip spot and packed him and thirty of his closest friends off to a holding cell until their parents came to bail them out.

"What, Dad?" Bennett wanted to know. "What happened?"

Davalyn reached up with hands and pantomimed choking herself. Cutter joined in with gagging noises, pulling on his own tie. "Teach me to leave the fan cover off when firing up an engine. Ripped my tie to itty-bitty shreds." Cutter chuckled despite his embarrassment.

"I'm surprised you ever had the nerve to put on another tie after that, Cutter McCall," Davalyn said.

"Well, if the sight of you coming after me with those hedge clippers didn't scare me off ties completely . . ." Cutter replied. He leaned over, pulled his collar away from his neck, and pointed at a two-inch scar on his neck.

"See that scar, Bennett? Took nine stitches, three weeks' worth of antibiotics, and a tetanus shot to heal."

"Hey, that wasn't my fault. I was only trying to help," Davalyn protested. "I would have cut you loose, too, if you hadn't moved out of the way."

"I was trying to save my neck," Cutter retorted. "Lucky for all of us, your dad heard the yelling and came out to the garage. Otherwise, we all would have been in serious trouble."

"He should have been around to stop you two clowns from this little honey," Davalyn retorted. She pulled up her sleeve, showing Cutter the long, oval scar on her forearm.

"Remember this?" she challenged him.

Cutter leaned forward, lightly tracing the outline of the scar with his index finger. "I remember, Dav," he said softly.

"So do I," she murmured. Then, realizing that they weren't exactly alone, she pulled her arm away. "I suppose I should thank you and Van for scarring me for life."

"And why is that?"

"If it hadn't been for you two, I wouldn't have developed this healthy respect for fire."

"And what happens when it burns too hot?" he suggested, moving even closer to her.

"Made me the woman I am today." This time, she didn't back away from him. She held her ground. Something in her very stance seemed to encourage his closeness. Maybe it was the way she met his gaze directly. Or the small smile on her lips that shared with him an unspoken secret. They continued talking for several more minutes, reminiscing. And in Bennett's mind, very close to kissing. They were so close—if either breathed too hard, moved in the slightest, they would touch.

Bennett stared openmouthed at his dad, the fork poised midway between the plate and his mouth as he watched the exchange between him and Uncle Van's sister. His daddy was a mack! He'd never seen Cutter in action before. Not like this. *Go, Daddy! Go, Daddy!*

"Well." Davalyn roused herself. "I'd better get back out there. Julian's probably wondering where I've gotten off to."

"Julian?" Cutter shook his head, blinking a little at her sudden shift in attitude. "Who's Julian?"

He felt as if the name should have been familiar to him.

"A friend," Davalyn replied. "I've mentioned him before, if you've been reading my letters like you said."

"Oh . . . oh yeah, Julian. Julian Blake."

Come to think of it, he'd also heard Donovan mention Julian several times in connection with Davalyn.

Julian was a lawyer. Maybe that was why he had a mental block against the man. Cutter wasn't feeling particularly friendly toward lawyers these days. He'd had a bellyful of them during his divorce proceedings with Angela. In his opinion, everything could have run so much more smoothly, a helluva lot more amicably, if it hadn't been for the lawyers prodding and pushing Angela into gouging him for everything they had worked so hard together to achieve.

Cutter tried not to buy into the stereotypes when it came to lawyers; he tried not to think of every cliché or lawyer joke in the proverbial book when Angela's lawyer contacted him and informed him that all communication would be coming through her now. They'd been together for too long to play those kinds of games.

Now that he thought about it, Davalyn had sent a couple of pictures to Van—she and this Julian at some of Austin's local hot spots. Davalyn and Julian partying at a blues club on Sixth Street, in hiking clothes following the trails of Mount Bonnell, dressed in appropriately corporate attire on the steps of the state capitol building. It was all coming back to him now.

"In case I don't catch up to you again, too busy with my duties as grieving hostess, don't forget to say goodbye to Mama before you go, Cutter. She'll only be here a few more days and then she's heading back to Silver Springs."

"Will do." He saluted, then turned his attention back to filling Bennett's plate. Bennett waited until after the swinging door had settled to a close before saying, "Uncle Van's sister is kinda nice."

"Yeah," Cutter agreed amiably. "Yes, she is."

"I think you like her," Bennett observed.

"Of course I like her," Cutter said, his tone matter-of-fact. "Davalyn's family. She's like a sister to me."

Bennett narrowed his eyes at his dad. He didn't think that his dad was deliberately trying to fool him. He'd always told him what a smart kid he was. The only other reason for that dumb answer was that maybe his dad just didn't know.

"Da-aad," Bennett said, drawing out the word, "I'm not talking about *that* kinda like." Bennett started to go into detail, using a couple of classmates as an example.

Cutter listened to the explanation with only half an ear. He moved to the swinging door of the kitchen and opened it just enough to peer out through the crack without being seen. Through a thinning press of bodies, he could just make out Donovan, Ms. Dana, and Davalyn grouped together exchanging pleasantries with one of the deacons of the church. He'd started to let the door ease closed again but stopped when someone else joined the group.

He watched as the man moved next to Davalyn and slid his arm around her waist, drawing her close. Was that her friend? Was that Julian Blake? Cutter could only see him from the rear, so he couldn't be sure. The man was almost Davalyn's height, about five feet seven, slender build, and seemed to fit the general look of the man who'd been in several of the photographs she'd sent. He was dressed in a sharp Italian suit. Expensive. Cutter could see the flash of gold on his Rolex band even from across the room. From the open, interested looks that several of the remaining female mourners gave him as they passed him, moved around him, edged closer to him, and insinuated themselves into the conversation, he was probably good-looking enough to be Davalyn's friend. The man in Dav's pictures had been very good-looking—if ladies went for that high-yellow, good-hair, Creole look. He looked of class, and smelled of money. To top it all off, he was a lawyer, too.

Cutter detested him on sight.

Six

"Thanks for putting Julian up for a few days, Van," Davalyn said as she readjusted the strap of an over-stuffed canvas overnight bag that was slung over her shoulder. She rested a rolling suitcase against the wall to avoid dragging it on the ceramic-tile floor of the entry. She'd helped Julian pack in a hurry, throwing in more than enough clothes for the week, as they tried to beat the midday checkout time at his hotel. The rest of his luggage was still in the trunk of his car.

"Ah, girl, you know you didn't even have to ask. There's plenty of room since Mama's gone back."

Nearly two weeks after the funeral, Davalyn had barely finished unpacking herself. Now she was trying to find room for Julian.

"Don't mean to be nosy. What's the deal with your condo, anyway, Julian?" Donovan asked.

"Incompetence," Davalyn responded for him.

"They told us something about a mix-up with scheduling the painting contractor and the new carpeting. If I'd known that they wouldn't be ready, Van, I would have made other plans. I could have gone back home to Dallas and stayed with my folks for a couple of days or kept my room a little while longer."

"I told him you wouldn't mind putting him up for a

few days, Van. It didn't make sense for him to drive all the way there just to have to turn around again. And the hotel . . . Well, paying that kind of bill is only fun for a day or two, and then it starts to get old."

Julian shrugged as if the money didn't bother him.

"There is a cheaper motel out on Highway 146, near Seabrook," Donovan began, but Davalyn glowered at him. "Just kidding, Julian. You know you're welcome here as long as you need to stay."

"It shouldn't be long. Davalyn made sure of that. You should have seen her talking to the leasing agent." Julian sucked in his breath. "She wasn't nice at all."

"What? Does my itty-bitty baby sister have a little bit of a temper-wemper?" Donovan mocked her, grabbing the fleshy part of Davalyn's cheek just below the cheekbone and tweaking until her lips made wet, smacking noises.

She pulled her head away, rubbing her cheek. "That's not funny, Van. And you can chill with that baby sister stuff. I'm a grown woman."

"She certainly wasn't kidding when she ripped that leasing agent a new one. The poor woman."

"Davalyn has this certain way of looking at you when she's really mad. She doesn't yell, but gets icy quiet. It's spooky. Trust me. You don't want to get on this lady's bad side," Donovan warned.

"All I wanted her to do was do her job. If she couldn't handle it, she should have just been honest with us. It's the dishonesty that I won't tolerate. Anyway, thanks again, Van. I appreciate you taking Julian in on short notice."

"I told you, it's not a problem, Dav."

"The leasing company said that they should be finished with the final touches on his condo by Monday.

Tuesday at the very latest," she promised. "And then we'll be out of your hair."

She reached up and tugged on one of the beaded cornrows that her brother wore. Davalyn found an odd sense of irony that she'd recently cropped off her shoulder-length hair and Donovan had allowed his to grow extra long.

"He can stay as long as he needs. It's your home now, Dav. Dad left it to you, too."

"We just hate to inconvenience you, Donovan," Julian said, putting his arm around Davalyn and pulling her tight to his side. His hand caressed her hip, leaving no doubt in Donovan's mind the claim he'd placed on Davalyn. "We could just as easily have kept our room at the Kemah Boardwalk Hotel."

"Your room," Donovan corrected, glancing at the hand that Julian had placed possessively on his sister. It didn't escape Donovan's notice that Julian hadn't said "suite" or "adjoining" or even completely "separate" rooms. After she'd gotten back from Silver Springs, she'd called him from the airport and said that she'd see him in the morning. It didn't take a genius to figure out that she wasn't going home, that she'd planned to spend time with Julian. Donovan hadn't objected. He just played "hear no evil, see no evil, speak no evil." But not today. Not in this house. Here he had a little something to say about the sleeping arrangements.

"Well, we've got plenty of room. Enough for everybody to have their own," Donovan said with a finality that encouraged without further explanation for Julian to drop his hand away.

Donovan smiled in confirmation when Julian got the message. There wouldn't be any of that bunking down together for Julian and Davalyn. Not under this roof.

That whirring noise in his ears was probably the sound of his dearly deceased dad spinning in his grave at the thought of Julian playing more than patty-cake with his baby girl.

Donovan had suspected that their relationship was something more than friends, but he didn't want to *know.* The pictures that Davalyn had sent him clearly showed that she and Julian were spending more time together than just casual friends. At the same time, she'd never come right out in any of her letters or phone calls and said that she and Julian were getting serious.

"I just finished a load of laundry, so there are fresh sheets in that linen closet down the hall. Julian—"

Donovan half turned, and pointed with his chin to guide Julian. "There's a guest bedroom down there. Down the hall, past that little table with the hall telephone, first door on your right. Make yourself at home." When he turned around, he pretended not to see the quick exchange of glances between Julian and his sister. If they'd discussed the sleeping arrangements before they'd arrived, Donovan had effectively rearranged their plans.

"See you in a bit, Davalyn." Julian blew Davalyn an affectionate kiss.

"In a bit," she echoed.

"I've some steaks and veggies on the grill. Should be ready in, oh . . . an hour or so. You guys can go on and get yourself settled in," Donovan said.

"Is that what smells so good? Need some help finishing up, Van?" Davalyn asked, continuing up the stairs.

"No, I think I got it all handled. But if you're volunteering, you're welcome to do the dinner dishes." Donovan followed after her.

"Dishes?" Davalyn scoffed. "You mean, you're not eating off paper plates and drinking from plastic cups?"

"No, ma'am. Since Julian's a guest in our home, we've got to use the 'good' china."

"When did you get to be so domestic, Van? You're a regular Martha Stewart."

She glanced over her shoulder in time to see her brother running his hand along the highly glossed wooden mahogany banister and frowning at the buildup of dust that had collected in the grooves of the carved railing.

"I gotta get Bennett over here. Maybe spray a little lemon-fresh Pledge on the bottom of his jeans and let him slide down the banister a couple of times," Donovan murmured aloud to himself.

Davalyn laughed at the image. "That poor kid. Between you and Cutter, how are you managing to bring him up as sweet as he is?"

"Just like Martha Stewart." He chuckled in turn. "We're doing all of the work with none of her dough."

"Isn't everything going all right at the shop?" Davalyn sounded concerned.

"Sure. We've got more business than Cutter and I can handle on our own. We just took on four new employees so we can keep the work going on extended hours."

"All that work that you guys put into that raggedy old Impala. I thought you'd never get it running. And now look at you. Making a pretty decent living out of fixing up other folks' junk heaps."

"Not too shabby for a couple of gearheads, huh?"

"Speaking of junk, what ever happened to that old car?" Davalyn asked.

"Well, we never got it running good enough to make it out to New Jersey to find Whitney Houston," Donovan said self-consciously. "It's still at the shop. Sometimes we park it out front, sorta like free advertising of what we do."

Davalyn shook her head. "You ought to send Whitney a fan letter and put that picture in it. Show her what kind of devoted fan you were, Van. You were stone crazy about that woman," Davalyn recalled.

"That was just the teenage hormones." Donovan tried to downplay the depth of his tender feelings for the megastar.

"No, it wasn't. I still remember when you called me at school, snifflin' and snottin' and cryin', when Whitney married Bobby Brown. Broke your heart."

Donovan stopped and sighed with exaggerated wistfulness. "If only she could have waited for me. I know I would have made her happy."

"You know, it's never too late to make your dreams come true, Van. You've been waiting for Whitney a long time. And with Bobby popping in and out of jail, now's your chance to step up. Represent. Show her what she's been missing all of this time."

"You've got issues. Anybody ever tell you that?" he teased.

"That's why I'm here, big brother. To get them all resolved."

As Davalyn pushed the door open, she paused dramatically in the entrance, soaking in the sights of her childhood. Not much had changed. Perhaps the wall paint had been freshened over the years. The pink-and-white wallpaper had been covered over with antique-white paint, then sponge-pattern swirls of sea-foam green, then back to white again—but a creamy, warm white Donovan had seen once in a popular interior-design-and-decorating show. He and Cutter had taken a cue from the show. Instead of swapping homes for a couple of days, they helped each other with some much-needed repairs and sprucing.

Her white and pink-peppermint-striped curtains had been swapped out, too, along with the giant pink faux-fur foot-shaped rug. But the white-and-gold gilt-edged canopy bed, oval mirror vanity, and claw-footed six-drawer chest had remained. Framed wall hangings of Davalyn's artwork, which spanned kindergarten through the second grade, still adorned the walls.

She also spotted a handprint of plaster when she'd first learned to write her name, a self-portrait depicting a family trip to the zoo, her first-grade spelling test marked with the teacher's smiley face for a perfect score, and a montage of prized trading cards. Donovan had made her feel really at home by pulling some of her old toys out of the storage closet. The toys now stood guard in new built-in shelves and seemed to perk up to attention as she entered the room.

Davalyn felt strange stepping into the domain of a long-gone eight-year-old. *Not quite gone,* she corrected. That funny eight-year-old girl was still part of her but buried down deep. She'd buried the girl she used to know, trying to hide the pain of separation from her father and her brother.

When her parents had divorced, her mother hadn't allowed her to take very much with her. She'd promised that she'd get Davalyn all new toys. And, for the most part, she had. Her Barbie collection, her jewelry maker, her paint set were set out in her new room, waiting to greet her.

By the time her folks were on speaking terms again, and her father agreed to ship some of her things to Maryland, she'd outgrown her need for most of them.

What was she going to do with an animated, talking teddy bear when she was allowed her own phone in her room?

But some things could not be replaced, no matter how she and her mother tried to replicate them. She wandered over to her window, pulled back the curtains and peered outside. Her room overlooked the backyard. Looking down, she could see the neatly mown grass, the flower bed, and the fence that separated her yard from Cutter's. The line of green-and-white honeysuckle and the buzz of bees and flutter of butterflies were barely a divider between the two homes. More like an extension of her family over into Cutter's. Daddy couldn't send that to her.

"Told ya it hasn't changed much," Donovan murmured, almost in her ear. "It's been here all this time just waiting for you to come back."

"And if I hadn't come back? What then?" Davalyn half turned, addressing her brother.

"The thought never crossed my mind. I always knew you'd come back, Dav. To tell you the truth, I was hoping that someday Mama would come back, too. I always hoped that somehow our folks would work it out. A ton of golden bricks would drop down on their stubborn heads and they'd somehow discover that they loved each other and couldn't do without each other. Or at the very least, they'd figure out that you and I should never have been separated. Not as kids. But they never did. Never did . . ." His voice, heavy with regret, trailed off.

"I'm here now," Davalyn said, holding out her arms to embrace her brother.

Donovan sighed. "You don't know how this makes me feel. I've finally got my baby sister back. Not just for a short visit with Mama calling every five minutes to check up on you, but back to stay."

"You're just saying that because you miss throwing things at me," Davalyn teased, leaning back and regarding him at arm's length.

"You're right," he didn't deny. "I miss that, too."

She plopped down on her old bed, bouncing a little and feeling the spring of the double-thick mattress cushion her weight. With a nostalgic sigh, Davalyn fell back, folded her arms under her head, and stared at the canopy overhead. Donovan flopped back beside her. "What are you looking at?"

"Nothing really." She shrugged. "Just thinking."

"About what?"

"About how strange it feels to be back here after all this time. At the same time, it feels so right. Like I never left. Does that make any sense?"

"A little. I mean, I look at you and I see a grown woman. I'm so proud of you, Dav. Look at how smart and pretty you turned out. At the same time, I still see my little sister and I can't help wanting to make up for all the mean things I said to you."

"I know you didn't mean them. That is, deep down in my heart, I knew. Just like I always knew that I'd be back here."

"And bringing company," Donovan replied, his tone dry. "So what's the story with the two of you, anyway?"

"What do you mean?" Davalyn avoided his gaze, fumbling with the corner of one of the overstuffed pillows.

"Don't play dumb with me. Is Julian your man or isn't he?"

"He's a friend," Davalyn hedged.

"Just a friend?"

"I didn't say that. He's more than that."

"Can't be too much more the way you were hanging all over Cutter after the funeral."

"I was not!" Davalyn protested. "I wasn't hanging on him. Was I?" She didn't sound so sure of herself.

"Enough so that old Miss Eugenia said something to Mama about it. Said that maybe she should have kept your little hot tail back in Maryland."

"Nuh-uh!" she denied. "You're just trying to yank my chain."

"Okay, maybe I'm exaggerating a little bit." He held up his thumb and forefinger about half an inch apart to show the distance.

"I was just glad to see him," Davalyn insisted.

"Sure . . . sure you were." Donovan intentionally made his tone seem as though he was agreeing with her in word only.

"There wasn't anything more than that to it, Van. Really."

"Really," Donovan echoed.

"Did he . . . Did he say anything to you about me . . . that is, about that day?" she asked hesitantly.

"Nope. Why?"

"Just asking."

Donovan thought he heard disappointment in her voice. "I don't believe it. You still holding on to that crush for him, Dav?"

"Oh, please! I am so over that."

"I don't know. The way you used to follow him around when you were a kid. Watching him at the time . . . It gave him the willies."

"I was only eight years old. I didn't know any better," she said defensively. "But I do now."

"Looks like your tastes *have* changed if Julian is the

kind of guy who jazzes you. Looks to me like he's more than that, Dav. Or wants to be. The way he was hanging on to you just now . . . That said to me he thinks you and he . . . well . . . you know."

"Julian and I are really good friends. And I care for him very much. Is that what you wanted to know?"

"Tell me," Donovan said, propping several pillows behind him. He leaned back, put both his feet on the bed, and gave Davalyn an open, interested expression as if he were ready for some good gossip. "Was it love at first sight?"

Davalyn sat up on one elbow to face him, too. She scrunched up her face. "I wouldn't exactly call it love. But we definitely had a connection. Julian and I met our first year of school at UT."

"Yeah, so you said in your letter. Was he the one that you called that high-yellow, stuck-up wanna-be?"

Davalyn laughed, then placed a finger to her lips. "Sh! Not so loud, big mouth. He'll hear you. The first time I met him, I didn't really like him. He was hanging out with this really snobby crowd. All of them had parents who came from money. Old money. New money. Didn't matter. All they did was sit around and talk about what trips they just came back from or their diverse stock portfolios. I was working two jobs and still taking a full load of classes. So, talking about how much money I could throw around really wasn't my game."

"But?" Donovan prompted. "You hooked up with him anyway."

"We found out we had some classes together and wound up in some of the same study groups. And when Julian's not with his friends, he's really, really nice. When you get to know him, you'll see. It just seemed kinda natural that we'd eventually go out together. I remember one summer, he took me home to meet his parents."

"Yeah, that was the summer that Cutter and I tried to get up to Austin to see you."

She reached out and punched him on his arm. "I wish you hadn't tried to surprise me. If you'd told me that you were coming to see me, I wouldn't have made other plans."

"Don't worry about it. It was spur of the moment. The important thing is, you had a good time."

Donovan didn't miss the shadow that suddenly fell across her face. Again she averted her eyes.

"You did have a good time, didn't you?"

"It didn't start off that way. I don't think his dad liked me too much, but his mom bent over backward trying to make me feel at home. The second time I went to visit, his dad was a little nicer. And by the third visit, they were dropping hints the size of bowling balls. Mrs. Blake had even gone so far as to start scouting homes for us in their neighborhood and Mr. Blake had Julian interviewing with some of his partners. They'd opened their home to me, so I didn't have the heart to tell them Julian and I aren't a couple."

"He feels the same way?"

"He's never said otherwise."

"I don't believe that. The man blew you a kiss, Dav."

Davalyn scrunched up her face. "I know. What's up with that? That's not Julian at all. We've been a couple for a long time. A couple of whats, I'm not sure."

"So"—Donovan's voice dropped to a conspiratorial whisper—"have you and Julian done it?"

"Excuse me?" Davalyn felt heat rising from her cheeks. She sat up, her expression properly indignant.

"Don't act like you don't know what I'm talking about, baby girl."

Davalyn's laugh was coy. "Yeah, I know what you're talking about. What I want to know is why you're asking me."

"Because I have to know whether or not I should go down there and kick his ass. Say the word, I'll do it, too."

"Oh, no, you won't!" She reached out and grabbed his belt loop as he started to climb off the bed. "You invited him to stay here, too, Van. You can't go back on your word now."

"My house, my rules," Donovan said stubbornly, inching forward and dragging her near the edge of the bed. For being so thin, Donovan was surprisingly strong. As he leaned forward, causing her to slide along the comforter, Davalyn hooked her other arm around the bedpost to stop her slide.

"My house, my rules, too," she corrected. She yanked back, causing him to flop backward onto the bed. "And for your 411, it's none of your business, bro, what I do with my private life." Davalyn lay beside him, panting slightly for the effort.

"Look at you, gettin' all grown-up on me and *everything*," Donovan drawled. "Well, it wouldn't have been too private if I'd let you and him share a room. Sound carries in this house. Some of these walls are paper thin. The last thing a brother wants to hear is the sound of bedsprings creaking, waking him up in the middle of the night."

"That goes double for me, *bruh*. Since we're sharing spaces, I'd better not hear any heavy breathing coming from your side of the house, either. If I'm not getting any, nobody's getting any."

"Man, that's cold!"

"No. What was cold was the way you sprang the sleeping arrangements on Julian like that. You could have at least given him a warning. Broke him in easy."

"What more did you want from me?" Donovan sounded hurt. "I gave him the room with the private bathroom. If he's got a problem with it, let him take a cold shower and get over himself."

Donovan stood, heading for the door.

"Where are you going?" Davalyn demanded, her expression suspicious. "You'd better not be going down there to interrogate Julian about our private business. The only grilling you need to be doing are those steaks and veggies."

"You're getting suspicious in your old age. I've got to go check on the food, don't I?"

"I'll be down to help you in a few minutes," Davalyn promised. "A few," she reiterated. She didn't want to give her brother the chance to corner Julian alone.

"Take your time," Donovan said. His tone was silky smooth. Which, of course, made Davalyn want to pick up her pace.

"I'll be down in two seconds," she corrected.

"Why? Don't you trust me?" Donovan was laughing as he closed the door behind him.

"Not as far as I can throw you!" Davalyn yelled through the door after Van had gone, rubbing the sore spot on her arm where she'd hooked it on the bedpost.

Davalyn climbed out of bed and sat down at her vanity table. She set out her hairbrush and curling iron, facial cream, perfume, vitamins. She set her birth control pills on top of the vanity as a reminder to herself to take one.

No, I don't think so. Davalyn immediately changed

her mind. Instead, she opened the drawer and dropped the pillbox back inside, stuffing the small box way in the back of the drawer, nestled between underwear she hoped Donovan would be too embarrassed or too modest to dig through.

"I can't believe that buttinsky asked me about Julian," she said aloud. "He'd better not be down there trying to wiggle any more info out of him."

She wasn't really worried. Julian wouldn't talk. He was as tight-lipped as they come. She just didn't want Van to put him on the spot like that. It really wasn't any of Van's business about her sex life anyway—even if there was something to tell.

Davalyn grimaced. If Van knew how much there *wasn't* to tell, he probably would have made an even bigger deal about her atrophied love life.

"Probably would grab a stack of cash out of the cookie jar emergency fund and rush right out to pick up the first gigolo on the street who'd perform for chump change," she said to her own reflection.

She had to giggle at the image of Van hanging out on some seedy street corner, waving cash in front of the "working boys" and having to dust off cookie crumbs before enticing some hot stud into a car for a little private party.

Other than the fact that it was glaringly illegal and mortifying if he was caught, it couldn't be any more embarrassing than Van asking Julian point-blank about them.

Davalyn propped her elbows on the vanity table and settled her face, with a heavy sigh, on her fists. What was even more pathetic was that for a split second, for just one insane moment, she'd once considered out of desperation to go prowling for action. She'd thought about it, considered the idea, and then quickly disregarded it. Whatever issues she had with Julian, that was still no reason to risk her health and her safety. Still for once . . . just once . . . she wished for something more.

She wasn't in love with Julian. She certainly didn't desire him, but she'd been with him for a long time. Maybe too long. The proverbial biological clock was ticking so loud, she expected her neighbors to call the bomb squad on her. Just once, she wanted to know what it felt like to lose herself in passion.

"So why am I still with him?" she asked herself.

Davalyn shook her head. A good question. A very good question. And once things settled down, she'd pose the question to Julian, too.

"Oh, why bother?" she asked her reflection in disgust. "I already know what he's going to say anyway."

She already knew what his answer would be—the same answer he always gave whenever she started to hint around that maybe it was time to change the nature of their relationship. Maybe she should stop hinting and come right out and say it.

They'd gone as far as they could go, hadn't they? What was the point of hanging on? If Julian couldn't give her what she wanted—what she felt she deserved—what was the point of wasting the rest of her years? Fertile eggs were dropping out of her body like a sky diver without a parachute. She had to *do* something.

Giving her reflection a determined nod, Davalyn changed out of the demure skirt and blouse she'd put on that morning when she and Julian drove to inspect his condo. For Van's barbecue, she changed into a more comfortable pair of faded, low-rise, hip-hugging, flare-legged jeans and a tie-dyed blue, purple, and green cropped top that stopped just above her belly button.

The top showed off the silver pierced navel ring accenting her slim torso and the colorful, half-dollar-size hummingbird tattoo fluttering on the small of her back.

After brushing on sheer, wine-tinted lip gloss, touching up her mascara, and running her fingers through her hair to fluff up her spikes and curls, she slid her feet into her sandals, clipped on a matching silver toe ring, then started downstairs after her brother.

"Van?" she called out. Turning left at the bottom of the stairs, she hurried down the hall, through the kitchen. The smell of char-grilled steaks wafting through the screened door made her mouth water and quicken her steps as she pushed open the door and stepped onto the back porch.

Davalyn stopped short. It wasn't Donovan at the grill, but Cutter poking at the charcoal briquettes to stir up the flame. Juices from the steaks bubbled over and through the slots of the grill, dropping onto the fire and sending up a tantalizing cloud of aromatic gray smoke. He poked at the steaks with a large two-pronged fork, testing them, while the other hand tilted a long-neck bottle of imported beer to his lips.

Davalyn stood in the doorway for a few seconds without announcing herself. She wasn't sure if she was more drawn to the smell of dinner on the barbecue pit or to the sight of the man preparing it. The way she was feeling now, it was a toss-up which she could devour first.

"Action," she whispered to herself. Then, as if cued by an invisible director offstage, Davalyn allowed the screen door to slam behind her. At the sound, Cutter's head snapped up.

"Bennett! How many times have . . . I . . . told . . . you . . ."

As he turned around, the reprimand died on his lips.

Davalyn stood under the comfort and shade of the wooden lattice awning, crossing her arms at her waist.

"I'm not Bennett," she announced. Her gaze shifted from the steaks sizzling scrumptiously on the barbecue pit back to Cutter again. She approached him slowly, deliberately, moving into the sunlight. She stopped just inches away from him and leaned carefully over the pit to take a whiff.

"Umh-umh-umh . . . that sure does looks good."

Seven

Took the words right out of my mouth.

Cutter pressed his lips together to keep from voicing that thought aloud. He stood at the grill, fork poised in midair, as he watched her approach.

"Sorry about snapping at you, Dav. I thought you were Bennett."

"You thought I was Bennett?" Davalyn echoed. She didn't know whether to be insulted or concerned. She thought she was lookin' kinda sexy in her homage to the 1960s flower child style and Cutter thought she looked more like an eight-year-old boy? What was wrong with that picture? "I think you need to get your eyes checked."

No, I don't, Cutter denied silently with certainty. He saw just fine. Maybe even looked harder than he should have been. He was glad for the dark sunglasses perched on the end of his nose and the muted light streaming through the patio cover. Anything to keep her from seeing just how hard he was looking. Pushing his sunglasses farther up to conceal his eyes, Cutter saw perfectly well how that cropped top clung to the generous curves of her breasts. Cutter wondered if Davalyn knew that in certain light, that thin cotton top was semi-transparent. It didn't take X-ray vision to see that she wasn't wearing a bra, either. Or if she was wearing one, it was more decorative than functional. Probably one of those little silky, wispy things that molded to her like second skin. One that might go completely transparent when dampened by the moisture from her body.

Whoa, boy. Cutter found himself once again reining in runaway thoughts. What was the matter with him? This was Van's sister. His baby sister. Another side of him couldn't help but notice that there was nothing babyish about Davalyn now. Except maybe those wide, baby-bearing hips.

"I'm glad I'm not your son," Davalyn continued. "From the look on your face, Cutter, I thought I was in for a spanking."

She's teasing me, Cutter thought. *Maybe even flirting.*

"I don't spank." Cutter spoke brusquely to get the image out of his head of his hand pressed firmly and often against Davalyn's tight bottom. This was bad. This was very bad. Thoughts like those muddying his thinking were enough to get a good old-fashioned beat-down from big brother Van if he ever got an inkling of what was going on inside Cutter's head. And if he kept having thoughts like those, Van was going to find out sooner or later. They shared everything.

Even if he did manage to keep his mouth shut, Van was bound to catch him looking at Davalyn. How could he not find out? Cutter found that with each passing moment he liked looking at her—long and hard.

"I was about to get on him about slamming that door. If I've told that boy once, I've told him a thousand times to be more careful. I've already had to fix the mesh on Van's screen door twice, and just last week I put a new set of hinges on my own."

"Oh, lighten up on him, Cutter," Davalyn said. She reached for a handful of potato chips from a bowl on the picnic table and popped them one by one into her mouth.

When she dusted off the salt from the chips on the back pockets of her jeans, Cutter averted his eyes. Okay. So, she was wearing a bra. With her hands behind her, the material of that top straining ever so slightly, he saw the gossamer-thin, lace-edged lavender outline of the bra strap resting against her skin.

"I'm not being hard on him," Cutter denied. "Just tryin' to bring the boy up right. So when he goes out in public, folks know he's had at least a little home trainin'. When he goes out, I want folks to say, 'Look at Cutter's son. Look how well behaved he is.'"

"Instead of 'There goes Cutter's son. Somebody call the cops,'" Davalyn suggested. "How quickly they forget. I seem to remember my dad having to replace a few window screens more than once because of a couple of somebodies that kept sneaking out in the middle of the night to go drag racing," Davalyn said, thoughtfully tapping a well-manicured fingernail against her temple. "As far as cops go, that officer was very polite every time he escorted you and Van home."

"Oh yeah, Officer Wilder," Cutter said nostalgically. "I wonder what ever happened to him. He was pretty patient with us."

"See!" she challenged. "Patience is a virtue."

"That was different." Cutter grinned at her. "We weren't being careless back then."

"Just sneaky," she amended.

"Adventurous," Cutter corrected.

"Hardheaded," Davalyn volleyed.

"We sure were a couple of cutups. Ah, those were the days."

"Don't get too lost in your reverie, Cutter. You're burnin' our dinner to a crisp," Davalyn warned.

"Don't blame me. Blame your brother. He's the one runnin' around here in a 'Kiss the cook' apron." Cutter reached for an old bottle with the top poked full of holes to shake out Van's secret recipe of water, vinegar, and spices.

"Where is Van, anyway?" Davalyn asked, looking back toward the house. She had a momentary panic attack. What if he carried through with his threat to interrogate Julian? She considered going after him, to drag him out here by his braids if she had to.

Cutter shrugged. "He called me and told me to show up for dinner. Asked if I had any extra speaker wire. Said something about pulling out some old giant speakers, the ones that stand about this high." He held out his hand about four feet off the deck. "So, I sent Bennett over here with a coil. But that was about fifteen minutes ago. I guess they're still workin' on it. The next thing I know, I'm watching my dinner go up in flames. I could see the smoke from the pit from my back porch," he said, setting the large two-pronged fork on the side table with the other grilling utensils, including a small bucket filled with cedarwood chips. He made himself busy, poking at the embers, sprinkling on more spices.

Waving her hand over the open pit to dispel the plumes of rising gray smoke, Davalyn coughed delicately. "Now, that's what I call putting our tax dollars to work. Your dedication as a firefighter absolutely amazes me, Cutter. Risking life and limb to rescue that poor charred T-bone steak from a horrible, flaming death."

"Shame to let a good piece of meat go to waste," he agreed.

Davalyn started to giggle.

"What's so funny?"

"My brother and you. You two crack me up."

"How's that?"

"My brother, a man who can hot-wire cars but can't hook up a speaker system, and you, a volunteer fire-fighter who can't control a barbecue. Now tell me that you don't think that's funny? Go on. I dare you."

Cutter dipped his chin to his chest, peered at Davalyn over the rim of his sunglasses. "Funny in a pathetic, cruel-twist-of-irony kinda way. Yeah. It's hilarious."

"Come on, laughing boy. Let me give you a hand," she offered.

She reached past him, her shoulder lightly brushing his chest as she leaned over to pick up the fork he'd just put away.

"Nuh-uh," Cutter said quickly, leaning away from the point of contact. "That's all right."

His reaction to her touch surprised him. He hadn't taken this much care around the open flame of the pit. "I think between Van and me that we can handle it."

"Yeah, I can see how well you're handling it." Her tone dripped with sickly sweet sarcasm as she poked at the T-bone steak. When instead of sizzling, the steak crunched, she faced him with raised eyebrows. "The fire's too hot," Davalyn assessed.

"Is that your unbiased, professional, expert opinion?" Cutter quipped.

"Well," Davalyn said, placing her chin between her thumb and forefinger and circling the pit, "judging from the burn pattern . . ."

"Uh-huh," Cutter encouraged.

". . . and the accelerant," she continued, pointing to the lighter fluid resting on the side table, "and given the propensity of the human male of the species to resist following even the simplest of directions." She then tapped the warning label on the side of the grill that advised against leaving the grill unattended.

"Hey! I thought you said unbiased," Cutter objected.

"No, *you* said unbiased," she corrected him. "But I am still claiming to be an expert."

Cutter gave a noncommittal grunt.

"Anyway, given that particular character trait, my analysis of the scene is—" Davalyn paused for dramatic effect.

"You'd better not keep the insurance adjusters waiting this long for your expert fire scene analysis," Cutter warned her.

"Even with the combined cooking knowledge of you and Van, you two still can't cook worth a damn."

"And that's your expert opinion?"

"Do you want me to put it in writing for you?"

"That's all right. I think I've got the gist of it." Cutter laughed. Seconds later, the air crackled with a burst of static, made them wince with a high-pitched whine, and then the blare of zydeco music.

"See there? My boy redeemed us. Got the music goin'," Cutter said. "We're in for some good times now."

"Maybe." Davalyn was skeptical. "It all depends."

"Depends on what?"

"On how many times you step on my feet when you dance with me."

"Dance with you? Who said I was askin' you to dance?" He sounded amused until Davalyn wrapped her arms around his waist.

Cutter sucked in his breath. "Wait a minute. Hold up. . . . What do you think you're—"

"You burned my dinner," Davalyn interrupted

smoothly. "You have to make up for it in some kind of way."

Ignoring his protests, Davalyn dragged him away from the grill toward an open area on the wooden deck.

"I gotta watch the steaks."

"It's not as if they're gonna do tricks. They'll be fine for a few minutes. I haven't been dancin' since finals my senior year in college. Folks in Silver Springs know a lot about rock and roll, and alternative music like ska, and you might even find a decent blues bar closer to D.C., but they don't know squat about zydeco. I heard this group once in Austin on Sixth Street. They were awesome! For a minute, I thought I was going to quit school and become a groupie."

She began to move, keeping perfect time with the lively zydeco rhythm.

Cutter didn't move. Kept his feet planted firmly on the deck. "Sorry to disappoint you, Dav. But I don't dance," he said stiffly, grasping her by the elbows.

"Don't dance? What do you mean you don't dance? It's not against your religion, is it? I don't remember any commandment that says, 'Thou shalt not get your swerve on,'" Davalyn teased, moving closer to him, then backing away.

"Cut it out, Davalyn." Cutter tried not to sound irritated, but failed.

Davalyn stopped in midtwirl, noting the pained expression on his face.

"Come on, Cutter. Dance with me." Her tone was enticing, teasing. "It's not as if I'm asking you to do the macarena. I'm in a good mood for the first time since Daddy passed away. I just want to let go for a while."

"Then why don't you start by letting go of me?" he retorted, physically pulling her hands away.

Davalyn took a surprised step back. "Sor-*ry*. I didn't mean to get your briefs in a bunch," she retorted.

"I'm not pissed," he denied.

"Coulda fooled me."

"I just don't wanna dance. Is that all right?" He didn't want her that close to him. He didn't want her to know just how much she affected him. If she continued to press against him, it wouldn't be an easy thing to hide.

Davalyn lifted her arms in acquiescence. "Fine. We won't dance."

"Maybe later." He tried to appease her.

A few moments of strained, uncomfortable silence passed between them. Cutter didn't like it. He didn't like it at all. Choosing not to talk because he didn't have anything to say was one thing. But not talking because he didn't like putting a voice to the thoughts in his head was another. He didn't mean to upset Davalyn.

But what bothered him more than upsetting her was admitting to himself that dancing with her, having the opportunity to hold her close to him again without a hundred curious eyes staring at them as folks had done after the funeral, was on his mind. He wanted to touch her. Couldn't think of anything else for the two weeks she'd returned to Maryland.

The thought of seeing her again, touching her, was burning inside him. He imagined himself as well done as those T-bone steaks, complete with grill lines across his backside.

"I guess I'll . . . uh . . . go inside and see if Van needs any help," he mumbled, moving sideways toward the kitchen door.

"No, you stay here and stomp out the flames of what's left of our dinner. I'll go." She paused again, then said, "I need to check on Julian anyway."

That stung him. He'd almost forgotten about Van's houseguest. Conveniently forgotten.

"You go do that," Cutter said stiffly. "Ask him real nice. Maybe he'll dance with you."

Davalyn folded her arms across her chest and replied, "I don't *have* to ask."

Cutter knew what that meant. Julian was Davalyn's man. She wouldn't have to cajole him to hold her.

"Fine," he said, resenting the fact that she'd brought up another man's name in front of him.

"Fine," Davalyn tossed over her shoulder. As she disappeared inside, the slamming screen door made Cutter wince.

"Stop slamming that door or you will be in for a spanking!" he bellowed after her.

He stopped short when the door opened once more and Julian came out. Instinctively, Cutter tensed, preparing to react. He wondered if Julian had heard or witnessed any of the exchange between him and Davalyn. Kinda difficult not to. It wasn't as if they were whispering. But if Julian had heard, he didn't give Cutter any indication.

Eight

Cutter thought that Julian might have heard the conversation between him and Davalyn, but he couldn't be sure. He kept telling himself that it really didn't matter. He shouldn't worry. Yet, all during the dinner, he kept waiting for an opportunity to feel Julian out. He kept wondering, if Julian had heard, why hadn't he said anything? Why hadn't he come to Davalyn's defense, since it was so obvious that he'd upset her? What kind of man was he?

But there never seemed to be a good time to draw Julian out. Besides, how do you tell a man, "I'm having visions of your girlfriend in her underwear"? There was no easy, sane way to do it without expecting a confrontation. Knowing that Julian could be planning to confront him didn't stop him from thinking about Davalyn.

Every time the idea popped in his head, he shifted uncomfortably, as if he were sitting on live barbecue coals. He shifted his gaze from Julian to Donovan—another source of conscience-pricking irritation. Cutter couldn't quite get his lips to tell Donovan that he was having more than brotherly feelings toward Davalyn, either.

In between the small talk and the potato salad, cracking jokes and breaking bread, Cutter waited for his opportunity. Right after dessert, Cutter thought he had the right time. Davalyn had taken Bennett to clear the table. Donovan was cleaning the grill.

In the full-bellied, sated kind of silence that followed, Cutter leaned back in his chair, chewing a minted toothpick absently. Thinking of nothing, staring off into nothing, he was content just to sit there and digest the meal.

The breeze coming off Galveston Bay stirred the poplar and pecan trees scattered around Van's backyard. The sound of the wind whistling through the trees was answered by the chimes hung under the eaves of the back porch. This late in the evening, cicadas had started to hum. Their cry, rising and falling, was loud enough to drown out conversation one moment, and a low, barely discernible hum the next. Nature's symphony. The scent of cooking food thinned, chased away by the heavier, sweeter scent of honeysuckle. Full stomach, full senses, Cutter wanted to lie back in a swinging hammock and let its gentle rocking lull him to sleep.

While he was still debating whether to get up, Davalyn came out of the house with Bennett in tow. One of Bennett's storybooks was tucked under her arm. She crossed the backyard and climbed carefully into the hammock. Bennett eased next to her, didn't seem to mind when she put her arm around his shoulder. Together they started to sway back and forth. Cutter could hear his son reading out loud, Davalyn helping him over the harder words. He smiled. *Looks like they hit it off really well.* Too bad it was at the expense of his perfect napping spot.

When he turned back around, he realized that Julian had been watching Bennett and Davalyn as well. More than that, Cutter had the distinct impression that Julian was watching *him* watch them.

Julian also leaned back in his chair, but he didn't look comfortable or relaxed. Cutter couldn't exactly figure out what kind of look the man had. It wasn't one of jealousy. He didn't look as if he wanted to confront him, but he did look as if he wanted to talk.

Cutter had tried all evening to find a way to approach Julian with tact, finesse. There was no easy way to do it. Besides, he wasn't one for beating around the bush anyway. It wasn't his style to waste time.

Julian opened his mouth, then shut it again without saying a word. He glanced across the deck at Donovan, then back at Cutter.

"Something on your mind, Julian?" Cutter asked softly. Nothing confrontational in his tone. He said it blandly, as casually as if he were asking Julian to comment on the weather.

"Ye-es," Julian said hesitantly. He leaned forward. "Got a minute, Cutter? I do need to talk to you."

"Go on," Cutter said, gesturing for Julian to start talking.

Julian shook his head. "Not here. Not now. It needs to be just you and me. Do you get what I'm saying?"

Cutter nodded once. This was it. What he'd been expecting all evening.

"Van," he called out over his shoulder, "I'm takin' Julian over to my place to see the boat. He's thinkin' about gettin' one for himself."

Van turned around. "Really? I didn't know you were interested in boats, Julian." He sounded surprised. Surprised and amused. Julian didn't strike him as being a hard-throttling, wind-in-your-hair, sea-spray kinda guy. Cutter's boat was sweet. A Chaparral SS-180. They

didn't come much sleeker. Much faster. He didn't imagine that Julian would let anything ruffle those high-cost
tailored suits. Even his casual clothes spoke of wealth.
How Julian had managed not to spill red barbecue sauce
on his white silk shirt—Donovan spent a good part of
the dinner watching, wondering, and waiting for a splat-
ter to ruin that pristine material.

"I guess that's another interest that Cutter and I
share," Julian said, rising from the table.

"We'll be right back," Cutter promised, also standing.
He noded toward the fence. Through that gate, around
the corner, and across the front yard, Cutter made his
way toward his garage.

Midway across the yard, Julian reached out, laid a
hand on Cutter's shoulder to stop him.

Cutter turned around, instinctively shrugged Julian's
hand off him. He thought he saw a look on Julian's face.
A curious mixture. A brief flash of anger, followed by
an apology. And then Cutter wasn't sure, but he also
thought he read a profound sadness. Hard to tell. The
emotions swept so quickly over Julian's face, it might as
easily have been the shadows of a passing cloud.

Cutter was all at once wary, suspicious, and curious
as to why Julian wanted to talk to him alone.

"All right, Julian," he said easily. "Nobody's around
now. So talk."

"I'm not sure exactly how to say this," Julian began
hesitantly.

"Say it plain," Cutter suggested. "It's usually the best
way."

"I'm a lawyer," Julian said with a wry smile. "I spent
three years training the plain talk out of me."

"But I don't have three years to stand out here while

you work on getting it straight." Cutter made a swirling motion with his hand, urging Julian to get to the point.

"It's about Davalyn." Julian said this as if her name explained it all.

"What about her?" Cutter played dumb, waiting to see if Julian would own up to eavesdropping on his and Dav's conversation before dinner. Maybe not much eavesdropping was necessary. Toward the end, their conversation had gotten a little heated. In other words—loud.

"You and Davalyn have been friends a long time," Julian said as a matter of fact. "Since you were kids."

"You took me away from Van's dinner table to tell me that?" Cutter was incredulous, trying not to sound disgusted. He made an effort to inject a little patience into his tone. The man was obviously working his way up to something and finding it hard to say. "Tell me there's something more you wanted to say to me."

Cutter should have been used to that reaction from people by now. Though he'd slimmed down considerably since his teen years, he hadn't reduced in height. Some folks still found it difficult to approach him, to strike up a conversation. If he'd had a dollar for every time some stranger crossed the street to avoid passing him, Cutter figured he could retire by now. As he stood here, staring at Julian, he willed himself to relax, to make himself appear less imposing.

"Wait. There's more," Julian said sharply. He took a step closer to Cutter, as if to stop him from going back. Cutter almost laughed. Unless Julian was a lot stronger than his 130 pounds implied, he didn't think there would be any contest if Cutter decided he really wanted to end this conversation. He could push past Julian with little or no effort.

But Julian's stance didn't seem confrontational. Just the opposite. More imploring than threatening. Cutter squashed the instinctual response that made him react negatively to Julian.

"That's not *all* I wanted to say," Julian continued. "Davalyn and I are friends, too. Good friends."

"I know that, too. It's pretty obvious . . . the way she talked about you in her letters."

"She talked about me?" Julian sounded pleasantly surprised. "In letters to you?"

"To me and to Van. Sure. She sent pictures and everything."

"So, she talked about me," he repeated, looking away. He took a deep breath, then met Cutter's gaze squarely. "But it can't be anywhere near how she talked about you."

"She talked about me to you?" It was Cutter's turn to repeat.

"Like a broken record." Julian's mouth twisted in blatant sarcasm.

"You mean she talked about Kemah, about her brother, Van. . . ." Cutter just wanted to be sure that he understood.

"And *you*," Julian stressed.

Cutter shook his head. He couldn't understand it. Julian and Davalyn were together. A couple. Inseparable. He wondered what kind of man Julian was to let his woman go on and on about another man. If Davalyn were his woman, he wouldn't let her interject a man who wasn't her brother into the conversation as much as Julian indicated she'd talked about him. He'd put other things on her mind . . . enough to keep her thinking about him and only him. If Davalyn were his . . . If only.

Cutter folded his arms across his chest. "Why are you

telling me this, Julian?" Cutter asked. "If you think I've encouraged her, led her on—"

"I'm not accusing you of anything. Or asking for a confession," Julian said tightly. "You don't owe me a thing."

"Then why'd you bring me out here?"

"Maybe to overstep my bounds. To ask you to do me a favor."

"A favor? What kind of favor?"

"Like I said, you don't owe me anything. And I've got no right to ask you anything. But . . ."

"But you are going to ask me anyway."

"I have to. I don't have a choice." Julian's voice was tinged with regret. "Have to," he repeated.

"What is it you want, Julian?" Cutter said impatiently.

"You mean besides Davalyn?" Julian snapped.

Cutter glanced toward the Bowers house. "I still don't see how I can help you, Julian."

"Why do you think Davalyn came back here, Cutter? Not just for her father's funeral. Why'd she come back to Kemah to stay?"

Shrugging his shoulder, Cutter offered the only reason he felt comfortable suggesting. "She got a job offer. A good one."

"Not better than the one she got in Austin. If she'd stayed there, she could have been making almost double what she's making here."

"Double?"

"That's right. Double. But obviously, she valued something else more than money. Some*one* else. She came back because of you."

"You don't know that." Cutter shifted uncomfortably. "She came back because she wanted to come home."

"Home? Come on, McCall. You're smarter than that. This hasn't been her home for twenty years. I see the way she looks at you. She wants you." Julian's jaw tightened, and Cutter thought that he would grind his teeth to a pulp.

"Like I said, I haven't given her any reason to think that I see her as anything more than a kid sister. She's a friend of the family."

Julian paused, as if considering both Cutter's claim and his own next words. "Then it shouldn't be too hard to grant my favor, should it? I need you to stay away from Davalyn. Can you do that?"

"We practically live in each other's houses."

"Friendship can only go so far, McCall. Especially between a man and a woman. If you really are just a friend, then you won't have any problem backing off. Don't make her choose between you or me. Don't put her in that position."

"What do you mean back off? I've never pressed, Julian. If you've been listening to all that talk from Dav about me, then you should already know that."

"If that's how you feel, I can accept that. It's how she feels that concerns me. I can't believe she's never—"

"She's your woman," Cutter said tightly. "I'll respect that for as long as that situation continues."

Julian let out a long breath. "I know that I can't compete with you, McCall. Before now, I've never tried. All while we were in undergrad school together, when she talked about you, I let her talk. As strange as it sounds, it brought her closer to me. I was willing to listen to her. Now that she's back . . . Well, she doesn't need to talk to me anymore. She has you in the flesh. I didn't think it would bother me . . . losing to you. But it does."

Cutter opened his mouth. He wanted to apologize,

but couldn't quite bring himself to do it. He hadn't done anything to Julia—either intentionally or unintentionally.

"I don't know what to tell you, Julian."

"I just need more time with her," he told Cutter. "Just a little more time."

"You do what you need to do to keep her, Julian," Cutter said, walking away. "You won't find me in your way."

Nine

Davalyn didn't have any trouble finding her sorority sisters, even though they'd taken a table all the way in the back of T-Bone Tom's. The restaurant, noted for its steak and seafood combinations, was one of their favorite meeting places. Good food, live music, and its extended hours—staying open to nearly two in the morning every day—was the perfect place to plan their community service event.

However, with the weather still being so hot, no one really wanted to concentrate on Kwanzaa, an event that was nearly three months away. After eating, catching each other up on what was happening in their lives over a couple of pitchers of chilled margaritas, the ladies of Alpha Kappa Alpha were ready to unwind.

Not that they weren't a serious-minded group. They were. The professional women who made up her alumnae chapter were very serious when it came to representing their sorority. Raising awareness for women's issues, communicating health risks to African-Americans, mentoring young women, fund-raisers for the disadvantaged—their lists of achievements, their service to the community, went back since the sorority's inception. They took their responsibilities as community leaders very seriously, along with some of

the most highly celebrated women of their sorority—
actresses and activists, doctors and poets, athletes and
astronauts. The roll call of women who were in the top
of their field and made a difference in their community went on.

But that didn't mean they didn't like to have their fun,
too. The women that Davalyn thought of as friends and
sisters worked hard and played hard. The 100 percent
all-out effort that they gave showed in everything they
did.

It was time for play now. Davalyn recognized that as
soon as she joined them. Kimmy Dupree was standing
in front of the stage, urging the live band to stop playing all of that rock and roll and bust out with some
old-school jams. Kimmy made an imposing figure
standing there—as tall as Davalyn, twice as wide, and
three times as loud. She wasn't drunk, just boisterous.
She could be heard over the band, even though she
didn't have a microphone. Margot Tate, the self-
appointed voice of sophistication, had taken off her
shoes and was trying to show Angelique Wyatt the latest dance step. Nydia and Nia Gilbert, the identical
twins, were up on the stage, performing an air guitar
routine along with the band. Rashida Samir was left to
hold the table and watch their purses. As the designated
driver for them tonight, she didn't mind. She'd been in
the emergency room at the University of Texas Medical
Center, trying to revive the victims of a boating accident. Right now, she needed a little alone time. The only
one missing from the group was Tonia Andrews. Davalyn didn't think the other sisters minded too much.
Tonia was a little on the uptight side and was frequently
the voice of doom-and-gloom in their efforts.

Davalyn pulled up a chair, grateful that they'd gotten a table under one of the taller cottonwood trees.

"Hey, girl," Rashida said in greeting. "I already ordered for you. Salad with grilled chicken strips and an extra-large lemonade."

"That sounds good, so good." She looked around. "Looks like we're just about all here."

"This is it. Nola Rogard said that she wasn't going to be able to make it. And Tiffanie just doesn't have the time. She said that she'll catch us on the next go-round, when we're planning the event for black-history month."

"If this is it, then we should get started. I've got a few ideas. . . ."

Rashida turned in her seat, put two fingers between her lips, and whistled sharply. She waved the rest of the ladies over, while Davalyn set out copies of the presentation that she'd made—complete with pie charts, samples, and a timetable for when everything would have to be pulled together.

Margot called the meeting to order, effectively getting their minds back on the task at hand. Once they were all in agreement about their next action items, then they could get back to the serious business of resuming their fun.

Davalyn passed out her presentation. "I figure, there're enough of us here to each take a Kwanzaa principle and run with it," she suggested. "Now, the lists you see on page four are just suggestions on some of the things that we can do. After we've been assigned a principle, we can decide what we can do to best present that principle."

By the time Davalyn's food arrived, the sisters were well on their way to deciding their plans.

"I bet I can guess which principle Nia's going to take," Kimmy said with a sly wink.

"How do you know I want to take *Nia?* I may not want purpose. Suppose I want creativity?"

"I think Rashida should take that one," Margot suggested. "Remember that time she sponsored a beautification fund-raiser for the Moody Gardens?"

"Rashida?" Davalyn asked, asking permission to assign her the task. "Do you want to take *Kuumba?* "

"Sounds good to me," she agreed.

"Nia, are you cool with your namesake?" her twin, Nydia, asked.

"Of course I am. Y'all know I was just kidding y'all."

"Then I'd better take *Imani*"—Angelique laughed—"as long as we're taking our namesakes. If Angelique doesn't say 'faith,' I don't know what does."

"Which one do you want, Nydia?" Kimmy asked.

"I'll take *Ujamaa.* I'm pretty tight with some folks with the chamber of commerce. I think we can get some black-owned merchants to donate what we need for the ceremony," Nydia replied.

"Margot?" Davalyn looked over at her.

"I'll take *Kujichagulia,*" she said, sliding her feet back into her designer shoes.

"That leaves just two more. *Umoja* and *Ujima.*" Davalyn marked off her list. "Any preference, Kimmy?"

Kimmy shrugged. "Sign me up for whatever. I'll do whatever's necessary to make this a success."

"You know the Deltas are trying to plan a ceremony, too, don't you? So, this one had better be kick ass, whatever we do," Margot reminded them.

"Or we could join with them," Kimmy suggested. "The more hands we put together, the better this event is likely to be."

The rest of the sisters all exchanged glances, then said almost in unison, "She takes *Ujima.*"

"That leaves me with *Umoja,*" Davalyn said, checking off the last of the list.

"I've been in touch with the director of Jimmie Walker's Community Center," Kimmy told them. "The place is ours if we need it."

"Oh, I can see it now!" Nia said excitedly. "We can string some lights around that covered entry."

"Use the main hall to set up some exhibits," Nydia added.

"And get a caterer to serve some authentic African dishes," Kimmy said, smacking her lips. "Gotta feed the stomach as well as the spirit."

"No goats," Margot said, turning up her nose. "I'm not eating anybody's goat."

"I'll eat it," Kimmy retorted.

"Okay, ladies," Davalyn said, turning their attention back to the planning. "We have our assignments. Next week when we meet, let's narrow down what we plan to do to present each principle. And while you're at it, think about where we can get Kwanzaa items to use as decorations. A *kinara,* the *mkeka,* items like that."

"On-line," Rashida said. "There are plenty of Web sites that provide Kwanzaa-related items."

"If we can, let's see what we can do locally. Isn't that the spirit of the holiday?" Angelique objected.

"But we have to think globally, too. Share the wealth with our brothers and sisters around the world," Margot reminded them.

"There's plenty enough for us to do to make sure everybody gets recognized and compensated," Davalyn said. "Are we gonna do this or what?"

"Let's do this!" her sisters shouted, joining hands.

Ten

Davalyn moaned, then raised her hands to press her fists against her eyelids.

Thud ... Thud ... Thump! Thud ... Thud ... Thump!

The noise coming from next door jolted her out of a sound sleep.

"Come back!" She languidly lifted her hand, calling back hazy images that were rapidly fading from memory. Davalyn couldn't recall the dream in its entirety. She knew that it had something to do with Denzel Washington, Boris Kodjoe, Vin Diesel, Shemar Moore, a deserted-island paradise, and *mountains and mountains* of whipped cream. Whatever the dream had been, she knew that she didn't want to be awake now. Not now!

Turning over in her bed, her back to the half-open window, Davalyn jammed her pillow over her ears. If she tried really, *really* hard, squeezed her eyes shut and thought sensuous thoughts, maybe she could get back to whatever fantasy world she'd created for herself. No such luck. There was nothing sensual about the sound of hard work. The hammering coming from Cutter's backyard was as labor intensive as she'd ever hoped to hear so early in the morning.

Davalyn sighed. "Sorry, boys," she lamented. The

frolicking foursome would just have to wait until the
cover of night to visit her again.

Fumbling for the alarm clock on her nightstand,
Davalyn gave an enraged cobralike hiss at the glowing
red LED numbers, then spat out a stream of colorful ob-
scenities.

"Four o'clock in the freakin' morning," she swore.
"I'm gonna kill him."

She'd think that after three months of living next door
to Cutter again that she would have gotten used to his
odd habits. When he got it into his head to work, nothing was going to stop him. Not the absence of sunlight,
not the neighborhood ordinance against loud noises,
and certainly not the fact that the rest of the world might
not share his work ethic.

She didn't have to be at work until nine today. Davalyn had every intention of sleeping up to the point where
she could just stumble out of bed, snooze through a
shower, tug on her clothes, and race against the traffic
lights to get to her office—all with seconds to spare.

But he was ruining all of that—making her wake up
long before she wanted. Davalyn had almost convinced
herself that she could sleep through the hammering
when that annoying noise was replaced by the completely unignorable whir of an electric circular saw
tearing through planks of plywood.

Davalyn threw back the covers, shivered, then pulled
the covers back up to her nose. A cold front must have
swept through Kemah last night. The thin cotton cover-
let, more decorative than functional, seemed to
suffocate her in the warmth of the early evening. Now it
was barely enough to keep her own body heat from
being sucked into the chilled air of her room.

Davalyn half twisted, peering across the room. No

wonder it was so cold. She'd slept with the window open again. Maybe that's why Cutter's backyard work seemed so loud. A light, intermittent breeze rattled the aluminum miniblinds, sending the curtain sheers billowing away from the windows like fully unfurled clipper ship sails.

Van had warned her about sleeping with the window open. Said that it wasn't safe.

"Some of these knuckleheads out here don't care if you're on the second floor or the seventieth floor, Dav. We get a lot of traffic through here and not all of it tourism on its way to the boardwalk. If they want in, they'll find a way to get in."

"I should be so lucky," Davalyn had quipped. "I don't think I've had a date in weeks."

"That's no way to find a man. I'm serious, Dav. Keep that window shut and your curtains closed."

But Davalyn couldn't help it. She spent all day at work, tramping around burned-out shells—structures completely decimated by unforgiving flames. The acrid mixture of smoke, ash, standing pools of water, and charred remains of property stayed with her, even after she'd showered. It clung to her clothes and her hair; debris was often wedged under the soles of her work boots.

Whenever she got the chance to take advantage of clean, crisp air to soothe the scents in her nose, she did it—even if it meant suffering through an assault on her ears.

More pounding. If it was possible, it seemed even louder, more intense. Davalyn swung her feet off the edge of her bed. Shivering, she wiggled her feet around, searching by feel for her faux-leopard-skin fur-lined house shoes. She still couldn't quite manage to keep her eyes open.

Dragging the cotton duvet off the bed to wrap around herself as she shuffled to the window, Davalyn jerked on the dangling nylon cord to open the slats of the mini-blinds. The sun was not due to rise for another hour or so. The sky was pitch-black, pinpointed with a sprinkling of stars. A full moon was high overhead, but its light was muted, filtering its way through wispy, low-hanging dark gray clouds that spread out across the sky like strands of overstretched cotton balls.

Her windowpane was cool to the touch as the cooler weather front took Texas temperatures from nearly eighties in the midday to near forties in the late evenings and early mornings. Her breath condensed on the window, fogging it.

As she peered through the window to the yard below her, only a small corner was lit by a halogen utility lamp resting on a metal folding chair. She peeked through the blinds, watching as Cutter moved quickly and deliberately around two sawhorses supporting a four-foot-by-six-foot piece of pale yellow plywood. His back was to her as he extended a measuring tape from one end to a point, then marked a spot on the wood with a square pencil he kept tucked behind his right ear. He measured once more, lifted the tape from the plywood. The echo of the tape recoiling with a metallic *snap* back into its case carried through the yard.

Cutter stuffed the tape into the front pocket of his multipocketed work belt before picking up the saw again and trimming the plywood to the marked length.

Davalyn winced, as much from the noise of the saw hurting her ears as she did for the memory of her ill-mannered swearing. Cutter wasn't out at the crack of dawn just to annoy her.

"Bennett's birthday present," she murmured. Now she remembered. In three days, Bennett would be nine years old.

"November the fourteenth," Bennett had reminded her almost every day since her arrival. Van had planned a birthday party at Bennett's favorite restaurant—the Aquarium. Bennett was fascinated by the two-hundred-gallon fish tank that spanned multiple floors of the restaurant. Cutter, though, had wanted to surprise his boy with a tree fort. Not a prefabricated one that he could slap up in a couple of hours, but one that he'd designed himself. He'd shown the plans to Van and her over a week ago, excited as much for himself at the prospect of working with his hands on a different kind of project as he was in anticipation of the look on Bennett's face when he saw it.

"This is gonna be so cool. Take a look at this, folks," Cutter had said, spreading the plans so that she and Donovan could ooh and ah. He'd drawn and redrawn the plans several times on graph paper. Cutter had been brushing off stray eraser dust as he laid the plans out on their backyard picnic table.

The fort design had shown a split level, covering five of the heaviest branches of the pecan tree that old Calvin McCall had planted over thirty years ago. The highest level had an opening cut into the ceiling.

"A moon roof so Bennett can use the telescope that I got'em." Van grinned his appreciation and patted Cutter on the back. The fort had a rope ladder leading to the lowest level, which could be pulled up, and a tire swing. This tree fort would take days to complete.

Trouble was, Davalyn remembered, Cutter was also

on duty this week. Typically, he would have to be at the fire station by seven in the morning. Unless something drastic happened or one of the other volunteers didn't show, he might be called out even earlier and would often be on until seven that night. Maybe even later. That didn't leave much time for construction. He probably wouldn't be as far along as he was now if his ex-wife, Angela, hadn't agreed to keep Bennett past her designated weekend. She would take him to school in the morning and pick him up in the evenings. The price for all her generosity? Cutter had grudgingly agreed to let Bennett spend Christmas Day with her family, without Cutter. A high price. Cutter didn't want to miss seeing his son's face on Christmas morning as he tore through his presents. Davalyn sensed how much that sacrifice cost him.

Normally, if Cutter was on call, Donovan would baby-sit. Or Davalyn. But Cutter didn't want that this time. He didn't want to ruin the birthday surprise. Still, if he was going to get the fort finished before Bennett's birthday, he was going to have to start working a lot earlier than four o'clock in the morning.

Oh no. Davalyn quickly dismissed that thought from her head. *We're not having any of that.*

Four o'clock was bad enough. Any earlier than that and she would never get back to her dreamworld. And she was definitely going back. A soft, secret smile touched her lips. "I wonder if there's any way I can substitute coconut body oil for whipped cream in my dream," she said aloud.

Pulling the blinds closed again, Davalyn turned away from the window. Without giving herself time to talk herself out of it, she changed out of her pajamas, slid on a pair of jeans and a sweatshirt, a pair of warm socks, and thick-soled shoes. After splashing water on her face and swishing her toothbrush over her teeth, she tied a bandanna over her head and trudged downstairs.

She took out two wide-handled ceramic mugs from the kitchen cabinet, spooned instant coffee and sugar into them, added water from the tap, and then heated the concoction up in the microwave. While pastries were warming in the toaster oven, she unlocked the back door.

"Choo!" She sneezed as a puff of fine sawdust tickled her nose and throat. The screen door was coated with the dust blown from Cutter's yard to hers. *"Achoo!"*

Laying the impromptu breakfast out on a serving tray, covering it with a dishtowel, Davalyn pushed the door open with her shoulder. As soon as she left the warmth of the kitchen, she was starting to have second thoughts about her spontaneous generosity. It was cold out there! Her breath hung in puffs of white mist. She expected that in Maryland, not here. Texas gulf coast winters were typically brief. In fact, if you sneezed and blinked, you could miss a cold snap. Not so today.

"Leave it to me to pick the one morning it was actually cold outside to play delivery girl. Now I know why Cutter was working so fast and furious," she grumbled aloud. "He's not hurrying to finish Bennett's present. He's hurrying to keep his buns warm."

She was careful as she headed for Cutter's backyard. It was still dark and the stone path that wound through her yard was slippery with a light frost. Davalyn stepped onto the grass, feeling it crunch beneath her feet as she crossed over to the back fence.

Cutter hadn't seen her yet, hadn't heard her. The buzz saw was making short work of another piece of wood.

When the high-pitched whine faded and another piece of wood dropped to the ground, Davalyn gave a short, sharp whistle to draw his attention.

Cutter straightened, then turned around. When he pulled the safety goggles from his face, Davalyn grinned at the coating of sawdust dusting his cheeks, chin, and hair.

"Hey there, you!" she called out to him. "Knock it off."

"Go on and cuss me out," he called back, wiping a bead of sweat from his forehead with his shoulder, smearing his face even more. "I've already heard it from some of the other neighbors."

"I'm too sleepy to come up with a curse good enough for you," she lied. She'd actually come up with some very creative curses when he'd snatched her out of the arms of the dreamy Shemar Moore and back into the cruel, empty sheets of her bedroom.

Davalyn lifted the breakfast tray so that he could see and whisked off the dishtowel with flair. "Ta-dah!"

"What's this?" He leaned over, sniffing as steam from the still-warm coffee curled up past the vine-coated fence. He looked up at her. His eyes smiled at her, crinkling up at the corners.

"Take it." Davalyn passed the tray across the fence to him, trying to sound gruff, but failing miserably. She wasn't mad at him for waking her up. How could she stay mad? Not when he looked at her like that with those big, soulful puppy-dog eyes. Knowing that he was giving up his own much-needed rest to give something special to his son made her even more sympathetic, more tenderhearted toward him.

Davalyn felt herself melting as easily as the icing over the warm toaster pastries.

"You brought me breakfast?" He sounded pleased.

"A bribe," Davalyn corrected. "Anything for a little peace and quiet this morning."

He grabbed the tray and started to back away, but looked over his shoulder when he heard the metal fence rattling. Instead of taking the long way around to get to his yard, Davalyn had grabbed the top rail and was digging her feet into the vine-covered chain-link fence. She hauled herself up, then over the top.

"Careful, Dav," Cutter warned just as she exclaimed, *"Oooh!* Ouch! Just great. . . ."

Quickly Cutter set the tray onto the ground, grabbed her by the waist as she brought her other leg over and tucked in her bottom to clear the V-shaped fence spikes lining the top of the fence. Davalyn slid down into Cutter's arms. The chill of the early-morning air was driven away as his arms drew her close to his chest.

"Next time, I'll walk around," she promised, wincing at the tender spot on her inner thigh. One of the spikes had dug into her leg as she brought it over, and it didn't exactly tickle.

"You all right? Did you hurt yourself?" he asked, his brow wrinkled with concern.

"Just a flesh wound. I'll live. Just give me a minute to collect myself."

"Sure." Cutter nodded, then knelt down to retrieve the breakfast tray.

Davalyn leaned forward, trying to examine the tender spot in the near darkness. Her hand went involuntarily to the source of the sting, gingerly massaging.

When Cutter looked back over his shoulder at Davalyn, his eyes zeroed in on the slow, circular motion, mesmerized by the sight of her slender hand working its way around her inner thigh.

Ah, hell, Cutter thought. His own hands clenched as a wave of raw desire caught him unprepared. The breakfast tray rattled in his grasp as he clamped down harder on the aluminum handles. Coffee sloshed over the rim of the mugs, soaking the toaster pastries into an icing-coated, soggy mess. He set the tray down again with a clatter, trying to mop up what he could with the paper napkins she'd provided. But the more he tried, the worse the situation became. It was bad enough trying to clean the spill in the dark. And it certainly wasn't made any easier when his eyes found their way time and time again to Davalyn's inner thighs.

Davalyn's head lifted, pinning him with a curious stare. *What is his problem?* She'd gone through all this trouble to bring him instant coffee and prepackaged pastries and this was how he showed his gratitude? Feeding the ants? She followed the line of his gaze, and when comprehension dawned on her, she snatched her hand away.

Shrugging apologetically, Cutter turned his attention with more focus back to the breakfast tray. He was disgusted with himself. He must be slipping in his old age, getting slower.

In the three months since she'd moved back, he'd managed to play it cool, keep his thoughts about Davalyn mostly to himself. After all, a promise was a promise. And he'd promised Julian that he wouldn't encroach on his relationship with Davalyn. When he'd made the promise, he didn't see a problem with it. Cutter had convinced himself that his feelings for Davalyn were transitory. That is, whatever he was feeling was what any man would feel for someone who had Davalyn's natural endowments. In a word—lust. Had to be just plain, good old-fashioned lust. Thoughts that could easily be controlled.

Between raising Bennett, managing the auto shop with Van, and his KVFD calls, he was kept on the run. When he climbed into bed at night, he was too exhausted to think of anything but the next day's business.

Sometimes their paths crossed at work. But by the time any of the investigators were allowed at a fire scene, Cutter's job was all but done. They only had time for a few words in passing—Cutter verifying that it was safe for her to begin the investigation—before he climbed back onto the pumper truck and reported back to the station. With all of that, who had time to think lustful thoughts?

But every now and then, when the mood was just right, he let himself slip. Instead of worrying about everybody else, Cutter let himself think about taking care of his own needs. It was times just like these, unexpected moments that he and Davalyn shared together, when he let his guard down. It was times like these when he could allow himself to think, to feel for her.

Yet those moments were rare and brief. If ever he got too fanciful in his head, reality usually stepped in to slap some sense into him. It wasn't going to happen. It just wasn't going to happen. She was Van's sister. Julian's woman. His friend. It just wasn't going to happen. It wouldn't be right.

Eleven

"Are you all right, baby girl?" Cutter cleared his throat, adopting the tone he sometimes used with Bennett. Paternal. Concerned. Even a little scolding. "Did you hurt yourself?"

Davalyn was amused. *I know he didn't just try to go all brotherly and platonic on me!*

She'd seen the heated look he'd given her. Had immediately recognized it for what it was, even through her sleep-fogged brain. Any other time, she might have missed it. She might have passed it off as her own imagination. Not this time. She knew what she saw.

"What if I wasn't? Were you gonna offer to kiss it to make it better?" Davalyn chewed her lip to keep from laughing. Poor Cutter. He was trying so hard to be gallant. And she wasn't making it any easier for him.

Cutter stood up, turned toward his workbench. "That's Julian's job," he said tersely.

Julian? Davalyn mouthed to herself. She wondered what made him bring him up.

He reached for a coffee mug, ignored the now-lukewarm taste as he swallowed several times. He had to brush the sawdust from his hands before reaching for a pastry. Frowning, he let the soggy pastry fall to the tray with a small sound of disgust.

Squashing a grin, Davalyn moved next to him and picked up a mug, too. "Speaking of jobs," she said, quickly changing the subject, "what can I do to help? That's really why I came out here. Though I have to say, it looks like you're doing pretty well on your own. Not bad, Cutter. Not bad at all."

She raised her eyes to the tree fort, admiring Cutter's handiwork. He'd finished the first level and was well on his way to finishing the second. Already he'd put up the floor and wall frames for a second level.

"I could still use a hand to put on a few finishing touches."

"Finishing touches? You mean like gingham curtains or lace doilies?" Davalyn suggested.

Cutter snorted in a mixture of laughter and derision. "Lace curtains in a tree fort? Hell, no. Not unless you want Bennett to be the most-talked-about, made-fun-of, or beat-up kid on the block."

Davalyn elbowed him in the ribs and gave him a broad wink. "I was just teasing you, Cutter McCall. Trying to lighten the atmosphere a little. A moment ago, you looked so serious."

"Well, some things are no laughing matter."

"Such as?" Davalyn prompted, though she already had a pretty good idea what he was alluding to. He was still bothered that she'd caught him looking at her. Not just looking, but thinking. He didn't want her to know that he saw her as something more than Van's little sister.

"Dav . . . back there at the fence . . ." he began, shifting uncomfortably, staring down at his foot. "I . . . uh . . . I didn't mean to disrespect you. You know I would never treat you that way."

Davalyn wanted to sigh in frustration. *That was exactly the problem,* she thought. Not that she wanted to be disrespected. But she didn't mind him looking. Didn't mind at all. She wanted him, too. And if he managed to touch her every now and then, she could handle that, too. But so far, he'd been completely hands-off.

She reached out, laying her hand gently on his shoulder. "I know that, Cutter," she said sincerely, giving him a reassuring squeeze. "If I thought that you meant to hurt me, do you think I'd still be out here, risking triple pneumonia, to help you out with Bennett's tree fort?"

"I guess not," he admitted reluctantly.

"You'd better believe I wouldn't. I'd be back upstairs, curled up under my covers so fast, your head would spin faster than your buzz saw. Now let's see what we can do to get this fort finished."

"Bennett's gonna flip his lid when he sees this." Cutter eagerly clapped his hands, then briskly rubbed them together in childlike anticipation.

"You probably won't get Bennett to sleep in his own room for weeks. So don't even try," Davalyn said over her shoulder as she stepped away and started to fit together some pieces of precut wood. She hummed a little to herself as she referred to Cutter's sketches next to the pile.

"Is this what I think it is?" she asked incredulously, lifting the paper and rattling it at him. "An entertainment center?"

"For his PlayStation. A little outdoor safety-rated extension cord and it's on. With a little more practice, I think I'll be able to beat him in Fists of Fury. He's already beaten me half a dozen times, so I'm asking for a rematch."

"Oh, brother. And I thought I was spoiling him with that stack of Yu-Gi-Oh game cards that I searched all over creation to find."

"Maybe I've gone a little overboard." The smile on

Cutter's face was a mixture of embarrassment and nostalgia. "But when I was a kid, I would have done anything for a tree fort like this."

"Why didn't you just build one?" Davalyn wanted to know.

"'Cause my old man always said no. That's why."

"Since when did you let what your father said stop you from doing anything you wanted to do?" Davalyn sounded surprised. She couldn't imagine a little thing like authority standing in Cutter's way of getting what he wanted.

"You make me sound like I was trying to buck him every chance I got. There was a time when I actually respected and followed everything my old man said, you know."

"So what changed you?"

"Puberty," Cutter retorted. "When I hit six feet, he stopped hitting me."

"Oh . . ." Davalyn let out a long breath. It hung in little puffs of white around her mouth. "Just curious, Cutter. What was his reason for not letting you have a tree fort?"

"He said, and I quote, 'Only monkeys play in trees. Some folks say it took us a million years of evolution to get out of the trees. And it took boycotts, freedom marches, and an act of Congress to stop some of those same crazies from calling us monkeys to our faces. And you want me to help you jump right back into those same trees we supposedly climbed out of? Hell, no. Besides, you would only fall out and break your fool neck and I ain't gonna take time off from work to bring you to the hospital.'"

"Your father was a mean old man," Davalyn announced. "When I was playing in the backyard, did you know that sometimes he used to throw watermelon rinds over the fence at me?"

Cutter twisted his face in reluctant remembrance. "I can't lie, Dav. That wasn't always him. Sometimes it was me and Van."

"You!" Davalyn exclaimed, taking a mock swing at him, which Cutter easily ducked. "I should have known."

"But old Calvin had his issues, too. All I can say is that he was my father, doing the best that he could to keep me in line. Safe. Out of all the things he said to me, what I got out of it was he didn't want to see me fall, to see me get hurt. I wish it didn't take as long as me becoming a grown man, a father of my own, to see that in him. By the time Bennett came along, he didn't have such a hard time showing that he cared. He really loved that boy. His first grandchild."

"It must have made him so proud," Davalyn said.

"When Bennett was barely a year old, just learning to walk, my old man used to take Bennett up to the job, push him around in his stroller. And woe be unto anybody who didn't confess that he was the smartest, cutest, most wonderful grandbaby in the world. Anybody who said otherwise was just daring old Calvin to open up a can of whup-ass. You couldn't ask for a better baby-sitter than that . . . . er, that's present company excluded, of course."

"Of course," she said, her tone smarmy. Davalyn didn't have to wonder how much of old Calvin McCall had rubbed off on his son. "You're not afraid of Bennett falling?" She craned her neck to find the top of the tree fort. "It's so high off the ground."

Once it was finished, the roof of the upper level would disappear into the highest branches of the pecan tree.

"I hope he doesn't fall. But the thought has crossed

my mind a couple of times," he admitted. "I've got a plan for that."

"A plan?" Davalyn chuckled. "What are you gonna do, Cutter? Nail bumpers to Bennett's bottom?"

"See those posts over there?" He pointed out a stack of long wooden beams, wrapped in a plastic blue tarp lying beside his back porch.

"Uh-huh." She nodded. "What about them?"

"I'm planning a two-foot ledge that runs around the outer edge of the fort as a guardrail. I picked up some orange netting. You know, like the kind they use at construction sites. And I'm gonna nail some from the rail to the floor. And then I've got mulch and play sand that I'm gonna put in a three-foot-by-three-foot perimeter around the tree." Cutter talked excitedly, demonstrating with his hands how he planned to lay it all out. "It may not stop him from falling, but maybe he'll have fewer broken bones if he does. Until he gets used to climbing up and down the rope ladder, I'll be up there with him when he plays in it."

"Yeah, right." Davalyn crossed her arms across her chest and said, "He's a nine-year-old boy. You don't think he knows how to climb? You just need an excuse to play up there, too, Cutter McCall. I think you're gonna spend as much time up there as he will," Davalyn predicted. "Go on. Admit it."

Cutter spread his hands. "What can I say? I'm a little kid at heart."

"Big kid," she amended.

"Tell me you're not curious to see what it's like to be in the treetops, too." He nudged her back.

"Curiosity is one thing. Crazy about the climb is another." She waggled her finger at him.

"You wanna see what it looks like from up there?" He

set his mug back onto the tray and pointed at the hanging rope ladder.

"You mean me? Climb up there? You must have sawdust for brains," Davalyn scoffed.

"C'mon, Dav." Cutter grabbed her by the hand and pulled her toward the tree. "This is gonna be kickin'. You'll see."

"The only thing kickin' about me and that tree fort is me, kicking and screaming, if you try to get me up there." Davalyn dug in her heels and tugged against him.

"I promise I won't let you fall."

"Gravity says otherwise," she retorted.

"This may be your last chance to get up there."

"A risk I'm willing to take."

"Pretty soon Bennett and crew will be up there, complete with a 'He-Man Woman-Hater's Club. No girls allowed' sign painted on the door. This is your last chance to get a little bit closer to the sky. It's an awesome feelin'. A little like flyin'."

"How about if I take your word for it?" Davalyn hesitated.

"Chicken," he taunted, then clucked at her.

"That's not gonna work on me, buddy boy. You're not gonna goad me into climbing up there."

"I could always swing you over my shoulder," he threatened. "I'm a firefighter, Dav. I've got a license to carry and not afraid to use it."

Davalyn burst into open laughter, then clamped her hand over her mouth when she realized it was still a little too early in the morning. Her voice carried in the still air now that Cutter had laid his circular saw aside.

"All right, fine. But if I fall down and break my neck, I'll haunt you for the rest of my days."

"I won't let you fall," he repeated.

Davalyn stared up at the tree fort, then back at Cutter. His expression was sincere, his dark eyes encouraging. She had no choice but to trust him.

"Ladies first." Cutter gestured at the rope ladder. Davalyn grabbed one rung, then another. He held the ladder steady, anchoring it as she slowly made her way to the top.

"Watch your head," he warned as she raised her hand to push aside the trapdoor. The hinge was new, freshly oiled so it barely made a sound as she swung the door open. The door made a soft thud and a *whoosh* of air as it landed on the indoor-outdoor carpeting that he'd laid on the floor.

Davalyn moved aside as she heard Cutter coming up behind her. She rested, cross-legged on the carpeted floor, with her back against the wall. She closed her eyes, trying to get used to the feeling of being two stories off the ground with little more than branches and leaves around her.

"Well?" Cutter prompted, grinning at her, as he settled next to her. "What do you think?"

"It's . . . uh . . . high." She gulped.

"It's supposed to be. A tree fort is no fun if it's only a couple of inches off the ground."

"Nothing wrong with keeping your feet on solid ground," she insisted.

"Not to a nine-year-old boy. A low fort would let all of his enemies overrun him before he had a chance to barricade himself in."

"What kind of enemies does a nine-year-old have?" Davalyn asked.

"Stupid, stinky girls," Cutter responded promptly.

Davalyn narrowed her eyes at him. "Say what?"

"Those are his words. Not mine," Cutter said, raising his hands in protest. "Don't shoot the messenger."

"I take it this means you haven't had 'the talk' about girls with him yet?"

"As long as he's thinkin' that girls are stinky, I don't need to."

"Poor Bennett." Davalyn shook her head, covered her eyes with her hand. "Some little girl is going to break his heart, all because his dad was more interested in building a skyscraper tree fort than talking about the birds and the bees."

"We'll talk when the time is right. I'm not willing to admit that my son is having those kinds of thoughts about girls."

"Cutter, do you know that kids these days are experimenting with sex as early as junior high school? He's only got a few more years before he's there."

Cutter groaned. "Are you tryin' to give me a heart attack, Dav?"

"Better now than becoming a grandpa by the time he's in the sixth grade," she retorted. "Sometimes, when I'm visiting with a class, talking about what I do . . . I can't help wondering if I'm getting through to them, or talking over their heads, or if I'm falling on deaf ears. . . . I look into their eyes and I see that some of those kids are way too sophisticated for their own good. Especially the girls. They're developing a lot faster these days. Their raging little hormones are practically setting off school sprinklers."

"So how old were you when your folks gave *you* the talk?" Cutter wanted to know.

Davalyn could hear the laughter in his question. He was teasing her again. She cleared her throat and faltered. "Well, actually, I . . . um . . . already knew a lot about it by the time Mama got around to talking to me. But I didn't let her know that I knew."

"Oh?" Cutter's mouth quirked and Davalyn knew that he was fighting not to laugh in her face. "Old Calvin told me that girls matured faster than boys. Is that true?"

She felt the urge to wipe that smirk right off his face.

"You tell me. I knew it all by the time I was eight. And I have you and Van to thank for that."

Cutter nearly choked. "What do you mean—me and Van?" he sputtered.

"Breathe, Cutter. Breathe," Davalyn said, patting him on the back between the shoulder blades. "And no, I didn't go rummaging through those girlie mags you and Van had stashed in the garage, underneath that stack of *National Geographic* and *Popular Mechanics.*"

"You little snoop!" He pointed at her. "I told Van somebody was going through that stuff. He didn't believe me."

"It wasn't me! Like my pops believed you guys were doing all of that reading in the garage to better your mind. Hah!" Now it was Davalyn's turn to laugh. "I picked up a lot just listening to you and Van."

"Snooping and eavesdropping? You were one busy little girl."

"I didn't have to eavesdrop," Davalyn said, puffed up and indignant. "You two clowns were just loud. Sometimes I could hear every word you said."

Cutter leaned close and asked in a conspiratorial whisper, "So what did you learn?"

"That you, Cutter McCall, have a one-track mind. You wouldn't shut up about that Angela Bennett. Just went on and on and on." She pretended to slump as if completely numbed by his obsession.

"You remembered all of that?"

"Of course I remembered, Cutter. A person doesn't forget what love looks like. And you . . . you really loved her, didn't you?"

He shook his head, then turned to stare out the open window of the tree fort. "I would have given her the moon if she'd asked me to get it for her."

"What happened between you two? If you don't mind me asking. Everybody thought you made the perfect couple."

Cutter's shrug was nonchalant. Almost too blasé. Davalyn felt that she knew him well enough to sense that he was uncomfortable. It showed in the nervous, self-conscious way he picked at sawdust on his jeans, avoiding her gaze. "I dunno. We just didn't work out. It be's that way sometimes."

"I'm sorry," she said softly. "I know it still hurts."

"Thanks for the sentiment. But like you said before, by now it's only a flesh wound. I've come to accept that Angela and I, for whatever reason, just weren't meant to be. It sounds crazy to me when I say it, or even think it, but it's true. As hard as it was trying to make it work, I wouldn't have traded a minute of it. She taught me a lot. Maybe more than I would've wanted to know," he said ruefully. "But I learned fast."

"And, in the end, you've got a wonderful kid to show for all that effort," she encouraged him. "Something good came out of it, huh? Just look at Bennett. He's a wonderful kid. And I'm not just saying that, so you can keep that can of whup-ass closed."

Cutter's voice changed. The edge was gone. His expression softened. "Every day with him I learn something new. Keeps me on my toes, moving too fast to look back and regret what might have been."

"Really? You have no regrets?" Davalyn sounded

doubtful. "Sometimes people say that because it sounds good. Gives meaning to what could very well have been a pointless exercise. But do you really mean that, Cutter? Can you look back on such a painful experience and honestly say that you wouldn't do things differently, if you had the chance?"

Cutter sighed through his nose and was silent for several seconds, considering his words carefully.

Davalyn didn't push him for a response. Instead, she drew up her knees, hugging them tight to her chest, and watched the first rays of morning sun warm the sky. Pitch-black faded to deep purple, then pale mauve. She hadn't meant to goad him, or to pry. She wanted to know. She wanted to know what would make a man cling so desperately to a loveless marriage even when it was killing his soul.

"Maybe some," Cutter finally answered, just when she thought he'd let the prying question pass. "I regret saying some things in anger, doing some things outta revenge. For a while, I know I became a stone-cold son of a bitch. But I'm only human, Dav. Just a man. When a man keeps getting pushed away, sooner or later he's faced with two choices. He either pushes back or he chooses not to go back."

"And which did you choose?"

"Not to go back. She kept pushing me away, so I never went back."

"Did you ever cheat on her?" The question popped out of her mouth before she could call it back. Davalyn bit her lip, then murmured, "Sorry, Cutter. That was out of line. None of my business."

"You're right," he said tightly. "It is none of your business."

"Sorry, Cutter," Davalyn murmured again, her voice cracking. "I didn't mean to—"

"Forget it," he said curtly.

Davalyn unfolded her long legs and started to crawl toward the rope ladder. The emotional brick wall he'd instantly erected around himself was a clear indicator that she'd overstayed her welcome. She didn't look forward to the climb down, but she would rather face a rope ladder in the dark than the uncomfortable silence brought on by her prying questions.

Why'd I have to go there? Davalyn berated herself. Cutter had let his guard down before her and she'd managed to reopen a wound that had barely begun to heal.

Cutter clasped his large hand on her shoulder and squeezed gently to stop her progress.

"Where are you going, Dav?"

"I think I should go," she whispered, barely able to speak around the tightening of her throat.

"Why?" he demanded. "Don't you want to wait around for an answer? Or do you think you already know me that well? Have you already made up your mind about me?"

She shook her head. "Tell me, Cutter. I want to know."

"I *never* cheated on Angela."

"Not ever?"

"Nev-er," he repeated emphatically.

"Did you want to?"

"Jeez, Davalyn. You don't give a guy a break, do you? Why would you ask me something like that? What kind of question is that?" Cutter said, throwing up his hands.

"A nosy, prying one," Davalyn admitted.

"You're damned right it is. I didn't bring you up here to pry into my private life."

"Then why did you bring me up here?"

Cutter had no answer for that. Not a simple one anyway. He enjoyed the view from up here and thought she might, too. It was a little bit of a haven for him and he wanted to share it with her. He didn't count on sharing a piece of himself that he hadn't even allowed her brother, Donovan, to see.

"Do you want to leave?" he asked, his voice pitched soft and low, nearly a whisper, as if he was afraid of the answer.

Davalyn shook her head no. She didn't want to go. Not yet. As uncomfortable as the moment was, she wanted this time with him. The alternative was going home, climbing back into her cold bed, and trying to get back into a fantasy world. No, she didn't want that. It was cold out here. But Cutter was here, too. Flesh and blood. She could talk to him, touch him. He was no fantasy.

She was silent for a minute, listening to the sound of the pecan tree branches brush against the wall of the fort. A few overripe pecans fell, peppered against the roof in staccato bursts.

She settled back against the wall, a little closer to Cutter this time. Her shoulder brushed against his. Davalyn shivered—whether from the chill seeping through the wall or her unexpected pleasure at being this close to him, she couldn't be sure.

"Cold?" he asked.

"A little. But I'm all right," Davalyn said quickly to assure him. She didn't want him to suggest that she should leave.

Cutter shifted, lifted his arm, and laid it across her shoulders. "That better?"

"Yes. Thanks."

A moment later, he drew her closer to him, his left hand absently caressing her arm. Davalyn leaned her head against his shoulder, keeping her eyes trained on the pale glow of her window visible from the tree fort's side window.

"I can see my house from here," she observed. "And that's my room."

Then she gave a little gasp. "Can you see me all the time when I'm in there? Will Bennett be able to when he's playing up here?"

"He will if you don't keep your curtains closed," Cutter said dryly.

"All I need is a gang of preadolescent Peeping Toms staring at me."

"You should keep your blinds down anyway. Not all Peeping Toms are preadolescent, you know."

"Yeah, I know," she responded.

"What?" Cutter tried to sound shocked and failed. He pointed to himself. "You mean me?"

"Tell me you haven't looked a time or two." She dared him to tell her an untruth.

Cutter gave a guilty chuckle. She already knew the answer to that one. He *had* looked. And she'd caught him at it. "You'd better keep your blinds down," he repeated.

Leaning her head back against the wall, she said softly, "Maybe . . . maybe I don't want to close my curtains. Maybe I *want* someone to look."

Slowly, carefully, as if she were fearful of frightening a skittish wild animal, she took Cutter's hand and laid it against her thigh. It was near the spot she'd stabbed when she'd climbed over the fence separating their yards. When Cutter tensed, she felt his muscles contract as he held her. She intuitively knew a tiny war was being waged in the very fiber of his flesh. Stay or go? Run or hold fast? Davalyn didn't give him a chance to pull away. She settled the battle for him by removing any doubts of what she wanted. She kept her hand firmly over his.

Cutter kept his eyes focused on a distant spot outside. He had to stare straight ahead. If he looked at her, it would be over. He'd either bolt headfirst out the window like the Cowardly Lion from *The Wizard of Oz,* or do something worse—stay and face the fact that maybe it wasn't a good idea for Davalyn and him to be alone. He didn't want to think about that now. He didn't want to listen to the whispers of caution warning him. More than whispers. Big, freakin' alarms as jarring as the ones that roused the station crew of the fire department to action.

He clenched his teeth, forcing the inner noise down deep. Because if he listened, he'd do what was sensible. He'd get up, climb down that rope ladder, and put the distance of two adjoining yards between them. But he didn't want to be sensible. Instead, he let his senses rule him. He let the sweet smell of her hair wash over him. She smelled like summer. Like sweet honeysuckle on the vine, untouched by the air, sharp and crisp, announcing the start of winter. He let the sound of her breathing—a slow exhalation of warmth—draw him closer for comfort.

It took a while for him to find his voice. And when he did, it sounded raspy to his own ears. "Maybe more than look?" he suggested.

More silence. Countless heartbeats marked the time before she answered, *"Maybe."*

"Davalyn—" Cutter said, his voice strained. This was all wrong. They shouldn't be here. As soon as she'd passed him that breakfast tray, he should have insisted that she get back inside. Go back to bed where she was warm—and safe.

"It's been two months, Cutter," Davalyn interrupted.

"I've been back for two months. Why haven't you asked me out?"

"Two months, two weeks, three days . . . not that I've been payin' much attention."

"Liar, liar. Pants on fire," Davalyn taunted.

If only she knew how close to the truth she is, Cutter thought. As long as he was content to only look, he could fool himself into believing that he was behaving as any normal red-blooded, healthy male would behave. She was a beautiful woman. Beautiful in mind and spirit, with one helluva head-turning body.

As long as he could keep physical contact with her as incidental, casual, platonic, even brotherly, he was fine. He could keep his thoughts under wraps without having to settle for a teeth-chattering cold shower. And he had his promise to Julian as his shield. He'd promised that he'd keep away for as long as their relationship remained intact. Could he assume by her actions now that the situation had changed? If they continued as they were, there would definitely be a change. Nothing would ever be the same between them—that is, if he continued as he wanted. He couldn't shrug it off, pretend that everything was cool. All one big happy family.

Not this time. This time, he'd crossed the line. There was no mistaking his intention, what he wanted. He'd crossed and there was no turning back. Nor did he want to. Two months, two weeks, three days . . . he hadn't thought of any other woman but Davalyn since that time. Hadn't dated, hadn't called anyone, hadn't joined any of his other friends in group gatherings, hadn't been to any of his on-line chat rooms.

He squeezed, the warmth of his hand filtering through her jeans.

Davalyn gasped, her breathing not quite so even now.

She squeezed his hand, communicating her intention before moving his palm over her thigh in slow, small circles. His hand, though large and calloused, was surprisingly gentle as she encouraged him to massage her leg. She guided him along in a definitive, unmistakable direction. Higher up her leg, deeper into her flesh. Each rotation widening. Each rotation warming her, so that by the time he cupped his hand, closing over the V-shaped juncture of her thighs, Davalyn felt branded. She lifted her hips, arching her back to meet his caress.

Cutter twisted sideways, squaring himself to her. He faced her on his knees with his free hand supporting her on the small of her back, drawing her into his chest. His other hand still had not released his prize. Instead, he slid his hand under her sweatshirt, palm against the flat of her stomach, fingers pointed downward until they worked their way under the waistband of her jeans. Only a wispy swatch of lace separated them. There his caresses continued. Skilled. Intimate. Relentless.

"Touch me, Cutter. Please touch me," Davalyn whimpered, a shameless expression of need. She reached up and wrapped her arms around his neck for support, having no strength in her legs to support herself. She was liquid fire—where he was touching her was the proof. Fingers soaked, making it easier to push aside her panties, slide into her. First one finger, then another, moving in and out, easy and unhurried.

Cutter lowered his head, kissing her at the pounding pulse on her neck. Tender at first, then intensifying as he followed along her jawline. He caught her full lower lip between his teeth, nipping gently.

Davalyn opened her lips to him. The farther he probed, the harder she pushed back. She kissed him, working her tongue to match the rhythm of his caress. She matched him, stroke for stroke, keeping them in sync until impatience set in and she changed the tempo. Deeper, more desperate, she reset the pace. Without realizing that she had, she pulsed against his hand, rotating her hips closer to him until his hand was trapped between their bodies.

His response was instantaneous. Cutter jerked his hand away from her waistband, the bulge in his jeans receiving the benefit of Davalyn's open invitation as she ground her hips against his groin.

"How long has it been?" she muttered against his lips.

"More than two months," he managed to get out as she kissed him. She kissed his lips, touched her tongue to his jawline.

Cutter lifted his chin, giving her access to his chin, the sensitive skin at his throat.

"Two weeks. A couple of days. A few hours. Wasted minutes. *Damn, baby girl!*"

The last exclamation was yanked unwillingly from him when Davalyn lifted his sweatshirt, ran her tongue in the indention from his navel, up his sternum, then swirled lazily around a dark nipple.

"Too long," she murmured sympathetically, sliding her hand up and down the front of his jeans.

"Watch what you say," he teased her. "It might go to my head."

"I should be so lucky," Davalyn retorted.

Cutter laughed softly. He shrugged out of his sweatshirt, bunched it up. Easing her backward, he slid the shirt under her head to protect it. At the moment, that was the *only* thought of protection that had entered his mind.

As he settled over her, Davalyn struggled with the clasp of his belt. Fingers stiffened by the chill air worked against her. She managed to work the belt loose, pulled it free from his pants, and tossed it to the floor, only to have the attached pager suddenly go off with an unsympathetic, untimely alarm.

Cutter cursed—a single four-letter frantic word that communicated both his frustration and his desire. He scrambled for the pager as it vibrated against the carpeted floor, pressed a button on the side, and squinted at the small glow of the LCD panel.

"What is it?" Davalyn asked, her voice stricken.

"It's the fire station," he muttered. "Reminding me I'm scheduled to come in."

"Now?" All of her disappointment poured into that one word.

"Yeah. Now."

Davalyn caught her lower lip between her teeth, cursed, repeating the word that Cutter had expressed seconds before. Cutter sat down beside her, his breath ragged as he fought to regain composure. Beside him, Davalyn flung her arms over her eyes.

"Well," she said with a sigh, "do you want to say it, or should I?" Her tone was tinged with bittersweet amusement.

"Say what?" His expression was puzzled.

"Saved by the bell," she said ruefully, blowing out a heavy sigh, then smothering a giggle at her own pun. "Get it? Fire station? Alarm bell?"

"That's not funny, Dav," Cutter retorted. "Do you have any idea what almost happened here?"

"Yep. And have known since I was eight." Her tone was flippant.

Cutter cursed again and zipped up his pants. As she sat up, he shrugged back into his sweatshirt.

"Go home, Dav," he insisted, sounding very much like he used to when she was eight and he wanted to get rid of the pest. A little too late. He wished that he'd said those words to her when she first brought him the breakfast tray.

Davalyn started for the rope ladder and hesitated. It was a long way down. Somehow she had to get over her apprehension or get run over. Cutter *had* to respond to that call. She'd almost cleared the floor, was about to swing the trapdoor closed, when she changed her mind and popped her head back inside.

"Probably just as well we were interrupted, Cutter. I'd love to have been a fly on the wall when you tried to explain the carpet burns on your butt to all your crew at the fire station."

She didn't wait for a response, but allowed the trapdoor to slam shut. She couldn't be sure, but she thought she heard Cutter laughing as she descended.

Twelve

The early-morning sun gave more than enough light as Davalyn navigated back to the safety of the cold, solid ground. She looked up as her feet touched the ground, but didn't see any sign of Cutter. He wasn't coming down after her. She didn't know whether to be pissed or relieved.

"The least he could do was walk me home," Davalyn muttered. She didn't think that pager alarm going off had killed his chivalry as well as his passion. But on second thought, following her home would lead to more awkwardness, more strained conversation, more denial, desperate wanting and strategic retreats.

"Later," she called up to him, knowing that it would seal the fact that he couldn't avoid her forever. Her final salutation was both a threat and a promise.

To get back home Davalyn took the long way around. She'd been stung twice that morning—once physically when she'd climbed the fence, the other emotionally when she'd wanted to climb Cutter. She didn't feel like putting herself at either risk again. So she walked around until she came to the gate leading to her own backyard, trudged across the grass and back into her kitchen.

It was six o'clock in the morning. By now, Donovan was awake. He sat at the kitchen table, dressed in the dark

blue coveralls he usually wore when working at the auto
shop, dipping unbuttered toast into his hot chocolate. The
front page of the morning paper was spread over the
kitchen table. When Davalyn stormed inside, slamming
the door, the newspaper rattled. A few flyers advertising
holiday season sales fluttered to the linoleum floor. In a
couple of weeks, it would be Thanksgiving. Davalyn
wanted to scream. She wasn't feeling very thankful right
now. She was feeling hot. Bothered. Cheated.

Donovan shifted around, draping his arm along the
back end of his chair. He glanced down at his watch. It
was a little early for Davalyn to be up. Not that she was a
slacker. But on those mornings when he knew she could
sleep in, she took full advantage of those rare times. He
also knew that Davalyn worked out in the evenings, so she
wouldn't have been out for a morning run.

He took in her appearance, from her mud-covered
shoes to the sawdust-covered clothes. His gaze moved up
to the downward turn of her frowning full lips.

"Where have you been?" he asked.

With barely a break in her stride, Davalyn stomped
across the kitchen floor. She wasn't going to answer, not
sure how she should.

"Dav?" Donovan pressed.

She paused at the kitchen door, her back stiff and
straight to him. Davalyn whirled around. "Where have I
been?" she echoed sarcastically. "I'll tell you where I've
been, big brother."

She wanted to tell him that she'd been stranded on a
fantasy desert island with four of the sexiest men on the
planet. She was soaring with the stars one minute and
straddling a weed-choked fence the next. She'd been
taken on an emotional roller-coaster ride, rocketed to
the highest heights of pleasure and then sent plummet-

ing to reality, all in a couple of hours. But she didn't say any of those things to him. In the cold, cruel light of morning, the events that had just transpired didn't seem real to her. Didn't seem rational.

Who would believe that she'd been out climbing trees at four o'clock in the morning? Who'd believe that she'd almost made love to the boy next door—the boy she'd loved for as long as he'd been the boy next door? She'd held on to that love through the years. Neither distance, puberty, nor his giving his heart away to another woman had been able to change how she felt about Cutter Mc-Call. Who'd believe that something as tiny as circuits and wires could come between her and her will to consummate that love? So she answered him with the only answer that made sense.

"Fighting fires, big brother," she finally responded, her voice tinged with regret. "Just fighting fires."

When the fire alarm sounded, Cutter was in his gear as fast as the next man. He shrugged into his jacket, slammed on his helmet, and was at the pumper truck before the station chief could urge them on.

"Let's go! Move it!"

The chief's voice boomed over the sound of the Klaxon, reminding anyone who might have any doubt that this was not another practice drill, but a bona fide emergency.

Instead of taking the wheel as Cutter normally did, he motioned for Jerry Jeffries to drive instead.

J.J., or Junior, as he was sometimes called, was the lanky, good-natured, self-nominated mascot of the fire station since he was the new man on the crew. Had signed up about six months ago and was usually relegated to checking gear and crowd control.

When Cutter gestured for him to climb into the cab, he lifted an eyebrow in surprise but didn't say a word. He simply slid into the driver's seat, slammed the door shut, and cranked up the engine.

Cutter picked up the radio and confirmed the address with the dispatcher. The GPS monitor mounted on the dashboard of the pumper truck lined out a route for them.

He nodded at J.J. "You heard it, Junior. Let's roll."

J.J. eased the truck into gear, made a cursory check of cross traffic. The flashing yellow caution light positioned outside the station was blinking red, warning cross traffic to hold while the truck exited the station.

J.J. watched Cutter out of the corner of his eye. Nothing in his outward appearance gave any indication that anything was out of the ordinary, but J.J couldn't help wondering. Cutter almost never let anyone else drive. The truck belonged to the city of Kemah, paid for by a special bond election, voted on by the residents. But ask anyone at the station and they would all agree that the brand-spanking-new Pierce Dash Pumper was Cutter's baby, his pride and joy. No one knew their way around that truck better than Cutter did—from the light bar flashing on top to the dual exhaust rumbling from the rear.

They'd all been trained on the truck, so J.J. didn't feel at all apprehensive about handling Cherry Bomb, as the station crew had affectionately dubbed her. What did concern him was why Cutter had given up the wheel. He figured that nothing short of two broken arms, blinding in one eye, and a clubfoot would stop Cutter from driving her. He was both driver and mechanic. J.J. thought if anyone could conduct a love affair with an inanimate object, Cutter could. So what had soured?

Careful to keep his eyes on the road, J.J. shot Cutter a concerned glance.

"You all right?" he asked, keeping his tone light, conversational.

"Yep." Cutter's reply was short.

"You sure?" J.J. didn't quite buy the answer. He'd only been a volunteer at this station for six months. But Cutter had taken him under his wing, shown him as much as anyone. With all of the time they'd spent together in training, J.J. thought he knew as well as anyone when something was bothering the big man.

"Yep," Cutter repeated.

"Just checking."

"Why? Don't I look it?" Cutter asked, also keeping his gaze trained ahead. Anyone riding on the passenger side was another set of eyes, looking out for motorists or pedestrians who might not have seen or heeded Cherry Bomb's approach warning.

"I dunno." J.J. shrugged.

"Then why'd you ask me?"

"Why'd you let me drive?" J.J. countered.

Cutter grinned at him. "You don't think it's about time, Junior?"

"Long past time," J.J. responded, fondling the smooth grip of the steering wheel. "I was ready from day one."

"There you go, then." Cutter tapped him on the head. "Consider it an early Christmas present."

It seemed a simple enough explanation. Too simple for such a complicated question. Why had he let J.J. drive? Why had he given up control?

His mind flashed back to earlier that morning. Nothing but residual fallout from his conversation with Davalyn. J.J. was enjoying the benefit of an earlier time when control seemed to be beyond his grasp.

Cutter's gut wrenched. Davalyn! God, if ever there was an example of careening out of control, kissing Davalyn was it. It was like responding to an alarm. Racing full speed ahead, barreling down the street in this truck toward imminent danger, with his hands off the wheel. Every sensible brain cell in his head warned him against it. It was stupid, dangerous, figuratively playing with fire. He knew better.

At the same time, the lure of the forbidden quickened his blood. The same way responding to an alarm did. He didn't take this job lightly, though he was a volunteer. If anything, he took it more seriously, because he knew the consequences if he didn't. The damage to property, the potential loss of lives. Maybe even his own. He knew what it meant every time he climbed into this truck, but he kept doing it time after time.

Cutter would have liked to believe that he did it because he thought he was doing something good, being noble, making a difference in the community. The same way he volunteered his time to participate in various ministries in church. Youth choir, though he couldn't carry a tune. Bible study, even though he didn't like to read. But sometimes, when he was really honest with himself, he recognized that he'd joined the Kemah VFD for a purely selfish reason. It was for the pure adrenaline rush the job gave him. It was the thrill of being in the middle of the action. He needed it. He craved it just as surely as he needed air. And it scared him to think that Davalyn's touch had invoked in him this same feeling. If she could do that with just a touch, a simple kiss, how was he going to resist her? How was he going to keep his promise to Julian? How was he going to be able to walk away from her? He couldn't walk away from the VFD. *Or could I?*

Cutter had to know. So he experimented with J.J. He

tried a baby step, tried giving up just a tiny part of what made him look forward to volunteering. He let J.J. drive.

"Show time." J.J. broke into his thoughts, indicating a column of thick black smoke billowing upward into the morning sky. They'd ridden with the windows down. And the unpleasantly familiar acrid smell of charred brick, metal, and insulation stung his nose, made Cutter's eyes tear. He blinked rapidly, clearing his vision.

J.J. eased the truck past the street blockade set up by the Kemah Police Department, following the directions of the uniformed officer waving him away from the gathering crowd of spectators and closer to the house, nearly a fourth of it engulfed in flames.

Cutter picked up the radio once more, relayed back to the dispatcher the time of their arrival, then climbed out of the cab to get his assignment from the station chief.

"Matheson, get that line connected. McCall, you on point. Danvers, back him up. J.J., help that officer back those people up off the tape. Clear the perimeter. Toomey, Burleson, masks on. I've been told the house is clear, but let's make sure. Hustle it up, people. Come on, let's go!"

Six men, six different directions, but all carefully co-ordinated as masterfully as an orchestrated performance with the station chief treating each crew member as a finely tuned instrument. Each one with a function—and if anyone was out of tune with the others, he could turn the operation sour in an instant.

Matheson fitted one end of the hose to the hydrant while Cutter uncoiled. He grunted, tugged, careful to shake out any kinks in the line, and then laid it against his shoulder. Once the water was turned on, it would come rushing through the fire line with enough force to knock a grown man over. He'd seen it in training films and in enough newsreels from the 1950s and 1960s when such a force was turned against men just like himself. He wanted the line as straight as possible, to keep a buildup of nearly one hundred pounds per square inch from working against him.

He looked over his shoulder, waiting for Danvers to take up his position behind him. So far, the fire was contained to one room on the bottom floor. With luck, low winds, and skill, the KVFD would keep it that way.

Cutter looked back at Matheson. He snapped down his face shield, widened his stance, and took a firmer grip on the hose.

"Open 'er up," Matheson shouted, giving the go-ahead to start the water flow. The slack hose snapped suddenly taut as if jerked from the opposite end. Cutter, however, held it firm against his shoulder, by now used to the bruising crush, directing the spray toward the area the chief indicated would be the main point of entry.

For a brief moment, angry flames flared out on either side of the door, unwilling to give in to its nemesis—water pouring forward with enough force to crush a man's chest. Cutter squinted as ash and backspray clouded his visor. But he moved forward, step by step, as skillful as a surgeon, taking out fire-destroyed sections of doorway to make the way clear for the crew.

He sensed, rather than saw, Danvers pick up the slack behind him, making it a little easier to manage the hose. Only a little. He could still feel the hose throbbing in his hands, just a bad grip away from leaping away from him—almost as if it were alive with a mind and a will of its own.

Sometimes Cutter thought that the struggle to put out the flames was as much a struggle of man against the elements as it was element against element. Fire and rain. If he wasn't careful, wasn't conscious of what he was doing, the high-powered hose could be just as much of a threat as the flames wearing away the building in front of him.

As he moved cautiously forward, closer to the burning building, he instinctively took in a deep breath. Oppressive heat pressed down on him even as he felt the cold inrush of air from the oxygen tank strapped to his back burn his nose and lungs. Training taught him to breathe normally, regularly. Instinct wanted him to do otherwise. He felt his pulse quicken, spurred on by an odd mingling of panic and pleasure. He had sense enough to have a healthy respect for the damage an unmanaged flame could do. Each time he stepped into what he sensed was the very core of the burn, he fought against the urge to get the hell outta there. After all, what sane individual would willingly step into this unfeeling, unrelenting chaos?

At the same time, he knew that with the crushing force of the water spewing in front of him, his crew members behind him to back him, that fire had better know when it was time to retreat. Knowing that for a brief time, he was master of two of the most powerful elements on this planet was enough to make him almost drunk with power. There was nothing like it. Nothing he could eat, drink, sniff, or shoot up could give him this high, this odd contradiction of vulnerability and invincibility.

Nothing. No thing. And up until this morning—no one. He couldn't say that anymore. Because there was one who had taken him to this extreme. Davalyn. She had ignited him, frightened him, and, at the same time, strangely fulfilled him. Davalyn Bowers. God, if he could take back this morning, he would. How did that old song go? Something about turning back the hands of time? If it was in his power, he'd do it in a heartbeat. He'd turn back time and undo what he'd done.

Cutter had gone over what happened that morning again and again in his mind. He'd rationalized his actions and given himself excuses for behaving as he had. He was tired. He was lonely. Truth was, he was horny—hadn't been on a date in months. Some kinda record for him. Yeah, that had to be it. He hadn't had any in a while, and Davalyn was close. Convenient. Willing. Didn't matter who she was. At that moment, any woman with a pulse would have done.

All of those rationalizations sounded plausible. He'd even come close to convincing himself that nothing had really happened. It was a kiss. A simple kiss. Something men and women did every day. Where was the harm in that?

It all sounded plausible while the thoughts echoed in his head. However, he couldn't bring himself to say the words out loud. He wouldn't let his mouth give credence to his mental self-delusions.

Something *had* happened. She'd touched him, and not just between the legs. She'd touched his heart. Though, not kindly at first. Whatever gave her the idea that he'd cheated on Angela? So, he'd dated a little after the divorce. So what? What did they expect him to do? Join a monastery? He was no saint, he admitted. But he wasn't a dog, either. She'd hurt him with that accusation. And without hesitation, he'd let her know that. Didn't even occur to him to shut his mouth, as he sometimes did with Donovan when the conversation between them got too deep. Donovan knew him well enough to know when to press and when to back off, but Davalyn had no such boundaries. Somehow she'd managed to get him to open up. To talk about matters that he'd carefully locked away, kept hidden so that he could function from day to day.

He had to keep his feelings squashed. Dealing with the

pain of his failure, his inability to keep his family together despite his best effort, was too much. Anger and disappointment, frustration and futility. Sometimes it came at him from all sides, driving him back so that he had to retreat into himself to regroup. If there hadn't been Bennett, the one pure source of unconditional love in his life, he didn't know what he would have done. Donovan was his friend, but he had his own life, his own issues. As much as he wanted to be there for Cutter, he wasn't always around. And there were some types of pain a friend couldn't soothe—even a good friend like Donovan. And then there was Davalyn.

"McCall!" Someone was at his right elbow, pounding at his back to get his attention. Danvers was shouting and pointing across the room.

There Burleson was advancing, gesturing toward a section of wall where resistant flames found pockets of oxygen and flared up at sporadic intervals. "What's the matter with you, McCall? Get your head out of your ass and move that line!" Danvers snapped.

Cutter cursed under his breath. This was exactly what he didn't need. The distraction, this inattention to duty. He snapped back to the here and now, aimed the hose in the direction Burleson indicated. Ceilingward, in a sweeping motion, back and forth, working his way down, then back up again. Where the flames went, he went, pursuing, dousing, drenching until the hiss of dying flames and the rise of gray steam indicated that he was back on the job, and handling his business.

Thirteen

It was a competitive, male-dominated business. So, whenever Davalyn showed up at the scene of a fire, ready to start her investigation, she always put on her hardest, no-nonsense persona. She had a job to do. Get in, take notes of the fire scene, collect the evidence, and get out. Today was no different. That's what she told herself as she waited outside the perimeter marked off by the police.

When Davalyn stepped out of her red Ford Ranger, she zipped up her dark brown leather bomber-style jacket against the sharp wind, tugged on her gloves, and grabbed her clipboard with her checklist and blank report forms. Her personal digital assistant that she used to e-mail the camera images back to the office was tucked in her jacket pocket.

She scanned the area but didn't see any sign of a fellow investigator whom she sometimes partnered with—Mason Scott. There was time before she could begin the investigation, so she wasn't concerned that he hadn't shown yet. Mason was always running a little behind. In her opinion, he had a little too much on his plate, trying to be investigator and trainer as well. She didn't have quite enough experience to go that route yet. So, she stayed focused on the job.

Because the Kemah VFD was still searching for hot

spots, last pockets of resistant flames that flared up as the wind shifted directions, she took a few minutes to start entering some of the information on her report form. Davalyn leaned against her truck, holding the clipboard with one hand, occasionally taking sips of her double mocha from Starbucks.

"Ms. Bowers."

"How's it going, fellas?"

When a couple of officers passed her, she nodded once, acknowledging them, but didn't strike up a conversation. There would be time to talk later. She'd learned early on in the job that the last thing the victims wanted to see and hear were officials yakking it up in the midst of their misfortune. To inspire in them a sense of proficiency and professionalism, she always strived to maintain the appearance of efficiency—to outward appearances, that is.

Her insides told a different story. Her heart was fluttering inside her chest as wildly as if it were being buffeted by the high winds. It wasn't the sight of the burning building that stirred her. Or even the sight of that family, pathetically huddled in blankets, standing beside the ambulance. The fire had started early in the morning while they were still asleep. The presence of a private-security cruiser told Davalyn that it was probably the family's alarm system that had saved their lives. She'd seen the commercials often enough. How peace of mind against burglary, fire, and other medical emergencies could be bought for a few dollars a month.

Davalyn's heart went out to them as it always did. Knowing that fire had ravaged someone's home or business, or even taken a life, always moved her. But she could always take small comfort that she was there to help provide some of the answers when the victims could finally form the questions How? Why? What do we do next?

But it wasn't the sight of the family, either, that had her stomach tied up in knots. It was Cutter. Cutter Mc-Call. He was one of the firefighters who'd moved in and out of the structure. Even with his gear—the heavy jacket with the reflective stripes across the back, the helmet, and the soot-covered faceplate—and his back to her, she recognized him right away.

Davalyn tried to keep her mind focused on her work, tried to keep her eyes lowered. But she couldn't. Time and again, she found herself staring at Cutter and wishing that he would look up at her, too. She knew that he was busy, that he had a job to do as well, but she wanted him to notice her. More than notice her. She wanted him to give her some sign that he felt her presence as keenly as she felt his.

Even now, hours after his kiss, she still felt him. Involuntarily Davalyn reached up and touched her cheek. She thought she could still feel the rough whisker burn of Cutter's unshaven cheek grazing against hers. She caught her lower lip between her teeth, convinced that she could still feel his mouth, firm and demanding, over hers. The thought of his kiss burned in her stomach, and it made her feel with agonizing freshness the press of his calloused palms against her stomach. Davalyn instinctively drew in a deep breath, half expecting to feel Cutter's curious fingers exploring past her waistline, beneath the flimsy elastic of her panties.

Davalyn swallowed hard.

Get over yourself! she mentally snapped, reaching for her cup of coffee. But her hands were trembling, telling all the world that her calm exterior was a lie. Cream and coffee spilled over the hood of her truck, beading on the high-gloss exterior but running into the crevices of the front grille and headlights, and splattered over her vanity license plate that read BURN OUT.

"Just great," Davalyn muttered, then reached inside the cab for the box of tissues that she kept tucked in the compartment that flipped down, dividing the bench seat.

"I told you that you were drinking too much coffee," Mason Scott admonished from behind her.

Davalyn twisted around, glaring over her shoulder at him. "Just don't stand there looking all smug, Mason. Help me get some of that coffee off my grille. If Van sees how I've ruined his custom detail job, it'll be me splattered on the front of that grille instead of my double-shot mocha latte."

"You could always get someone from the KVFD to wash it off with the power hose," he suggested. Mason was only half joking. He'd visited her brother's shop a couple of times and had seen his passion for cars. Maybe his concern went deeper than passion. More along the lines of fanaticism.

"Never mind." She shook her head. She sopped up as much coffee as she could, going through several tissues, then wadded up the soggy mess and handed it to Mason. "Here, make yourself useful."

"Useful?" Mason said in mock indignation. "While you've been sitting around on an extended coffee break, I have been busy. Just got through talking to the chief. He's cleared us to work."

"Cool. Good work, Mason. Let's get at it." She collected her clipboard, pen, plastic evidence bags, and digital camera. Then they headed for the police line, showing their credentials to the officers in charge before crossing the tape.

"What's the word on the suspected cause?" she asked.

"Fire started in the family room, near the back of the house." Mason gestured. "Could be electrical. The family had already started decorating for the holidays. Had lights strung up everywhere. On the staircase, along the mantel. If there was an outlet to be had, it had an extension cord plugged into it, too."

"Extension cord? Good Lord."

"Somebody ought to tell these folks that the only thing those extension cords are good for are spankings of naughty children."

When his bad joke didn't get a response, Mason waved his hand in front of her face.

"Hello? Earth to Davalyn? Did you hear what I just said? I said to use extension cords to beat children—"

"I heard what you said," Davalyn said.

"But you're not all over me."

"I'll chastise you later, Mason. I've got a lot on my mind right now."

"Well, shake out the cobwebs, lady. It's show time."

Part of the reason she had such a hard time concentrating was that she had a bad case of the "don't wannas." She didn't want to be here now. She didn't want it to *be* now. She wanted to push back the sun, forcing it to the horizon so that it appeared to be the crack of dawn, with frosty stars still dotting the sky.

Davalyn didn't want to be carefully picking her way through the ground floor of a stranger's house, stepping through the collecting puddles of water and ash. She wanted to be high up in the trees, sheltered by the four walls that Cutter had built with his own hands. Nor did she want to be grasping her elbows in a self-embrace to keep out the wet wind that whipped through the ravaged walls. Instead, she wanted to be wrapped up in Cutter's arms, his warmth suffusing her, driving away the prewinter chill.

She crossed the threshold, ducking her head just a little to avoid grazing a fallen support beam, and stumbled over a brick partially hidden by pooled water.

A hand, quick and steadying, reached out to grab her elbow and kept her from falling. "Whoa there. Easy."

"Clumsy." Davalyn muttered a terse curse. She should have been more mindful. She knew better than to approach a fire scene without all of her senses keenly tuned. But it wasn't her assistant giving her the warning. It was the source of her distraction.

Davalyn looked up into Cutter's face. He still had on his helmet, but the Plexiglas faceplate was flipped back, showing a face that was covered with sweat and grime. But to her, it was as handsome a face as she'd ever want to see.

"Thanks, McCall," she said, trying to keep her tone level, professional, even though she felt as if the air were being squeezed from her lungs. Her professional training was her shield, her savior. When she was on the job, she called every city official by their last name if she knew it. Even the one who just hours before had touched her in more places than her elbow.

"Don't go through the hall, Ms. Bowers." Cutter took his cue from her and remained deferential. "Part of the stairway has collapsed, blocking the way. Cut around to the kitchen to get to the family room. That's where we suspect the fire started." He pointed out the direction.

Mason took the lead. "How's it goin', Cutter?" Mason was a little more familiar as he moved ahead. He'd been inspecting for the KVFD for a lot longer than Davalyn and knew everyone on a first-name basis.

"Same ol', same ol'. You know how it is," Cutter responded. Half of his attention was focused on keeping an eye on Davalyn as she made her way through the burned-out hull.

"Yeah, I know how it is," Mason said, not missing Cutter's preoccupation.

The chatter was brief, almost obligatory. Enough to maintain working relationships, but not enough to get in the way of work. Davalyn let Mason and Cutter do most of the talking. She snapped the photographs, took her notes, and indicated when she thought she had enough evidence to send to the lab. The damage had been contained to a few rooms of the house, so the full investigation took just under an hour. Though her findings seemed to support the fire chief's theory of where and how the fire had started, she still took her time to make sure she performed a thorough investigation. She had a job to do. It was her signature on the final report.

She'd gathered up a stretch of molten extension cord and decorative lighting, carefully coiled them, and dropped them into an evidence bag. Davalyn then pulled out a permanent marker and labeled the bag with her name, identification number, and the street address where this sample had been taken. She then dated the bag.

After a bit, she called out to Mason. "All done here. Time to go," she announced, heading for the entrance again.

"So? Was the chief right?"

"Seemed to be," Davalyn said cautiously. She wouldn't say for certain until she'd submitted the evidence to the lab for final analysis. Their findings would appear on a report that was submitted to insurance companies.

Her caution about prematurely reporting her findings

was something else she'd learned early on the job. Even when she thought she was 100 percent certain of the cause of a fire, she never, ever, ever announced those findings until a separate, independent laboratory confirmed her assessment.

She'd heard horror stories of graduates before her who, confident of their own abilities, had gone in front of the media and announced their findings only to be publicly proven wrong later. In such a competitive business, you weren't doing yourself any favors by speaking too loudly or too assuredly without backup.

So, whenever Davalyn had to face the media, she always couched her assessment in words like "appears to be" or "seems to suggest." If she worried that she didn't come off confident or knowledgeable, she let her consistent track record speak for itself.

"Last one back to the office buys the coffee," Mason teased her.

"You don't drink coffee," she reminded him.

"Judging from that stain on the front of the truck, neither do you," he quipped.

Davalyn didn't look in Cutter's direction as she turned to go. She counted herself lucky that she could take a few steps without her rubbery knees giving her inner turmoil away.

But she wasn't getting away. Not that easily. Not completely unscathed.

"Ms. Bowers," Cutter called out to her. "Got a minute?"

"Just barely," she said, glancing at her watch.

"It'll only take a minute." He fell into step beside her. Out of the earshot of anyone else.

"Clock's ticking, McCall," she said.

"It's about Bennett's party this Saturday."

That stopped her in her tracks. She turned to face him. They were both on the job. Why was he taking the time to air their personal business in front of almost everyone? "What about it? You're not canceling, are you?"

He paused. "Naw. Nothin' like that. I just thought you should know . . . That is . . . if you wanted to, you could invite Julian to the party."

"Julian?" she repeated.

"Yeah, you remember him," Cutter said, his tone edged with sarcasm. "Your boyfriend."

When Davalyn didn't respond, Cutter went on. "Just thought you wanted to invite him along. You bring your friend. I'm bringing someone, too. A friend."

"Oh." Davalyn exhaled slowly, deliberately, and hoped that it didn't sound as if she'd just been hit in the stomach with a cannonball. "Okay."

"Okay?" He lowered his head and peered into her eyes.

"Okay," she repeated stiffly. "What time's the party supposed to start again?"

"Dinner's at six. And after that, we're taking Bennett around the boardwalk. He gets a kick out of the train ride."

"We? As in you and your friend are taking him?" she clarified.

"Uh-huh."

"Oh." Davalyn wished she could think of something wittier, or at least more coherent to say. It took some effort, but she forced herself to sound cordial, rather than sound as if he'd just ripped apart her innards. He was going to spend most of Bennett's birthday with someone else. Not even his ex-wife. Never mind that she'd been the one caring for Bennett when no one else could.

Never mind that she felt as close to that boy as if he were her own. Don't even mention the fact that she was looking forward to spending Bennett's special day with him.

"Okay, McCall. We'll see you then."

"You and Julian," he stressed.

"Me and Julian," Davalyn repeated.

She turned sharply, grinding charcoal beneath her booted heels as she made it back to her truck. Davalyn climbed behind the wheel, but she didn't drive off immediately. She lowered her head, grasping the clipboard with both hands to steady herself. If she didn't trust herself to hold the board without trembling in anger and humiliation, she certainly didn't trust herself to grasp the steering wheel.

She wasn't sure how long she sat there, shellshocked.

What the hell just happened here?

This morning, Cutter was all over her. Just inches away from being all inside her, too. *Now he's telling me to bring my own date?* It didn't make sense. Or maybe it did. Davalyn's shoulder slumped. There were some not-so-subtle hints that he'd dropped all along the way. She just didn't want to pick up on them.

When they were all hanging out—she, Van, and Cutter—she hadn't wanted to count how many times Cutter's cell phone had rung. How he turned away to answer it, never offering apologies, just picked up on their conversation as if nothing had ever happened when the call ended. And what about the additional baby-sitting requests? They weren't all because he had to work. When he dropped Bennett off, he looked too clean, too sharp, to be heading out to work. Though some of those requests had slacked off considerably in the last few months, they hadn't ceased altogether.

Davalyn had never questioned him about his comings and goings. She'd teased him, made fun of his impeccable taste and fashion sense, but she always had cheerfully agreed to baby-sit whenever Van couldn't. After all, what were friends for? It's what they were, after all. Just friends. Or so she'd thought.

She didn't feel like a friend now. She felt used.

"Damn you, Cutter McCall," she said aloud, slamming her hand on the steering wheel. What was the matter with him? Why was he running the streets, looking for something he already had? He should take a lesson from Diana Ross's Dorothy in *The Wiz*. Everything he needed was here. Right here. Didn't he know what he had in the palm of his hand? Didn't he know that she was all he could ever want, and more?

Lifting her head, Davalyn reigned in her anger. She squashed it. Doused it with a cold splash of reality. So what . . . So what if he didn't want her? He didn't know what he was missing. If he didn't know a damn good thing when he had one, then he deserved whatever skank he could find to take her place.

"Screw you, Cutter McCall," she said aloud. "You're nothing but a coldhearted son of a—"

The warning Klaxon of the pumper truck as it pulled away from the scene drowned out the sound, if not the spirit, of Davalyn's vehement cursing.

fourteen

"Sonofabitch!" Cutter snapped, and let the razor fall to the sink in a splash of sudsy water. He leaned forward, fishing for the supposedly nonslip grip handle with one hand, and clung with the other hand to the towel that was starting to unwrap from around his waist.

"Ooh . . . Dad! You cussed!" Bennett sat on the toilet, pointing to the disgusted image of his father in the mirror as he carefully watched Cutter's grooming ritual. He'd come in, just after Cutter had stepped out of the shower, his towel wrapped around his waist, to tell his father about a phone call. The bathroom was thick with steam, so Bennett stood on tiptoe and flipped the switch to start the old vent whirring. He'd forgotten all about the call when Cutter started to rummage under the sink for his shaving utensils.

Usually, if his dad was going out, he was already at Uncle Van's before he got a chance to watch him get ready. And his father had banned him from his bathroom after he'd caught Bennett with a face full of shaving gel, shaving off the only easily accessible hair on his face. His eyebrows were coming back in nicely—or so Aunt Dav had told him just last week. So, Bennett considered it a rare treat to be able to sit there and watch him like that. Even over the loud, metallic whirring fan vent, he could hear the frustration in his father's tone.

"I know, little man," Cutter said, ripping off a piece of tissue and sticking it to the slowly bleeding spot just below his Adam's apple. "I'm sorry. I said a really bad word." He pointed the dripping shaver at his son. "Don't you let me catch you saying it, either."

Bennett screwed up his face. "Don't worry about that. Mama said that she was gonna put soap in my mouth the next time she heard me repeat something you said."

Cutter gave a reluctant smile. He was going to have to be more careful. Bennett's sharp eyes and ears were picking up more and more these days. Every time he thought his son wasn't paying attention, something came out of Bennett's mouth that wound up biting Cutter in the end.

"She's right. Good little boys don't cuss."

One of the few times he agreed with anything Angela said or did when it came to their son.

"But big bad boys do." Bennett smiled up at his dad. A big, bucktoothed grin as his permanent teeth had finally come in after a summer of gap-toothed grins.

"Go on and get out of here." Cutter tried to sound severe, but failed. He turned on the faucet and splashed water on Bennett. "Go get dressed, Bennett. I'll be in there in a minute to check your buttons and fix your tie. You're a big boy now. No more clip-ons. Uncle Van bought you a real silk tie."

Bennett opened his mouth, then gave up the fight. This was another one of those times when he was going to lose the fashion fight. He decided to save his arguing tone, just in case his dad tried to order something gross for him at the restaurant.

"Oh, I forgot to tell you. Aunt Dav called when you

were in the shower, Dad, and said that she was bringing a guest. Asked if that was all right."

Cutter paused in midstroke. "It's fine," he said, then swirled the shaver in the water with brisk, agitated strokes. "Just dandy." He muttered more to himself than in response to Bennett. He didn't know why he was so irritated. Inviting him was what he'd asked her to do. He supposed she was confirming that he was going to show up—and in the process giving him the extra jab that made this all so hard.

"How can she bring somebody else to the party? We can't all fit in the truck, Dad." The last Bennett had "accidentally" heard about his birthday plans, they were all going to the restaurant together. Him, his dad, Uncle Van, and Aunt Dav. Uncle Van had just finished working on a '65 Mustang and they were going to put the top down and cruise around Kemah so that everybody could see them. Dad had called it free advertising.

"We won't have to. They're meeting us there. Uncle Van and Aunt Dav and her friend Julian Blake. You remember him from the barbecue, don't you? When Aunt Dav moved back with Uncle Van."

"Yeah, I remember him. The punk."

"What did you say, Bennett?" Cutter said, whirling around to pin Bennett with a hard stare. Now where did that come from? Angela couldn't blame him for that one. He may have slipped with a few other nasties. But that was one word that he would never, ever use around Bennett. That much was certain.

"I s-said . . . he was a punk," Bennett stammered. "He acts like one anyway."

"Sit down, Bennett." Cutter pointed to the toilet.

"Yes, sir," Bennett mumbled, taking up his seat again.

No doubt in Bennett's mind. His dad wasn't joking. He was serious—punishment time serious.

"Bennett, those are very ugly words you're using. Ugly, hurtful words. No way to talk about your aunt Dav's friend. Do you understand me?"

"But Dwayne said that when a grown man switches when he walks that—"

"I'm not interested in what Dwayne says," Cutter snapped. Bennett's best friend had a lot of influence over him, Cutter knew. But not as much influence as his father should have. "It's what I'm telling you that's important. You will not use those words again or, so help me, you, me, and this bar of Dial are going to become very well acquainted. Do I make myself clear?"

"Yes, sir."

"Your friend Dwayne doesn't even know Julian. So how can he judge him? That's called prejudice, Bennett. You know what prejudice means, don't you?"

Bennett hunched his shoulders. "I dunno."

"Yes, you do." Cutter's tone reminded him that he'd better come up with an answer quick.

"It means hate."

"That's right. It means to prejudge. And usually involves hate and ignorance. And that's not how I'm raising you. I'm not raising you to judge someone before you get to know them."

"Yes, sir."

"Now get out of here. Go get dressed. We're running late and we've got to pick up Miss Shayla. Remember?"

This time, Bennett made his displeasure obvious. "I didn't invite her to my birthday party."

"*I* did," Cutter replied, a slight edge to his voice.

"Why'd you do that, Dad?" Bennett complained. He'd only met Miss Shayla a couple of times, for a couple of

minutes each time. Not enough time to really get to know
her. Certainly not enough time to make him want her at
his birthday party. He supposed that was enough time for
him to make up his mind about her. So, it really wasn't
prejudging. Something that seemed to really bug his dad.

Bennett didn't like her. Didn't like her at all. Not the
way she smiled at his dad. And especially not the way she
didn't smile at him. Bennett caught on quick that whenever Miss Shayla came around him, she showed him her
teeth. Big, pretty, superwhite, superstraight teeth. But that
didn't mean she was smiling at him. She was always
showing those teeth at him—but looking at his dad while
she was doing it. Like she was smiling just to make Dad
happy. To get on his good side. It wasn't working. Bennett
thought that maybe his dad knew what she was doing.

He didn't like the way she didn't make his dad happy.
Not really happy. He smiled when he was around her, but
that didn't mean that he was happy. Not the way he was
when Aunt Dav came around. He didn't have to force
himself to laugh at Aunt Dav's jokes. Not the way he did
with Miss Shayla. Sometimes Bennett got the feeling that
Dad and Aunt Dav shared jokes even when they weren't
talking to each other. Like they knew what each other was
thinking, agreed what was funny, and could enjoy each
other without having to say it out loud. Bennett had seen
them pass looks and then, for a reason that wasn't obvious to him, just start laughing. Sort of like the way Dad
and Uncle Van were together sometimes when they were
hanging out or working at the shop. Dad could hold out
his hand and Uncle Van would slap in a tool without Dad
ever having to ask. They worked like that all the time.
Sometimes even finishing each other's sentences.

Dad and Aunt Dav were like that. But not quite the
same. Bennett couldn't put it all together just yet. But he

knew that his dad liked Aunt Dav in a way that was different from the way he liked Uncle Van. It was a nice difference. He didn't mind Aunt Dav coming to his party at all. It was the only girl he didn't mind being there. So what did they need Miss Shayla for?

"Go on, Bennett," Cutter urged. "Or we're gonna be late."

"Yes, sir," Bennett mumbled, then slid off the toilet seat. As he pulled the bathroom door closed behind him, Cutter could hear Bennett muttering, "I still don't see why I couldn't invite Dwayne to my birthday party, but we gotta go get that . . ."

Cutter couldn't hear the rest of the sentence. Didn't really want to. He already knew how disappointed Bennett was. Dwayne was Bennett's best friend. When Cutter had told him that he was going to have a party, Dwayne was the first person Bennett thought of. Cutter couldn't blame him. Bennett and Dwayne were best friends and had been since Bennett was in kindergarten. But Dwayne had a nasty case of chicken pox. He'd caught it from another kid at the birthday party Angela had given him the week before Bennett's actual birthday.

Cutter didn't figure the rest of the guests could have a good time sitting at the same table with an itchy, feverish, Benadryl-lotion-covered nine-year-old.

That explained why Dwayne couldn't be there, but it didn't explain why Shayla had to be there. The key word being "had." Cutter went out of his way to track down Shayla's number. Hunted high and low for it, overturning couch cushions, checking the pockets of jeans that he hadn't worn in a while, even called a friend of a friend of a friend for her number. Out of all of the women he could have called, he had chosen Shayla Morgan.

He knew that she would be the least pissed at him for

not returning her phone calls. He'd been polite, cordial enough when she called him, even though he kept the phone calls brief. As pleased as he sounded to hear from her, he'd always had a plausible excuse why they couldn't hook up. Excuses like his son was sick, or he had to pull overtime at the shop. Maybe he was on call at the KVFD and wouldn't feel right leaving her stranded if he had to respond to an alarm.

Cutter wasn't stringing her along. He honestly didn't want to hurt her. From the couple of dates that they'd gone on, he knew that she was looking for something more from him—something that he wasn't prepared to give. She was so sweet, so willing to please. He couldn't, in good conscience, ask Shayla out when his thoughts were of another woman, but he had to now. He had to ask Shayla out so that he could get Davalyn out of his head.

Cutter blew out a heavy, frustrated breath, which bubbled between his lips. *Davalyn! See what you've reduced me to?*

Before Davalyn had come back into his life, he didn't mind dating several women at once. Every one of them knew it was all about the kicks. Every one of them knew that there were others. He said so up front so that there could be no misunderstanding. And, if ever he got the inkling that one of them was thinking that she could change his mind, could hook him, he immediately backed off. No pretenses. No hard feelings. No harm. No foul. He wasn't ready, or the type, to pretend that he was feeling something that he wasn't in order to get the fleeting, easy sex they readily offered him.

That didn't mean that sometimes the situation didn't get a little out of control. He was human. Saying no didn't come as easily as he thought. Not after a fine meal, smooth wine, and baby-sitters who didn't mind keeping

Bennett until late in the evening or sometimes until the next day.

But he was always careful to use protection. Each time. Every time. He was protecting his health and his future. No matter how heated the moment got, if it ever progressed to that moment, he either used a condom or he used the door. Simple.

So where was that simplicity, that conviction, when it came to Davalyn? How in the hell had things progressed so far, so fast? If it weren't for that page from the station, Cutter had no doubt in his mind that he and Davalyn would have made love—five o'clock in the morning, two stories up, covered in sawdust, and as Davalyn quipped, ready to face the threat of indoor-outdoor carpet burns on his behind. Not exactly the most romantic setting. But the moon and stars as his witness, he wanted her and would have gladly accepted the consequences to have her. Cutter had never known such recklessness. Not even with his ex-wife.

When he was a teenager, all he could think of was Angela Bennett. With Donovan's help, he went after her with a single-minded purpose and grand plan. Eventually it worked. He wooed her with his heart, wowed her with his skills, and eventually won her with his persistence. Not an easy task, but systematic and predictable once he and Van figured out what Angela wanted in a man.

Not so with Davalyn. There was nothing predictable about that woman. Not the way she made him feel. And certainly not the way she made him act. She'd gotten to him. Made him want her in the worst kind of way. Made his very skin crave for her touch to the point where he'd abandoned reason and rationale. He was just a heartbeat away from sublime pleasure and ultimate disaster.

Cutter gripped the edge of the sink. His fingers

pressed so tightly into the porcelain lip that he thought
he heard it crack under the pressure. Even now, a few
days later, the memory of her touch excited him. Evidence of his arousal pushed painfully out against the
cotton towel around his waist.

He closed his eyes, telling himself that he was trying
to block out her image.

*Focus, Cutter. Focus! Think of something else. Anything else! Anyone else. Shayla. Francine. Bethany.
Saundra. Ruth.*

A parade of names. A swirl of faces. Each one special in her own way. But none of them were Davalyn.
None of them. Closing his eyes only made her image
sharper, more acute. His vision wasn't the only sense
she affected. Not only could he still see her, but he
heard her as well—the quickening of her breath against
his cheek when he touched her. The smell and feel of
her skin, fresh and floral, like a warm summer's day.
She always reminded him of summertime.

Cutter groaned. Hadn't realized that his hand strayed
beneath his towel. His eyelids flew open as he snatched
his hand away with a sizzling curse. Bennett wasn't
around, so he took full advantage of the solitude and
gave free rein to his frustration. This was ridiculous. Insane. One woman shouldn't have him strung out this
way.

It was one of the reasons why he had called Shayla
Morgan and invited her to Bennett's party. He needed to
prove to himself that this thing with Davalyn, whatever
it was, wasn't any different from any other relationship
he had with his other women friends.

Sure, Davalyn turned him on. That much he'd admit.
But it was physical. All physical. A biochemical, physical reaction to her incredible body. It was just her body

that attracted him, and he found it hard to keep his eyes from straying to her full hips or the generous swell of her breast. But he also enjoyed dueling with her rapier wit. She was well read and up on any topic he wanted to talk about—either current events or historical. No topic was taboo. Politics. Religion. Davalyn's comedic sense of timing was dead on. She knew exactly how to set up her jokes to catch him off guard. He wished that he had a dollar for every time she caught him midswallow or midswig, to send him into a fit of unexpected laughter.

He supposed that it was cosmic justice. When they were kids, he used to tickle her until she was gasping for air, calling out to Van to come to her rescue. Davalyn was often in his thoughts even then. He spent hours thinking of ways to get to her and took pride that he was never disappointed. Now the tables had turned. And he was racking his brain trying to find ways to get her out of his thoughts. That told him that *maybe* his reaction to her wasn't all physical.

"But it has to be," Cutter said aloud to his reflection. "It's just the thrill of the chase. The curiosity factor. An ego trip. If I can get to her, I can have anybody."

He wouldn't accept any other explanation. Because the only other explanation he could find for behaving around her as he had was that he was in love with her. And he was *not* willing to admit that he was in love with her. He couldn't be. She was Van's sister. Julian's woman. And he wasn't the type to push up on another man's lady. So, it couldn't be love. Just couldn't be.

Fifteen

Davalyn couldn't decide between two equally attractive outfits. She stood in front of a full-length mirror hanging in front of her closet door, holding one outfit in front of her and then switching to the other, assessing the effect. The first outfit was a two-piece bright red tunic and skirt. A little tighter and a lot shorter than she remembered it being when she wore it about six months ago. With her irregularly shaped, multistrand pearl choker and high-heeled, strapped sandals, the red would make her feel very festive. More in tune with the holiday season.

The second outfit was a black silk pantsuit, with eight bright gold buttons running beneath the velvet-trimmed, double-breasted lapels. The black was more demure and would certainly keep her warmer this brisk November evening. And Julian liked black. Said it made her look sophisticated. She'd worn this outfit the evening of his open house for his law firm. If she chose this, he'd remember and know that she was thinking of him.

Davalyn felt a twinge of guilt. They'd both been so busy lately. A few phone calls and a couple of lunch dates had been about the extent of their contact this month. So when she'd called him to invite him to Bennett's birthday, the pleasure in his voice stung her. She'd been a little preoccupied with Cutter these past few weeks, but that didn't mean she should give up on her other friends. Davalyn was busy, yet she still found time to touch bases with her sorority sisters. An hour here, an hour there. Why couldn't she find time for Julian?

"Get your act together," Davalyn said aloud. That's what Margot had told her the last time she was late for a planning meeting. She was warned to get her priorities straight or let someone else take the lead. It was harshly said, but taken deeply to heart. If Julian truly was her friend, then she should do better by him. He'd been a good friend to her. More than a friend. He deserved better than that.

Holding the red dress against her again, Davalyn couldn't help but note that though Julian liked the black, she preferred the red. It was her favorite color. Trafficstoppin', head-turnin', jaw-droppin' red. And this dress was all that, and then some.

Or less, Davalyn mused, noting where the hemline fell on her. She hadn't grown any taller in the past six months. Still five feet seven. But the dress was certainly shorter than she remembered. It fell somewhere between her belly button and her knees. Closer to the former. It was the kind of length that made her walk slowly, stand erectly, sit carefully. The kind of dress that made men watch her—hoping that she wouldn't be so mindful. One small slip on her part and it would be that famous interview scene with Sharon Stone in *Basic Instinct* all over again.

"Who am I trying to impress?" Davalyn said with disgust, tossing the outfit on the bed. Not Cutter. His eyes wouldn't be on her tonight but on the "friend" he made a point of telling her that he would bring to the party tonight.

"Friend, my ass." Davalyn snorted, turning to see how much the red would cover if she wore it tonight. She knew what "friend" meant. It meant female flavor of the month.

Davalyn had tried not to listen when Donovan had told her in some of his letters that Cutter had changed since his divorce. Ever since she could remember, she'd always known him to be a one-woman man. *Angela. Angela. Angela.* If he wasn't talking cars, he was talking about that girl.

Obviously not anymore. He obviously found a way to pacify himself now that Angela had married someone else. Davalyn ground her teeth. Is that what she was? A pacifier? Something to tide him over until he found what he really wanted?

It took her a few days to get over the hurt, the embarrassment. But she was over it now. So over him. That's why she could go to this birthday party tonight, celebrate the joy that had come into her life that was Bennett.

She and Bennett had developed a special bond that was separate from her relationship with Cutter. That kid was cute, funny, reflective, saucy, and mannish at any given time. She didn't mind baby-sitting him when she could, even though she suspected that his dad was taking advantage of their friendship.

"But that's all it is," Davalyn said with regret. "Just friendship." They'd tested the boundaries of that friendship with that kiss and he, single-sidedly, decided that it wasn't worth it. Or maybe she hadn't stirred him as much as she had thought. She had thought that he was with her—step for step, touch for touch. As much as she wanted him, she thought he needed her. Could she have been so wrong? Could she have misjudged him so much? Maybe it was just wishful thinking? Had she seen what she wanted to see? Was she that deluded?

No! Davalyn vehemently denied. *I'm not wrong. He wants me. He needs me.*

It wasn't just about sex. If she'd judged simply by the urgency in which he touched her, she might not have been so sure. She would be the first to claim that she'd been swept up by the moment. Yet, something in his eyes told her otherwise, something primal. Pure. And tortured. It couldn't have been purely physical. He was fighting too hard to resist the pull.

Cutter was no saint. She never believed that. Whatever pedestal she'd placed him on was built on human frailties. Yet, if all he wanted was a quick lay, why did he stop? Why didn't he ignore the pager, satisfy himself, and *then* go into work? She'd asked herself those questions a thousand times.

He said that he'd never disrespect her. Wouldn't dream of hurting her. Was that all it was? Deference to his relationship with her brother, Van?

"Times like these make a girl wish she were an only child," she said dryly. She took one last, longing look at the red dress, then reached for the black pantsuit.

The sound of a huge diesel engine cranking up told her that Cutter and Bennett were already on their way to the restaurant. Davalyn made her way to her window, pushed aside the curtains. She didn't expect to be seen. Didn't want to be seen. She wasn't even sure why she went to the window. She just knew that she had to go.

Davalyn watched as Cutter's black Dodge Ram backed slowly out of the drive.

"Bye," she whispered, raising her hand in a half-hearted wave. Perhaps it was a little masochistic, watching him drive off, knowing that he was going to pick up another woman. Davalyn stood and watched anyway. Feeling that for those last few seconds, she still had a chance with him.

She wasn't expecting the truck to stop before pulling out into the street. With the truck left idling, Cutter climbed out and strode with long, hurried steps for the house. He was talking on the cell phone, his face animated, almost jovial.

Davalyn afforded herself a self-indulgent sigh. That man sure did clean up well. Even from that distance, she could tell that he'd cut his hair. Unlike her brother, who kept his hair long and cornrowed, Cutter kept his reddish brown hair cropped close to his head.

"Makes it harder to count all of the gray," he'd once joked.

Davalyn closed her eyes, remembering the sound of his voice, the look on his face during that conversation.

About a month ago, she'd stayed over late at his house, watching over Bennett while he was out. After making Bennett's favorite, fish sticks and tater tots with almost a whole bottle of ketchup, she ordered Bennett into the bathtub. Afterward, she played a few rounds of Legend of Zelda with him on his Game Boy, read him a few chapters of African folk tales about a much-too-clever spider named Anansi, then put him into bed around nine.

When Cutter had called to say that he was going to be late, Davalyn didn't question what had caused the delay. She closed her mind to the fact that he might be using the opportunity to spend a little quality time with someone else. She just made herself comfortable on his couch, a huge lodge-style sectional leather couch with plenty of overstuffed pillows to prop her up. A big bowl of white-cheese popcorn, several frosty cans of Vanilla Coke, and a stack of DVD movies—she was set for the long haul.

Cutter had finally come in, almost two o'clock in the morning, trying to be quiet. But Davalyn was already awake. Wired from the soda and too embarrassingly scared to go to sleep after watching several movies in which a ghoul named Jason hacked to pieces enough teenagers to fill Galveston Bay, she sat up as soon as she'd heard the jingle of keys in the lock and the door swing open.

"Cutter?" she called out, her voice tremulous. She pointed the remote control toward the television, turning down the volume.

Thud. Thud. Thud. The heavy fall of boots against the linoleum floor, slow and deliberate, grew softer, softer, then stopped altogether.

"Cutter, is that you?" Davalyn called out a little louder. She'd turned out all of the lights before she'd settled into the living room. Now shadows and echoes were playing tricks on her mind. She would have given a king's ransom for one of those "clapping" devices that would let her turn on the lights with a handclap. As skittish as she was feeling, she'd light up the whole house with enthusiastic clapping.

Davalyn felt her heart beat a little harder. Maybe it wasn't Cutter. Maybe it was that ghoul, coming for her. In a few days, it would be Halloween. Wasn't this how all of those slasher movies started out? An unsuspecting, stupid little baby-sitter calling out to the would-be murderer?

Davalyn let out a surprised shriek as Cutter spoke from the other side of the room—from the door that led to the breakfast area.

"What are you still doing up?" he asked, brushing fish stick crumbs off his pants legs.

"God, Cutter! You scared me!" Davalyn snapped, hurling a pillow across the room at him.

"I know." He ducked, laughing openly at her. He pointed to the television. "Which one is that one? When Jason is in outer space?"

"Yes," she said, settling back onto the couch cushions.

"I haven't had the time to watch that all the way through yet, but I read in the paper that all of the critics hated it."

"The best kind," Davalyn said, picking up the remote and starting the movie over. Cutter settled down next to her, stretching out his long legs on top of the combination ottoman/coffee table upholstered in the same leather as the couch.

"That stuff will rot your brain, you know," he said, picking up the cover to read the credits.

"It's your movie," she reminded him.

"That's how I know," he replied, leaning forward and grabbing a handful of popcorn. He tossed a kernel into the air and caught it in his mouth on the first try. "First-hand knowledge."

Davalyn picked up a few kernels, tried to imitate him, then gave up when most of the popcorn kernels bounced off her face, landed on the carpeted floor, or slipped unexpectedly down the front of her blouse.

"Do you let Bennett watch these?" Davalyn asked to deflect his attention, then turned aside to shake the popcorn out.

"Nope. Of course not. This vice is all mine."

He started to lean back, but Davalyn picked up another pillow. Cutter raised his hands in a defensive posture. "You're not gonna hit me again, are ya?"

"You deserve it for scaring me." She thumped the pillow into his chest. "What were you thinking, sneaking up on me like that?"

"Sorry, baby girl." He tried to look contrite, but his dark eyes were shining with too much mischief for her to fall for it.

"Yeah, right. Somehow I don't believe you." She reached for another pillow. "But I'll forgive you just this time. You look too tired to fight about it anyway." When he leaned back, she put the pillow under his head, then curled up her legs and rearranged a blanket over her.

"I *am* tired," he said, then smothered a yawn behind his hand.

"Rough night?" she asked.

"A lot of pranks," he said. "This close to Halloween, a lot of folks out there have got a really sick, twisted sense of humor."

"What happened?" She sat up, her expression interested.

"We responded to this one call. Strangest one yet. It took us four hours to dig out a man whose wife had a truckload of sand poured on him because she was tired of him tracking beach sand through her house. A neighbor saw the cloud of dust rising from her backyard, thought it was a fire, called 911, and we were dispatched to the house."

"You're lying!" Davalyn exclaimed, trying not to laugh.

"If I'm lyin', I'm fryin'." He held up his hand to

swear an oath. "I didn't know whether to dig him out or build a sand castle."

"What happened to the husband?"

"He's all right. A couple of bruised ribs and one hell of a sand rash."

"And the woman?"

"She's now spending some quality time in the care of a few Galveston UTMB doctors who can help her work out her passive-aggressive issues."

Davalyn looked askance at him, not sure whether to believe him or not. She didn't smell alcohol, so he hadn't gone out drinking with "the boys" after leaving the fire station. No makeup smudges on his shirt, so there was no obvious evidence that he'd been with another woman. And his hands didn't look as though they'd had a vigorous cleaning from that harsh soap Van kept at the shop.

Content that he was back with her, Davalyn said thankfully, "At least there were no fire alarms." She glanced at her pager sitting on the coffee table. "Thank goodness. Hasn't gone off once."

"Thank goodness," Cutter echoed—yawning, stretching, and settling deep into the cushions of the couch.

Davalyn rested her head on her folded arm on the back of the couch cushions. She watched as Cutter's eyes fluttered closed, his breathing becoming deep and regular. He, too, looked peaceful.

"You're going to miss your movie again," she whispered.

"I'm willin' to make that sacrifice for a little sleep," Cutter responded drowsily.

"Poor baby," she said, spreading a portion of her blanket over him, too. She felt oddly maternal. Just as she had when she'd tucked the covers around Bennett. "You need to slow down, Cutter. You're running yourself ragged."

"I'm gettin' too old for this," he agreed, running his hand over his grizzled head. "Gray hairs are poppin' out like weeds more and more every day."

"You could always dye it," Davalyn teased him. "Wear some of that wash-in/wash-out temporary hair stuff that covers just the gray."

Cutter grunted. "With as many showers as I'm takin' after each call, I wouldn't get more than one or two good days of color out of the box. Not worth the effort. No, thanks. I think I'll just grow old gracefully."

"You're not getting old," Davalyn answered in denial. "You're becoming more distinguished." She reached out and ran her fingertips lightly over his skin, just over his right ear.

"That's just a politically correct word for old," Cutter retorted. He folded his arms across his chest, balling up his fists and tucking his hands under his armpits.

"Age isn't anything but a number." Davalyn recognized his defensive stance. She pitched her voice low, soothing, continuing to massage his temples.

"In my case, a very big number and getting bigger all the time."

"If you're blessed, it'll keep getting bigger."

"Every man's prayer," Cutter replied, tilting his head and opening one eye to peer at her. Davalyn saw the mischievous gleam return and instantly recognized that he wasn't necessarily talking about age anymore.

"You're awful!" she exclaimed, jerking the pillow out from under his head and hitting him with it. "I've had it with you. I'm going home."

"Hold a minute, Dav. I'll walk you back."

Davalyn uncurled from the couch, slipped on her shoes. Cutter helped her shrug into her jacket.

"Thanks for watching Bennett for me," he said quietly, his voice almost directly in her ear.

"No problem. He's such a good kid."

"Yeah, I think I'll hang on to him for a little while longer."

"Hang on to him for a little while longer . . ."
The words were echoing in her mind when Cutter came out of the house carrying a small wrapped package with a big bow and a bundle of flowers wrapped in dark green tissue paper. He'd almost forgotten Bennett's present. Davalyn had recognized the irregularly shaped package immediately. She'd wrapped it herself when Cutter had come over yesterday, all thumbs and paper cuts, asking for a little help.

Her amusement rapidly turned to annoyance when she also recognized the other package in his hand. Flowers. Roses, to be exact. A dozen long-stemmed red roses. Those weren't for Bennett. They could only be for his "friend."

As she stood at the window, Davalyn felt each tiny thorn on all twelve long stems prick her heart. She clutched the window curtains, her breathing ragged and painful.

"You certainly know how to charm a girl, Cutter Mc-Call," she whispered. She didn't think he saw her. He certainly couldn't have heard her. Yet, something caught his attention and made him stop. Stop and stare. Cutter lifted his head and looked directly at her.

Davalyn gave a startled curse, then backed away from the window.

"Great," she snapped. "Just great." She wasn't going to a birthday party but to a pity party. She felt sorry enough for herself. She didn't want Cutter going to that party feeling sorry for her, too. So what if he didn't want her? She was smart, attractive. Any man would be lucky to have her. Any man.

"Keep your roses and your friend, Cutter McCall," she said.

Her mind made up, Davalyn let the pink satin robe fall to the floor, then reached for the red outfit.

Sixteen

Donovan reached for the red sports cap with the Houston Rockets logo, but Bennett screwed up his face.

"What?" Donovan put the hat on his head, bill cocked to the side. "You've got something against basketball?"

"It's *aw-ight,*" Bennett drawled. "But I like the Texans better." He picked up a gray football jersey with a red-and-blue bull logo. He'd been milling around the gift shop located on the bottom floor of the Aquarium restaurant with his uncle Van for what seemed forever. Saturday night, the foyer was packed. Some of the overflow had gone outside to kill time. But Uncle Van had said that he didn't want Bennett out in the cold, wet weather, so they remained crammed like sardines into the gift shop.

"Football it is," Donovan agreed, and walked up to the gift shop cash register and fished in his pocket for his wallet.

"Hey, Uncle Van, what do you think of this one?" Bennett called from the rear of the shop. He stood on tiptoe, held up a cut-glass and porcelain dolphin figurine leaping from a wave of iridescent blue, green, and crystalline foaming white.

"Nice," Van said distractedly. "But it doesn't match your jersey."

"Not for me," Bennett said. "For Aunt Dav." Worming his way through a press of bodies, he joined Donovan at the cash register. "I was thinking I could get it as a Christmas present for her."

"How much is it?" Donovan asked, turning the figurine over to check the price on the porcelain base. "Ouch!" he said, glancing at the salesclerk. "Put that back, Bennett. And be careful. Don't you drop it."

"Come on, Uncle Van," Bennett wheedled.

"I don't know. Maybe you'd better ask your dad if you can get it."

"Can't. He's outside with Miss Shayla." Bennett made a face, stuck a finger down his throat, and made gagging motions.

"Well, they'll be back in a few minutes. They didn't go too far. They've got that flashy-blinky thing that will let them know when our table's ready."

Donovan had offered to keep Bennett inside the restaurant, rather than kill time walking around the boardwalk, so that Cutter and Shayla could have some adult conversation. He'd noted Bennett's irritated tone but didn't respond to it. Not yet. He put it in the back of his mind to have a little talk with Bennett later to find out where the anger was coming from. This was the first time since his dad had started dating again that Bennett had ever expressed displeasure at the idea. What was it about Shayla that made Bennett put up his defenses? Shayla seemed like a nice enough girl to him. Real nice.

"Come on, Uncle Van. I haven't got a present yet for Aunt Dav and this one is perfect. She loves dolphins."

"That's a whole lot of Christmas there, little man. You sure you want to pay that much?"

"I'll go halfsies with ya." Bennett offered his best compromise.

"I'm observing Kwanzaa this year. You gonna give me a gift this nice for *karamu?*"

"Aunt Dav has been tellin' me all about Kwanzaa, Uncle Van. I don't think it's about how much money the gift costs. It's the thought that counts. How about if I make you something instead?"

"Unh-huh." Donovan tried to hide the grin that tugged at the corners of his mouth. "That's a pretty slick argument you got there, little man. Are you sure that Julian hasn't been schoolin' you, too? I don't think any lawyer could present a better case than you did for buying that for Dav."

"Where are they, anyway?" Bennett complained. "And when are they gonna take us to our table? I'm starving!" He clutched his stomach and swayed as if about to faint from hunger.

"Come on. Let's get out of here before you break something. Then we'll all be giving homemade gifts this year."

"So are we gonna get that dolphin?"

"We?" Donovan raised an eyebrow at him.

"You," Bennett amended. "But I'll pay you back."

"All right, I'll get it. But you'd better put my name on the Christmas card, too."

Donovan handed the salesclerk his credit card, tried not to groan when the price came back in the high double digits. The clerk carefully wrapped the dolphin in thick wads of white wrapping paper and placed it in a small cardboard box. She reached for a gift shop bag, added some additional shredded paper for good measure. Donovan couldn't help thinking that with what he'd paid for Davalyn's gift, that packing paper had better be lined with gold.

"Here you go, sir. Thank you and come again."

"After I win the lottery," Donovan said, lifting his chin in salute as he took Bennett's hand and led him from the gift shop. He stepped out in time to see Cutter and his date, Shayla Morgan, reentering the restaurant.

"Just in time, Cutter. Your boy's about to break the bank," he called out.

"Wanna see what I got Aunt Dav?" Bennett said loudly. He held up the plastic bag, dangling it in front of his father.

"Maybe later," Cutter said, narrowing his eyes. He wasn't fooled by Bennett's innocent enthusiasm. He knew exactly what Bennett was doing. From the moment they'd picked up Shayla from her beachside condo, Bennett was a chatterbox. *Aunt Dav this and Aunt Dav that!* At one point in the almost endless stream of accolades, Bennett made it very clear to Shayla that Aunt Dav wasn't his aunt at all, but a woman who lived next door to them and was at his house almost *all* of the time.

Cutter had to admit, the boy wasn't exaggerating. If she wasn't at his house, Cutter was over there. Maybe even more so than when just Van lived there—if that was at all possible. The four of them—Cutter, Bennett, Donovan, and Davalyn—one big happy family.

Only, Cutter mused, *Dav isn't so happy.* He could feel waves of sadness from her window washing over him before he headed out. He didn't know what made him look up when he did. A feeling. A presence. The timing of it almost creeped him out. Raised the hairs on the back of his neck. He could actually *feel* her watching him.

How he wished she'd never brought him breakfast that morning. He regretted ever asking her to follow him to Bennett's tree house. If he could undo that kiss, he would. He should never have kissed her, not like that. He should never, ever have touched her. Not like he had. There wasn't a hint of brotherly affection in that embrace. He couldn't even pretend. He'd wanted her in the timeless way a man wanted a woman.

He couldn't undo what he'd done, but he could certainly watch his step moving forward. Cutter told himself that keeping an eye on Bennett was a good way to start. Between curbing his son's obvious infatuation with Davalyn and by taking the edge off his own by dating Shayla, he might stop himself from making any more critical mistakes.

"Is it time to eat, Dad? I'm hungry," Bennett complained.

"I know, I know." Cutter glanced at his watch. When they'd first arrived, the hostess had informed him that it would be about a ten-minute wait. That was over twenty minutes ago.

"Just hang on a little while longer, Bennett. I don't think they'll seat us without all of us being here, and Dav and Julian should be here any minute now."

The front doors swung open again. Cutter instinctively looked over his shoulder. "See, here they are," he said.

For the second time that night, he felt something reach inside him, squeeze his insides. Was it curiosity that made him look up when the doors swung open? Was it coincidence that it should be Davalyn? Or was it something else? It had to be something else. It could have been anyone walking through that door. Patrons were coming and going all the time. Somehow he'd known that it was her. He'd just known. He'd felt her. It was hard to explain. But he felt glad she was here. More than glad, excited to see her. She excited him. At the same time, she settled him. Made him feel that when she was there, everything was as it should be. Everything was all right.

" 'Bout time," Bennett muttered.

"Bennett," Cutter said, his tone rumbling with parental warning. "Remember what we talked about. Mind your manners."

"I'm mindin', I'm mindin'."

"It's not too late to give you that birthday spankin', you know." Cutter hooked his arm around his son's neck, drew him close, and rubbed his knuckles briskly over his head.

Bennett squirmed but didn't really try to get loose. "Cut that out, Dad! You're gonna make me have an electric shock."

"Over here, Dav!" Donovan lifted his hand and waved them over. "Where you have you been, girl? We've got a nine-year-old kid here that's about to gnaw his arm off from starvation."

"Sorry we're late," Davalyn said breathlessly as she approached the group. "The parking lot was packed, even for a Saturday night. We had to park all the way in the boonies. But we made it." She brushed Cutter's hand aside, laid a hand affectionately on top of Bennett's head. "Couldn't miss Bennett's big night."

"It's all right," Cutter said carefully, trying not to feel the electric current that passed from Davalyn's warm hand to his when she'd touched him.

"They haven't called to seat us yet." His eyes swept over her, noting her flushed cheeks and ruffled hair. Her flustered look *could* have been due to the brisk walk, the crisp November air. Could have been. But as he stepped up to Julian, offered to shake his hand in greeting, he thought he saw traces of Davalyn's lipstick at the corner of Julian's mouth. The light in the foyer was dim, but the pale greenish glow from the oversize aquarium reflected iridescent glitter caught in his mustache.

"How's it going, Julian? Haven't seen you in a while." He clasped Julian's hand, maybe a little harder than he'd meant to do.

Julian squeezed Cutter's hand back, with equal force. "Actually, it's going very well. I've got a few pending cases that should bring a little of attention to my practice."

Davalyn linked her arm through Julian's, pressed herself against his side. "Julian's been working a lot of long hours, dedicating himself to the firm."

"Congratulations," Cutter said. "That's what I like to hear. Another brother's success story."

"The world needs more brothers who know what they want and commit to making it work," Davalyn said smoothly, deliberately looking with affection at Julian as she spoke. Davalyn didn't look at Cutter, didn't wait to see what effect her response had on him. She'd promised herself that she wouldn't turn into the world's biggest bitch tonight. This was Bennett's night and she wasn't going to ruin it.

Cutter stepped back. "Where are my manners?" he said, holding out his hand and ushering his "friend" forward.

"You weren't here for the introductions earlier. This is Shayla Morgan. Shayla, this is Davalyn Bowers, Donovan's sister, and her *dedicated* friend Julian Blake."

"How do you do?" Julian took her hand, though admittedly not with as much force as he'd shaken Cutter's.

"Hi, Shayla." Davalyn mustered as much genuine politeness as she could. She surprised herself by just how pleasant she actually sounded. That effort came from a very severe pep talk that she'd given herself earlier.

"You are not going to hate that woman on sight, Davalyn Bowers," she'd told herself. "It's not her fault that Cutter prefers her to you. Maybe she's better for Cutter. Maybe she's an awesome woman. You never know. You might like her. You two might even become friends. Don't scratch her eyes out the minute you see her."

So when the crucial moment came, Davalyn had already programmed herself to try to get along. As she stood there before her competition, she tried not to hate. Still, that didn't stop her from doing a careful analysis—picking at Shayla, body part by body part.

Shayla Morgan seemed nice. So, Davalyn vowed that she wasn't going to hate her flawless skin, her movie-star, laser-whitened, capped smile, or her high, round breasts—made to seem even more touchable by just the right amount of cleavage showing from the modestly plunging neckline. Shayla Morgan wasn't beautiful—not drop-dead gorgeous like Angela Bennett had been. Nor was she as tall as Davalyn. In fact, she seemed kinda short. Five feet three in heels. As he stood next to her, his arm around her waist, Cutter towered over her.

Shayla had impeccable taste in clothing. Davalyn noted with a critical eye that her clothes were well tailored. However, she could probably stand to drop a couple of pounds. The jacket and slacks combination was designed to fit an expanding waistline. *And that color doesn't do much for her, either,* Davalyn mused.

The charcoal-gray-and-white coat dress was expensive, probably from some designer shop, but it made her looked washed out. That was Davalyn's impartial opinion. That wasn't hating. She wasn't hating the girl. Shayla Morgan was cute. Long, straight hair, recently permed, parted in the middle, that fell to her shoulders in silken ebony layers. Long, mascara-coated lashes framed hazel green eyes, dimples in her cheeks, carefully lined pouty lips. In a word—perky.

"Hi," Shayla said brightly. "So you're Aunt Dav. Bennett has been talking about you nonstop. It's so sweet. I think he's caught a hard case of puppy love for you, Davalyn."

Bennett groaned at that remark, which made Shayla giggle again. Davalyn wanted to groan. Maybe the woman was nervous. A grown woman shouldn't giggle. Davalyn suspected that Shayla couldn't help it. She was *sooo* perky. When she spoke, everything either sparkled or jiggled. God, how she hated perky! *Not Shayla,* she mentally corrected. *I don't hate the woman. Just her perkiness.*

"Bennett's my buddy," Davalyn said, winking her eye at him.

"I've got a present for you, Aunt Dav," Bennett said proudly.

"For me?" Davalyn was genuinely touched. "Bennett, you shouldn't have spent your money. It's your birthday, not mine."

"Don't worry, baby sister," Donovan spoke up, his tone wry. "He didn't spend too much."

"Uncle Van," Bennett said out of the corner of his mouth, elbowing Donovan into silence. "It's right here." Bennett showed her the gift shop bag. "But you can't have yours until Christmas."

"What a coincidence. I've got one for you, too. But you can have yours now, birthday boy." Davalyn reached into her purse and pulled out a small package. "Here you go."

"Can I open it now?" he asked excitedly, digging his fingers into the wrapping paper.

Cutter closed his large hands over his son's. "Not now, Bennett. Wait until after dinner. I think our table is ready now."

The hostess waved them over.

"You can go on up now." She indicated the darkened spiral staircase winding up to two more floors. "Sorry for the wait, sir."

"No problem," Cutter said, but his attention wasn't on the hostess. Out of the corner of his eye, he watched as Julian reached up toward Davalyn's coat collar and helped her shimmy out of the long black wool coat. He'd whispered something to her, causing her to laugh out loud. She threw back her dark head, resting against him for a moment, exposing her long throat encircled by a pearl choker. It was a warm, open laugh that made other patrons also waiting to be seated turn to stare at her, smiling a little in infectious humor.

Maybe it was her laughter that caused a few to turn and look, but it was considerably more than that causing a few more to gawk at her openly. Cutter couldn't blame them. Couldn't blame them at all. He was doing a considerable amount of staring himself.

Her dark coat opened to a flash of crimson. Davalyn was stunning. Absolutely stunning. In that dress, she seemed to light up the cool, dark ambiance of the restaurant foyer like an emergency flare—sizzling bright red, glowing with energy, and bound and determined to get attention.

"Man, now that's what I want under my tree for Christmas. . . . "

"Come on over here and sit on Santa's lap. . . ."

"I've got something in my Christmas stocking for you. . . ."

Cutter overheard snippets of conversation all around him, behind him. He turned, glowering. He wasn't sure who'd said what, but two or three jokers who'd maneuvered to get a better look at Davalyn felt Cutter's looming presence, and they suddenly found something more interesting to look at in the stirring waters of the aquarium several feet away from him.

He jammed his hands in his pants pockets to keep himself from snatching that coat out of Julian's hands and throwing it over her. What the hell did she think she was doing? Coming out in this weather dressed like that—didn't she know she could catch triple pneumonia? Why couldn't she have chosen something more appropriate for his son's birthday dinner? That wasn't a dress. She was wrapped in cellophane disguised as Lycra and lace. That dress . . . that dress . . . That skintight, curve-hugging, legs-all-the-way-up-to-your-neck-showing dress wasn't meant for nine-year-olds. Hell, it wasn't even meant for ninety-year-olds.

"Lawd, have mercy." An elderly gentleman in a three-piece black suit, with a head full of snowy white hair, peered over the rim of his glasses at Davalyn. "Take off ten years, and a case of Viagra, and . . ."

Cutter didn't listen to the rest. He moved off, taking deep breaths to steady himself. How could he set an example for Bennett, remind him to respect his elders, when he himself was entertaining thoughts of asking the old man to step outside for a hard lesson in respect and manners?

"Let's go, folks. Our table's ready," he said curtly, avoiding Davalyn's gaze. He took Bennett's hand and ushered Shayla ahead of him. Donovan fell in behind him, followed by Davalyn and Julian.

Don't look back. Don't look back, Cutter repeated as a mantra as he climbed the stairs. He wouldn't embarrass Shayla by letting everyone know that he'd also wanted to stare. He bit his lip to hold back laughter when he heard Donovan scolding his sister. He obviously wasn't too pleased with her fashion choice, either.

"When you wake up, hacking and coughing, in the middle of the night from a bad cold, don't be expecting me to bring you honey and lemon tea, baby girl," he warned.

"You won't be hearing me tonight, little boy," Davalyn called back sweetly.

"Don't worry, Davalyn. I'll bring you all the tea you need." Julian's voice echoed in the stairwell, causing Cutter to almost miss a step. The intimation was clear. After the party, Davalyn didn't plan on going home tonight.

"Hey!" Donovan said, spinning around and pointing his finger at them. "Now, you know that you didn't have to go there."

"You started it," Davalyn retorted.

"I'm finishing it," Donovan shot back.

Cutter had to turn around now, had to step into his familiar role as mediator. He told himself that he was turning around to keep the peace between them. It had absolutely nothing to do with the fact that the desire to watch Davalyn climb those stairs was burning him up on the inside.

"All right, children. Behave yourselves." The bass in

his voice seemed even more menacing while rumbling in the stairwell.

"Yes, sir," Donovan, Davalyn, and Julian said in unison.

"I promise I'll be good," Davalyn said, moistening her lips with her tongue and pinning him with a direct stare.

Cutter swallowed hard, turning quickly around and taking the next couple of steps in a hurry as if fleeing for his safety.

Shayla giggled. "Your friends are so crazy, Cutter. They must be a blast to hang around."

"You don't know the half of it," Cutter murmured, blinking his eyes to drive out the mesmerizing vision of the sway of Davalyn's hips as she carefully navigated the stairs in those high-heeled red sandals.

Yeah, he thought ruefully. *A real blast. A virtual inferno.*

Seventeen

Cutter congratulated himself on how cool he played it all evening. He managed to keep the conversation easy, light, and flowing. He'd kept everyone engaged, participating in the conversation. Even though Bennett was the little man of the hour, Cutter was the one who worked the hardest to keep the atmosphere festive. Bennett was too busy digging into his presents. He wasn't concerned about whether anyone was feeling slighted, left out of the conversation—but Cutter was. He especially wanted to make sure that Julian and Shayla felt included. There were too many in-jokes among him, Van, and Davalyn. And why wouldn't there be? They all practically lived together.

It was worse than some sitcom. Only, their day-to-day interaction was constant. It was real. It would have been so easy to fall into old habits, to speak in half sentences and innuendos and know that the Bowers siblings would immediately get what he meant.

He didn't do that. He shared his attention among all of his guests, even though one in particular stayed just on the edge of his awareness. Always in his thoughts—Davalyn.

When the evening first started, he had to admit that Davalyn had thrown him off his game when she took off that coat. He had a hard time looking at her, of meeting her gaze. He'd never seen her like that before—so blatantly sexual. It was a hard concept to grasp. This wasn't quite like when he'd kissed her in the tree house. Then her sexuality had been a private moment. Her expression of femininity had been meant for his eyes, and his eyes only. Now she was showing the world what she was capable of. Not that she wasn't always attractive. Davalyn was a very attractive woman. She took care of herself. Worked out as often as she could. Ate the right kinds of foods. Got her beauty rest. Paid attention to her physical appearance—her hair, her skin, her nails.

But she made sure that she groomed her mind and spirit as well as her body. She was well read and could hold a conversation on almost any topic he could throw at her. Or when things got too hectic, she had no trouble shutting out the world to spend a little time in silent reflection, deep meditation, or even a fervent prayer.

Still, even with all of that, Cutter knew that she did those things for herself. It wasn't for show. It was all a part of who she was. She was beautiful on the inside, so that communicated itself to the outside world.

Tonight, however, there was a lot more going on inside Davalyn than her standard self-maintenance. And he wasn't the only one who'd noticed her, he wasn't alone in his fascination. In between the salad-and-breadsticks banter, the main course, the opening of presents, and the after-dinner coffee, he watched the effect Davalyn had on several patrons in the restaurant.

He could almost follow the ripple effect when she got up from the table to take Bennett over to the restaurant's namesake aquarium to watch the exotic fish. Heads turned and stayed turned as she sauntered by. When she leaned forward toward the tank to point out an interesting specimen hidden among the coral reef, Cutter heard the clatter of silverware falling to the floor and the heated exchange between the man and his female companion. It was something about throwing him in the bay for chasing after every piece of ass in the state and his vehement denial that he was even watching that girl's butt.

Cutter draped his arm behind Shayla's chair and turned his attention back to the conversation at his own table. It wasn't too hard to pick up the thread. Shayla was going on about her aspirations of becoming a singer.

"Don't sign any contracts before you've had them carefully reviewed by a lawyer," Julian suggested. "Too many young talents sign away their rights and wind up with little or nothing, even though their records are going platinum and their concerts are raking in millions."

"I don't know any lawyers," Shayla said, pouting.

"Sure you do." Julian smiled, smooth and sweet as the whipped topping on his cheesecake. He reached into his inner jacket pocket and pulled out a business card. Holding it between his index and middle fingers, he passed it across the table to her. "When you're ready, Shayla, you give me a call. Anytime. I'll be more than happy to review your contract."

"This is so exciting," Shayla said, bouncing in her seat.

"You know, I thought about becoming a lawyer," Donovan said.

"Yeah, right," Cutter said in derision. "Was that before or after you thought about becoming a roadie for Whitney Houston?"

"You like Whitney?" Shayla gasped. "Oh, I absolutely love her! That gal sure can *sang*. Some people say I sound like a cross between Whitney, Mariah, and Ashanti."

That did catch Donovan's attention. "You've already got a recording contract, Shayla?"

"Not yet," she admitted. "But my agent says that it's only a matter of time. He says I've got talent."

"You're gonna give us a demonstration, Shayla?" Donovan asked.

"Here? Now?"

"Sure, why not? If you're so good, let's see if you can shatter the glass in that aquarium."

"Donovan!" Cutter threw back his head and laughed. "Cut it out. Don't embarrass the girl."

"Okay, I'll settle for this glass of water on the table," Donovan quipped, tapping his knife against his water glass to make it ring.

"Don't listen to him, Shayla. He got bounced on his head one too many times when he was a baby," Cutter joked, dismissing him.

"What? You're sayin' there's something wrong—wrong—wrong with me?" Donovan shot back, jerking his left shoulder up and down several times to imitate a nervous tic. "I'll be fine as soon as I take my medication."

"Ooh, y'all are just too funny." Shayla snickered behind her hand.

"Seriously," Donovan said. "Give us just a taste."

"It's all right, Cutter. I don't mind." Shayla looked back and forth between them. She sat up straighter in her chair, took a sip of water, and cleared her throat. "Okay, here it goes. It'll be a little rough since I haven't warmed up yet."

"Wait," Julian said, looking around. "What's that? You hear that?"

"I don't hear anything," Shayla said.

Julian leaned down, picked up Davalyn's purse, hanging by its strap on her seat, and dropped it onto the table. "Davalyn's pager," he said, feeling the purse vibrate through the cloth.

"You think she's been called to work?" Donovan asked, twisting around in his seat to try to get her attention. She'd moved around to the far side of the tank and couldn't see them.

"Could be," Cutter said. He checked his own pager, but it was silent. He wasn't on duty tonight anyway.

"Somebody should check," Donovan suggested. "Open up her purse, Julian. Check her pager."

"No, I don't think I'll be rummaging through her things," Julian said, eyeing the purse as if it were a snake ready to strike.

"Cutter?" Donovan looked to his friend.

"No way. Don't look at me." He raised his hands. "You're her brother. You open her purse. Or take it to her."

"What do I look like? A punk? I'm not carrying a bright red purse through the restaurant."

Julian sighed in resignation, then reached for the strap. "Fine. I'll—"

"I can't believe you macho men are so insecure in your masculinity that you won't even touch a woman's purse," Shayla said, picking it up. "I'll take it to her."

"I think she took Bennett back that way, where we came in, near the rest rooms," Cutter offered.

"I'm not likely to miss her," Shayla quipped. "Just follow the trail of drool left by all those tongues hanging out." She hooked the strap on her arm and slid her chair back.

Cutter half rose, helping to slide the chair out from under Shayla as she stood. He watched her make her way to the far side of the restaurant floor. He had half a mind to call her back, to face ridicule by carrying that bright red purse to Davalyn himself. He wasn't sure if letting Shayla take that purse to Davalyn was such a good idea. What if they started to talk? Compare notes? What if they put their heads together and found him lacking? He was trying to do the right thing by both of them. He didn't want to be found lacking.

Wasn't he careful in his attention to Shayla? Wasn't it obvious that he was doing his best to help her feel part of the party crowd? He thought Davalyn was doing the same thing for Julian. He couldn't count how many times she mentioned his name, shared some story about his latest successes.

"What's up with you, Cutter? You look like you're gonna burn a hole in that fish tank," Donovan commented when Cutter didn't respond to his name being called several times.

Cutter blinked and looked over at his friend. "What? Sorry? What were you saying?"

"I was asking whether or not you and Bennett are going to come over for Thanksgiving."

"Nuh-uh," Cutter said distractedly. "Angela's aunt Bessie invited us over. She usually sets out a monster spread, so I think I'll hang with her folks for a while."

"I told Dav not to try to cook anything. I'll be out of town, too."

"Uh-huh," Cutter responded, but he was only listening with half an ear.

"Me, Darnell, and Jose are thinking about heading up to Big Bend State Park to get in some climbing."

"That sounds fun." Cutter craned his neck, trying to

catch sight of Shayla, Davalyn, and Bennett. *Where are they? They should be on their way back to the table by now.* Cutter fretted.

"Dav and I have already made plans for that weekend anyway," Julian interjected.

That got Cutter's full attention. "What kind of plans?"

"We're driving up to Dallas to have dinner with my parents."

"Oh," Cutter repeated. He lifted his coffee cup to his lips. Swallowing several times, he tried to clear the sudden tightening of his throat. "How long you gonna be gone?"

"We haven't nailed down plans," Julian said coolly. "But I imagine that we'll be gone through Sunday. She's already cleared her work schedule. Does she need to clear it with you, too?"

Cutter shrugged. His outward appearance was nonchalant, as if the verbal jab didn't bother him a bit. Inside, he was starting to seethe. Without the ladies at the table, keeping the conversation civil, Cutter felt a definite shift in tone. As if the testosterone levels had been cranked up a notch or two.

"Not really. I was hoping that she could watch Bennett for me on Saturday."

"Sorry." Julian smiled blandly. "I guess you'll have to find someone else for a change. Tell me something, McCall, what did you do before Dav?"

"I was the sitter," Donovan spoke up, spooning a huge wedge of cheesecake into his mouth. It never occurred to him that the conversation between Julian and Cutter had shifted—in both tone and context. They weren't talking about baby-sitting anymore.

"But I'm not free next Saturday, either. If I'm lucky,

I'll be clinging to a rock face with nothing but blue sky above me and sharp jagged boulders beneath me."

"Looks like you're stuck like chuck, McCall." Julian sighed. "Too bad."

Cutter wasn't fooled by his display of disappointment. And he wasn't impressed by Julian's obvious play to put him in his place.

"Don't worry about me and Bennett, Julian," Cutter replied. "Somehow or other, I always get what I need." As he took another sip of his coffee, his eyes never wavered from Julian's. He wanted his meaning to be perfectly clear. No chance of misunderstanding. It had taken him all evening to figure it out. Now that he had, he wanted to share that knowledge.

Cutter was in love with Davalyn. He loved her on a level and with an intensity that he didn't think possible. It took an entire evening of watching her interact with Julian to make him realize that. Was he jealous? Sure he was. What red-blooded male wouldn't be? Had she used Julian to make him jealous? That he wasn't so sure of. Maybe it didn't matter. The result was the same. He'd come to his senses.

He almost wanted to laugh out loud. Three months ago, he would have been ready to swear on a stack of Bibles that his relationship with Davalyn was purely platonic. You couldn't have gotten him to admit that what he felt for her was more than honest affection. When that honesty had turned into a lie, he couldn't say. How and when he'd started fooling himself, he couldn't figure out. It kinda snuck up on him—hit him on the back of his head like a cast-iron skillet. Now it was all crystal clear to him. The truth was ringing in his ears, loud and blaring and as easily identifiable to him as that red dress.

As he watched Davalyn cross the restaurant floor, Cutter felt as if his entire body had been set ablaze. It wasn't just a physical desire that he felt for her—though he couldn't deny that she affected him that way. If it were only about someone to share his bed, he figured any woman would have done. Even Shayla. She was pleasant, attractive. But that wasn't what he wanted. Watching the two women side by side, and noting his reaction to the both of them, he looked at Shayla and all he could think of was how soon he could take her back to her condo. He wondered how could he get her out of here without letting her realize how quickly he was trying to end the evening with her.

His attention switched back to Davalyn and his scheming mind went into overdrive. How was he going to get her away from Julian? After flaunting another woman in her face, how was he going to convince her that she was the only one that he wanted?

Davalyn hustled up to the table. She reached for her coat and tossed it over her shoulders. "I hate to eat and run, folks."

"What's wrong, Dav?" Cutter asked.

"I've got a page from my assistant. I have to go to work."

"I thought you had someone cover for you tonight?" Donovan asked.

"Well, plans change." She shrugged.

"You're *not* going to a site dressed like that," Cutter said. The tone of his voice surprised even himself. It wasn't a question. It wasn't even a suggestion. It sounded to everyone at the table like a direct command. Even Donovan had to raise an eyebrow in surprise. If he'd used that tone with her, she'd have him in a headlock so gripping that even The Rock couldn't get out of it.

Davalyn raised a finely arched eyebrow in response. Turning her back deliberately on Cutter, she faced Julian and said, "Julian, could you bring the truck around? My bag's in there."

"With your change of clothes," Julian said, purely for the benefit of fanning the flames of Cutter's jealousy.

"This is the key to the lockbox. My duffel bag is on the driver's side. I'll wait for you downstairs."

"Be back in a bit," he promised. He rose, then leaned down to brush a butterfly kiss against her cheek. Cutter averted his eyes and thought he'd crushed his temporary dental filling with the grinding of his teeth.

"I'm sorry I can't celebrate the rest of your birthday with you, Bennett. But you go on and have fun without me. Make sure your dad takes you up on the Ferris wheel like he promised."

"You were supposed to go up on that ride with me," Bennett reminded her.

"No . . . I don't think so." She wrinkled up her nose at the thought. "Me and heights don't get along." Davalyn glanced at Cutter, wondering whether he would think about her and the tree house.

"We'll have to get you off the ground in stages," Cutter replied. And Davalyn knew that he knew what she was thinking.

"Night, folks." She waved. "Nice meeting you, Shayla."

"Nice meeting you, too," Shayla called as Dav walked away.

Nice. Too nice. Cutter didn't want to hurt Shayla's feelings, but the overwhelming need to talk to Davalyn alone, for just one moment, outweighed his conscience and his caution.

"Excuse me, folks. I'll be right back. I've got to . . . uh . . ." He pointed vaguely in the general direction of the rest rooms.

"Number one or number two?" Bennett piped up. He just wanted to know how long he had to sit and wait until they could leave the restaurant and play some of the games on the fairway. Sometimes at home, after a good meal like the one they had tonight, he'd known his dad to spend enough time in the bathroom to read an entire newspaper from cover to cover.

Cutter didn't have to say a word. He just flashed his son a look that said it all as he started for the bathroom. Cutter headed for the alcove, thought about ducking inside, then sneaking out again. He quickly discarded that idea. Too much skulking around. That wasn't really his style. Besides, he didn't have much time to waste. Davalyn could be already on her way to work. He took the stairs, heading for the lower level, two and three stairs at a time.

A couple heading up the stairs, seeing the big man barreling toward them, squeezed against the sides of the stairwell to get out of the way.

"Excuse me," Cutter threw over his shoulder when the man made a low objection. "Watch it, bruh."

When he'd almost reached the bottom of the stairs, he saw Davalyn sitting on one of the bench seats. Holding her coat around her shoulders, she sat and watched the entryway doors as patrons entered or left the restaurant. She looked worried, even a little melancholy, as tightly wrapped in her own thoughts as she held her coat around her. The image seemed out of place. With all of the laughing, openly adoring couples and families that milled around, the dark beauty in the red dress seemed unapproachable.

When the doors opened and the brisk wind flapped her coat lapels, she shifted on the seat, turning her body away from the main force of the wind.

If Cutter had any thoughts of turning away, escaping before she saw him, the thoughts scattered as if driven like autumn leaves on the wind.

"Cutter?" Davalyn rose, took a step toward him. "What are you doing down here?" Her expression brightened, if only for a moment.

"A helluva good question." His tone was dry.

"Then maybe you ought to get back to your friend until you figure it out." A mask of slow, boiling anger shut down over her face. "She'll be wondering where you are." She started to walk away, but Cutter closed the distance between them. He reached out, grabbed her a little too roughly. His fingers closed around the soft part of her upper arm.

"What do you think you're —" Davalyn began, but she never got the opportunity to complete the sentence. Or the thought, for that matter. Anger melted way, disappearing like icicles under a warm spring breeze as Cutter snatched her to him and lowered his head. He sealed his lips to hers. Only, there was very little warmth in that kiss. It was all-consuming heat, fueled by suppressed anger, frustration, and desire.

Davalyn's breath caught in her throat. She couldn't move, couldn't breathe, couldn't think to breathe. She couldn't remember how. Everything and everyone else faded. Every thought of pulling away disintegrated. She stood there, their bodies barely touching. He hardly needed the hand on her arm holding her close to him. His mouth to hers, Cutter kept his mouth moving over hers with deliberate slowness. Nothing else existed but the pleasure of his kiss, the sheer, unbridled, unfiltered emotion it communicated. It was part pleasure, part punishment. It was calculated and manipulative, honest and heartrending. No one knew better than she did what he was telling her with that kiss.

When the catcalls from onlookers became too intrusive, Cutter pulled himself away. "This is crazy," he murmured. "You know that, don't you?"

"I know you've got a woman upstairs waiting for you," Davalyn returned. Cutter groaned with the regret weighing heavily on his heart.

"Don't you think I know that?" He ran his hand over bristly hair. "Dav, we've got to talk."

"Why? So you can tell me how this shouldn't happen? Again! That line's getting very old, very fast, Cutter."

"Just listen to me. Hear me out."

"It's not the time, Cutter. What if Julian comes back? He'll think—"

"Screw Julian!" he said savagely, his voice low and tight. "I don't give a rat's ass about what he thinks."

"Am I'm supposed to stop caring about what he thinks, how he feels, because you say so? That's not fair, Cutter."

"Davalyn, I didn't come down here to pick a fight. I just want to talk to you."

"We wouldn't even be having this conversation if you hadn't told me to bring him. You were bringing someone else tonight. Isn't that what you told me?" she said, stabbing him in the chest with her index finger.

"I know . . . I know, baby girl," he soothed, closing his hand over hers. "And I'm sorry. I just wanted you to know that."

The double doors opened and, by reflex, both Cutter and Davalyn turned to see who it was. Not Julian. Cutter could feel tension draining out of Davalyn's shoulders.

"Promise me that when you're done with work, you won't go home with him tonight, Dav."

"Cutter, don't—"

"You gotta promise, Dav," he insisted. "Don't do . . . anything . . . until you and I get a chance to talk. Really talk."

"What about Shayla?"

"As soon as I can, I'm taking her home."

"To her house," Davalyn clarified.

"And then me and Bennett are going home. Alone. I promised him we'd sleep in the tree house tonight."

"It's chilly out there, Cutter."

"So, we'll take an extra blanket." He paused, looking down at her with that gleam she'd come to recognize. "You could always come up after work and help drive away the chill."

"I'm afraid of heights," she reminded him. "Remember?"

"I can help you with that, baby girl." Cutter grinned at her. "Give you something else to think about while you're up in that tree with me." He pulled her close to him, making it very obvious by the placement of his hands, the way he nuzzled her neck, that he was letting the world know that Davalyn was with him.

Davalyn leaned away, narrowed her eyes at him. Tried to frown. "You sure you wouldn't rather be cuddling up to Shayla?"

"You already know the answer to that," he replied, placing both hands on her rear and drawing her closer, sealing his hips to hers.

Davalyn cleared her throat and tried to pull away. "Everybody's watching us, Cutter."

"I guess some conversations are better held in private." He released her, but not by much. "Promise me that you'll call me on my cell when you get in tonight."

"What if it's really late? I don't want to wake up Bennett."

"It doesn't matter. I want to see you again tonight. Promise me you won't go home with Julian."

"Cutter . . . " Davalyn hesitated. As much as she wanted to hear these words from him, she wasn't going to hurt Julian. "We'll get our chance to talk, Cutter. I promise we will. But I have to talk to Julian first. Try to understand."

"Do you mean talk?" he asked. "Or *talk?*" He punctuated his last question with a subtle thrust of his hips.

Davalyn broke away, making sure to sever all physical contact with him, as she said, "Just talk."

That answer seemed to appease him, if not completely satisfy him.

"Just let me get through Thanksgiving at his parents' house," she said. "I owe him that much for being such a good friend to me."

"Just through Thanksgiving," Cutter relented. "And then it's you and me. Dinner for two, a good bottle of wine, smooth jazz at this place I know in Houston . . . and"—he paused dramatically—"what ever comes after. You down with that, Dav?"

Davalyn paused, realizing that however she answered would forever change their friendship.

"What ever comes after," she agreed.

berry sauce around her plate, Lucinda reached over

Eighteen

Davalyn had every intention of sitting down with Julian and having a heart-to-heart talk with him right after Thanksgiving. Only trouble was, she feared she didn't have the heart to do it. No time seemed like the right time.

While visiting his parents, Julian didn't seem to notice how distracted and detached she was. He was too busy showing off how he'd come into his own since graduating from law school. With a beautiful, sophisticated woman on his arm, a thriving business, he could do no wrong in his parents' eyes. And that's the way he wanted it. That's really why she was there. She was nothing more than something to dangle on his arm like a charm bracelet, all bright and glittery and decorative.

She couldn't count how many times during the miserable weekend, while everyone was laughing and joking and full of good holiday cheer, she wanted to run screaming from the room. It was all so phony. A big, fat lie. She was pretending to feel happy and content and glad to be among friends. But she wasn't.

At one point Sunday evening, she thought Julian's mother, Lucinda, might have had a clue. She might have felt her internal suffering. As Davalyn sat at the dinner table, pushing leftover dressing and homemade cranberry sauce around on her plate, Lucinda reached over and touched her hand.

"Are you all right, dear?"

Davalyn looked up and smiled blandly. Finally! Somebody had finally noticed that she wasn't turning flips with joy. "Yes, ma'am. I'm all right. I'm just not hungry today."

"You sure you're not coming down with something? This is a terrible time for flu."

"I think I just snacked too much during the day, Mrs. Blake. You know that holiday binge cycle. This time, my eyes were much bigger than my stomach."

"Don't let that innocent look fool you, Mother. Dav can put it away when she wants to," Julian teased.

"Gee, thanks, Julian." The smile she sent back was as warm as the congealed mashed potatoes and gravy on her plate.

"Just in case, I've got seltzer and vitamin C tablets in my medicine cabinet. You take what you need, honey. Unless, of course"—Lucinda smiled warmly at Davalyn—"you can't take any medicine."

"Excuse me?" Davalyn asked, not sure that she understood what Lucinda meant. Did she mean to ask if she was allergic to medicine?

"You sure there isn't another reason why your stomach's upset, honey? Something you maybe want to tell us? Or maybe you want us to wait another nine months or so to find out."

Julian's father, Jonathan, raised his eyebrows, but said nothing. He glanced over at Julian, who sat back in his chair and smiled, shrugging his shoulders.

Davalyn stared at Julian, disbelief written clearly over her face. They thought she was pregnant? Was that it? Had Julian told them she was pregnant?

"It's probably just a virus," Davalyn said stiffly. "It'll be over in days, not months." She wanted to be good company. She didn't want anyone to fret about her. However, she was finding it harder and harder to hide her feelings. She'd come to Julian's home because she'd promised that she would. She had to keep her promise. Several times during the weekend, though, she wondered if she was honoring the spirit of the promise by wishing all the time that she were elsewhere.

She could have been camping with Van. They were family. Shouldn't they have spent time together? But her thoughts were also on Cutter. What might have happened if she hadn't gone away for the weekend? What was going to happen when she got back? That answer depended on whether she came clean with Julian.

It was Cutter she wanted. Always had. Always would. If she didn't say something soon, something drastic, to break off with Julian, she'd be stuck in this awful triangle forever. She couldn't do it. She just wasn't going to do it. Life was too short to live a lie. Her father went to his grave, too proud to admit that he still loved his wife. He would have done anything to get her back. He'd waited too long, too late.

Davalyn didn't intend to live the best part of her life desperately in love and alone. And now Julian was spreading lies about her? It was time to do something.

"Julian, maybe a little walk will make me feel better."

She interrupted his discussion about his latest client and the fat retainer that had been dropped on the table.

Davalyn wanted to gag. Julian had only been out of law school for two years. She didn't know what kind of client would trust that much money to a lawyer with limited trial experience. As a lawyer himself, his father should have known something about that story didn't quite ring true. Unless, and she wouldn't put it past him, Jonathan Blake had something to do with Julian's inexplicable success.

"Sure . . . sure," Julian said, acknowledging her. "Go on."

"I don't know the neighborhood very well. Maybe you should come with me, Julian," Davalyn insisted, tilting her head toward the door.

"Just walk around the gardens in the back," he suggested.

"Julian," Lucinda said gently, "I think Davalyn is trying to say that she'd like some company."

"There's a game on in about ten minutes, Mom. You ladies don't go for that kind of entertainment. You can keep her company, can't you?"

Davalyn seethed. "Ten minutes, Julian," she said. "Just give me ten minutes."

He turned toward her, recognizing the frosty edge of her voice. "Sure. Let me get your jacket. It's chilly out there."

"Not nearly as cold as it is in here, Jules," his father muttered just loud enough for everyone at the table to hear.

"Don't tease, Jon," Lucinda scolded. "You'll only make it worse. Let the lovebirds handle this on their own."

Lovebirds! Davalyn wanted to run from the room. Instead, she rose slowly from the table.

"Excuse me," she said politely, laying her linen napkin across her plate. She didn't necessarily speed-walk to get away, but she wasn't waiting for Julian, either. By the time he caught up with her, she was already through the kitchen, past the breakfast area, and out the back door, heading to Lucinda's prized rose garden. There were very few blooms left on the carefully cultivated branches. Thorny limbs, trimmed back to a few branches, looked thin and bare in the pale moonlight.

Davalyn shivered. Whether from the cold or from the image, she wasn't sure which. She felt a little like those rosebushes, all bare and prickly. All she needed was a loving hand to help her blossom. Cutter's hand.

When Julian moved toward her, placing his coat around her shoulders, his hand grazed her neck. Davalyn flinched away from him.

"What's wrong with you, Davalyn?" Julian asked. He couldn't help but notice her response.

"I want to go home, Julian," she said bluntly. No preamble. No softening. Straight out.

"We are going back tomorrow."

"Not tomorrow night. Now," she insisted.

"Why? What's wrong?"

"Everything. I shouldn't be here. It's Thanksgiving week. My first one back and I didn't even spend it with my family."

"You spent it with my family, Dav. Like you promised that you would," he protested.

"I shouldn't have made that promise. I don't know what I was thinking when I did."

"It didn't bother you then. Why should it bother you now?"

"You know why," she said tightly. "Do I have to spell it out for you?"

"It's not Donovan you're trying to get back to, is it? It's Cutter. You'd rather be with him than with me, wouldn't you, Davalyn?"

Her silence confirmed his answer. "God, all I asked is that you spend a little time with me and my parents. Ex*cuse* the hell out of me if that's asking too much."

"I know what you asked me to do . . . and what I agreed to. But I can't anymore. I just can't. Please don't get me wrong, Julian. You've been a really good friend to me. And because you've been so good to me, I've done everything I know to make you happy. But now, things have changed. Trying to make you happy is making me miserable. And I don't want to be that kind of person."

"Is being my friend that painful for you, Davalyn? Do you love him that much, Dav, that you'd kill our relationship?"

"Relationship?" The laughter that burst from Davalyn was harsh. "Julian, our relationship, or friendship, is based on a lie. You know that, don't you? What kind of relationship is that?"

"You didn't see anything wrong with it while we were in school."

"I guess because it served us both. I was so focused on getting through school that having you around helped to ease some of the pressure. If I used you, I'm sorry. But you used me, too. And I went along with it. So, I can't blame anybody but myself, but it's over now. It has to stop. I can't go on like this . . . pretending that you and I have something that we don't. For God's sake, Julian. Your mother thinks that I'm pregnant! That I'm carrying your baby. I can't let her go on believing that about me. About you. Why don't you just tell them that we're not together?"

"I can't! Do you know what my father would do to me if he found out that I . . . That is . . . that I don't . . ."

Davalyn shook her head. "You can't even bring yourself to say it. You've been living a lie, being false to yourself for so long, you can't even be honest with yourself."

"Dav . . . I just need a little more time."

"How long, Julian? Nine months? What happens when after nine months there's no baby? Then what?"

"We could . . . uh . . . say that you miscarried . . . the strain of helping me with my law firm . . . the hazards of your job. They'll buy it. They like you."

Davalyn's mouth dropped open. "You're crazy. You've absolutely lost your mind."

"I'd lose that before I lost my parents' love and respect, Dav."

"You're their son. You can never lose that from them."

"You don't know how my father is, Dav. You have no clue. He's rigid and narrow-minded. My mother thinks she's a liberal, but she really isn't. In my family, there isn't any such thing as alternative lifestyles. You follow their rules, their way, or you're out. Plain and simple. No love, no acceptance, no money."

"Is that what this is about? Money?"

"Who do you think gave me those retainers, Dav? Some anonymous benefactor with loads of cash? No. It was my father. He called in a few favors and . . . Well, you can figure out the rest for yourself, can't you? How do you think I could afford to keep such nice offices and pay a staff, even though we don't have cases? It's because of him. And if I disappoint him, all of that goes."

"I'm sorry, Julian. I'm really sorry. I care for you. I really do. But I'm in love with Cutter—you've always known that."

"I was hoping that it was just some sort of leftover preadolescent fantasy. That as soon as you got to be around him more, that the appeal would get old and you wouldn't care so much for him."

"That didn't happen. But I guess the real question is, what happens if you meet someone . . . someone that you want to share your life with? How are you going to handle your father then?"

"I won't tell him. Just keep on going as I'm going. You just promise to show up a few times, a few family dinners, some social engagements. Everything will be fine, Dav. I promise you it will."

"No, it won't!" Davalyn snapped. "I'm not putting my life on hold anymore, Julian. You're a grown man. If you're not free to choose who you want to love and how you want to love, then don't expect me to be bound with you. It's your lifestyle. Deal with it. But having me on the side—"

"Do you think it's any different between you and Cutter now?" Julian snarled. "You think he's sitting at home, mooning over you because you're not there? News flash for you, Davalyn. You're just *his* thing on the side! While you're here, playing the good little girlfriend with me, he's getting his jollies off with some other woman. A lot of other women. He probably has more numbers stored in that cell phone than—"

Davalyn didn't realize that she'd slapped Julian until she felt the stinging in her hand and saw his head rear back. He reached up to massage the area.

Tears stung her eyes. "I'm so sorry, Julian. I didn't mean to . . ."

Julian stepped back, brushing off her apology. "Truth hurts, doesn't it, Dav? But I have to admit, not as much as that slap."

"Julian, you know I'd never do anything to hurt you. I'd rather cut off my right arm than hurt you. It's just that you have to end this. You have to tell your father the truth. We're not in love. We're not together. We never will be."

"Everybody's got their secrets, Dav. We all have our

own version of the truth. Even you and your family. Nobody wants to tell you, Dav, not even your brother . . . that your boyfriend's an asshole. A jerk. Doesn't care who he uses or how. All he's looking for is the next easy lay . . . and you fell right into his hands."

"You and your so-called alternative lifestyle—I guess that makes you an expert on assholes, doesn't it, Julian?" Davalyn shot back.

"Cheap shot, Dav. I guess that means you and McCall are made for each other, because he's certainly brought you down to his level. You want to go home tonight. Fine. Pack your stuff. I'll take you home."

"We're both upset," she said, her voice shaking. "We've said and done some things I know we'll regret. Speaking for myself, I know that I have. I didn't mean to try to cut you down or to take shots at you, Julian. It's just that I'm upset that you can't talk to your father. I don't understand. I would give anything to be able to talk to my father. Anything."

"You don't talk to Jonathan Blake. You listen. He does all of the talking and none of the listening."

"You have to make him understand." She walked up to him, laying her hand on his arm and gently squeezing. "I'm sorry that I got angry with you and said those hateful things. I don't hate who and what you are, Julian. I hate the fact that you can't be *true* to who you are. That's what I'm angry about. You're living a lie and it's hurting you. It's hurting me, too."

"Do you think I like sneaking around, pretending in front of my parents that I'm something I'm not? You think I chose this life. I didn't, Dav. It chose me. It hounded me, tortured me, made me know that I was different until I finally accepted."

"You say that you've accepted, Julian. But you

haven't really. Not if you're being completely open and honest. In this day and age, you don't have to hide. You shouldn't have to."

His mouth twisted in irony. "You say that like just wishing it will make it true. This ain't Kansas, Dorothy. You can't click your heels together three times and make it all right."

"Maybe you've been hiding the truth for so long, that you're afraid. Your parents might be more liberal and accepting than you think they are."

"Twenty-nine years under their roof and rules, Davalyn. I think I have a pretty good grasp of how they'd react. My mother would start to wonder how she'd failed me, would probably tell the pastor and they'd conduct marathon praying sessions over me. Like I was possessed by some kind of demon. I've seen how so-called upstanding members of the church can freeze you out, the endless gossip, the intentional snubs. They'd make my parents feel uncomfortable, unwelcome in the church they founded. I know my father would stop talking to me altogether. Our communication may not be the best, but it's all that I have. I'm not going to let that go. I'd rather live a lie for the rest of my life than lose his respect."

"But, Julian—"

"No, Davalyn!" Julian made a curt, slashing motion with his hand. "I'm not going to say anything. Not yet. I can't. I know you're trying to help. But you don't know what the hell you're talking about. You don't have a clue what it's like to live in my shoes. People talk about freedom of choice and tolerance, but it's all just lip service. As soon as they find out, or even suspect, they'll never look at you the same. I've already seen it happen with some of my friends. If they had kids, they stopped calling, stopped bringing their kids by—as if they're afraid their kids would catch something just by being around me. Or like I was some kind of pervert or pedophile. I would never, ever hurt a child, Dav. That's not who I am. But how do you explain that? How do you break through a mind-set that says, 'Well, if he's freaky one way, you know stalking children is the next step'?"

"That's ridiculous!" Davalyn snapped.

"You say that because you know me. Others who I thought knew me and trusted me didn't feel that way. I can only thank God that they've broken off all contact with me; otherwise I wouldn't have been able to keep quiet about my lifestyle."

"Julian, what happens when you do meet someone and you want to share your life with him? How are you going to keep it quiet then?"

"How do you think I'm going to meet anyone, Dav? As far as having a social life goes, forget it. Gay bars are hunting grounds for the homophobic. As soon as everyone finds out, you'll be looking over your shoulder for the rest of your days, wondering if some idiot is going to jump you, pound you to a pulp. Probably the same idiots that are fighting their own inclinations. I'm a big, fat, walking target. A rich, gay black man. It just screams, 'Open season. Grab a bat and come beat me to a bloody pulp.'"

"I didn't know, Julian. I didn't know how much you've suffered. I'm so sorry."

"Will you stop apologizing? I know you didn't know. I didn't want you to. Which exactly proves my point, Dav. Sometimes it's just better to keep your family and friends in the dark."

"Listen, Julian, even with all that you've kept from

me, nobody knows what a wonderful person you are more than I do. If you want me to, I'll help you talk to your parents. What's that they say in legal circles? I'll be your second chair. We'll do it together. Maybe I can do some research, find some literature or counselors who could talk to them. We'll sit them down, someplace casual and nonthreatening, and lay it all out for them."

"Then afterward we can watch a couple of episodes of 'Will and Grace,' join hands singing 'Kumbahya,' and everything will be right with the world, huh, Dav? That's only on TV. Only on TV is being gay fashionable. Unless, of course, I want to become a hairdresser or an interior decorator."

"I'm trying to help you and you're being sarcastic."

"A little self-deprecating humor. I know all the stereotypes. I'm only trying to be realistic. If I have to tell them now—disappoint them—it'll kill them. And I'd do myself in before I hurt them, Dav. I mean that."

"You don't mean that," she said sharply. "Come on, Julian. Let's go back inside. I'm tired. Maybe things will look better in the morning. Don't you make any rash decisions until you've had some time to think about what I've said."

Davalyn started for the house, then turned back when she realized that he wasn't following her.

"Aren't you coming in, Julian?"

"Not yet. I want to stay out here for a while. I'll take your suggestion and think about you . . . and what you've said."

"All right, then. Don't stay out too late. It's cold out here. I'll see you in the morning." She turned, started back up the gravel path, and was met halfway by Julian's father.

"Mr. Blake," Davalyn said, a little surprised to see

him. She wondered whether he'd heard any of the conversation. She couldn't tell by the expression on his face.

"Temperature's dropping," he said. "I didn't want you to catch a cold standing out here in this wet weather."

Davalyn smiled. He seemed so concerned. This didn't fit the image of the man that Julian had painted. "I was just going in," she said.

"So did you two patch things up? I know my son can be a little difficult sometimes."

She shrugged. "We talked. We have a better understanding, but there's more talking that needs to be done."

"That's what I thought," he said, staring off down the path.

"Julian needs to talk to you, too, Mr. Blake," Davalyn said softly. She could have said more. At the same time, she wondered if she'd said too much. If Julian didn't want to talk to his father, she had no right to force the issue. Yet, she was moving on with her life. She couldn't do that yoked to him as she was. Someone had to take the first step.

"Good night, Mr. Blake. It's been a long day. I think I'll go up to my room now."

"Good night, Davalyn. Pleasant dreams."

Nineteen

"Thanks for letting me sleep up here, Dad." Bennett snuggled down deep within the heavily insulated sleeping bag. Only his nose and big, dark eyes could be seen poking out from the bright red nylon sleeping bag. Another gift from Davalyn in her signature color.

Cutter stopped in the middle of spreading out his own sleeping bag. He couldn't help thinking about Davalyn. That color screamed of her. It reminded him of their conversation in the restaurant when the sight of her in that red dress nearly knocked him flat on his butt. It reminded him of how he'd invited her up to this tree house before it was finished and almost made love to her near that very spot where Bennett now lay. Mostly, it keenly reminded him of how much he was now missing her.

"You know that when school starts up again, I'm not gonna let you sleep up here, Bennett," Cutter admonished him.

"Except on weekends," Bennett amended.

"And if you haven't received any bad conduct notes from school."

"Only if I get some for things that weren't really my fault."

"We'll see how that goes." Cutter didn't make any promises. He turned back to spreading out his sleeping bag and hoped that Bennett didn't see him pressing his lips together trying to keep himself from laughing.

He was actually very pleased regarding Bennett's conduct in school. First positive sign was that he was going to school instead of trying to find ways to ditch. *That is a promising start,* Cutter mused. Bennett was bringing home his homework, participating in class, and was well liked by other students. That was a lot more than Cutter ever did when he was in grade school.

He'd been told that all parents' nightmare was to have a kid just like him. In his case, if Bennett had been more like him instead of his ex-wife, he would have to go along with that statement. But Bennett was a near-perfect blend of them both. He had his mother's natural grace and social skills without any of her social snobbery. That allowed him to make friends easily—and keep them. Didn't matter if they were the richest kids in school or the poorest. Bennett counted them all as part of his "crew." That was something Angela never could get past. She'd taken one look at Cutter, from his home-done haircut to his thrift-store shoes, and summed up his net worth.

Like him, Bennett had his overwhelming curiosity about how things worked. And, like him, Bennett was no angel. He had no illusions about that. He'd been up to that school more than once to sort out why trouble sometimes seemed to find his son. He was still trying to figure out how Bennett was involved in releasing a box full of huge Texas-size flying tree roaches in the girls' bathroom. No angel, indeed. But Bennet was a gift from God, of that much he was certain. Cutter woke up every morning thankful for the gift and completely amazed that he'd gotten through another day without completely warping his son. Maybe he shouldn't break his arm trying to pat himself on the back with his success so far. He still had a good eight to ten more years of Bennett living under his roof to do enough damage.

"Wanna pass me another piece of that sandwich, boy?"

"You want the turkey or the chicken sandwich?"

"Please . . . I don't want to hear the word 'turkey' again for at least another year." Cutter groaned. He'd seen enough turkey since Thanksgiving to make him sick of the stuff—and the sit-in-the-bottom-of-the-stomach stuffing that went along with it. "Just give me the chicken."

"Uh . . . I took a bite of it already. Still want it, Dad?"

"That's all right. I'm used to your germs."

"Stuck my finger in it, too," Bennett said impishly.

"Only made it sweeter. Now hand it over."

"What if I told you I spit on it?"

"That's nasty, Bennett. Are you trying to tell me that you want the chicken sandwich? Just come right out and say it, son. Tell me that you want the chicken sandwich."

"I want the chicken sandwich," Bennett repeated.

"Too late! I already called dibs!"

Cutter lunged for the blue-and-white Coleman ice chest, which was stocked full of food, juices, water, and snack cakes, and reached for the lid. Bennett was almost directly under him and brought up his knees and caught his father in the chest. He kicked out, throwing Cutter off balance. Cutter controlled his fall, made sure not to crush his son beneath him. Even as he was falling on his side, Bennett had wiggled out of the sleeping bag and was crawling toward the ice chest.

"Oh, it's on now! Where do you think you're going?" He wrapped his arms around his son, digging his fingers into his stomach and waist to find the most vulnerable tickle spots.

Bennett laughed, a high-pitched, hysterical giggle that made Cutter laugh, too.

"N-n-no fair!" Bennett gasped. "I called no tickling!"

"When did you do that?" Cutter stopped tickling, but he didn't let go of his son, either.

"Last week," he said, gasping for air. "When we were at Uncle Van's house and you wanted the remote control so you could watch football and I wanted to watch cartoons."

"How come you can remember that, but you can't remember to take out the trash?"

"Da-aad," Bennett complained.

"Never mind. Go ahead and take the last chicken sandwich. I'll just choke down another turkey."

Bennett reached for his sandwich, tossed his father his, followed by a couple of packages of low-fat mayonnaise.

"Cranberry, apple, or orange juice?" he offered.

"Which one didn't you spit in?" Cutter asked suspiciously.

"None of 'em." Bennett grinned at his dad.

"The apple, then."

Munching on his sandwich, Bennett scooted near the window. "Cool!" he exclaimed softly. "The neighborhood's turned on the Christmas lights. Come see, Dad. It looks so different from up here. Kinda like Santa's Tinseltown at the mall."

Cutter crawled across the floor to join Bennett at the window. From their vantage point on the first level of the tree house, Cutter could see almost half a mile from any of the windows in all directions, except on Donovan's side, where his view was blocked by one of the few two-story houses on the block. If they climbed up to the second level, then they could see more. Especially with the skylight he'd cut out so that Bennett could stargaze with the telescope Van had given him for his birthday.

"With all of these lights, Santa should have no trouble finding this neighborhood, huh, Bennett?"

"Can I sleep out here Christmas Eve, Dad? Huh? Can I? I want to see if I can use my telescope to see Santa coming."

"He might not come if you're still awake, son."

"I could take a really quick peek, then go to sleep really fast."

"Hmmm . . . you can't fake it, Bennett. You have to be asleep for real."

"I know. But this may be my only chance to see him. Can I sleep out here? Please?"

"If it's not too cold. We'll see. Now finish your sandwich so you can brush your teeth and go to bed."

"Brush my teeth? Out here? How am I gonna do that?"

Cutter dragged out a small bag that had Bennett's toothbrush and a small tube of toothpaste. "If you don't want to go back inside to brush, do it out here, rinse with bottled water and spit out the window."

"And you called me nasty," Bennett said under his breath. "And if I have to go to the bathroom?"

"I'll leave it up to your best judgment how to handle that. Just wake me up if you need to go back to the house."

"Like for a number two?"

"I really don't need to know the details, son."

They sat in silence for a while after that, finishing their snack, watching the neighborhood rooftops and the chaser lights that flashed, blinked, or winked outlining them. White lights or strands of multicolored ones, big bulbs that glowed as bright as neon or tiny ones that twinkled like stars, strands that hung down like icicles, pointing to elaborate lawn decorations depicting every winter scene from secular Santa and his reindeer to the traditional Nativity manger scene.

If it weren't for Davalyn insisting that he at least put up a welcoming wreath on his front door, Cutter thought that his house might have been the only darkened, undecorated house on the block. Everyone else had started putting up their decorations the first of November. Even before then. Right after Halloween. Between working at the shop, his volunteer duties, and working on Bennett's tree house, he just couldn't find the time. He found the energy, though. Davalyn's enthusiasm was infectious.

While Davalyn was busy setting up a Kwanzaa display in her front yard, complete with a flagpole attached to the support column displaying her sorority colors and the striped *bendera,* he made a quick run to the local thrift store and picked up a couple of strands of lights and tacked them around the eaves of the front porch and around Bennett's tree.

"Couldn't stand to be left out of the neighborhood decorating contest, could you, Cutter?" she'd teased him.

"I just got tired of you calling me Scrooge," he retorted, standing back to admire his handiwork.

She'd come over to him and wrapped her arms around him in a quick squeeze. "Good job," she praised. They'd stood for a moment, his arm draped casually over her shoulder, her arm around his waist. It was a small thing that he'd done, but she'd smiled at him as if it were a grand gesture. He wasn't used to that. He wasn't used to a woman being satisfied with the thought. With Angela, it had been all about the effort.

More. More. More. Give her more. Davalyn just wanted to be with him. She just wanted to know that he *wanted* to be with her.

Davalyn. He sure did miss her. Cutter didn't know how much time had passed as he watched the moon track across the sky. He wondered was she missing him, too. Was she looking up at that same sky, the same moon, and wondering whether he was thinking about her? Cutter wished. It wasn't on the first star of the night, but that didn't dim his wishing power. He wished hard and strong. Wished for that woman to come home soon.

Maybe he dozed a little, too. The next thing he knew, he was startled awake. His head jerked up.

As he looked around, a little disoriented at first, it took him a while to realize where he was. The tree fort. He finally noticed that Bennett was leaning against him, snoring softly through his nose. His arms were wrapped around his son, shielding him from the cold seeping through the walls. Carefully, gently, trying not to wake him, Cutter maneuvered until he was able to get Bennett back into his sleeping bag. He crossed over Bennett, starting for his own sleeping bag, but a single noise caught his attention. The muffled echo of a car door slam. It sounded close. Next door maybe. Was that Van coming home early from his camping trip? Cutter doubted it. Van was so psyched about the trip. He couldn't imagine Van coming home any minute sooner than he had to.

Turning his wrist over, Cutter checked his watch. The luminescent paint added to the hands and letters cast a faint greenish glow. Two o'clock in the morning. Cutter rolled over onto his side and pulled his sleeping bag over his shoulder. He closed his eyes, breathed deeply.

But somehow, sleep escaped him. A tickle in the back of his neck, a tightening of his stomach. What was it that wouldn't let him relax? He twisted his head, checked on Bennett. His son was breathing deeply, caught in the throes of a nine-year-old boy's dream. Eyelids fluttered rapidly and every so often his mouth worked, as if he were trying to speak. Cutter grinned softly in the darkness.

Probably scheming on a way to get over on his old man, Cutter thought. He could remember a dream or two of his own when he got the upper hand on old Calvin McCall. The good feeling coming from that dream lasted him all day.

Since daylight was a few hours away, Cutter tried to settle down. He told himself that there wasn't anything wrong. No reason why he should feel uneasy. Yet, even as he thought, the words didn't ring true. He sat up, rubbed his hand over his bristly head and stubbled jaw. When he reached for another bottled water, he saw the light in the upstairs window of the Bowers house.

Davalyn! She was home! Carefully Cutter skirted around Bennett and moved to look out of the Plexiglas window. He could make out a shadow moving behind the drawn curtains of her bedroom window. Once . . . twice. Back and forth. Back and forth. She'd disappear for a moment, then return to the window. Her shadow loomed large, then faded. Moments later, it was back again. It didn't take Cutter long to figure out that Davalyn wasn't just preparing for bed. She was pacing.

Shaking his head, Cutter unscrewed the cap and raised the bottle to his lips. After several passes of watching the shadowy image of Davalyn crossing in front of the window, Cutter dug his cell phone out of the corner pocket of his duffel bag and dialed the Bowers house.

It took a couple of rings—almost as if she were debating whether to answer it. He watched the shadow silhouetted against the window stand stock-still for a moment. Finally, after about the fifth ring, she moved away.

He opened his mouth to greet her and was savagely interrupted.

"Leave . . . me . . . alone!" Davalyn said tightly, carefully enunciating each word. The phone slammed down, leaving a ringing in his ears.

"Now, what was that all about?" He pressed the redial button.

"I thought I told you to—"

"Dav?" Cutter interrupted her.

Cutter heard the catch in her voice. "Cutter . . ." Her voice was flooded with relief.

"Yeah, it's me. Who else would be calling you at this time of morning?"

"What are you doing up?"

"Couldn't sleep. You know, you really should turn off your lamp if you're gonna go pacing back and forth like that. I can see almost every move you make."

He peered out of the tree house window just as Davalyn stepped to the window and peeked through the blinds.

"You and Bennett having a sleepover?" she asked, waving at Cutter through the window.

"Uh-huh. I promised him that we'll stay up here as many times as we can while he's on Thanksgiving break, while the weather holds."

"But you're not sleeping."

"Nope. I heard your truck drive up."

"Better than having a next-door Brink's security man."

"What are you doing back so soon, Dav? I thought you and Julian were spending the weekend together. You weren't supposed to be back until Tuesday."

"Well, plans changed," Davalyn said bitterly. There was no hiding the anguish in her voice.

"Is everything all right, Dav?" Cutter asked.

She shook her head; then not sure he could see the subtle movement through the window, she spoke into the phone. "I have to admit, I've had better holidays, Cutter."

"Wanna talk about it?" he asked softly.

"No. Not really." Her voice cracked.

Cutter could tell by the sound of it that she'd been crying. He felt his heart squeeze in his chest. It wasn't the fact that she was crying that upset him. He'd seen her cry before—at movies with sad endings, or movies with happy endings. Love stories. War stories. She even cried at commercials. This was different. This wasn't something that had made her cry. It was someone. Julian. He sensed it without her having to tell him.

"I'm coming over there anyway. I'll be down in a minute."

"Don't, Cutter. You're supposed to be sharing this moment with your son."

"It's two o'clock in the morning, baby girl. He's sound asleep. I don't think he'll miss me for a few minutes."

She hesitated, wanting to talk but not wanting to infringe on his family time. "I'm fine, Cutter. Really. You don't have to come over."

"Then come over here," he suggested.

"You mean up in that tree fort?"

"Why not?"

"You know why not. Are you forgetting what happened the last time I came up there, Cutter?"

"You know better than that, baby girl," Cutter replied. The huskiness of his voice reached through the airwaves, grabbed Davalyn in the pit of her stomach, and sent up a flock of butterflies. "I couldn't forget. Even if I wanted to." His voice was a hoarse whisper. Maybe because he didn't want Bennett to overhear. Maybe it was because he was afraid. By saying the words out loud, he gave them weight. Substance. Veracity. Once the words were out there, he couldn't call them back—and he didn't want to.

"Then that's why you know it's a bad idea."

"Dav, all I'm offering you is a chance to talk. You sound like you need a friend. I can be that for you. If you need me, I'm here for you. Just as a friend."

Davalyn leaned her head against the cool pane of the glass.

"I could use a friend right now," she admitted.

"Then grab an extra blanket and come on over. I'll be waiting for you by the tree."

"Ten minutes," she promised.

"Make it five."

Twenty

Davalyn sat for at least twenty minutes, huddled in her blanket. Her back was against the tree house wall on the upper level. Cutter sat next to her. They'd climbed up to the second level so that they could talk without waking Bennett. So far, very little talking had actually taken place since Davalyn met him at the bottom of the tree. He didn't speak, either, or encourage her to speak. He knew that when she was ready, she would share what was bothering her.

That's the way it usually went between them. Sometimes they could talk for hours on end. Sometimes they were content to sit in silence. This was one of those times. Only, Cutter knew that Davalyn wasn't content. She sat quietly, but she was apprehensive, bothered. He could see it in the tightness around her mouth. She was holding back.

Cutter did what he could to make her feel at ease with him. He'd promised that he would be there for her as a friend. And that's what he planned to do. He wouldn't talk, wouldn't touch her until she let him know that she was ready.

"I think . . . I think he'd been drinking." She'd lowered her head to her knees, so her voice came out muffled.

It was on the tip of Cutter's tongue to ask, "Who?" yet, somehow he knew. So he didn't interrupt her.

"We'd had an argument, so I came home."

"Because of the argument?" It was too simple an explanation for him. There had to be something more.

"Sort of. Not really. I don't know. More than that," she said, sounding irritated and confused at the same time. "He told his parents that I was pregnant. Pregnant!"

"With his baby?" Cutter said tightly.

"No, Elvis's baby. Of course his!" Davalyn said sarcastically.

Cutter hated himself for asking, but there was no way he could avoid it. "Are you?"

"Am I what?" Davalyn asked.

"Are you pregnant?"

"Cutter!" Davalyn exclaimed, thumping him in the chest. "How could you ask me that?"

"I had to ask, baby girl."

"No, you didn't. You didn't have to go there."

"Why would he say it if there wasn't a chance?"

"Because he's an idiot!" she snapped. "And so are you. For the record, I am *not* pregnant."

"It's a natural assumption. You do eat a lot sometimes."

"That makes me a glutton. Not pregnant."

"So, you and Julian had an argument. You've known each other a long time. You've never argued before?"

"Not like this," Davalyn confessed. She drew her knees up, hugged her legs close to her, and rested her chin on her knees.

"What happened, Dav?" Cutter urged her. "What could be so bad to make you want to pack up in the middle of the night?"

"Like I said, he'd been drinking. A first for Julian. He takes a glass of wine every now and then with dinner. Nothing hard. But last night, something got into him. I'd gone to bed early. I don't think he did. Next thing I know, he's pounding on my door. It was either let him in or wake up the whole house. When I went to the door, I could smell it on him when he . . . he . . ." Davalyn stopped, then shook her head as if she didn't want to think about it. She certainly didn't want to talk about it.

"When he *what?*" Cutter said tightly. "What did he do to you, Dav?"

Davalyn closed her eyes. "Nothing. I wouldn't let him. I told him to get out. He wasn't thinking straight. He wouldn't listen to reason. I know it must have embarrassed him in front of his folks when I threw him out. But what else could I do?"

"You threw him out of your room. You two had separate rooms?" It dawned on Cutter the implication of Davalyn and Julian having separate rooms. Maybe it was because they didn't want to share a room in his parents' house. A family of lawyers—Cutter imagined them a little traditional, maybe even old-fashioned.

Or maybe they had separate rooms for another reason. Maybe they were having troubles. Had that kiss at the restaurant driven a wedge between them? He admitted that he was only thinking of himself when he'd kissed her. Consequences, *schmonsequences*. He'd wanted her. And the fact that she already had a man didn't matter to him. If she and Julian had broken up, so much the better for him. But Julian obviously meant a lot to her. If he'd caused her any pain, Cutter was more than willing to do his share to even the score.

"Of course we did. Why would you think otherwise?"

Cutter shrugged. "I dunno. I just figured you would. He's your man."

Davalyn shifted around to face Cutter. She reached up and laid her hand gently on his cheek. "Cutter," she whispered. "Julian's my friend. A good friend. A close friend. But that's all we are is friends."

"But I thought that you and he . . ."

"I know," she said in exasperation. "That's what everyone was supposed to think, Cutter. Truth is, he isn't my type . . . and I'm not his. That's all I can say about that subject for now."

"So, if you two aren't really together, why the front, Dav? Why did you go up to Dallas and spend the weekend with him? You could have been here. I . . . I wouldn't have gone to Angela's if you had stayed here."

"Oh, it's all so complicated. But I had to go. I made a promise to him back in the summer that I would. I couldn't break it. But when I told him that I was tired of playacting in front of his parents, he got angry."

Davalyn got really quiet when she realized that Cutter was doing more than just listening. He was thinking, plotting. She could almost see it in his expression.

"Did he hurt you, Davalyn?" Cutter questioned in a tone that she had never heard from him before. Ice cold. Dark with menace.

"No," Davalyn said quickly. "God, no. I told you, Cutter. I threw him out before anything happened. Then I called a cab and took the first flight back I could get."

"Friend or no friend, he had no right to put his hands on you, Dav."

"He didn't. He never has. Do you understand what I'm trying to say to you, Cutter? Julian has never touched me that way." She leaned close and spoke so softly that he wasn't sure he'd heard correctly. "No one has."

Cutter blinked. "What did you say?"

"I said, no one has ever touched me, Cutter. No man. I've . . . I've never been with anyone."

"Never?" he repeated.

"Nev-er," she said with the same conviction he'd spoken when she'd asked if he'd been unfaithful to his ex-wife.

"But . . . why not? I mean . . ." Cutter had a hard time voicing his thoughts. Davalyn was an incredible woman. Beautiful. Intelligent. Confident. She knew what she wanted. That kind of self-assurance should have had those undergrads thronging after her. Wasn't there one on that entire campus that she could have fallen for?

"After seeing what my folks went through, the pain they inflicted on each other, I swore that I would make sure the man I gave myself to . . . my heart to . . . would be the one. The only one. No breakups. No divorces. No do-overs. My man and I are going to be in it for the long haul, so he'd better be the right one."

Cutter sat back, absolutely stunned. He covered his mouth with his palm, shaking his head in absolute astonishment. "I don't know what to say."

"You don't have to say anything." She shrugged.

"But that night . . . up here . . . when we almost . . . Jeez, Dav. I had no idea! God . . . how could I have been so stupid!" He slapped his forehead with his palm.

"I didn't say the perfect one, Cutter. I said the right one. I was ready to give myself to you because I know in my heart that's who you are."

Cutter stood up and moved away from her. He couldn't face her. Didn't want to think about how closely they'd flirted with disaster. Thank the Maker that he'd been called to duty. Otherwise, there was no doubt in his mind that he would have taken her without regard for protection or propriety or even her own pleasure.

Davalyn watched his back, watched him struggle and wage war with his doubts. On one side was Cutter the man. A man who had feelings, desires. A man who had licked the wounds of his divorce and had decided that the search for companionship, even love, was worth the risk of a few more emotional battle scars. On the other side was Cutter the friend—the man who believed it was his responsibility to shield her, to protect her, and to support her. The man who had his own code of honor, who could not bend to his personal desires, no matter how strong or compelling the reasons to go against that code.

Davalyn shrugged the blanket from her shoulders and stood up. She walked over to Cutter, wrapping her arms around his waist. She didn't let go, even when she felt his back stiffen, heard the inrush of his breath.

"You should have told me, Dav." His voice was filled with anguish and recrimination.

"If I did, it would have freaked you out. Just like you're freaking on me now."

Cutter brought his hands from the wall and covered her arms with his. "You're damn right that I'm freakin', baby girl. I know what would have happened. You're not on birth control, are you?"

"I have them, but I haven't started taking them yet."

"Uh-huh . . . and I didn't have condoms with me. That was stupid of me to even think about making love to you without them. It doesn't take long to make a baby, Dav."

"Nine months," she teased, giving his waist a little squeeze.

"Wrong. Nine months to grow one. But only seconds

to plant one. A lifetime of responsibility of caring for one."

"I'm ready for that responsibility, Cutter," she assured him.

Cutter thought about all the times that he'd left her with Bennett. He thought about how quickly they seemed to have bonded. Bennett cared for her—that much was certain. But her letting him into her life wasn't decided in the heat of the moment.

"Maybe you are. Maybe you aren't. The time to find out isn't after you're pregnant. That's exactly what would have happened if we'd gone on."

"Did you want me, Cutter? I have to know."

"Is that a trick question?" He turned his head to ask.

"No. I just wanted to know. That night up here in the tree house, was it just the sex or was it me? Did you want *me* or would any woman have done?"

Cutter spun around and drew her tight to his chest. He lowered his head, hooking his chin behind her shoulder. "There's no other woman I want more than you, Davalyn Bowers. Not a one."

"Even if you could get Angela back?" Her voice trembled. "Even if you could fix things between you?"

"Let me tell you something about me and Angela, Dav," Cutter began. He sat down, easing Davalyn next to him. With his arms draped around her shoulder, he drew her close to him. "When I married Angela, I still wanted what a child wanted, Dav."

"She's all you used to talk about. I remember like it was yesterday."

"I'm a man now. A grown man, with a grown man's wishes. I swear to you, since you've come back, Dav, I've never once wished that Angela and I were together again. We have a history. That means we have a past. The only thing between us now is Bennett."

"I had to know," she whispered. "Because I've wanted you ever since I was a child, Cutter McCall. For as long as I can remember. As a child, I wanted you, and as a woman, I want you even more. Only now, I'm old enough to know what that means. I love you, Cutter. Always have. Always will. That's why I left Julian. He knows how I feel about you. It frightened him. Threatened him. He knew that I could never feel for him what I feel for you. I got tired of pretending that I could, so I got out of there."

Davalyn felt dampness on her face and realized that she was crying. Cutter smoothed her face and wiped away her tears.

"You waited . . . waited for me?" he asked. He couldn't imagine a greater sacrifice, a more precious gift she'd offered to him. "I wish that I'd waited for you, Dav. So we could have shared together."

"I didn't know that's what I was doing at the time. Waiting for you, that is. I just knew that every time I thought of letting someone touch me, I panicked. It wasn't right. None of them were right. None of them were you. I know there were a couple of guys who thought I was being a tease. Lord knows, I thought I was ready. I felt ready. So incredibly ready," she said. "A couple of times I almost went through with it. But each time, I backed down. I couldn't stand the thought of another man touching me."

Davalyn backed away, lifting her chin, and regarded him with dark, luminous eyes.

"That makes two of us," he said through clenched teeth. "When you showed up late to the restaurant, looking like you did in that dress, I could have wrapped my hands around Julian's neck and squeezed him to the last breath."

"You were jealous!" She laughed softly.

"That's not funny, Dav." He was stung. "I was suffering."

"You had Shayla," she reminded him. "You didn't look like you were suffering too much."

"It wasn't the same. She wasn't you."

"You've got that right." Her tone was taunting. She scooted away from him, reached for the hem of her sweater, and pulled it over her head.

"Whoa, boy," Cutter said under his breath. "Wait a minute, Dav. Weren't you the one who was afraid that something might happen if you came up here with me?"

"That was before I knew you loved me, too."

"I never said that I—"

"Tell me you don't?" she challenged. "Tell me you don't love me." Davalyn raised up on her knees, reached for the snaps of her low-rise jeans, and slowly undid them.

"You're not being fair!" he complained. "I can't think with you doing a striptease."

"All's fair in love and war. You'd better say it, Cutter. Three little words. Come on, you can do it." She hooked her fingers at her belt loops, swaying her hips slowly back and forth.

"Lawd have mercy," Cutter muttered.

"Not the three words I wanted to hear, but you're getting warmer," she said, sitting on her bottom again, pulling out one leg. And then the next.

"Warm ain't the word, baby girl," he said with chagrin, easing his jacket off his shoulders.

"Come on, Cutter," she urged. "Let's start with something easy. Tell me that you like me. You do like me, don't you?"

"I like you," he repeated quickly.

She kicked her jeans aside. "Good. That's a good start." Davalyn reached behind her, undid the clasp of her brassiere. It was the dead of winter, yet her flushed skin barely felt the chill of the air. When she unhooked her brassiere, the cold air touched her nipples, making them pert and alert.

She slid the undergarment off her arms and tossed it at Cutter. He snatched it out of the air, then balled it up in his hands. She cupped her hands over her breasts, lifting, massaging, and kneading her flesh. Her gaze never left his.

"The next step is to tell me that you want me. Say it, Cutter. Tell me that you want me."

Cutter moved toward her, but she avoided his desperate grasp.

"You know that I do, Dav. Why are you playing with me like this?"

She was teasing him, taunting him, pushing him past his limits.

"This isn't a game, Cutter. I'm playing for keeps," she retorted. "I want you to say it before you touch me. Say it to me before, during, and after. Because I'll accept that you might lie to me once to get what you want. I'm putting a lot of pressure on you. If I were a man, faced with a gorgeous, hot woman like me, I'd lie to get what I want, too."

Cutter laughed, knowing that it was painfully true. Every word of it.

"I'd even expect that you might say it during. Caught up in passion, in the heat of the moment, you might tell me that you love me. That is, if I didn't work you so hard that you wouldn't have the breath to speak."

"You're that sure of your ability?" He raised an eyebrow at her.

"Aren't you?"

"The way things are looking now, I'd say that was a definite possibility. Once we start, there won't be much time for talkin', baby girl."

"That's what I thought," she agreed. "But I know you, Cutter McCall. I know what kind of man you are. I don't believe that you could say it three times if you didn't mean it."

"For someone who isn't experienced, you seem to know a lot about what turns a man on, baby girl."

"You sound like you don't believe that I'm still a virgin." She didn't sound angry at all. "Sounds incredible to my own ears. A twenty-seven-year-old virgin. Unbelievable. Not many of us left in the world. But, if you tell me that you love me, and mean it, and if I believe you mean it, you'll find out the truth soon enough. If you can't say it, then I'll put my clothes on and I'll go. We can go back to being just friends, neighbors. Living that awful, painful lie when we both know that it's not what we want."

She lay back against the blanket that she'd brought from her house. One hand continued to cup her breast; the other hand slid palm downward, over sternum, over navel, underneath the waistband of her panties.

Cutter dropped to his knees beside her. "I just have to know . . . How close did you come to those other men making love to you, Dav? Just how far did you let them get with you?"

Davalyn took her hand in his, placing it at the warm, moist V at the junction of her thighs, to satisfy his morbid curiosity. He was jealous—jealous of nameless faces who might have gone where he hadn't. Done what he didn't.

"This is how close I came to having *sex* with other men, Cutter," she said honestly. "Not love. I said I was a virgin. I didn't say that I was a saint."

"I want you, Dav. Lord knows that I do. But this may not be the best time. You're still upset after your fight with Julian. Besides, Bennett can wake up. I told you that I don't necessarily walk around with condoms on me all the time."

"I've got some. Do you want me to go get them?"

"No!" he said, almost in a panic.

"What does a girl have to do to get a guy's attention?" She laughed at him.

"Oh, you've got my attention, all right. My complete attention," he said ruefully. "Besides, I thought we were going to do this right. A real date. Dinner. A movie. A baby-sitter. The works."

"I'm impatient. I've waited for so long."

He sighed heavily, lying down next to her. Spooning her into the hard lines of his body, Cutter murmured into her ear, "Just hang on a little while longer, Dav. I promise. When it's right, there'll be no stopping us."

He raised a bit and kissed her affectionately on her cheek. "It's because I love you so much that I don't want to rush, baby girl. I want it to be right between us. No hurries, no fears, no regrets."

"You love me," Davalyn echoed. Her heart pounded in her chest. "Oh, Cutter, tell me again. I need to hear you say it so I know that I'm not in one of my fantasies."

"Yes, I love you, Davalyn Bowers." He leaned on his elbow, staring down into her eyes. "You don't know how hard I fought it. I didn't even want to admit it to myself. But I do love you, Dav. It scares me how much."

Davalyn reached up and hugged him tightly around the neck.

"I love you," he said hoarsely. "I'll say it a thousand times if you want me to. A thousand times a thousand."

As she lay next to him, feeling the pounding of his heart, his nature rise, she tried once more. "You sure I can't change your mind? Tempt you to . . ." Davalyn began.

"Sh!" Cutter said suddenly, laying his index finger against her lips. She questioned him with raised eyebrows.

"Hear that?" he said, straining his ears. It didn't take long. Within seconds Davalyn heard it, too. The wail of sirens. Fire engines.

Cutter shot up, crossed the tree house floor in a couple of steps. He leaned down to peer out the window.

"Next street over. Five, maybe six houses down," he judged.

"The Jensens?" Davalyn gasped. "Or the Romanos?"

"I can't tell for sure," he said, pushing open the window and leaning out. "But it's ugly. I can smell it."

When he turned around, Davalyn had already put on her sweater and was stepping back into her jeans.

"Where do you think you're going?" he asked.

"Same place you are." Davalyn recognized the look on his face and knew that no matter what was going on between them, he would be there for his station.

"You're not on call," he reminded her. "You're supposed to be on holiday break."

"So are you, but you're still going to the scene."

"Somebody's gotta stay here with Bennett, Dav. Van's not here to baby-sit."

Davalyn paused. Theoretically, she couldn't start an investigation until after the fire had been tapped out, but this was her neighborhood. If there was anything she could do to help, she would.

"Then wake him up. Wrap him up in my blanket. We'll bring him with us. He can stay in the truck, out of the way. I'll stay with him until it's my turn to work. Just give me time to grab some gear from my truck."

Cutter accepted her suggestion as the best compromise. "Meet me out front when you're ready," he said as he reached for the latch to open the door.

"Next time, McCall, you're not getting away so fast," she promised him. "I don't care if the flames are licking at your toes, you're going to stay and finish what you started."

"Lickin' toes," he repeated, running his tongue suggestively over his full lips. "I love it when you talk dirty to me, baby girl."

Davalyn choked back a laugh as she hunted underneath the covers for her shoes.

Twenty-one

Davalyn poked at the remains of a Christmas tree with the toe of her thick-soled boot. She bent down and picked up a charred doll. A gift, probably, for Mrs. Jensen's great-granddaughter. The tree was artificial and supposedly flame retardant. But nothing could withstand the destructive energy of the fire that had nearly gutted the home of the Jensens.

She knew the Jensens. They'd moved into the neighborhood when she was six years old. An elderly couple, kept mostly to themselves. But at Halloween, their house was always the most decorated house on the block. They didn't just come to the door when you yelled, "Trick or treat!" They invited you in. You could always count on a Dixie cup of hot cider and cinnamon sticks from Mrs. Jensen. For Thanksgiving, Mr. Jensen kept a live penned turkey that the neighborhood kids could come and feed and help donate to a petting zoo instead of munching on for Thanksgiving dinner.

As Davalyn tapped the stylus against the screen of her Palm Pilot, taking notes on the fire scene, Mason gathered evidence.

"That makes four," Mason commented.

"Put them in the lockbox," Davalyn said distractedly, thinking that he was referring to the evidence bags that he'd collected for her.

"Four fires this month in this area," Mason clarified.

"What are you talking about?" Davalyn looked up at him.

"I'm talking about the rash of fires in this area. Or haven't you noticed?"

"I guess I've been too busy investigating them to pay attention to their spread."

"You don't think it's strange that fire trucks have been called out four times in the month of November alone? All electrical. Granted, one of them was due to a space heater, but the others . . . strands of lights. Every last one of them. Damn shame that a few cheap twinkly lights can cause all this damage."

"More tragic than strange." She brushed the idea aside. For now, she was focused on this fire, this tragedy. This one had hit too close to home. By the time she, Cutter, and Bennett had piled into his truck and driven around the corner to the police barricade, the Jensens' wood-frame home was fully engulfed. Orange flames shot into the predawn sky, blotting out the moon and stars with thick black smoke. Cutter had gone immediately to the Jensens, huddled in blankets and their nightclothes, staring in disbelief and horror as their home tumbled to the ground before their eyes.

The look of disbelief and profound sadness snapped Davalyn out of the detached mode she sometimes went into when she was working a scene. They were an elderly couple. Retired on a fixed income. She wasn't sure if they had insurance. Even if they had, an insurance check couldn't replace the memories they'd collected in that house. Priceless memories.

This was the one time that Davalyn could not push the faces to the back of her mind. She knew these people. Felt the pain of their loss.

She bent her head back to her PDA, called up records of fires since she had started her job as an investigator late this summer. "More than four," she noted. There were several fires on which she had not been the lead investigator but were still tracked on her computer. She pulled up a report summary of each one.

"Since the start of November, there have been at least seven fires that the cause was ruled as electrical. Why didn't I notice this before?"

It irritated her that she hadn't seen the pattern. She should have noticed this. That was her job. Granted, as Mason had said, a few of those recent fires had been caused by space heaters. One had been caused by a candle left burning, and one good old-fashioned case of arson. Davalyn had been suspicious of that fire from the moment she arrived on the scene. Even after the building, a local pawnshop, had been completely destroyed, she could still smell the gasoline that had been splashed around the building. After her preliminary report suggested arson, she'd turned the investigation over to a certified arson investigator, someone who specialized in suspiciously set fires.

Maybe the types of fires were spaced out enough to where the pattern wasn't immediately obvious. She'd grouped them all mentally as just those kinds of things that happened when the weather turned colder. It was either accept the fact that the pattern wasn't intuitively obvious or face the fact that her head was so into Cutter McCall these days, she couldn't focus.

"Makes you think, doesn't it?" Mason lifted his eyebrows at Davalyn.

"Sure does," Davalyn agreed. "When we get back to the office, we're going to—"

"I know, I know," Mason muttered. "Call the lab and get the 411 on those strands of lights we sent for analysis on those electrical fires."

"You know me so well." Dav grinned and patted Mason on the cheek with a gloved hand.

"I know you well enough not to ask you any more questions right before I want to go home," he complained. "You need me to pull the full records on all of those fires, don't you?"

"I've got reference dates here in my PDA if that will help speed things up." She held up her hand to show him the tiny black-and-silver computer.

"Any chance that this can wait until a more decent time of morning?" Mason checked his watch. Five o'clock in the morning. The sun wouldn't be up for another hour. The bed that he'd crawled out of to respond to this alarm was calling to him—loudly and insistently.

"The sooner we figure out if the fires are connected in any way, the sooner you can take all the credit for figuring it out, Mason."

"Right now, I'd trade that glory for my thermal blanket and my lady curled up next to me."

"The blanket, I can take care of. The snuggle bunny you'll have to get on your own."

When he grimaced at her, Davalyn linked arms with him. "Come on, Mason. Look at it this way. Which would you rather do—lose a little sleep over the guilt of knowing that we might be able to stop more of these fires from happening or lose sleep over the excitement of knowing that you could be the next hometown hero? Might even get you a well-deserved promotion."

"Why? So I can be assigned to a wider coverage area? Risk never getting any sleep . . . or sex, for that matter, with regularity ever again?"

"It's not as bad as all that, is it?"

"Uh-huh. Tell me something, Davalyn, when was the last time you were on a date? A real date."

"I know things have been busy around here lately. But 'tis the season, you know that, Mason. Wintertime is our peak time for alarms."

"When isn't it our peak time?" He grumbled, then ticked off on his fingers as he continued. "In the summer, we get the careless brush fires. Folks flickin' their cigarette butts out the window, or freakin' illegal firecrackers shooting left and right. In the fall, it's the trash-burning kind of fires. Folks ought to know better. High winds, dry grass, lots of sparks. What do they think is going to happen? And for winter, we get this crap. Freakin' twinkling Christmas-tree lights."

"I'm sure the Jensens had inconveniencing you in mind when they decorated their tree for their grandkids, Mason," Davalyn said sharply. She looked out of what used to be the Jensens' living-room bay window and saw Cutter with a consoling arm around Mrs. Jensen. Her distressing wails had started afresh now that she could see that there wasn't much that could be salvaged from her home.

"Let's go, Mason," Davalyn said curtly. "We can talk about a career change on the way back to the office." If there was a connection between the fires and faulty lighting, she wanted to find it, and find it fast.

"Wait a minute. Why are you going in? This was your weekend off. You aren't even supposed to be here."

Davalyn shrugged. "I was already in the neighborhood. I might as well work the scene."

"Brownnoser," Mason teased. "You bucking for the Investigator of the Year Award?"

"I'm trying to make sure that you don't get called from your bed any more times than you have to, Mason," she shot back. "How's that for motivation?"

"Works for me," he agreed.

"Good. I'll pull the files from the computer at the office; you get on the phone and start calling in favors. Wake up a few lab techs and get them started on researching those cords. The first thing I want to find out is if their United Laboratories labels were authentic. If we can find out what lot the lights were sold from and where they were sold, we might be able to figure out whether they should ever have made it to store shelves in the first place."

"Whoa . . . whoa . . . hold up there, Sherlock Holmes. Aren't you getting a little ahead of yourself? You're stepping into areas that other agencies maybe should be looking into."

"We'll notify all the proper authorities as soon as we get our facts straight," she promised.

"Something tells me that it's going to be a long day."

"See you back at the office. I'm going to check in on the Jensens before I head in."

Mason held out his hand, laying it gently on Davalyn's arm. "Please give your neighbors my condolences. No time is a good time to have your home destroyed. But somehow, it always seems harder this time of year."

"I'll tell them," Davalyn promised. "Better watch

yourself, Mason. You might get a reputation as a caring human being if this keeps up."

"Don't let me fool you. It's just the sleep deprivation talking."

"And just when I was beginning to think there might actually be a heart beating under all of that bluster."

Twenty-two

As Mason headed back for his car, Davalyn stepped over the wall and crossed the front lawn.

She approached Cutter, asking, "Where are the Jensens?"

"Across the street at the Romanos'. No sense in them staying out here in this weather. Mrs. Romano is trying to get in touch with a relative. Mr. Jensen said something about having a son in Houston." Cutter stomped his booted feet to keep the blood circulating. He folded his arms, tucking his hands under his armpits.

"Speaking of sons," Davalyn said, glancing over at Cutter's truck. Bennett was wide awake now, wrapped up in Davalyn's blanket. His face was pressed against the glass on the driver-side window. She waved once. Cutter turned around, too, then gestured for him to lie down again.

"Yeah, I know. There's school tomorrow. I'd better get him back to bed."

"Not to the tree house," Davalyn said quickly. She pressed her lips together, wondering how much she should say without any definitive proof to back up the suspicions that Mason had raised.

Cutter recognized the look of indecision on her face, read in her eyes her concern.

"What is it?" he whispered.

Davalyn shook her head. "Not here, Cutter. Let's go where we can talk."

He grasped her by the elbow and started walking back toward his truck.

"What's the problem?" he asked, his tone low.

"I can't say for sure," she said, "but Mason pointed something out that we need to look into. It might take some other agencies to probe deeper."

"What's that got to do with the tree house?"

"The lights," she said, her tone strained. "The white lights that we strung up around the tree and along the balcony. Mason noticed that we've had three fires in this area that have all been electrical."

"And a couple of space heaters and a votive candle, if I remember."

"I know, I know. We've had our share of fires lately. More than Kemah deserves. But at least three fires with strands of Christmas lights as the suspected cause. It's not a smoking gun, no pun intended, but it's something that made Mason sit up and take notice. I'd feel better if we took the lights down from around the tree house. Just until I've done some more research."

"This whole neighborhood is lit up like Santa's workshop. You gonna go ripping down everybody's decorations?"

"No, of course not. At this early stage in the investigation, I can't even put out a public warning or initiate a product recall request. I don't have all the facts yet. All I can do is go on camera and remind everyone to be extra careful. You know, the usual warnings that somehow always seem to go unheeded by someone. Don't leave candles burning unattended. Make sure your live trees are watered. Turn off and unplug the lights. Don't leave them burning overnight." Davalyn used her on-camera voice and expression—a practiced mixture of sympathy and professionalism.

"I don't want to see any more of my friends and neighbors like this, so I'm starting with you and Bennett. I might be risking a little professional misconduct and bad judgment by leaking those suspicions without proof, but I'm willing to take that risk. I'm not playing with the lives of people I care too much about."

She wanted to hold out her arms, to hug Cutter close to her. She couldn't. She'd already received a few strange stares when she and Cutter arrived on the scene together. Any other time, she might have been able to explain the situation away. Not at three in the morning. Mason had been savvy enough not to mention it. But she could almost bet that by the time she arrived at the office, there would be at least half a dozen theories about what they were doing together.

Cutter took half a step toward her, then realized that they were under the watchful gaze of half the neighborhood.

"Thanks for the heads-up," he said.

"No problem. When I find out more, I'll let you know," Davalyn promised.

"You let me know if I can do anything to help, baby girl. You need somebody to help back you up, I'm there for you."

"I know you will be. Just keep an eye out on the next alarm. If it's electrical, I need to know ASAP. I'm putting my office on alert as soon as I get some information back from the lab. Now come on, McCall, let's give everyone something else to talk about by letting them see me drive away with you."

"Oh yeah. I can hardly wait for the tongues to start

wagging back at the station." Cutter rolled his eyes comically. He followed Davalyn around to the passenger side and held the door open for her. By the time he'd made his way around to the driver's side, he noticed the guys from his station gathering, pausing in groups of twos and threes from their work of shoveling through the debris. Some were openly pointing at Cutter.

"It's started already," he said aloud as he put the key in the ignition and started the engine.

"Started what, Dad?" Bennett asked through a sleepy yawn. Cutter made a face. He hadn't realized that Bennett was paying attention to their conversation. He wasn't sure he had an answer for his son.

"Stirring up a mess," Davalyn said quickly, grinning over Bennett's head.

Cutter chuckled softly. "You know they're gonna have a field day with this."

"I know," Davalyn agreed. "Are you okay with that?"

"Are you?" he challenged.

She shrugged. "If this is going to work, I'm going to have to be."

"Okay, then," Cutter said slowly. There was still a hint of doubt in his voice. "Just tell me how you want to play it."

"For keeps," she whispered to him.

Cutter turned his attention back to the road, but not before Bennett saw his dad give the kind of smile he only gave when Aunt Dav was around. Whatever it was that she had said to him, whatever it meant to him, it seemed to be the right thing. That tight-jawed, squinty-eyed, vein-popping look that he got when something stressed him out eased from his face. Aunt Dav had said something to him to take that look away.

Bennett leaned back and closed his eyes. He didn't

need to see anymore. Even if he did try to stay awake to listen, he didn't think he'd understand much of it. They were doing it again. Talking to each other without saying a whole lot. Almost like they had their own special code. Grown-up talk.

Bennett was glad that his dad seemed to settle on a woman who could talk to him like that. It had taken a while, and Bennett noticed what seemed to him a lot of women before his dad could focus on one. It would probably make his dad upset if he knew just how much Bennett really did know. It wasn't because he didn't try to hide some of it from him. He knew that his dad made sure that Bennett stayed out of it. The long list of ladies almost never came to the house while he was there, though the phone was always ringing. If not the house phone, then his dad's cell phone. And then there were the gifts that mysteriously appeared in the mailbox or on the front porch or left in the glove box of his dad's truck. His dad seldom said anything about the gifts or the women who left them, but sometimes when he was talking to Uncle Van at the shop, stuff slipped out. A name. A description. A decision on whether he'd call her back.

Strange, Bennett thought. But there weren't nearly as many calls since Aunt Dav started coming around. Not nearly as many presents, either. Bennett didn't think his dad minded. When he did call those women back to "thank them," he didn't always sound very grateful for the presents. Bennett didn't blame him. Some of the gifts, like candy or cologne, he could see his dad using.

Bennett especially liked it when he shared the candy with him. But other stuff he couldn't see his dad having any use for. Like that time he was searching for a flashlight in the glove box and wound up pulling out a pair of black underwear with a flower and candy tied to it with a long red ribbon. That was one time his dad *didn't* let him have the candy. Just muttered something about not sure where it had been and tossed the whole gift into the trash. Later that night, he'd heard him on the phone for one of the shortest conversations that he'd ever had. Like he was calling back because he *had* to. Not because he wanted to. He couldn't hear exactly everything that was being said, but Bennett knew by the tone. His dad laughed, but he wasn't happy. He was polite, but not friendly.

He didn't have to try too hard around Aunt Dav. Didn't have to try hard to be funny, thoughtful, or attentive—or any of those things that he'd seen his dad trying to be with some of the other women that he'd dated. Like that Shayla. He didn't have to try around Aunt Dav. He just *was*. That's why Bennett could almost rest easy between Dad and Aunt Dav. No matter what was going on, she could make it right. She would make it all right. *Almost all.*

The only thing that bothered Bennett about Dad and Aunt Dav was that he wished that they would make up their minds and decide that they were dating. That was the one conversation they couldn't seem to have. Friends. Pals. Buds. Play brother and sister. He'd heard it all coming out of their mouths. Couldn't they see that there was more going on between them than that? Why couldn't they? He could see it with his eyes closed.

"Come on, little man," Cutter said, gently shaking Bennett's shoulder. "Time to get you up to bed."

"Back to the tree house?" Bennett yawned and mumbled sleepily.

Davalyn and Cutter exchanged glances over his head.

"We'll have to finish the camping out next weekend," Cutter promised. He opened the door and stepped out, gathering Bennett up in his arms, blanket and all. "I promise."

Bennett was too sleepy to complain.

"Night, Bennett. Sleep tight," Davalyn hailed him.

"Don't let the bedbugs bite," Bennett murmured.

Davalyn pointed a finger at Cutter. "You too, Cutter. Big boys also need their rest."

When instead of heading for the house, she turned in the direction of her parked truck, Cutter called out, "Where do you think you're going, baby girl?"

"To the office. Mason's waiting for me, remember? That thing we were talking about before?" She raised her index finger and pointed at the lights surrounding the base of Bennett's tree house.

"Let him wait. You need to get some rest. You just got in from Dallas. You don't need to be on the road."

"Don't worry about me. I'm wide awake," she said, but not too convincingly. An irresistible urge to yawn made her tighten her jaw. Davalyn's vision blurred as her eyes became teary.

"Yeah, right. Any fool can see that you're dead on your feet, baby girl. You're not going anywhere until you've had at least a couple of hours of sleep."

"Stop fussing over me, Cutter. You need to get Bennett out of this weather and back into bed."

"Don't make me have to tie *you* to a bed, Dav." As soon as he'd said it, Cutter rolled his eyes at Davalyn's snort of laughter. He knew exactly what she was thinking.

"I love it when you talk dirty to me." She had whispered the same words he'd said to her as they were leaving the tree house. Then she blew him an affectionate kiss.

Cutter turned to his house, but not before Davalyn

saw the ear-to-ear, boyish grin on his face. He glanced back over his shoulder, watching her fit the key to the lock of her own front door and disappear inside. He didn't continue to his own home until the door closed firmly behind her. Then he climbed the short flight of steps, his boots barely making a soft, rhythmic thud over the wooden porch and up to the front door. Bennett stirred a little, mumbling in his sleep, as Cutter shifted to jingle the keys in his hand, searching for the house key.

"I know, little man," Cutter murmured, patting his son on the back to ease his dreamy concerns. He managed to get the door open, stepped inside, then kicked out behind him to shut the door again.

Cutter turned, started up the staircase leading to Bennett's room. Bennett's legs dangled long, swinging against Cutter's thighs as he walked. "Boy, either you're gettin' too big or I'm gettin' too old to pack you around anymore."

He pushed his son's bedroom door open with his elbow and set Bennett on his bed. Pulling the covers up over him, he checked in on him one last time. In another hour, it would be time to rouse him for school. Cutter didn't relish that idea. Thanksgiving break was over. It didn't seem fair somehow to make him go through the day all groggy and grouchy because he'd been dragged out of bed to a fire scene. Cutter nodded, making up his mind to let Bennett skip school this one day. Instead, he'd take him to the shop with him and let him sleep as long as needed.

"Speaking of work," Cutter muttered. It might not be too late to catch Dav before she headed out. Not that he thought he could stop her from going. He couldn't. Once she'd mentioned the possible danger from the lights, she'd had that determined look in her eyes—the same look she got when she wasn't going to take no for an answer. The same look she gave him when she insisted that he wasn't going to put down another nonsense word when they were playing Scrabble without her going to the dictionary and challenging him. It was the same look she got when she promised that she wasn't going to let him drive on her to the basket goal when they were playing one-on-one hoops. She'd rather plant her feet and take the blocking foul rather than make it easy for him to get past her. It was also the same look that made him keep his money in his pockets so that he wouldn't pay for her meals when they all went out together. Stubborn. The girl was just plain stubborn. It was one of the traits that drew him to her. She knew what she wanted. Made it very clear. And what she wanted was *him!*

Cutter took the stairs, two and three at a time, hoping he could get to her before she pulled out of the drive. All thoughts of getting her to try to catch up on sleep had gone out of his head. All he wanted to do was see her again.

He swung open his front door, not exactly running but not taking a leisurely walk, either, and stood at the end of her drive. He arrived in time to see the flash of brake and reverse lights as she put the truck into gear and started to back out of the driveway.

Davalyn's eyes met his in her rearview mirror as Cutter slammed his hands on the tailgate of her truck to make sure that she was aware of him.

She reached for the gearshift, put the truck in park, but didn't turn off the engine.

"Knucklehead," Davalyn murmured, but she was

smiling, shaking her head as she pressed the control to lower the window.

Cutter approached the driver's side, leaning in. Resting his forearms on the door.

"What is it, McCall?" Davalyn said, using her businesslike voice.

"I just came out to tell you to be careful this morning, Dav."

"You came all the way out here to tell me that?"

He shrugged. "Sure. Why not?"

"Let me let you in on a little secret, McCall. I'm a big girl. I can take care of myself. Can tie my own shoes and everything."

"You're teasing me. But I know you haven't had much sleep, Dav. I don't have to tell you what the statistics say about folks who drive on just a couple of hours' sleep. I don't want to have to respond to a call about a driver who fell asleep at the wheel and wound up a charred mess on the highway."

"Cutter, sometimes you say the sweetest things," Davalyn teased. She laid her hand gently on his cheek. "I'll be fine. I'll grab some coffee, keep the windows down, and turn the radio up loud."

"Call me when you get there to let me know that you've made it, baby girl."

"I promise," she said earnestly. Davalyn started to reach for the gearshift, but Cutter leaned in—filling the cab of her small truck. He filled her sight with the breadth of him, her nostrils with his unique scent. And when he touched his lips to hers, he filled her heart with sheer joy. Davalyn knew what that simple gesture meant. There was no conflict in his desire to kiss her. No second-guessing. No wondering if he was doing the right thing. He was doing the only thing he knew to show her how much he cared.

His caring communicated itself in that simple kiss. A sweet caress that spoke more of patience than passion. It was a kiss that was practiced but not mechanical, thorough but restrained. Cutter's hands remained firmly planted on the door. His knuckles tightened in his effort to maintain his distance at an invisible barrier.

Davalyn leaned into him, deepening the kiss, testing the barrier. She opened her lips, easing her tongue past the edge of her teeth to touch his lips. *Ummmm* . . . Her mind drifted, carried upon the wave of emotion. *He tastes so good. So good.* She wanted more. So much more. Davalyn moaned against his lips, communicating her frustrated desire. "Maybe I won't go in to work so early," she muttered, unclasping her seat belt.

Immediately she sensed the change in Cutter. She felt him stiffen, as jolted by a surge of electricity. His fingers clamped so tightly on the door, she imagined him having the strength of the Incredible Hulk to crush metal and fiberglass to a mangled mass. She had no doubt that he would have pulled away if she hadn't reached behind his head and drawn him even closer to her. She twisted sideways in her seat, pressing her breasts against his chest. Subtly, seductively, she moved up and down, creating a mounting friction that was both pleasure and pain. The heavy fabric of her sweatshirt was a silent whisper on the early-morning air as she moved against him.

"Ah, baby girl. This is crazy," Cutter growled. "I can't keep doing this! Somethin's gotta give."

"I'm giving. I'm giving," Davalyn said, her tone strained. "You're just not taking, Cutter."

"Is that what you want?" Cutter said raggedly. "For me to take you?"

"Hello!" Davalyn said, knocking him on the back of his head with her knuckles. "What do I have to do? Draw you a map? Have it play out on the six o'clock news! I'm in agony in here, Cutter. Literally climbing the walls of this truck. And it's all your fault, damn it. You and your good-bye kiss. You knew damn well I couldn't let you get away with that."

Cutter reached in. His arms wrapped around her back. He leaned back, literally pulling her from the cab, his mouth never leaving hers. He didn't stop pulling until she was out of the truck and her feet rested on the concrete driveway.

Yet Davalyn hardly felt her feet touch the ground, would have sworn in court that she was floating on cloud nine. All she knew was that she was in Cutter's arms. She was where she wanted to be—where he had to have her.

As Cutter pressed her back against the door, Davalyn vaguely remembered hearing the low hum of the motor and the vibration of the engine racing. Something told her to reach inside, turn off the key. Conserve fuel. Protect the air.

"Wait . . . wait," she gasped, leaning back, and stretching her arm for the key. Cutter's hand, caressing, massaging her rear end, was a distraction. Her fingers fumbled at the ignition. When she couldn't reach it, she straightened and maneuvered Cutter around so that she could open the truck door. His lips never left hers. He knew what she was trying to do, but he couldn't bring himself to release her long enough to do it.

Instead, he hooked his arm around her waist and shifted his knee so that Davalyn's legs parted. She was unsteady, unbalanced, but he held on to her, even as she felt herself falling backward onto the cloth cushions of the truck seat.

The keys jingled, slapping against the steering column as Cutter eased his bulk inside the tiny cab, settling over her. He reached behind him and shut off the engine. Mouth to mouth, chest to chest, thigh to thigh. Two bodies, one long line. Davalyn reached between them, easing the pressure and constriction of Cutter's jeans as her fingers worked to unclasp his belt. When her fingers touched his skin, a moan wrenched from Cutter's lips. Davalyn felt the shudder that rippled through his body.

"Maybe we should go inside," he suggested, looking toward Davalyn's house.

"We *are* inside," she insisted. "Come on, Cutter. Don't do this to me again. Nobody's around. No one can see us. Bennett's asleep. Donovan's out of town. There's just you and me and . . ." She reached above her head and opened her glove box. Cutter didn't have to guess what he'd find. He reached inside for the box of condoms resting on top of the collection of maps, proof of insurance, and paper napkins from the many fast-food restaurants she frequented.

"You carry these around for the hell of it?" He growled his charge with more than a hint of jealousy.

"Check the box, McCall," she retorted. "Never been opened." Davalyn grinned at him, her dark eyes sparkling with mischief. "Just like me."

Cutter swore. Instead of calming him, cooling him, her admission made him want her even more. He removed the plastic outer wrapper from the box, took out a single packet, and then set the box on the dashboard within easy reach. He stared at the packet for several seconds, waging a debate.

Davalyn didn't say a word. Didn't try to sway him one way or the other. But the longer he sat there, she knew the further he was withdrawing from her emotionally. It was only a matter of time before he withdrew from her physically as well.

With a sigh, heartfelt and heavy, she decided to end the debate. She sat up and kissed him on the cheek. Closing her hand over his, she folded his fingers around the condom.

"Hang on to this," she whispered. "When you're ready, let me know. You know where I'll be."

The look he gave her was filled with gratitude. And something else. She didn't get the chance to question him when the truck suddenly flooded with light.

"Oh, crap," Cutter said, shielding his eyes to look into the rearview mirror. "Van's back."

Twenty-three

For most of the morning, all Cutter saw of his closest friend was of his back. It didn't matter from what angle or from what area of the shop he was coming from, whenever Cutter saw Donavan, Van turned away from him. The silent treatment was a noticeable change from early this morning, when Donovan had exploded when he saw him and Davalyn together. If it hadn't been for Dav, literally dragging Donovan, Cutter was sure that they would probably still be swinging at each other even now.

Cutter had taken mostly a defensive posture, backing away and deflecting most of Donovan's strikes. He didn't want to get mad. Even when Donovan had landed a lucky punch on the side of his head, he'd kept his cool. It wasn't easy. That last punch had actually stung him, made his vision blur, but the names that Donovan had called him hurt more than the punch. He knew that if he had gotten mad and swung back, he could probably take Donovan with a single punch. Maybe two. Break him in half with a little effort. His friend was wiry, but tough. Still, he'd never wanted things to go that far.

He had never fought with Donovan. Not physically, that is. They argued all the time over stupid stuff—which basketball team had the best point guard, whether or not KFC really did use experimental animals in their special recipe chicken, which comedian was funnier— Eddie Murphy or Richard Pryor. Those were the kinds of arguments that got superheated, could go on for days, and usually ended up with them laughing hysterically after forgetting what the argument had been about in the first place. But they never, ever resorted to putting hands on each other.

As kids, they used to scrap all of the time, but that was when they were both closer in size, weight, and body build. A fight now could do some serious bodily damage.

If their nonverbal arguing was noticeable to the rest of their employees at the shop, Cutter didn't know. One thing he did know, you couldn't run a business that way. By lunchtime, things were getting worse. And Cutter knew that there was no way he could hide the rift between him and Donovan from the rest of the employees. The message was loud and clear—something was up between the bosses. The rumor mill started spinning, fast and furious, when Donovan used their people to pass messages along to Cutter. Sometimes verbal. Sometimes written on little yellow sticky notes. Van made it pretty obvious to everyone that he didn't want to talk to Cutter right now. He couldn't even stand to look at him.

This was a series of firsts for Cutter. Van had never been *that* angry with him. Then again, this was the first time that Cutter had ever given him reason to be. They'd always shared everything. Apparently, Cutter thought ruefully, sharing his sister only went so far. Cutter could understand Van's apprehension. He loved his sister and had often said that he didn't think any of the guys she'd presented as friends or dates were good enough for her.

Something was always wrong with them. Too tall. Too short. Too stupid. Too stuck-up. Now that Cutter had put himself in the contention, Van had looked at him and suddenly found him lacking.

Cutter shook his head. He'd just have to convince his friend that whatever flaw he thought he saw, whatever flaw he actually had, he could change. He would change for Davalyn. He would just have to get over it. Because he wasn't going to give up either Bowers sibling. They were each intricately part of his life. Without either, he didn't know what he would do.

Marquez, the youngest and most inexperienced of their employees, wasn't quite sure what to do when he brought the last message to Cutter. Couldn't help reading what the note said when he passed it to him, even though he tried his best to appear as if he hadn't. The message was a single word. A single word that compared Cutter to a definitive piece of male anatomy.

Cutter crumpled the note in his hand. "This is crap," he muttered. And it had to stop. Anything Van had to say to him, he could say it to his face. Though the irony of him not being able to tell Van that he'd fallen in love with his sister escaped him at the moment. It escaped him in a cloud of heat and steam, which he imagined poured out his head, as he said, "Marquez, do me one and keep an eye on Bennett for me, huh?"

"Sure thing, boss," Marquez said, glad to perform any task that would get him out of the middle of this mess.

"He's in the break room watching cartoons." Cutter indicated with a nod toward the area. He reached into his pocket and pulled out a couple of bills. "Take him across the street and get him some lunch, will ya? He likes his burgers plain. Just meat and bread."

"Just meat and bread," Marquez repeated.

Cutter glanced up at the office, where he thought he'd seen Donovan go. "And if he wants to play a little while in the play area, let him play as long as he wants. Don't worry 'bout your time sheet. Lunch is on me."

Cutter crossed the main work floor and went up the metal stairwell that led to a row of offices that overlooked the production area. He took the stairs slowly, trying to appear calm. His booted feet sent ringing echoes throughout the work floor as he brought his foot down hard. Cutter's hand clamped down on the handrail, seeming to pull himself up each stair, almost as if he could squeeze out his anger before he reached the last step. Out of the corner of his eye, he could feel the eyes of employees watching him. Some of them openly. They simply stopped whatever tasks they were performing and tracked his progress.

He approached the frosted glass door stenciled in large letters with the name of the company and Donovan's name in smaller letters beneath. His impulse was not to bother with knocking, just fling the door open and barge through. He restrained himself. If he didn't show respect for Van, even through his anger, he could bet that how he treated his friend would be picked up by the employees.

So, with more effort than he imagined he could ever muster, he stopped short of putting his fist through the frosted glass as he knocked before entering.

"Yeah? What is it?" Donovan called through the door. Cutter almost grinned. That was more words than he'd spoken to him at a single time all morning. That had to count for something.

Cutter turned the knob and pushed the door open. He stepped through, closing the door behind him. Then, holding the crumpled sheet up in front of him, he said, "I got your message."

Donovan had been on the telephone when Cutter entered. He spoke into the receiver, pointing at the guest chair across from his desk. "Sure, that will be fine. Bring the car to the shop and we'll take a look at it . . . unh-huh. Unh-huh." He cradled the phone between his ear and shoulder and shuffled through papers on his desk. Pantomiming a writing motion, he then pointed at the pen tucked into the front pocket of Cutter's work coveralls.

Cutter passed the pen to him while Donovan turned over an invoice and started to scribble some numbers on the back. "Sure. Not a problem. See you then. Looking forward to it."

While Donovan placed the phone back on the receiver, Cutter took a seat, stretched his legs in front of him, and folded his arms across his chest.

"Guess who that was," Donovan said, indicating the phone.

Cutter shrugged his broad shoulders, partly to convey his disinterest and partially to ease the knot of tension that had settled with agony between his shoulder blades. "I haven't got the foggiest idea."

"That was your friend Shayla."

"Shayla? What did she want?"

"She's got a friend who has a car, an MGB Midget, that she wants looked at. It's got a little rust and the upholstery is patchy. I told her to come on by."

"Good."

"Maybe not. Maybe you shouldn't be here when she gets here, Cutter. I don't want her to make a fool out of herself trying to get to you when it's obvious you don't care about her."

"That's not fair, Van."

"Hey, I'm just keeping it real, bro. You don't care for anybody but yourself."

They sat in relative silence for several seconds while Donovan collected his notes and Cutter collected his thoughts.

Cutter finally broke the silence. "It wouldn't be the first time I've been called out of my name, Van," Cutter said softly. "But not by you. Not like that."

"What else am I supposed to think?" Donovan retorted. "I come back and find you screwing my baby sister."

Cutter leaned forward in his chair. "What's the matter with you, Van? I told you that nothing happened."

"What's the matter with me? What the hell's the matter with you? I saw you . . . had the condoms all laid out on the dashboard like some kind of lunch buffet line. You didn't even have the decency to go inside the house. Just whipped it out . . . out there in the open for everybody to see like she was some back-alley whore."

Cutter shot up, knocking the chair halfway across the room. His jaw clenched, forcing out each word. "It wasn't like that, Donovan. So help me . . ." He pressed his lips together and clenched his fists. "Look, say what you want about me. I can take it. But don't you talk about Dav that way. She's your sister, but that doesn't mean you're the only one who can love her."

Donovan stood up, too. Planting his hands on the desktop, he leaned into Cutter's face. "Don't you lie to me, Cutter."

"Have I *ever* lied to you, Van?" Cutter asked, his voice strained and earnest. "Tell me. Have I?"

Donovan opened his mouth to speak, but Cutter stopped him.

"I'm not talking about that time you were in the fourth grade and I took your lunch. I'm talking about being truthful when it really matters. You know me better than I know myself. Could I lie to you, and you not know it?"

Lowering his eyes, Donovan couldn't meet Cutter's gaze. "I *do* know you, Cutter. You're my friend, my brother. But I know how you are with the ladies. Since losing Angela, you go through them like water. I love you, man, but I don't trust you with my sister. I don't want you messin' over Dav like you do those others."

"First of all, I didn't lose Angela. I let her go. I had to. Being with her was killing me. Our being together was hurting Bennett. I wasn't going to put him through what you and Dav went through because your folks didn't have the good sense to get out sooner."

"What gives you the right to judge my folks, Cutter? They took you in like you were one of the family."

"I know that. Don't you think I'm grateful for everything Mr. Bowers did for me? He gave me a job. Helped me through night school. Helped me build a future for myself and my son with this business. Your mom made sure that I had something to eat every day. I'm not saying they didn't love me. But look at them. Look how they couldn't hold their love together. Their bickering made you want to run away to chase after some singer."

"Some singer? Oh, so you wanna dis Whitney now, too?"

"Don't try to change the subject. We're not talking about Whitney Houston. We're talking about Dav."

"No, we're not. That subject is closed." Donovan made a slashing motion with his hand. "I'm telling you, Cutter, you keep your hands off her. Just stay the hell away from her."

"I'm not going to do that, Van. I can't."

"What do you mean, 'can't'? You will, Cutter. I swear you will, or I'll break my foot kickin' your ass."

"Then you'd better get used to walking on crutches," Cutter retorted. "Because I'm not giving her up. Not for you. Not for anybody."

Donovan blinked and sat down limply in his chair. He rubbed his hand over his jaw. "You really mean that, don't you?"

"Yeah. I mean that. I care about her, Van. I would never hurt her . . . or disrespect her."

"But you touched her. You touched my sister. You put your hands on her. What kind of brother would I be if I let you do that?"

"Last night when you showed up, I admit it looked a little . . . suspicious. But you have to believe me. The only thing that happened between us was the decision to dial it down a little, back off . . . until . . . well . . . until the time is right between us. You get what I'm sayin'?"

"You really care about her, Cutter?"

"I'm in love with her, Van. I can't put it any plainer than that."

"When did all of this happen? Where was I? How come I didn't know? I mean, we all hang out together. Pretty much live in each other's houses. How come I couldn't see this coming?"

"I don't know when it happened. I can't say for sure. I've always had feelings for Dav, I guess." Cutter shrugged. "Even when we were kids, something was there. But she was always a kid, you know. A seventeen-year-old doesn't look at an eight-year-old the same way. But when that eight-year-old suddenly turns twenty-seven, things change. I've changed. Why haven't you seen that, too?"

"Tell me something, man," Van began hesitantly.

"Anything."

"Was it her idea or yours? I mean, did you push up on her or did she come on to you?"

"It wasn't like any of that, Van. I wish I could explain it. One day, we just looked at each other and we kinda knew. We just knew. That doesn't mean that I jumped all over her the first chance I got. I thought long and hard about what it would mean if our relationship changed. I mean, we're family. We're friends."

"And?"

"And what if we crossed that line and it didn't work out, could we go back to being just friends? I thought about that for a long time."

"Almost never happens."

"That's what I thought. But I care about her, Van. I want to be with her. I'll just have to make sure that if we do this, if we get together, I don't screw up. This time, I'm gonna make it right. I swear I will."

Donovan watched Cutter's eyes. If Cutter had been right about one thing, Donovan did know him. He could look into his friend's face and know when he was trying to pull a fast one. He knew when he was full of it. And he knew when his friend was telling it straight. Donovan hadn't seen this look in a very long time. Not since they were so much younger. Cutter was in love—deeply, inarguably. It happened to be with his sister. He couldn't wish a finer woman on his friend.

"Oh, man," Donovan groaned. "So what happens now? Are we just gonna have to build a tunnel connecting our two houses? We might as well. We practically all live with each other anyway."

"So are you okay with us?" Cutter asked.

"I guess I'm gonna have to be. Dav's a grown woman.

She can make her own decisions. But if you hurt her, Cutter . . . If you ever give her a reason to cry, I'm coming after you. Don't forget, I know where you live."

"You know that works both ways, don't you? Just to let you know, sometimes I can hear you guys yelling at each other over there."

"We're that loud?" Donovan made a face.

"Let me put it this way, if you don't want her borrowing your shirts, why don't you just buy her some like them? And cut out all that rasslin'. If she says the word, I'll be over there to take you down."

"You'll try," Donovan snorted. "I almost had you on the ropes this morning, Cutter."

"You must be crazy," Cutter shot back. "The day you can take me . . . "

And so the argument went on for the rest of the day. *But at least,* Cutter thought each time he and Donovan verbally sparred with each other, *we are talking to each other again.*

Twenty-four

When Julian called her at work, Davalyn's first impulse was to hang up on him. She read the number that flashed on her cell phone caller ID and groaned.

Not now. I don't have time to deal with this right now. She had enough on her mind. With Donovan and Cutter going at each other, pressure to discover a link—if any—between the recent fires and the strand lights, and pulling off the Kwanzaa performance at the community center, she had enough to think about.

She let the phone ring until she knew the voice mail would pick up. The phone was silent for a few minutes, then started to ring again.

"You're not gonna answer that?" Mason's voice was muffled through the partition separating their cubicles.

"Nope," she called back.

"Why not? Did you and your firefighter boyfriend have a little fight or something?" Mason put the clues together—the rumors he'd heard about Davalyn and Cutter arriving and leaving together at the last alarm, her tense expression when she stormed in this morning, and her heated discussion with her brother on the phone not long after she got in. Words like "grown woman," "causing a scene," and "get a life" had made their way through the thin cubicle wall.

"Mind your own business, Mason," Davalyn said. She wadded up a piece of paper and lobbed it over the top of the partition.

"You missed," he informed her. When the phone started to ring for the third time, Mason thumped on the wall. "You wanna do something with that, Davalyn? How's a man supposed to get any work done around here?"

"You can start by closing down that solitaire game you've been playing for the past hour," she retorted.

"How'd you . . ." he began.

"Too many mouse clicks," she said knowingly. "Next time, try tapping on the keyboard a couple of times to throw me off. Wouldn't hurt to have the printer fire off a couple of sheets every now and then, either."

Davalyn flipped open her phone. It was Julian again.

"What is it, Julian? This isn't a good time to talk." She tried to brush him off, not give him a chance to bring up the incidents of this past weekend.

"I really need to see you, Dav. Just let me try to explain."

"I already know what happened, Julian. I was there, remember?" she whispered crossly, glancing over at the cubicle partition.

"But not for all of it. You don't know what happened after you left."

"I don't need to know. That's between you and your folks. I don't want to have anything to do with it anymore."

"You mean with me?" he asked shakily.

"Whichever way it plays out." Davalyn didn't have to try too hard to make herself sound cold.

"Please, Dav. Please! Don't give up on me now. I need someone to talk to. You're the only one who understands. Can we meet somewhere to talk? Go out for coffee or something?"

"I . . . I don't know, Julian. I've got a lot of work to do." She hesitated.

"I won't keep you long. I just want to talk to you. Just talk. You see . . . I've told them. I told them both. Told them everything."

"Oh, Julian," Davalyn said softly. She didn't have to ask what he was talking about. He must have finally opened up to his parents. "How did they take it?"

"How do you think?" he said, his voice ragged with emotion. "That's why I have to see you. You're the only one who ever made me feel like I wasn't a freak. Can you meet with me, Dav? Please."

"Uh . . . okay, sure. Where do you want to meet?"

"You pick the place." His voice was flooded with relief. "I'll come to you."

"Fine. There's a restaurant on Highway 146. T-Bone Tom's. Is that okay with you?"

"I think I know where it is. See you there around twelve-thirty, then?"

"Twelve-thirty," Davalyn repeated, then noted the lunch appointment on her PDA. Not that she would forget the appointment. Julian's tone was so imploring, she didn't think she would be able to get it out of her head. Davalyn was meticulous about the time she kept. Between her hectic work schedule and her sorority charity work, she wanted to make sure that all time was properly accounted for.

"Yo, Mason!" she called to him over in the next cubicle. "I'm heading out to lunch. Be back in about an hour."

He stood up so that she could see his eyes and the

tip of his nose over the gray partition. "I should have that lab report back for you by then."

"Can I bring you anything back?"

"Yeah, you can bring me back some chicken-fried steak." He smacked his lips. "Umh-umh-umh, that's what I want."

"You got it."

"And a large iced tea."

"Iced tea," she repeated.

"And a side order of hush puppies. No, make that peas . . . No, I want . . . Hmmm, I wonder what the vegetable of the day is."

"Why don't you call ahead and I'll pick it up before I head out?"

"Well, you offered," he said, sliding down out of sight again.

Davalyn saved the files on her work computer, then shut it down. She slid her arms into the sleeves of her leather jacket and slung her purse over her arm. "Be back in a bit."

When she stepped outside, Davalyn braced herself against the gale wind coming out of the north. It brought with it a chilling cold that cut through her clothes straight to the bone. She lowered her head, bowing to the force of the wind, and increased her pace to her truck.

As she sat inside, allowing the engine to warm a little before pulling out, Davalyn cursed her decision to go out in this weather. Normally, when the temperature turned colder, Davalyn loved weather like this. Gulf coast Texas winters weren't exactly a picture-perfect winter wonderland. No fresh powder snow. Few opportunities to play ski bunny, snuggling up to her favorite ski instructor after a full day of downhill racing or more radical snowboarding. On any given street in Kemah or along Galveston's seawall, you could find decorations draped across verdant green palm trees. Joggers, bikers, or skaters flitted by in shorts and tank tops. Christmas tree vendors hawked their wares to convertible SUVs, the tops pulled down to let the salty gulf breeze flow through. Depending on which weather front passed through, temperatures ranged from the eighties one day to the sixties the next.

So, at the first opportunity, when the weather dropped below sixty degrees, it was the perfect excuse to pull out the seasonal clothes. She could shake out her long-sleeved shirts and her turtleneck sweaters and wear her leather pants without feeling overdressed. She might be dressed for a winter blizzard in the morning and have to strip to lighter clothing in the afternoon, but just knowing it was winter gave Davalyn's spirit a lift. It was the season of giving and forgiving. Which is why, she thought ruefully, she had agreed to see Julian again. He'd screwed up, yeah—but who hadn't in a lifetime? If she considered herself his friend, if she cared for him, she would hear him out. She would treat him with the respect and sympathy that he'd always shown her when she needed a shoulder to lean on.

Davalyn adjusted the heater so that it wasn't blowing full force, then put the truck into gear. Twenty minutes later, she was circling the parking lot of the restaurant. It was more crowded than she thought it would be for a day like this and it took her a while to find a spot.

She was grateful for her sport truck's tight-turning radius as she pulled up, then backed into a spot nestled between a van with the Texas Department of Transportation logo painted on the side and a truck and trailer carrying cutting crew equipment. As she squeezed from the driver-side door, Davalyn was careful not to snag herself on the protruding rakes, picks, and shovels stacked inside green heavy-duty plastic trash bins secured to the trailer with rope and wire meant for clothes hangers.

As she pushed open the door to the restaurant, Davalyn's mouth started to water at the fresh-baked smells wafting from the kitchen and the dessert display counter. Top that with the heavier scents of grilled T-bone steaks, shrimp po'boys, chicken-fried steak smothered in white cream gravy, jumbo shrimp bubbling in seafood gumbo, steamed vegetables, and fresh-brewed coffee still percolating and Davalyn was tempted to call Mason back and tell him that she'd be back in considerably more than an hour. He might not see her again until after the dinner hour.

"Can I help you, hon?" The greeter approached her.

"Two, please. Nonsmoking," Davalyn answered.

"Booth or table?"

"A booth is fine. Can you put me close to the door? I'm waiting for someone. I don't see him here yet."

"Not too close to the door, hon. That wind's nasty out there today."

"Ooh, I know it," Davalyn said, rubbing her hands together. "It must be close to forty degrees out there."

"Thirty-eight. Weatherman says it may drop to below freezing tonight. And just when my tea roses were starting to take on a second bloom."

She gestured for Davalyn to take a seat. "Here you go, hon. Somebody will be right with you to take your order."

"Thank you." Davalyn picked up the menu, but she already had an idea of what she wanted. She'd seen the dish when she passed by another table. A huge bowl of chili topped with cheese and onions. Plenty of onions. If that didn't keep Mason's nose out of her business, nothing would.

She set the menu down and folded her hands on top of the table. As if that gesture were a secret sign to the wait staff, her server came up to the table, pencil and ordering pad already in hand.

"Good afternoon, ma'am. Welcome to T-Bone Tom's. I'm Frankie and I'll be your server today. Can I start you off with something to drink or an appetizer? Our special today is our appetizer sampler."

"Water with lemon, please," Davalyn ordered. "And I'd like to hold off on the rest. I'm waiting for someone to join me."

"Yes, ma'am. I'll bring your water right out. When you're ready to order, let me know."

Davalyn's booth was situated four rows back from the door. From there, she could watch the inbound traffic into the parking lot from the bay window that ran the length of the restaurant. Car after car passed, but none were Julian's. By quarter to one, she was starting to get concerned—and hungry. She waved the server over and ordered the day's special appetizer. Within ten minutes, a plate of delectable cheese sticks arrived at her table. There was more than enough for two. After Davalyn dipped the first one into the creamy white ranch sauce, she convinced herself that if Julian didn't get there soon, that appetizer was going to be demolished by one and only one.

At one o'clock, her cell phone rang. "Hello?"

"Hi, Davalyn. It's Julian."

"Where are you?" she demanded.

"Sorry, I'm running late. I got stuck behind an accident on Interstate 45. All but one lane was blocked off. But traffic's moving again now. I should be there soon. Twenty minutes or so. Go ahead and order for me. A salad or something. Vinaigrette dressing on the side."

"Okay. But once you get here, I'm sorry that I can't stay long. I'm working on something that's going to take a lot of effort and I need to get back to the office."

"Oh? What is it?"

"Just work stuff, Julian," Davalyn said. She didn't mean to be secretive, but without hard facts to back her up, she wasn't going to start rumors and put her professional reputation on the line. "Hang up the phone and drive, okay? We can catch up when you get here."

Davalyn ordered for both of them again, put in Mason's order for his sandwich and drink, then scaled back her munching on the cheese sticks. Twenty minutes. She could wait twenty minutes. By the time Julian arrived, their server had just set their orders on the table.

Julian approached their table, shrugging out of his full-length wool charcoal-gray coat. Davalyn's eyes swept over him. As Bennett would say, her spider senses were tingling. Something wasn't quite right, though she couldn't put her finger on it. It was Monday afternoon, but Julian hadn't been at the office. That is, he wasn't dressed in his usual work attire.

Instead of the designer suit in either navy blue or gray with subtle pinstripes, crisp button-down Van Heusen shirt, and silk tie, he was dressed today in casual cowboy chic. He wore a dark gray cotton turtleneck sweater, acid-washed blue jeans, and a wide black leather belt, with a silver cowboy buckle the size of her fist accenting his trim waist, and dark gray ostrich-hide boots. He hadn't shaved today, either. It looked as if he hadn't shaved in a couple of days. His smooth and creamy-as-butter complexion was darkened around the mouth and chin by the beginning stages of a beard.

Davalyn blinked. That wasn't Julian's normal style, but he seemed to be carrying it off well. She had to admit, he looked good in a bad-boy kind of way. Not that she went for that type. Or maybe she did. Something about that look he'd adopted was vaguely familiar to her.

Davalyn mentally shook her head. Maybe her mind was playing tricks on her. It was just a style. And Julian was, if anything, always stylish. Though, she'd never seen him this deliberately casual. Even when they were hanging out with their college friends, kicking back watching a football game, shooting pool, or having one of their all-night domino tournaments, he was always dressed like he'd just stepped from the pages of *GQ*.

He seemed comfortable with this new look, almost confident. It was the kind of confidence that exuded an understated sensuality that spoke loudly to the female patrons of the restaurant. She noticed a few heads turning when he walked by. Davalyn almost wanted to laugh out loud. If only they knew. Julian was as oblivious to the open stares he received by those women as he was to the plates of triple hamburgers or sizzling porterhouse steaks.

When he sat across the table from her, she was smiling.

"Cheese stick?" she said by way of greeting.

"Is this a peace offering?" he asked, lifting a fine eyebrow at her.

Davalyn shrugged. "It's hard to have angry words over fried cheese." She dipped a stick into the sauce again and popped it into her mouth.

Julian sighed. "Dav, about this past weekend—"

"Exactly," she interrupted him.

"Excuse me?"

"You said it, Julian. Past. Let's just put it behind us."

"I can't. I can't believe the way I acted. I don't know what got into me."

"Whatever it was, it was probably about one hundred eighty proof, costing about a thousand dollars a bottle."

"You know I'd never hurt you, don't you? Not intentionally. We've been friends for too long. And when you wouldn't talk to me, wouldn't even return my phone calls, I thought I'd lost you forever. I can't apologize enough."

"So why try? I know you weren't yourself, so I'm willing to let it go."

"I've been having nightmares, Dav. Thinking that I'm capable of . . ." His voice dropped to a low whisper.

Davalyn leaned in close, too. "Give yourself a break, Julian. You didn't rape me."

"But I could have," he insisted.

"I doubt it." She snorted. "If you hadn't gotten off me when I told you to, I was this close to turning you from bass to soprano."

"Ouch!" He grimaced, leaning back.

"I'm a woman in a tough, male-dominated business, Julian. Not that I expect anyone to ever get out of line, but I don't take anything for granted, either. I can defend myself if I have to. Though, with you, I never thought I'd have to."

"And you shouldn't have had to. But like you said, I was drunk. And pissed off. My father wouldn't stop pushing me . . . wouldn't stop telling me how to run my life. He has this old-fashioned, chauvinistic idea of what a man should be. And when he saw you ordering me around, making demands, it embarrassed him. No son of his was going to let a woman tell him what to do."

"You bought into that crap?"

"Something happens to me when I go home. I always feel like I'm twelve years old. I can't stand up to him."

"You said that you told them. What did you tell them?"

"Everything. I told it all. After you left, he started on me again, started calling me names. Weak, useless . . . It was ugly."

"I'm so sorry, Julian, that you had to go through that."

He shrugged. "I told you what kind of people they were. But they're my parents. I had to stay."

"But you didn't have to put up with that."

"Somehow, somewhere deep inside, I figured that out. I snapped. I started yelling back, pushing back in my own way. I told them how they didn't have the right to judge me, they didn't know me. The real me. That's when I let it all out. You should have heard me, Davalyn. You would have been proud of me."

"I am proud of you, Julian," Davalyn insisted. She reached out, took his hand in hers, and squeezed.

Julian closed his eyes, shook his head slowly back and forth. "You should have seen the looks on their faces. My mother just sat there, her mouth open. She couldn't even look me in the eye. And my father—well, I thought a vein was going to pop out of his forehead. He even had the audacity to ask if I was on drugs. Can you believe that, Dav? He'd rather think I was a crackhead than accept that I'm gay."

"Then what happened, Julian?"

"He threw me out. And when I got to the office this

morning, I found that the locks had been changed. I couldn't get in."

"Can he do that?" Davalyn asked, her expression horrified.

"It's his building. He can do whatever the hell he wants. My employees were on his payroll. Wouldn't even talk to me. All the meetings I'd scheduled this week, potential clients, were all canceled. My clients were steered my way by his firm. Everything I have is his. And now it's gone. Just like that!" He snapped his fingers.

"Julian, is there anything I can do? Anything I can do at all? Say the word and I'm there."

"Just be there for me. Be my friend."

"You know that I am," she said, raising his hand to her lips and kissing it. "If you need a place to stay, my house is open to you."

"Besides having you by my side, the only thing I'm thankful for is that the condo is in my own name and paid up through the summer. Otherwise, I'd be out of a job and a home. Besides, I don't think Cutter would like me hanging around you. He doesn't seem like the type to want to share you."

Cutter! Davalyn realized that she hadn't thought of him since morning. She wondered how Donovan and he were getting along. She'd meant to call to check up on them during lunch, but she'd gotten distracted by Julian and his problem.

"You're my friend, Julian. Like it or not, he's going to have to cope. Speaking of coping, are you going to be okay for a while? I mean, I hate to ask, but how are you for money? I've got some saved. Whatever you need, Julian, is yours."

"I'm not going to take money from you, Davalyn. My

father called me a lot of things, but one thing I'm not is
a bloodsucking leech. I'm not a moocher. I'm a grown
man. Time for me to start acting like one. I've got a degree and I've got my health. I'll make it."

"I said it once, I'll say it again. I'm so proud of you."

"I want you to remember that when you see me on
television, like all of those other ambulance-chasing,
contingency fee lawyers feeding off your injuries and
your fears to scrape up clients."

"Some of those lawyers are very good, Julian. Don't
knock them."

"Enough of my problems. What about you? You said
that you were working on something giving you problems?"

Davalyn shrugged. "I can't really say much about it,
Julian. I don't have all the facts in line."

"If it's confidentiality you're worried about, who am
I going to tell?"

"It's not that, it's just . . . well . . . Okay, here's the
deal. My coworker Mason noticed that we've been having a rash of fires lately. Several within ten miles of
my own neighborhood."

"Mason figured that one out all by himself?" Julian
had met Mason once or twice and had immediately determined that if he ever became a *Jeopardy* contestant,
he would love to go up against two others just like
Mason Scott.

"He may not be a quick thinker, but he's methodical.
He saw the pattern before I did. I have to give him credit
for that."

"Which was?"

"Strands of lights. Christmas tree lights, of all things.
Like the kind that twinkle and flash and glow. I'm having the lab determine if they were all the same kinds of

lights. From there, we'll see if we can backtrack where they were sold, who manufactured them. Until I know more, I can't initiate a public-safety warning."

"You can't sit on that information, Dav. People could get hurt, not to mention the damage to their property."

"I'm not planning to. Hopefully, we'll know something from the lab today and can notify the proper authorities, the media, anybody who'll listen so we can get those hazards off the street."

"How many homes would you say have been affected in the past, oh, two months?" Julian asked.

"I can't be certain. I have to look back through my records."

"And when will you do that?"

"I told you, I was working on that now. Why?"

Julian shrugged. "Just curious."

"A lawyer is never just curious, Julian. Not at your high dollar price per hour. When you ask a question, you're hoping for a decent return on your investment in time. So, why'd you ask?"

"Any way I can get a look at those records, Dav?"

"Only if they've become a matter of public record. I can give you some Internet link sites where you can pull up that kind of information. It might be sketchy. Some of the families are still working with their insurance adjusters, so I would say you wouldn't find very much."

"What about your notes?"

"Excuse me?"

"Your notes of the fire scene. Can I get a look at those?"

"What would you need to see those for?"

"So I can talk to some of the victims. Sounds to me they have a cause of action to sue. Either the manufacturer or the retailer who sold the defective equipment, I haven't decided which to name in the suit. Maybe both . . . Yes, that sounds better. If I make it class action, it'll make a bigger impact, so the media will pick it up faster. I'll call that consumer advocate reporter from Channel 11."

Davalyn sat back, staring across the table at Julian. She couldn't quite believe what she was hearing.

"What are you talking about?"

"I'm talking about getting some clients on my own, Dav. Isn't that what you were just encouraging me to do?"

"But I can't give you my records, Julian."

"Why not?"

"Because, for now, they're confidential."

"I won't name my source. I'll just say that my private investigator gathered the information for me."

"You don't have a private investigator. Your father took him off your payroll," Davalyn reminded him.

Julian grinned at her. "I was talking about you."

"I said I'd help you, Julian. And I will. But I won't break the law. When all the fire reports become public record, then feel free to interview and chase clients to your heart's content."

"By then, it'll be too late. As soon as the media gets wind of this, it'll be all over. Every shyster lawyer from here to Dallas will be out trying to get a piece of that pie. I'm just trying to get my share before the sliver gets too small to do me any good."

"I can't help you with that, Julian."

"You said you would do anything to help me." He was pushing.

"Don't be stupid, Julian. I'd do anything except help myself get fired."

"If Cutter McCall asked you to bend the rules a little for the sake of friendship, would you?"

"He would never ask me, Julian."

"Oh, I forgot. The perfect Cutter McCall never had a minute of trouble in his life. . . ."

"Funny, that's the same way he feels about you, Julian. You guys are so different, yet you think so much alike. Sometimes it amazes me. At least, I thought you two were different. What's with the new look, Julian?" Davalyn asked. The puzzle of Julian's new style tickling at the back of her head pushed to the forefront of her thinking.

"You like it," he said, making it more a statement than a question of her opinion.

She shrugged. "Yeah. I'm just surprised to see you dressed that way."

"I thought it might put you at ease . . . seeing that's the look you seem to be going for these days."

Davalyn's mouth formed a perfect O without making a noise. Now she got it. Now she knew why "the look" was so familiar. On any given day, Cutter might be dressed something like this. Jeans one day, cowboy boots another. She seldom paid much attention to what he wore. Cutter's clothes were a natural extension of who he was. He seldom dressed to make a statement. He didn't have to. He didn't dress for fashion; he dressed for function. Yet, it suited him. He dressed to suit himself, not because he worried about what others thought of his fashion choices.

That didn't mean that he was a slob—not by any stretch of the imagination. Davalyn had to admit that when he did clean up, like the night of Bennett's birthday party, the man looked damned fine. Julian had looked good, too, when he walked through the door. She noticed it right away, but now she understood that he dressed with a hidden agenda. He'd mimicked Cutter's style to get her attention, and maybe her support.

"Julian, you need to be who you really are. That's the man I know. That's the man I've chosen as my friend. You don't need to be anybody else for my support. But I'm still not going to break the rules for you. Not for you, not for him. You got that?"

"Got it," Julian said.

Davalyn checked her watch. "I've got to run now, Julian." She reached for her wallet, but Julian waved her aside. "I'll take care of lunch today, Davalyn."

"Are you sure, Julian?" she hesitated.

"It's a trifling twenty-dollar lunch bill, Davalyn," Julian snapped. "For God's sake, leave a man a little dignity."

"Fine. Have it your way. Next time it's on me, okay?"

"Fine," he echoed, then pushed his salad away, virtually untouched. He waved their server over and asked for the check.

Davalyn picked up her leather jacket. Julian stood up and helped her put it on.

"Make sure you stay in touch, Julian." She made him promise.

"Don't worry, Davalyn. You'll be hearing from me probably more than you want."

Twenty-five

Julian said that he would stay in touch, but Davalyn didn't hear from him for several days—even after she called him and left messages for him to return her calls. She just wanted to know if he was making out all right. She wanted to know whether he lacked for anything.

Two weeks went by before Davalyn finally heard from him. Even then, it wasn't a personal conversation—just an e-mail message that told her that he was extremely busy and would call her later. He didn't have any clients yet, but it was only a matter of time. She'd immediately written back, suggesting that maybe it was too soon to go out on his own. Maybe he should think about joining a firm. Start small, work his way up to partner. Being his own boss might sound attractive, but it might not be practical at that time.

He didn't respond to that e-mail, but Davalyn knew that he'd read it. She'd set the return receipt flag when she sent her message back so that she would be notified as soon as he'd opened it. When he didn't respond, Davalyn decided to back off.

"Let him sulk," she said in irritation. She wasn't going to jeopardize her job to help him. By not responding to her, he was only being stubborn, sulking like a baby. When he was ready to talk to her again, Davalyn was certain that he'd contact her.

Their conversation at the restaurant faded to a memory as she devoted all her mental energy into her own life. Her days were filled to capacity. Only days away from the Kwanzaa opening ceremony at the community center, the list of to-dos in her PDA threatened to overrun the limited memory.

"No . . . no . . . I think the programs with the *Nguzo Saba* inserts should go on the chairs," Davalyn said into her telephone. She cradled the phone between her neck and shoulder as she reached into the refrigerator for the carton of eggnog Donovan had left chilling since that morning.

"We can have someone at the front with extras if we need to," she continued. "But if we pass them out as folks file in, we're gonna cause a jam-up at the entry. It'll be smoother going if we let everyone come in and find their seats. Uh-huh. Uh-huh. I know it."

She then reached for a tray and filled it with enough mugs for Donovan, Cutter, Bennett, herself, and a face that she'd never thought she'd welcome into her small circle of friends—Shayla Morgan.

"It'll be bad enough with people milling around, looking for friends or family who've saved them seats. Some of the programs may slide off the chairs, but we'll let the cleaning crew worry about those."

"Come on, Dav, you're gonna miss the best part!" Donovan called from the den. He sat on the leather sectional, his arm placed comfortably around Shayla's shoulders.

Covering the mouthpiece with her hand, Davalyn shouted back, "Hold your horses. I'll be there in a minute, Van! It's not as if we haven't seen that movie a thousand times."

"You can never watch enough Whitney," Shayla agreed with him.

"A woman after my own heart," Donovan said. He'd invited Shayla over to the informal get-together. She came bearing gifts, a DVD of *The Preacher's Wife* and a small bottle of aged rum to add a little liquid holiday "cheer" to the eggnog.

Davalyn poured the mugs of eggnog and nodded as Cutter appeared in the kitchen. *Take this,* she mouthed to him, then turned back to the telephone conversation.

"Wait a minute, Kimmy. Who said anything about us coming in during the playing of the Negro National Anthem? You wouldn't go walking around at a baseball game while the National Anthem was being played, would you? What do you mean the program was printed that way? I checked the copy before we sent them to print. Oh, she did, did she? I know Margot didn't go off and change those programs behind my back. What else has she done that I expressly asked her *not* to do?"

Cutter stood at the entrance, grinning, mocking her with his hands on his hips and working his neck, while Davalyn picked up a mug and threatened to hurl it at him.

"We have two choices," Davalyn said after a frustrated sigh. "We can go against the program that we've been marching to for months and throw Tonia into a tizzy, or we can gather them up and reprint them. Uh-huh . . . no, I don't think so. Somebody should still be there. If not, I've got a key. I'll go over myself and pick them all up if I have to."

Cutter took the tray to the family room, but was back in the kitchen before Davalyn hung up the phone. He pointed his thumb over his shoulder, indicating the family room and the movie. It was the first time in a couple of weeks when their packed schedules allowed them all to be together like this.

Davalyn flashed him an apologetic look and mouthed, *I'm sorry.* But what else could she do? She couldn't proceed with a mistake in the program. It didn't look professional. Even though Kwanzaa was a celebration, it was a serious, dignified ceremony. She would not accept shoddy work from herself or her coplanners.

"Don't tell me," he said, folding his arms and leaning against the entry. "You gotta go."

"Kwanzaa starts in three days. These are the last-minute details that are killing us. I want to make sure that everything's right."

"So what now?"

"I'm going to the community center to see what I can do about fixing the problem."

"Then I'm going with you," he announced.

"Cutter, you don't have to do that." Davalyn felt bad enough that she had to miss out. She didn't want to involve Cutter, too.

"Sit down. Enjoy the movie with Bennett. Didn't you say that he was going to spend Christmas Day with Angela? You should be spending as much time with him as possible."

"And I will. But it's almost eight o'clock, Dav. Isn't the center closed now? I don't want you running around the center by yourself. It's nasty out there tonight."

"I won't be by myself. Kimmy said that she was on her way, too. If she can get in touch with the other sisters, I'm sure they'll show."

"Kimmy runs on CP time. You'll be there two hours

before she even gets in her car. I'd feel better if someone was with you."

"Are you volunteering?" She always welcomed his
company.

"I'm not talkin' Kriss Kringle, baby girl. Don't leave
without me. Just let me get my coat."

"Do you want to bring Bennett with us? I don't plan
to be there for very long."

"Nah, let him stay here." He glanced over his shoulder again. "From the looks of things in your family
room, Van and Shayla need a chaperon. With Bennett in
there watching over them, he'll make sure they behave
while we're out."

"Can you believe it?" Davalyn laughed, then clamped
her hand over her mouth. She didn't want her voice to
carry. "Van and Shayla."

"Stranger things have happened. You have to admit,
they make a good couple."

"You mean that, don't you?"

"Sure." Cutter shrugged. "Why wouldn't I?"

"I don't know. I just thought it might be a little awkward for you."

He shook his head. "What? You mean more awkward
than you and me?"

"You got a point." She nodded once.

"Van's my boy. As long as he's happy, I'm happy."

Cutter joined his friends in the family room. He
picked up his coat from the back of the sofa, warning
both Bennett and Donovan to behave while he and
Davalyn went out for a while.

Donovan raised his eyebrows. "Where do you think
you're going?"

"Dav has some list-minute details at the community
center for the Kwanzaa ceremony," Cutter explained.

"If you need us, you've got our numbers."

"I got your number, all right." Donovan wagged his finger at Cutter. "Don't be out too late. Remember, 'tis the season to be celibate."

"That's celebrate," Cutter corrected. "And we'll be back before you can say, 'Dudley.'" He directed their attention back to the movie and Denzel Washington's angelic character. Cutter could tell by Bennett's interested expression that he was paying more attention to what he and Donovan weren't saying as much as to what they were.

Bennett sat on the floor in front of the large-screen, high-definition television with a bowl of popcorn in his lap and a large, sticky candy cane licked until the bottom had became a sharp point stuck between his lips.

"Be good, Bennett. I'll be back soon." He leaned down and kissed his son on top of his head.

"Later, Dad," Bennett mumbled around the candy, barely turning his head.

"And no more candy for you. Somewhere, out there, your dentist is dancing for joy with visions of cavities at eighty bucks a pop swimming around his head."

"Would you believe that it's sugar free?" Bennett looked up, grinning with sticky pinkish lips.

"Not in a million years. Now watch your movie. See you kids later." Cutter gave a nod to Shayla as he went out through the kitchen.

Davalyn stood near the door, with her PDA in hand, jingling her keys. "Come on, Cutter. Let's go. Get the lead out."

"I'll drive," Cutter offered, wrapping his arm around her waist as he ushered her through the door.

"Thanks," Davalyn murmured, tapping the stylus against the screen. She pulled up a file, squinting in the evening light to read the information on the screen. "I knew I'd changed that program," she muttered. "Somehow they must have gotten the wrong file. How in the world did I—"

"You know, you pay more attention to that computer than you do to me," Cutter said. "I'm starting to get a little jealous, baby girl."

Davalyn looked up, smiling apologetically. "Sorry. I guess I have been a little one-track lately. I just want this program to go well. It's the first time I've ever planned something like this. You think you've got every detail covered and then something like this happens."

"Don't sweat it. We'll gather the programs all up and get the right ones printed before the ceremony."

"If we can find a printer that isn't closed or swamped with orders," Davalyn said, chewing nervously on her fingernail. "The first time we sent our request to the printer, they told us they had a backlog of wedding invitations to print. That's why we went to the simple flyer-style print job and hand-folded the things ourselves instead of the fancy creamy-colored ones with the gold lettering. *Oooh,* those were so pretty!"

"Think about it this way, you saved a little money."

"Yeah, but I'm still putting Band-Aids on paper cuts. If they tell us they can't squeeze us in now, I don't know what I'm going to do."

"Stop borrowing trouble, will ya?" Cutter admonished, holding the door open for her.

Davalyn climbed in, then leaned over to open the driver's side for him.

"It'll work out all right. I know if anybody can fix it, you can, Dav," he continued as he slid into his seat and buckled himself in.

"I knew there was a good reason why I let you hang

around, Cutter. You're so good for my ego. Thanks for the vote of confidence." She smiled warmly at him.

"Keep looking at me like that, baby girl, and I'll be stuffing more than the ballot box before long," he replied, raising his eyebrows lasciviously at her.

Davalyn burst into open, gleeful laughter. "Promises, promises. One of these days, Cutter, I'm going to call your bluff. And then what are you going to do?"

Cutter started the engine and allowed it to warm for a few minutes. "I'm not bluffing," he said quietly. He draped his arm across her shoulders and tried to pull her close. When the seat beat that was stretched across her lap got in the way, Cutter stabbed at the button to release the catch. "I've been tryin' to get you alone to myself all evening. There's something we need to talk about, Dav. Why don't we go inside?" He wasn't looking at Davalyn's home, but his.

She placed her hand against his chest. "I thought you told Van that we'd be right back after we left the community center."

"He knows me better than that." Cutter chuckled.

"So, you lied. Shame, shame, shame. And this close to Christmas. Bad boys get a lump of coal in their stockings for fibbing. Or didn't you know that, Cutter McCall?"

"Beats the lump right here," he said raggedly. Cutter placed her hand in his lap and squeezed gently. "Come on, baby girl. Why don't we slip over the back fence, hmmm?" He nuzzled her neck and whispered a few suggestions to her that had her squirming in her seat.

"Maybe Kimmy and the others can do without me for an hour or so," Davalyn suggested, lifting her face to him for a kiss.

Cutter leaned toward her, then stopped abruptly when

Bennett suddenly appeared on the passenger side, tapping on the window.

Davalyn and Cutter flew apart.

"Bennett!" Cutter snapped, lowering down the window. "I thought I told you to stay with Uncle Van—what are you doing out here?"

"Getting away from all the kissin'," Bennett replied, his face filled with disgust. His huff of displeasure hung in the air in soft white puffs of mist. "Kissin' in the movie. Kissin' on the couch. And now I come out here and catch you doin' the same thing."

Davalyn lowered her head, shielding her eyes with her hand. Her shoulders shook as she tried to suppress her laughter. Cutter slid his hand over his face, wiping away his grin.

"What do you want, son?" he repeated.

"Dad, can I go with you and Aunt Dav? Please?"

Cutter twisted his face to object, but Davalyn reached for the door handle. "Sure you can, little man. Climb on in." She lifted the seat, letting him settle in the small bench seat behind them.

"I promise I won't get in the way. So, if you guys wanna keep kissin', you can." He scooted up and rested his elbows on both headrests. His head swiveled back and forth, looking at his dad and then at Davalyn.

"Put your seat belt on," Cutter said gruffly.

"Yes, sir." Bennett sat back and buckled up as Cutter put the car in reverse and backed out of the drive.

The report on the radio had said to expect temperatures in the low forties. Yet, it mentioned only a 30 percent chance of rain. Davalyn had a good mind to call up the station and curse out that announcer.

The mixture of rain with sleet made driving dangerous. She stopped counting after she saw the fourth wrecker truck hauling away a crumpled car or truck.

"Maybe we should turn back, Cutter," she suggested. She kept her tone low, just under the loud vocals of Bennett as he sang to the music on the radio.

"We're halfway there," he said. "It's up to you. You want me to turn around?"

"Halfway there?" she repeated, biting her lip with indecision.

"Be there in about ten minutes," he judged, then adjusted the wipers to keep up with the heavier rain.

"We'll keep going. But keep an ear on the weather report. If it sounds like it's getting worse, we won't hang around the center for too long. Programs or no programs."

"Sounds like a plan."

Davalyn fell silent after that to keep from breaking Cutter's concentration. Though the weather was nasty, she trusted his skill and knew that he would do whatever was necessary to keep them safe on the road.

Cutter pulled up to the front entrance. "You two hop out while I go park," he said, leaving the engine idling.

"Button your jacket, Bennett," Davalyn directed over her shoulder. She checked that his hood was pulled over his head, then zipped up her own jacket. Setting her red wool Kangol cap on her head at a jaunty angle, she opened the door.

"Careful, Dav. That walk looks slippery," Cutter said, eyeing the walk suspiciously.

"Don't worry," she said. "If I learned anything in Maryland, it was how to walk on icy sidewalks."

Cutter grasped her by the elbow and pulled her close for a brief kiss before releasing her. "You ain't in Maryland anymore," he reminded her.

"I'll be careful. Come on, Bennett." She took his hand in hers and stepped carefully onto the slick path. Though her legs were much longer, she took smaller, careful steps to keep him from running ahead of her. She made a mental note to request to have the sidewalk sprinkled with anti-icing salt to try to avoid injuries.

She fished her keys out of her pocket and opened the entrance.

"Kimmy!" she called out to her friend. "Hello! Anybody here?"

"Don't sound like anybody's here," Bennett said, looking around the darkened main hall.

"She's probably running a little late. Come on. You want to give me a hand? We need to collect all of the programs from the tables and take them with us. That way, by the time your dad gets here, we'll be halfway done."

"All right, Aunt Dav," Bennett said, taking off in a sprint around the room.

"Wait, Bennett. Wait for me." She increased her pace.

Bennett ran, shouting to hear himself echo in the large, open room. His voice bounced off the walls as he raced up and down the rows between the tables, collecting the programs as he streaked by. Several of the flyers fluttered up in the air and settled to the ground.

Watching Bennett run reminded her of the time that she, Van, and Cutter ran up and down Galveston's east beach, throwing food scraps to the seagulls and watching them fly around in a circle and squawk for their attention. Van wanted to throw the birds tablets of Alka-Seltzer, knowing fully well that the birds' stomachs couldn't handle it. One or two tablets were enough to make the birds explode, but she'd cried so hard, made such a big fuss, that Cutter had stopped him. He'd even lifted her up on his shoulders so that she could toss the food scraps higher into the air. Davalyn was certain that she'd fallen in love with Cutter that day. Just like she was certain that she'd fallen in love with him the day before that one. And the day before that one. If she didn't fall for him at least three times a day, she was sure she wasn't getting her U.S. daily recommended allowance of her next-door neighbor. "My hands are full, Aunt Dav. Where do you want me to put them?" Bennett asked.

"Upstairs, there's a table draped with the kente cloth and a sign with the letters AKA." She pointed toward the loft. "There's a box underneath that table with some of our props for the ceremony. Can you bring that box down for me? Inside, there's a *kinara,* that's a fancy candlestick, and a box of candles. When you bring the box down, I'll show you how to put the candles together, in what order, and what they mean."

She collected the extra programs that he'd missed, then turned to the entryway, looking for signs of either Cutter or her friend Kimmy.

"Hey," Cutter hailed her as he entered, shaking the water off his jacket. "How's it going?"

"Bennett's been a big help. Next time, I know to have him on my committee when I have a huge project like this."

"No sign of Kimmy?"

"Nope. I was about to call her and tell her if she hasn't already left, don't bother. I don't want her to come out here in this weather if she doesn't have to."

"I'd be willing to put money on it that that idea has already occurred to her," Cutter said dryly.

"Oh, ye of little faith," Davalyn said. "Kimmy wants

this ceremony to go off without a hitch just as badly as the rest of us."

"Rest? What rest? The ceremony's in three days, but you're the only one I see out here, Dav."

"Yeah, I'm the only idiot who couldn't leave well enough alone." Davalyn laughed at herself. "The consummate perfectionist, I just had to drag us out here to fix those programs. But we're not going to be here long. Bennett's already collected most of them for me."

"Where is that boy, anyway?" Cutter asked, looking around.

"I sent him up to the loft," Davalyn said, pointing back over her shoulder. "He's getting out the candles for the *kinara.*"

Cutter shook his head back and forth and *tsked* at her.

"And just what is that supposed to mean? Why are you shaking your head at me?"

"I can tell that I need to help you work on your parenting skills. You left a nine-year-boy alone with a lighter and a stack of candles?"

"You don't think he'd—" Davalyn began, but Cutter had already brushed past her. His steps quickened to the sound of Bennett's frightened cry.

"Dad! Aunt Dav! Somebody, help! *Help!*"

Twenty-six

A wave of cold fear washed over Davalyn at the sound of Bennett's voice. Panic settled in the pit of her stomach and made her freeze for a second—only for a second while a thousand worst fears found their way to her imagination. What *could* she have been thinking? An active child left alone with easy access to matches and implied permission to experiment with them. It was a parent's worst nightmare. Though Bennett should have known better, brought up with fire safety rules drilled into his head from the time he could crawl, that didn't excuse her responsibility from making sure that he remained safe.

She stood rooted to the spot, fearing, dreading, regretting. Then something clicked in her brain. Something born of professional training and maternal instinct. She followed as Cutter sprinted past her. By the time they headed for the stairs, they were almost shoulder to shoulder. She let him take the lead to avoid stumbling over him.

As soon as they entered the loft, Davalyn quickly took stock of the scene. Every physical sense was alert to give her the information that she needed to react. Though smoke stung her eyes, she saw Bennett on his hands and knees, crawling away from the display table that was completely ablaze.

Good boy, Bennett, she thought. He had remembered something of his training. Stay low, away from the hanging layer of thick, choking smoke.

Raising her shirt to place it over her nose, mouth, and throat, she moved to intercept him.

"Bennett!" Cutter stood near the entry, frantically calling for his son.

"I've got him!" Davalyn waved to draw Cutter's attention to the far side of the room. She skirted around a row of stacked chairs. "Bennett, here I am. Come on, little man."

She reached down, grasped him by the waist, and gathered him up. Hugging him in her arms, Davalyn placed one arm under his bottom to support his weight—easily, naturally. She'd carried him like this more times than she could count. When he'd fallen asleep in front of the television, waiting for Cutter to come home, she'd picked him up off the floor and carried him up to his room just as she carried him now.

Davalyn started toward him.

"I've got him, Cutter," she assured him when he moved toward her. The look of relief and gratitude on his face pierced Davalyn's heart and brought fresh tears to her eyes.

She jerked her head in the direction of the blaze. *Go on,* she communicated without words. *Do your job.*

"Aunt Dav!" Bennett sobbed, his tear-streaked face pressed into the warmth of her neck. "I'm s-s-sorry. I d-didn't mean to. It was an accident."

"Sh . . . don't talk now. It's all right." She squeezed him tighter as she carried him out of the smoke-filled room. "Keep your head down, Bennett. Close your eyes."

Davalyn glanced over her shoulder, watching Cutter stoop and grab the metal legs of the table. The sound of metal scraping across the floor was barely heard over the burning snap of wood as he pulled the table away from the display behind it. Not soon enough. The seven-foot-tall, four-foot-wide, wooden trellis that had been used to present the *bendera* and other Kwanzaa symbols caught fire in several places at once.

"Cutter, be careful!" Davalyn warned. The wall started to sway, threatening to pitch forward on top of him.

"Get outta here!" he snarled, waving her out of the room.

Pushing the door open with her shoulder, she carried Bennett down the stairs toward the main entry.

"Dav! What the hell's going on here?"

"Kimmy!" Davalyn's voice was raspy and relief filled her as her sorority sister called out to her. "Here, take him out of here." She didn't take the time to explain but shoved Bennett into Kimmy's arms.

"You been smokin', Dav?" Margot said, wrinkling up her nose, waving her hand in front of her face.

"No, you idiot!" Kimmy snapped, already heading for the exit. "The place is on fire." She grabbed Margot's elbow and hauled her behind her.

"Call 911!" Davalyn shouted over her shoulder as she whirled around and started back toward the loft. She skidded to a halt in front of the kitchen, her eye catching the fire extinguisher case. Yanking the small red canister from the wall, she pulled the pin and squeezed the trigger, covering the wall and part of the sink in front of her with a frothy white foam. Davalyn didn't have time to check the tag that listed all of the dates the extinguisher had been tested. She only knew that it would have been useless of her if she'd gotten back to the fire and found the extinguisher was defective.

Sucking in a lungful of fresh air before going back upstairs, making sure she knew exactly where Cutter was before going forward, she used the rows of chairs as guides. Keeping her hand running along each row as she came behind him, she pounded him on his back to let him know that she was there.

Cutter whirled around. "Where's Bennett?" he demanded.

"He's safe," she assured him. "With Kimmy and Margot."

"I thought I told you to—" he began, but Davalyn shoved the fire extinguisher into his hands. No time for talk. He could fuss at her later for disregarding his order.

Cutter nodded, completely understanding. He turned around and aimed the hose at the display wall. Working his way in a sweeping motion, back and forth across the face of the trellis, with bursts of extinguishing foam, he circled around to the back of the display wall, trying to keep the flames from spreading.

Davalyn moved away to a safer distance, driven back by the hiss of steam and flying debris. One moment, Cutter seemed to have the blaze under control. The next moment, the flames spiked, leaping toward the ceiling. Davalyn didn't know whether to feel afraid or thankful when the blaze overcame his efforts. She settled on gratitude when the fire suppression sensors finally triggered the sprinkler system.

Finally! Certainly took long enough. She turned her face up to the ceiling, letting the icy water wash over her, and sent up a small prayer of thanks. She'd been careless, letting Bennett think that it was okay for him to play with the candles. It could have been worse. So much worse. Most of the damage would be smoke and water. No lives lost. No injuries.

No thanks to me, Davalyn thought glumly as Cutter approached her. He didn't have to say anything. She could tell by his expression that he was just as worried, just as frightened as she was. And Davalyn thought she saw in the tight downturn of his mouth an anger barely suppressed. She'd put his son at risk. His precious son. She didn't blame him. He had every right to be furious with her.

Davalyn folded her arms against her stomach, fighting the uncontrollable tremors brought on by her fear and the drench of icy water from the sprinklers.

Cutter trudged between the rows of chairs, dangling the fire extinguisher in his hand.

"Come on, Dav," he said, resting his arm against her shoulder. He drew her to his side to shield her from the force of the direct spray. "Let's get outta here."

As soon as he felt her tremble, he looked down at her, his face softening to concern.

"You all right, baby girl?" he asked, swiping at the water streaming down his face with his left shoulder.

She nodded. "You?"

"I could think of better ways to spend my day off."

"Oh, Cutter. I'm so sorry!" Davalyn burst out, pressing her face into his chest. "It's all my fault. I wasn't thinking. Bennett could have been hurt and it would have been because I was too busy."

"It's all right, Dav. It's all right," he soothed, squeezing her. Cutter dropped the extinguisher to the floor and stood, simply holding her. Davalyn stayed in his arms, content to be there, feeling safe and sheltered. She couldn't imagine what she'd done to be so deserving of his forgiveness. If the situations were reversed, she didn't know if she had it in her to be so compassionate.

"Bennett's fine," he said. "And it's all because of you." He placed his index finger under her chin to lift her face. His intention was to kiss her, to let her know that everything was going to be all right. Cutter shot her a confused look when Davalyn didn't look frightened or sad. Her dark eyes were shining. She bit her lip to keep the corners of her mouth from quivering up.

"You wanna let me in on the joke?" he asked, resuming the walk toward the exit.

"Us," she said. "You and me."

"What about us?" Cutter said, liking the way the word "us" sounded to him. He liked the way the word looked on her lips. Made him even more anxious to kiss her.

"You know we're never going to hear the end of this, don't you? The guys at the station are going to rag us to our graves."

Cutter stopped, considering the irony of the situation. He threw back his head and filled the room with his booming laughter.

It really wasn't a laughing matter, though. The community center director was understanding when notified and offered whatever assistance she and her sorority sisters needed. Still, Davalyn didn't know if they could get the center cleaned up in time for the ceremony. The walls on either side of the Kwanzaa display were blackened with smoke damage. The smell of charred wood permeated the air, the furniture, everything. Water from the sprinklers had completely destroyed the programs, even if she had decided to use them. It had taken weeks to collect all of their Kwanzaa symbols. Some of the materials were handmade and were donated just for this event. Her heart sank every time she thought what the fire had cost her, not only in lost time but in lost confidence. She'd been the project leader. Everyone pulled their weight, carrying out their assigned action items. Yet, she was ultimately responsible for the program's success. Or, as the case seemed to be, its failure.

She didn't know what she would have done if it hadn't been for Cutter and his unfailing support. He stood by her when she explained to the community center director how the fire had started. Hardly noticeable to anyone else, he saw her flinch when the fire trucks pulled up.

"Show time," Davalyn said, blowing out a heavy sigh. With his hand clasped firmly in hers, he made sure that if anyone even dared crack a smile at the situation, he pinned the culprit with a steady glower that promised a painful crack on the head.

When Kimmy and Margot crowded in on her, bombarding her with a thousand unanswerable questions, Cutter knew that Davalyn was struggling to maintain her composure. She had no answers for them but didn't want to appear helpless.

"What do you mean, you don't know? You'd better know, Miss *Thang*," Margot snapped after Davalyn expressed her doubt on whether they should proceed with the ceremony. "We've got city officials lined up, reporters from the paper and television, leaders of the church. Caterers starting to set up for at least two thousand. It's too late to call it off now."

"And where do you suppose we cram everybody, Margot? At the playland at Mickey D's? The Wal-Mart parking lot? Everywhere else is booked," Kimmy retorted.

"If you can't cancel and there's nowhere else to go," Cutter suggested smoothly, stepping between the two women, "why don't you see about making the community center work for us?"

"You got water on the brain, Sparky?" Margot sneered at him. "The place is toast. We don't have any programs. All of our decorations are gone."

"I know it looks bad now," Davalyn said. "Maybe it'll look better in the morning. First thing, we'll come back in and see what, if anything, can be salvaged. All right? We'll make the decision by midmorning. If there's nothing we can do, there's nothing we can do. I'll write up something tonight, just in case, and make sure it gets to the media if we have to cancel. With heavy enough radio coverage and some public-service announcements on the news, we should limit the number of folks who show up."

"Sounds like a plan to me," Cutter said.

"You'd agree with her if she'd asked us all to—" Margot began.

"Shut up, Margot," Kimmy cut her off. "All right, Dav. We'll play it your way. Everyone show up here tomorrow morning at six o'clock sharp."

"Six o'clock in the morning, Kimmy?" Davalyn couldn't help smiling. "That's a little early for you, isn't it?"

"I'll be here. And with bells on my butt." Kimmy grinned at her.

"I'd pay to see that," Margot grumbled. "All right. Six it is. My turn to bring the coffee and doughnuts."

Cutter and Davalyn didn't leave the scene until well after midnight. Wrapped in blankets and extra jackets,

Cutter, Davalyn, and Bennett piled back into her truck and headed home.

Davalyn didn't say much on the ride back. Wrapped in her blanket, she stared out the window, watching the street signs whiz by. Once or twice, she glanced behind her. Bennett was also wrapped snugly in a blanket and dozing. She reached behind the seat and laid her hand gently on him and readjusted the blanket to help him breathe easier.

When Cutter pulled into his own drive, parking Davalyn's truck behind his own instead of parking in her driveway, Davalyn raised a questioning eyebrow at him.

"Shayla's still over there," he said softly, and nodded toward her Mazda parked next to Van's Chevy truck.

"Bennett," Davalyn said, gently shaking the boy. "Come on, little man. You're home now."

Bennett mumbled something sleepily, then held out his arms as if he wanted to be picked up. Cutter unhooked his son's seat belt and gathered him up, blankets and all. Davalyn stepped out of her truck, leaned against the roof, and stretched out her hand to Cutter.

"Toss me my keys, will you, Cutter?"

"Why?" he asked, straightening. He tucked Bennett's blanket around him to shield him from the night air. "Where do you think you're going?"

"It's been a long day. I'm ready to crash," she said.

"What about Van and Shayla? You go up in there now, this late, you may walk in on something you don't want to see."

"I'll take my chances. I can go in through the back door and—"

"Nuh-uh." He shook his head. "You're over here tonight, Dav." Cutter nodded toward his own house.

"You boys. Always trying to cover for each other.

Come on, Cutter. Give me my keys. I just want to take a long, hot shower, climb into bed, and fall into a nice, deep coma."

"Nope. Not gonna do it. I gotta watch my boy's back."

"But—"

"No buts. You don't need to be over there. We need you over here tonight, baby girl. *I* need you."

"You what?" The words surprised her. Cutter didn't need anyone. Never had. He was always the strong one. Community volunteer. Father. Friend. Everyone's rock. He'd been all of those things for her tonight. Instead of pointing fingers at her, blaming her for putting Bennett in harm's way, he'd held her hand through it all. Yet, he'd said that he *needed* her. *Her?*

"You heard me," he said, giving her a crooked grin. He turned and started for his house. "You're here with me tonight, baby girl. And you may want to check your glove box before you come inside."

"The glove box," Davalyn echoed, ducking her head back into the cab. She pressed the button, then gasped in surprise when several boxes of condoms tumbled out of the glove box and onto the seat, spilling onto the floor.

"Ohhhhh . . ." She expelled a long breath of understanding. "You mean come inside."

Twenty-seven

"There are extra towels in the bathroom closet," Cutter said cordially. "Make yourself at home."

He was way too casual to ease Davalyn's raw nerves. He might as easily have told her to feel free to raid his fridge. She knew which bathroom he was referring to. It was the one that joined the master bedroom. His bedroom. She'd only been in there a handful of times, but never when Cutter himself was there. Once, while she was baby-sitting, she'd gone into his bathroom to find the hydrogen peroxide and bandages when Bennett scraped up his knees learning how to Rollerblade. She'd gone in another time when Bennett had stuffed too much tissue in the toilet. He'd called out to her for help, but not before water an inch deep soaked the bathroom rug and spilled over onto the hardwood floor of Cutter's bedroom. If ever Cutter had reason to question her parenting skills, it was that day.

"I'm gonna make sure Bennett's all tucked in," Cutter said, pointing over his shoulder. After leaving the community center, Cutter had taken Bennett immediately up to his room, stripped him out of his clothes, and eased him into his pajamas and into bed.

"Okay," Davalyn said, "give that little hellion a kiss

good night for me." She was surprised that he could sleep so soundly after all of that excitement.

"Will do." He started down the hall, then stopped and turned to address her. "Dav?"

"Yeah?"

"Keep the water running, baby girl."

Davalyn put her hands on her hips. "And what if while I'm in the shower, the water runs cold while I'm waiting?"

"Then we'll just have to find some way to warm it back up, won't we?" Cutter said, lifting an eyebrow at her.

"Oh," Davalyn said. "Ask a stupid question."

She pushed the door open to Cutter's bedroom, then closed it. But not all the way, she left it open just a crack. She didn't want to completely shut him out of his room. At the same time, she didn't feel comfortable having him just walk in on her, either.

Strange that I should feel this way, Davalyn thought. *This nervous, this apprehensive.* Wasn't this the moment that she'd hoped for? Wasn't this exactly the scenario that she'd dreamed about? Maybe she could have done without the fire, and the police report, and Margot's catty remarks questioning her ability to finish their project—but the end result was still the same. Cutter wanted her. He needed her. He made sure there was no mistaking his intention. Tonight he would have her. She could tell by the way he looked at her. Something in his eyes. Blatant. Deliberately sexual. Twice as hot as the fire that ravaged her Kwanzaa display.

Six months ago, she would have killed to have him look at her that way. Yet, she could tell by her heightened anxiety that, given the slightest provocation, she could open up Cutter's bedroom window, shimmy down

the trellis, and be back in her own room before Cutter
could say to Bennett, "Don't let the bedbugs bite."

It was different when she'd been the pursuer. When
she was in control, she didn't have a nervous bone in her
body. She knew that she'd wanted him. Didn't plan to
stop pursuing until she'd had him. Now Cutter wasn't
running from her anymore. No more hesitation. No
more doubt. She'd gotten what she wanted. But as her
father used to say, her eyes were bigger than her stomach. She didn't know if she had the guts to go through
with it.

This is silly, Davalyn berated herself. She was a
grown woman. She knew what she was doing. And if
she didn't feel comfortable, she didn't have to go
through with it. There was nothing stopping her from
turning right around, marching down those stairs, and
out the back door. Nothing but the weight of her own
desire tying her down to the spot.

Davalyn took a deep breath to steady herself. She
moved through the bedroom, ignoring the huge four-
poster oak bed that dominated Cutter's bedroom. She
figured she'd be paying attention to it soon enough.
Right now, she wouldn't let the lure of the plump down-
filled pillows or the handmade flying-geese-style quilt
distract her from washing the worries of the day away
from her. Then again . . .

She reached inside her jeans pocket and pulled out a
handful of the condoms that had spilled out of the glove
box. Nobody but Cutter could have planted them there,
though when and how she didn't know. And so many.
Why so many? Unless, of course, the man had some serious, lovemakin' marathon on his mind. What had he
said to her at the Aquarium restaurant the night he
begged her not to go home with Julian? "*A good bottle*

of wine, smooth jazz . . . and what ever comes after," she recalled.

No "what ever." She knew exactly what would come after. Would make sure of it. Davalyn slid the condoms under a pillow, patting the overstuffed, down-filled headrest before continuing onto the bathroom.

"Gonna wash that disaster right outta my hair," Davalyn sang as she stepped onto the glazed deep blue ceramic tile floor in the bathroom. She lifted her sweater over her head and stepped out of her shoes. She had to sit on the edge of the toilet to pry off her jeans. Cutter's shower was separate from his tub. She scooped up her soggy, sooty clothes and dropped them into the antique claw-footed tub, shoes and all. For the moment, she remained in her bra and panties while she opened the glass-front shower stall door and started the water. The shower tray hanging from the spigot head was filled with an assortment of soaps, shampoos, and Cutter's shaving utensils. One bottle caught her attention.

"Didn't expect to find you here," Davalyn murmured. She reached her arm inside the stall and lifted out a bottle of her favorite scented body wash. Honeysuckle. Not a scent she expected to find in Cutter's stash at all. Nothing manly or rugged about honeysuckle. If anything, she expected Cutter to use something with essence of pine or car exhaust. She twisted the cap, noting by its tightness that it had never been opened.

Just like me, Davalyn thought with poignant emotion. *But not for long.*

She placed the bottle back in its shower caddy, reached in front of her to unhook her brassiere. She tossed it across the bathroom, where it fell across the edge of the tub. Her matching pale rose floral nylon panties were the last to go.

The bathroom was completely misty with steam by the time she stepped underneath the spray of the water.

"Ummmm." Davalyn hummed deliciously, letting the water wash over her. Her dark hair was plastered to her skull as she moved her face back and forth. The water was too warm, stinging her across her shoulders and stomach like thousands of fiery pellets. But she didn't adjust the temperature. Not yet. She needed it that warm to relax her and drive away the chill that had settled into her bones.

Davalyn folded her arms across her breasts to protect them until she could get used to the temperature. She spun around, letting the jet spray pound her on her back. The water streamed down across her rear and trickled down the back of her legs. Smoothing her hands over her face and neck, down across her chest, and kneading her breast, Davalyn symbolically pushed away the coating of grime that she imagined settled over her skin. She pressed her palms against the flat planes of her stomach and continued downward on the tops of her thighs. She lifted one leg, scraped against her calf. Then she lifted the other, giving it the same treatment.

The water felt comfortable to her now. She reached for the honeysuckle-scented body wash, unscrewed the top, and poured a generous amount in the fluffy sponge that was crammed into the shower caddy tray. It didn't take long to work up a frothy foam. Davalyn stepped back away from the direct spray and passed the sponge over her entire body. That's how Cutter found her—eyes closed, completely covered in the slick, heady scent of the body wash.

She sensed, rather than saw, him enter the shower stall with her. She'd felt the cooler rush of air on her bare skin when the door opened. She heard the water hit him in the back and his small grunt of surprise at the force of it.

"Damn, baby girl! What're you trying to do? Cook us up in here?"

"Too warm for you, Cutter?" She murmured a small challenge.

He swelled up his chest, deepening his voice for a mock-gruff response. "Too warm. Naw. I'm a man. I can take it."

"A man," Davalyn repeated softly, tentatively reaching out to place her hands against his broad shoulders. "You certainly are. You are absolutely the most gorgeous creature I've ever laid eyes on."

"That's supposed to be my line," he said, lowering his gaze to take in her glistening form in its entirety. He wasn't disappointed. She was everything he imagined her to be—and more. So much more.

"Does it matter who said it first? As long as we're both in agreement," Davalyn proposed.

"Oh, I'm in agreement, all right. If I get in any more agreement, you may not get any sleep tonight."

"Promises, promises," Davalyn teased, all shyness suddenly gone. She saw the effect she had on him and reveled in her feminine power.

"Turn around," he commanded, taking the sponge from her hand. Davalyn complied, recognizing by his tone that he was feeling a certain power of his own. Forceful. Direct. Spare with words. It was a little like the tone he used when he was on the job at the VFD. When there was business to be done, there wasn't much time for chitchat. He had a purpose and would single-mindedly proceed until he'd accomplished his goal. In this case, it was the complete satisfaction of his woman that was on his mind.

Cutter moved the sponge over the small of Davalyn's back. Lower, lower, he paused at the tattoo that sometimes peeked out from the waistline of her jeans.

"What possessed you to get this?" he asked, tracing the ball of his thumb over the elaborate pattern.

Davalyn shrugged her slender shoulders. "I was in college, away from either of my parents for the first time in my life. I guess you could say I was sowing a wild oat."

"If I find the man who put his hands on you back here, you know I'm gonna have to beat him down, don't you?" Cutter played the jealous boyfriend to the hilt.

"That he was a she," Davalyn corrected.

"Hmmmph." He rumbled deep in his chest. "I guess I'll have to let it go, then."

"She did a good job," Davalyn twisted around, trying to see. "Don't you think?"

Cutter grinned at her. "An artist's work is only as good as the subject. If you ask me, your artist had some fine material to work with from the get-go. No way she could go wrong with you as her canvas."

"You are so good for my ego, Cutter McCall," Davalyn cooed. "You want me to do you now?"

"Excuse me?" The look on Cutter's face was classic. Sometimes Davalyn's bluntness caught him off guard.

"Wash your back," she clarified, indicating the sponge.

"Oh . . . fine. Sure. But not with this." He rinsed the sponge of most of Davalyn's scent and instead placed a bar of soap in her hands. Something a little less flowery.

Davalyn worked the sponge into a good lather, admiring the rich scent. Now that was more like it. More like the Cutter she knew. She then started to scrub across his back.

Cutter splayed his hands against the shower stall wall, giving her easy access to the corded muscles of his back, shoulders, and arms. Davalyn trailed the sponge over him, marveling at how the water followed the crevices of his cut lines. Water bounced off his biceps, trailed down the defined V-shaped trapezius muscles, and over the taut muscles of his glutes.

Lord, the man is fine! Davalyn couldn't help but appreciate what hard work, healthy living, and some generous endowments from the Almighty could do for a man. With little more than a thin sheen of soap separating them, Davalyn knew that she wouldn't be able to keep her hands to herself for too much longer. She stepped aside, letting the water wash the suds down the drain along with the last shreds of her inhibition. On impulse, Davalyn wrapped her arms around his waist. She pressed herself against him, trying to make him feel as much of her skin against his as humanly possible.

Cutter sucked in a deep breath. Davalyn heard him mutter a low curse, evidence that he was feeling the intensity of the moment as much as she. When she reached around him, her fingers closing possessively around his shaft, Davalyn felt the shudder that rippled through his entire body. It was sweet torture for them both, but she didn't stop. She didn't relinquish her prize. Instead, she slid her fingers up and down the length of him, cupping the tip, then back down again to its base. When he struggled for composure, his breathing ragged and strained, it spurred her on. Her caress became bolder, more insistent.

"Dav, please," he pleaded, grasping her wrist. "I can't take much more of this."

Davalyn ignored him. She wouldn't stop. Not yet. She fanned the flames of his passion by sweeping her breasts against his back. Back and forth. Up and down until her nipples swelled, tingled for attention.

"Yes, you can," she encouraged him. "You're a man. Remember?"

"Ummmm . . . yes. A man . . . I did say that, didn't I? You . . . ah . . . you're not . . . Jeez, that's nice. . . . You're not making it easy to forget."

"That means I must be doing something right." Davalyn widened her stance for stability on the slick tile floor, then bent her knees, making sure her thighs kept direct contact with his. She felt the muscles across his shoulders tighten as his fingers clenched as if to gouge deep scores in the tiles of the wall.

"Do you want me to stop?" She lifted on tiptoe and purred into his ear.

In response, Cutter shifted his hand from her wrist to cover her hand, guided her movements, and directed her caress. He set the pace, the direction, and by subtly squeezing her hand—the intensity. Davalyn smiled, resting her cheek against his back so that he could feel her emotion. It didn't take long for Davalyn to understand the pattern—or adapt it. In her reasoning, if she ever expected to become adept, she had to be prepared to experiment. She was. She wasn't afraid to test the boundaries of her sexuality. Waiting as long as she had, she had a world of love to give. And there was no one on this earth she'd rather share that emotion with than Cutter. No one. She was certain that he knew that, though he didn't say so. He didn't have to communicate how she made him feel. Not with words. Something as simple as a sigh, a low moan, or a barely perceptible shift of his stance spoke volumes to her.

His breathing changed dramatically, becoming shorter, harsher. Instinctively, Davalyn knew that he was on the edge. It wouldn't take much at all to push him off. Wouldn't take much at all. A simple rhythmic thrust of her pelvis against his rear, a subtle increase of her stroke . . .

Cutter's groan filled the shower enclosure, echoed off the walls as release came to him with uncontrollable force. He breathed deeply, filling his lungs, steadying his heart. Davalyn didn't know how long she stood there, holding him, calming him. She kept her arms wrapped around his waist. Cutter pulled his hands from the tile wall and massaged her forearms.

Finally he turned and looked over his shoulder. "You didn't play fair, baby girl," he said.

"Is that a complaint I hear?" Davalyn teased.

"Not coming from me, you didn't. But, Dav, I didn't want things to go like this. We were supposed to . . . you know . . . share together." He twisted completely around, and hugged her close. "I want your first time to be special, baby girl."

"It will be," she insisted. "I just made sure of that."

Cutter looked down at her, his frown showing that he was puzzled. "I don't get what you mean."

"I'll explain it to you. But first things first." She reached over and shut off the water. After running for so long, it had started to cool down. If they stayed in under its spray much longer, Davalyn imagined that eventually it would take on the icy feel of the water sprinklers from the community center. Besides, she was starting to feel like a prune.

"Sorry," Cutter murmured, rubbing her arms, back, and shoulders. He opened the shower stall and reached for a huge cotton towel. Wrapping them both inside, he snuggled next to her as he ushered her out of the bathroom and toward his bed. The huge towel was soft and freshly laundered. By the time they made it out of the bathroom, the towel had soaked up most of the water from her drenched skin.

Davalyn took the lead, easing herself onto the king-size four-poster bed. The mattresses seemed doubly high but firm. She felt a little like Goldilocks, finally finding the perfect fit, as she lay on her side, then patted the bed next to her. Cutter joined her and propped himself up on his elbow.

"You were saying?" he continued, trailing his fingers lazily up and down her arm.

She smiled at him. "You want to know why I . . . How should I say . . . took matters into my own hands?"

Cutter chuckled. "You do have a way with words, baby girl. Yeah, that's exactly it. I want to know."

"It's because I know you, Cutter McCall. You are the most giving, unselfish man I know. I also know that the minute you touched me, you wouldn't think about yourself. You'd give one hundred percent in seeing to my pleasure, my needs. Even at the expense of your own. That was just my way of letting you know that I wasn't going to forget about you."

"You did that for me?" Cutter sounded surprised, touched. He raised up, kissing her gently on the cheek.

"And much more before this evening is over," Davalyn promised, kissing him back.

"Hold that thought," Cutter said. "I'll be right back."

"Where are you going?" she called out in dismay.

"The word for tonight is 'patience,'" he said, laying his finger against her lips.

"Patience," she echoed.

"That's right, my dear. Patience."

Patience. Easy for him to say, Davalyn thought as she curled up in Cutter's bed. *He's not the one with what*

had to be the world's longest dry spell. Though, afte
that shower, she couldn't really say that she was in the
middle of a dry spell anymore. Standing there with hin
had drenched her—in more ways than one.

Grinning to herself, Davalyn extended her legs, feel
ing limber, relaxed, yet—at the same time—anxious
She'd waited this long. She could wait a little while
longer. But his sudden disappearing act did make her
curious. When he'd climbed off the bed, wrapped the
towel around his waist, and ducked out the door with
only a wink to tide her over until he got back, Davalyn
thought that he must be playing a cruel joke on her. He
knew how badly she was wanting him. She could imagine what it must be doing for his ego knowing that she
wasn't going anywhere. She was waiting on his leisure.

Davalyn rolled over and glanced at the clock. Almost
two in the morning. In just a few hours, she'd have to
meet Kimmy and Margot back at the community center
Patience? Yeah, right. She didn't have time for patience.
She was just about to go after him when Cutter poked
his head through the partially open door.

"Did ya miss me?" he asked.

"What do you think?" she returned.

"Don't worry, Dav. I'll make it worth the wait." He
then backed into the room, carrying a serving tray.

"What is all this?" Davalyn asked, sitting up and
peering at the tray with interest.

"I guess you can say that this is my way of saying that
I'm not forgetting about you, either."

He set the tray on the nightstand beside her. On top
of the tray several votive candles of various scents were
burning steadily. Cutter collected them and placed them
strategically around the room. He turned off the over-

head light, letting the candle flicker cast a warm glow over the room.

"Playing with fire, McCall?" Davalyn tried to sound gruff and professional, but she could barely do it through her laughter—and her growing desire.

"I'm not playin'," Cutter returned, pinning her with a stare that made Davalyn melt as easily as candle wax.

"So," she said, clearing her throat, "what else have you got over there?"

"You'll see," he replied mysteriously. "Remember? The word for tonight is 'patience.'"

"It's morning," she reminded him, nodding at the clock on the nightstand.

"Oh yeah . . ." He laughed softly. "It's been a long day for you, hasn't it, baby girl?"

She nodded, turning down her lips in an exaggerated frown.

"Lie down," he said, smoothing his hand over her pillow. "Let me see what I can do to help make it better."

Davalyn complied, lying straight with her hands placed nervously at her side.

"No. Turn over," he redirected. "I'll give you a back massage."

"You do that and you'll put me to sleep, for sure," she warned.

"I doubt it," Cutter said with more than a hint of confidence. His tone bordered on smug.

"Oh?" Davalyn said, turning her head to question him.

"Relax," he murmured, touching the back of her head to ease her onto the pillow. Davalyn folded her arms, resting her right cheek on top of her hands.

Cutter sat on the side of the bed and reached for a remote control in the nightstand drawer. He aimed it at an unseen spot beyond the room, filling the near silence with soft jazz music. Then he picked up a small, emerald-jewel-tone glass vial that he'd left warming beside one of the votive candles. Cutter unscrewed the cap and poured just a small amount into his hands, but even that little bit flooded the room with its soothing aromatic essence. Rubbing his hands together, he made sure that they were warm and well coated before reaching for Davalyn.

A contented sigh bubbled from Davalyn's lips as Cutter worked knots of tension from her shoulders. His hands were gently skilled as he moved back and forth, first one shoulder, then the next. He didn't speak as he worked; still, Davalyn always knew what would happen next. By removing a hand from one area and gently touching the next before applying pressure, he conveyed his direction.

Cutter shifted on the bed, concentrating his efforts on her lower back. His hands swept to her hips, then back again lower, across her rear. Davalyn pressed her lips together, moaning softly. She couldn't stop herself. The warmth of his hands coupled with the pressure against her rear pushing her down on the bed fueled her growing need.

"Shh . . ." Cutter whispered. "Patience." He applied more rubbing oil into his hands, scooted to the foot of the bed, and trailed his hands across her thighs. When she clenched, her rear and thighs tightening against his hand, his voice floated back through the darkness: "Relax, baby girl. You gotta relax."

"I'm trying," Davalyn returned. "But something inside is telling me—*Now!*"

"Nuh-uh. Not yet. We got time. All the time in the world," he insisted. But when his fingers touched her inner thighs and moved upward, Davalyn instinctively parted for him. As careful, as deliberate, and as controlled as Cutter was, Davalyn didn't think that he was prepared for the directness of her invitation. His fingertips explored upward between her legs, where she greeted him with a warmth and moisture that added her own unique essence to the room.

"Patience," Cutter repeated.

"I *am* being patient," Davalyn insisted.

"I was talking to me," he said. He added oil to his hands once more, then continued down the backs of her legs, across her calves. He smoothed over her heels and couldn't resist tickling the arches of her feet.

"Cut that out!" Davalyn buried her face in the pillow. She smothered her giggles, hoping that they wouldn't become peals of laughter. "Do you want me to wake up the whole neighborhood?" she gasped.

"The walls are soundproofed," he teased. "Make all the noise you want. Does nothing but puff up my ego when you're loud."

"You'd better have more than a puffed-up ego to make me scream, Cutter McCall," Davalyn retorted.

"That sounds like a challenge," Cutter said, looking over his shoulder at her.

Davalyn withdrew her feet from his grasp and turned over. She raised up on her elbows, tented one knee, and shifted the other leg farther apart.

"Or an invitation," she said huskily. "So why don't you do us both a favor and RSVP ASAP?"

"I told you, I'm not going to rush you, Davalyn," he said seriously. "I mean it. You don't understand. I don't want to hurt you."

"You can't hurt me, Cutter." Davalyn sounded certain.

He took her hand and placed it squarely in his lap at the base of his arousal. Slowly he guided her along the full length of him, giving her no doubt to his readiness. She took up the caress on her own, and was surprised—didn't think it possible—when she felt him lengthen. Feeling him respond as he'd done in the shower was one thing. Seeing it happen before her eyes was another.

"Yes, I can," he contradicted. She could hear the struggle for restraint in his voice. Through the muted light, she could see it in his face. "Trust me tonight, baby girl. Do things my way for now."

"So now what?" she asked. "I'm open to suggestions." Davalyn waggled her knee for comic effect.

"Lie back again, please, ma'am."

"Yes, sir. Lying back." She complied.

He sat for a few minutes, just staring at her without making a move to touch her.

"I can almost hear you thinking," she said softly.

"If that were true, you wouldn't be sitting there so calmly. You'd be slapping my face."

"Didn't know you were into the rough stuff, Cutter."

"I'm not . . . really," he amended. "I want to be gentle with you. That's why I'm taking the time to slow things down a bit. I have to."

"I might not be able to make you the same promise. I've waited too long for you. Do you know how many times I've thought about you, Cutter? Do you know how many times I've wanted to pick up the phone and call you? Just forget about my pride." She started to laugh, covering her face with her hands.

"What's so funny?" Cutter smiled, her amusement was infectious.

"I was just remembering this one time . . . when I was about sixteen . . . . no, I'd just turned seventeen; I had this crazy plan to use the money I made waiting tables, hop on a bus, and come down to see you. I'd even called the bus station to get the schedules. I wasn't going to pack a bag, because I only planned to stay one night. One magical, teenage-hormone-driven night. Everything I thought I needed was going to fit in one little bitty purse, if you know what I mean. It was the dead of winter, snowdrifts almost as high as the Greyhound bus, but I was going to come down here, wearing little more than my underwear and my boots and my overcoat."

"Jeez, Dav," Cutter began. "What happened? What stopped you?"

"Mama did," Davalyn said reluctantly. "She overheard me talking on the phone, asking one of my girlfriends to drive me to the bus station. She didn't know why I was going, just knew that I was up to no good. She grounded me for a month. I'm glad she never found out who I was coming to see, or why, or I'd probably still be in my room to this day."

"I'm sorry," Cutter soothed.

"Doesn't matter." Davalyn shrugged. "That was that same month that you and Angela announced that you were engaged anyway. So, I guess it all worked out the way that it was supposed to. I imagine that if I did make it down, you would have just turned me away anyway."

Cutter paused, then looked at her with a wicked gleam. "I like to think that I would have. But at seventeen, you were starting to get my attention. By then, you had filled out. If I remember right, you had the perkiest breasts."

"You were looking! You were noticing? Oh, now you tell me!" Davalyn exclaimed, reaching out to pummel him. Laughing, Cutter easily deflected her blows. He caught her up in his arms and stopped her protest with a kiss that took her token resistance away. Easing her back onto the pillows, Cutter slid into bed beside her. He reached over to draw the blankets over them, co-cooning them in the warm covers.

"I'm telling you now," he whispered against her cheek, "showing you the best way I know how. Do you trust me?"

"Of course I trust you. You don't even have to ask."

"And you know that I love you, don't you?"

Davalyn's throat closed up with unimaginable emotion. She nodded, squeezing her eyes shut tight.

"Baby girl, are you crying?" Cutter asked, his expression incredulous, even tender.

"I love you so much, Cutter," Davalyn whispered hoarsely. She squeezed him tighter in the embrace. "But I don't want to be your baby girl anymore. I want to be your lady. Your *woman*."

Cutter's mouth found hers in a kiss that was meant to comfort, but Davalyn's eager response changed the temperament and the tempo. She parted her lips, letting her tongue slip forward to taste and to tempt. What began as a long, leisurely exploration of each hidden corner of his mouth quickly became a frantic duel of mastery. Which one of them would delve farther? Whose lips could press harder? Was it her tongue or his that tasted sweeter?

No sooner had she thought she had the answer than she was suddenly distracted, not by a kiss, but by his caress. Tender one moment, then commanding—demanding that she yield herself to him. He had to know every part of her. Every swell. Every curve. Every valley. His hands knew her, had gained familiarity with her body during the massage. He wanted her to be pliant, even supple, to be comfortable with his touch. But now as he smoothed over her, his goal was not to relax, but to inflame. He had stoked the fire with his body massage. And he now was ready to set her ablaze.

Davalyn gasped for air, feeling the weight of her own desire crushing her like ten tons of air. She had to be free. She needed release! The kind only he could give. Clutching his shoulders, Davalyn arched toward him with a throaty moan of tacit permission. *Now, Cutter.* It had to be now. No more talk of patience or restraint. No more games. *Now!* Every instinctual sense in her body was telling her that she was ready. One way or another, she had to make him realize it, too.

Reaching between them, Davalyn guided him toward her. She shifted, easing the tip of his shaft inside her. Cutter moaned and started to surge forward, then jerked back again as if burned. His breathing was just as harsh, just as ragged as hers.

"Do that again, Dav, and you'll be carrying my baby just as sure as I live," he warned her. "I'm trying to protect you, and you're not making it any easier."

Davalyn reached under her pillow and pulled out a handful of condoms she'd stored there. Pressing a packet into the palm of his hand, she said sweet as honey, "Heaven forbid I be accused of making it hard for you, Cutter."

"You laughin' at me?" Cutter rolled away from her and sat up with his back leaning against the headboard.

"The thought never crossed my mind."

"You'd better not. Not nice to play with a man who's on the edge." He tore open the foil and withdrew the condom.

"Need some help?" she offered, reaching out.

Cutter gave a mock swat at her hand. "Nuh-uh. You just stay right there. You touch me again and I'm likely to send this rubber through the roof." A moment later he was snuggling next to Davalyn again, stroking her body and kissing her.

This time, when Davalyn touched him, guiding him, Cutter didn't withdraw. He didn't give in to the powerful instinct that goaded him to thrust forward. He settled between her thighs slowly, cautiously—one part of his brain remained focused on paying attention to her responses. Was she all right? Was his weight too much for her? Did she flinch? Was the undeniable tightness he felt close around him a painful reaction or was it simply the way she would conform around him? He moved his hips in short, controlled pulses. He didn't press forward until he felt her body give way.

Davalyn moved with him, matching his rhythm. Although this was her first time, she knew exactly what to do. No guessing. No indecision. No fear. She loved this man. Trusted him with all she had. She would give everything to him and know that her gift was cherished. Everything. She would hold nothing back. Davalyn lifted to meet him, encouraging him without words. She clung to his arms, his shoulders. And when passion overtook her, she threw back her head and cried out his name.

Cutter thrust into her swiftly, deeply, and prayed that he'd timed it correctly. As he broke through her barrier, he didn't give himself time to second-guess or regret, but drew back before closing with her again.

Davalyn gasped, then bit into his shoulder—the only indication that he'd caused her any discomfort, but she didn't stop moving her hips beneath him with a definite carnal grind. Her unabashed moans drowned out the voice in his head that had warned him to remain distanced, observant.

Cutter's caution caved under the overwhelming pressure of human nature and physical need. He increased his tempo, extended the depth of his thrusts as tenderness gave way to unmasked lust. Maybe later there would be time and opportunity for whispers of sweet nothings, or soft sighs with declarations of undying love, but for now, the room was filled with vocal sounds of their lovemaking—deep, guttural, feral in its intensity. Face-to-face, eyes boring into each other's souls, they fed the flames of their passion until finally consumed they let go the last of their inhibitions.

When release came to them both, it was unexpected, uncontrollable. Cutter's breath expelled from his lungs in sobs as he fell across her, gasping her name as fervently, as reverently, as a prayer. Davalyn's orgasm racked her entire body. She lay beneath him, trembling, dazed, and wondering how anyone could possibly share this moment with someone they did not love completely. She wasn't sure how long she lay there, stroking him, calming him. When she stirred, moving away from him, Cutter looked up in disappointment.

"Where are you going? You're not leaving now, are you?"

"I'll be back," she promised, nodding toward the bathroom.

"Oh . . ." he said on an indrawn breath when he heard water running in the bathroom. In a way, this experience was a first for him, too. It was the first time he'd ever been with someone who'd waited. He hadn't waited for Davalyn; and Angela certainly hadn't waited for him. Not that he judged Angela for not being a virgin when he married her. How could he expect more from her than he was prepared to offer?

Concerned, he got up and tapped softly on the bath
room door. "Dav?"

"I'll be out in a minute," she called back. Her voic
sounded strained.

"Davalyn, are you all right?"

"I will be," she tried to assure him.

Cutter wasn't convinced. "Can I come in?"

Silence for a moment. He thought at first that she
might refuse, then the door opened and she peeked ou
at him with wide eyes.

"It hurts a little," she confessed.

"Let me help." Cutter choked on emotion too compli
cated to fully express. She opened the door wider and le
him in. Cutter quickly took stock of the surroundings.

"Here," he said, rummaging in the cabinet for a fresh
towel. "And don't use that soap. Use this one. It's gen
tler."

"You keep it on hand for just these occasions?" Dava
lyn teased him. But there was an edge to her voice
Maybe she was testing him.

"Because Bennett's skin is sensitive," he corrected. He
moistened the towel, then added just a drop or two of the
soap. Davalyn took it from him, but didn't proceed.

"I'll . . . just . . . uh, be out here, if you need me," he
said, backing toward the door.

"Thanks," she said gratefully.

Moments later, she rejoined him, sliding underneath
the blankets and snuggling closer to him. "You'll prob
ably be sore for a while," he advised.

"Is that a brag, Cutter McCall?"

"Any complaints?" he returned.

"Not from this lady," Davalyn assured him.

Grinning, Cutter shifted his body to spoon aroun
her. "My lady," he corrected, smoothing over her hair.

"Good night, my man," she said through a yawn. "Sweet dreams, Dav."

He laid his own head down and had barely closed his eyes when the alarm clock suddenly blared, announcing the arrival of the next day. Davalyn's curse of dismay was drowned out by the sound of Cutter slamming his hand down on the snooze bar.

"Ready to get the day started?" Cutter asked, sitting up and swinging his feet off the edge of the bed.

"Not really," Davalyn replied, rubbing her tired eyes. "It feels like I just got to sleep." She pulled the covers up to her nose and tried to pull the pillow over her head.

"That's because we did." He laughed at her, jerking the pillow back. "C'mon. We're supposed to meet your sorority sisters at the community center. If we don't show up on time, you know Kimmy will nail us to the wall, don't you?"

Davalyn sighed heavily through her nose. "I still can't believe it all happened like that. All our hard work . . . gone . . . literally up in smoke."

Cutter leaned forward and tenderly brushed his hand over Davalyn's cheek. "You know it's not your fault, don't you, Dav? If anybody's to blame, blame me. I should have taught Bennett better than that."

"It was an accident. Just a stupid accident. I guess the son of firefighter is no less immune to that careless kind of danger than anybody else's kid. He was just being a typical, enthusiastic little boy. I'm just glad that he wasn't hurt."

"Tell Bennett that," he said. "I know he's gotta be feelin' pretty low."

"I will tell him. Right after we shower and get dressed."

"I'll go start warming the water." Cutter leaned forward and kissed Davalyn on the tip of her nose. When he walked into the bathroom, Davalyn snuggled down deeper into the bedcovers. Then she reached for the remote control to turn on the morning news. *What's happening in the world?*

Weather. Sports update. Davalyn surfed through several channels, getting snippets of all. Suddenly she called out, "Cutter, come here! Quick!" She sat up in bed and turned up the volume.

"What is it?" He came out with a towel wrapped around his waist and a toothbrush frothy with toothpaste in the other. Davalyn didn't answer right away, simply glared at the television screen.

"We, the sisters of the Kemah chapter of the Alpha Kappa Alpha sorority, would like to express our deepest regret. But in the interest of safety to the community, we must cancel the Kwanzaa celebration."

"Hey, that's Kimmy on TV." Cutter pointed, grinning at the screen. Davalyn narrowed her eyes at him.

"I can see that," she said in irritation. The smile was quickly wiped from Cutter's face.

Behind her stood Margot, who turned directly to the camera, pulling the microphone and focus away from Kimmy. "We'd like to thank all of our supporters for the generous contributions, the volunteers that have helped us to prepare for this event, and the facility director at the Jimmy Walker's Community Center. And we ask that you honor the spirit of the Kwanzaa observance by spending it with your families, your friends, and your neighbors, in your own way."

Not to be outdone, Kimmy concluded the interview by saying, "You can rest assured that we, the sisters of AKA, will be back next year, better prepared than ever to present the principles of Dr. Karenga. Thank you very much . . . and Happy Kwanzaa to all."

"Yeah, yeah, yeah. Happy Kwanzaa to you, too!" Davalyn said ungraciously, stabbing at the remote control to turn the television off

"You don't sound too happy," Cutter observed.

"That she canceled the ceremony without consulting me. No . . . I'm not," Davalyn confessed. "She and Tonia were always trying to do an end run around me."

"So, you're upset that she saved you from running around like a chicken with your head cut off to hold the celebration. You wanted to spend all day stressed out, irritated, overworked, and not having any fun. Is that it?"

"Well . . . now that you put it that way," she conceded.

"It's probably for the best that it was canceled, Dav."

"But we all worked so hard!" she complained.

"Isn't that what you're supposed to do? What was that principle? Kuumba . . . yeah, that's it. Wasn't that what your effort was all about?"

Davalyn paused, then looked up at him with a reluctant smile. "You know, you're too smart for your own good, Cutter McCall."

"And that's why you love me so much, darlin'," he said without an ounce of humility.

Davalyn's irritation melted away under his tender gaze. "I do love you, Cutter," she said, touching her hand to his cheek.

He took her hand in his, pressing his lips to it. "Look at this way. At least we don't hafta get out of bed so early."

Epilogue

Nine months later

Cutter propped a pillow behind Davalyn's back and tucked another one under her feet.

"How's that?" he asked, settling down next to her on the couch.

"Better, thanks. Now hand me that double-chocolate chip-and-mint pint of Hägen-Dazs."

"How many of those have you had today?" Cutter asked, looking around the family room at the discarded cartons of ice cream.

"Who's counting?" Davalyn countered belligerently. Six months pregnant in the middle of a Texas heat wave wasn't exactly making her the most charming person to be around.

"I'm not, but baby girl is. How do you even know that she likes chocolate?" He placed his hand possessively on Davalyn's swollen stomach. "What's that?" He then cupped his hand to his ear and leaned his head down to rest on her navel. "You say send you down some butter pecan?" He raised his head, dark eyes shining at her. "She says she wants some butter pecan."

Davalyn laughed and thumped Cutter on top of the head with her spoon. "We're out of butter pecan. I wen through the last of that yesterday . . . Unless . . ." She let her voice trail off meaningfully.

"Unless what?" Cutter wasn't fooled at all by her sudden shift.

"Unless you want to run out and get me some more?"

Groaning, Cutter fell back against the couch cushions. "Some more? But I just got comfortable."

"Never mind." Davalyn sighed. "I guess I don't need it anyway. I was perfectly fine with chocolate chip before you opened your mouth."

"What time are Van and Shayla supposed to come over?"

Davalyn shrugged. "I don't know."

"He's your brother. All excited about being Uncle Van again. Maybe he'll bring you some more ice cream." Cutter reached for the phone and dialed his next-door neighbor's house.

"Van, what's up? What time you swinging by, man? That late? Naw, you gotta do better than that. Your sister's driving me crazy craving butter-pecan ice cream." He turned away, ignoring Davalyn's icy glare.

"It's his fault that I'm in this fix, Van!" she shouted so that her brother could hear her. Cutter held the phone away from his ear, letting Davalyn listen to the sound of her brother's raucous laughter through the phone.

"Do us all a favor and make it a gallon," Cutter continued. "Better still, why don't you just back up to the creamery with a flatbed trailer and tell them to load it up? Yeah . . . all right. We won't start the movie until you get here. See ya then. Later."

"My turn to pick the movie," Bennett shouted from his favorite spot in front of the television. He sat shuffling through a pile of DVDs that he'd pulled from the cabinet.

"Not this one. Not this one. Seen it a zillion times. Bo-*ring!*" He pronounced judgment as he tossed each one aside.

"Careful with that!" Cutter exclaimed. He hauled himself off the couch to rescue the last DVD from Bennett's discard pile. "What do you mean boring? This one is the best one ever. A classic."

"Just you and Mom and a whole lot of kissing." Bennett screwed up his face.

"I like the kissing parts," Cutter told his son, rubbing him on top of his head. He glanced over at Davalyn. "It's our wedding," he told her.

"You and Angela's?" Davalyn mumbled, her mouth full of chocolate-chip-and-mint ice cream.

"Noo-ooo," Cutter said slowly, pointing to the label written in her own handwriting. "Ours. Yours and mine."

The spoon paused midway between the carton and her mouth. "But I thought . . . That is . . . Bennett said—"

"He said, 'Mom,'" Cutter finished for her.

Davalyn swallowed hard and blinked fast to hold back tears. "You didn't make him do that, did you, Cutter?" she whispered.

"We talked about it last night. He asked me if it was all right if he did. Since I'm his dad and you're about to have his sister, well, it just didn't seem right to him to keep calling you Aunt Dav."

"Is Angela okay with this? I mean, I didn't expect her to show up for the wedding. But she did. And she seemed cool about it. But this may be a little too much for her."

"Is it too much for you?" Cutter asked.

"Mom, is it all right if we watch *Spy Kids* again?" Bennett interrupted, holding up the case. "It's rated G."

"It's fine," Davalyn said, answering both her husband and her son.

"Go on and put the movie in, Bennett," Cutter told him. "By the time Uncle Van and Aunt Shayla get here, it'll be time for our movie."

Bennett pointed the remote at the television to change the channel when Davalyn suddenly cried out and sat up, clutching her stomach.

"What!" Startled, Cutter sat up, too. "What is it?" His heart suddenly leaped into his throat, fearing the worst.

"Look!" she exclaimed, gesturing wildly at the television. "It's Julian. No, Bennett, turn it back. Where's the volume? I can't hear what he's saying."

Cutter's head swiveled, his attention focused on the screen. He'd caught an image of the impeccably tailored Julian Blake. Behind him was bookshelf upon shelf of law books. Cutter couldn't tell if they were real or just props for his commercial.

"Bo-*rrrrinnng*," Bennett complained again, raising his hand with the remote.

"Hold up," Cutter said in a tone that brought no more argument but plenty of attitude from the nine-year-old. He sat, cross-legged on the floor, with his pouty cheeks resting on his fists.

"Who's that guy next to him?" Cutter wanted to know.

"I don't believe it. . . . That's Julian's father."

"The old man who kicked him out on his can because he—"

"Shhhh!" Davalyn shushed Cutter, partially so that he wouldn't complete his sentence and partially to hear her friend's commercial pitch.

Julian sat on the corner of an expensively crafted desk and stared into the camera. He was the very model of professionalism, mingled with a believable amount of compassion. "Have you been injured on the job? Could your medical ailment have been prevented? At the law firm of Blake and Blake, we share your pain and will help you get the restitution you deserve. No case is too small." His image gave way to some of his supposedly satisfied clients, all claiming huge settlements. Davalyn wasn't surprised to see at least one testimonial claiming that faulty Christmas tree lighting had destroyed her home. She knew after that day they'd argued in the restaurant that if he couldn't get the information from her, he'd get it on his own. Well, she thought in resignation, good for him. She hoped that he was happy.

It hurt her to have to deny him access to her reports. But as much as he was dear to her, she just couldn't compromise her work ethic. Too many people had lost too much because of those damned faulty Christmas tree lights. They were a menace. And she was glad to be a part of getting them off the street. Though, she had to admit she felt like the proverbial Scrooge when she had to go on television and announce to the local news anchor how dangerous they really were.

The investigative reporter breaking the story pulled every heart-tugging trick in the book to make the manufacturers appear as careless, money-hungry conglomerates. Mixed in with a few disadvantaged children who only had the twinkling lights under an empty tree to look forward to, and it became a virtual race to see who could bring the manufacturers to court faster. The glaring publicity and the pressure for her to testify became so great that at one point Davalyn considered changing jobs. She was glad that even through all of that, Julian hadn't pressured her to become an expert witness for his practice. He did it all on his own.

Cutter and Davalyn exchanged glances. He took her hand in his, squeezing gently. She certainly was happy.

"You can turn it off now, Bennett," she said, lying back against the cushions. Cutter settled back with her, swirling his finger on the outer rim of her ice cream carton. He started to raise his finger to his lips, but Davalyn stopped him. Instead, she pulled his hand toward her own mouth. The tip of her tongue licked away the rapidly melting cream from his forefinger.

"Careful, Dav," Cutter said low, a half smile playing sensuously on his lips. "That's how we got into trouble the first time. Remember?"

"Just making sure you don't forget," she said.

"That ain't likely to happen," he retorted.

"What time did you say Van and Shayla were coming over?" Davalyn asked, looking back toward the door.

"Not for at least another hour," Cutter said, reading her thoughts perfectly. He stood up, then held out his hands to Davalyn to help her from the couch. "Bennett, you be a good boy and sit here and watch your movie."

"More kissin'," Bennett muttered under his breath as his parents exited the room, snuggling and giggling, acting more like teenagers than the kids in his movie.

Davalyn looked back over her shoulder at her son. *Her* son. He had claimed her, making it all right to be as possessive as she wanted to be.

"Do you think we're setting a bad example for him, Cutter?" she asked, worried about leaving him all alone like that. "What do you think he thinks about us?"

"What? You mean, him witnessing two people who are so totally into each other? Two people who cherish him as much as they treasure each other? Two people who'd give their lives for him, support him in all that he does, wrong or right . . . giving him direction, affection and guidance? Yeah, I can see where that would warp him for life."

"All right. You've made your point," Davalyn said, lifting her face to his for a kiss. "Now that I'm his mom, I just want to be sure to do right by him . . . by you both."

"You're his mother, and my wife. Even before I put that ring on your finger, you were everything he needed you to be. And you're still doing everything he needs you to do. You've given me everything I could ever ask for. And I love you for it, baby girl."

With his arm curved around her waist, she allowed Cutter to lead her upstairs. Feeling completely cared for in the warmth of his embrace, she took her place by his side, secure in the knowledge that this was where she always belonged, and where she would forever stay.

Dear Readers,

First I want to take a moment to thank you for all of your continued support. Your comments and suggestions are helping me to become a better writer. In my last book, *Hearts of Steel,* I introduced you to the Johnsons—a close-knit family with ties so strong that they would do anything to secure each other's happiness. That love was so expansive, it couldn't be contained— spilling over into Shirley Hailstock's *A Family Affair* and Eboni Snoe's *The Ties That Bind.*

In *Winter Fires*, you have met the Bowerses and the McCalls. Maybe not related by blood, but no less willing to go the extra mile for each other. *Winter Fires* expounds on the idea of the community as family and our duty, our privilege, to see that all are cared for. I hope you enjoyed it.

As always, I'd love to hear from you. Keep those suggestions coming! Drop me a line at geri_guillaume@ hotmail.com. Until the next time we meet, God keep you.

ABOUT THE AUTHOR

Geri Guillaume is the pseudonym for Krystal G Williams. Ms. Williams was born in Jackson, Mississippi, in 1965. She received her undergraduate degree from Rice University, Houston, Texas, where she double majored in English and legal studies. She is currently a full-time technical writer and mother of two. Her motto, "Too many words, not enough paper," has helped her to publish several contemporary romance novels, a play for her alma mater, and a family reunion planning guide. Ms. Williams currently makes her home in Houston, Texas.